GRIFF DRISCOLL
AND THE
SHARDS
OF
ESSENCE

ISBN: 979-8-9861099-2-3 (Paperback)

ISBN: 979-8-9861099-3-0 (E-book)

Cover by Christian Bentulan

Edited by Michaela Bush

First published in United States in 2026

www.BrandonHarriman.com

To the "Girl from the Coffee Shop": I still can't believe I'm married to you. Thank you, Annette, for supporting me and believing in this story.

To Jayce and Haley, who keep my life full of adventure and joy.

To my parents, Jay and Teri, who showed me the love of God and always cheered me on.

ACKNOWLEDGEMENTS

Writing a book has always been a dream of mine. To me, saying I wanted to be an author was like a five-year-old saying they wanted to be an astronaut. It felt out of reach. Impossible. But I've been incredibly blessed to have the right people around me who pushed me, provided insight and refused to let me quit. I'm thankful to everyone in my circle who has helped me not only publish one, but now TWO books!

To my readers: Writing a story is a deeply personal ordeal. To share it with the world is both wonderful and horrifying. But my readers have been so very kind, and to know there are people who are excited about the stories I've shared truly feeds my soul.

Lastly, I'd like to thank Brandon Sanderson. I hope he reads this! Not only do we share a first name, but his stories have given me countless hours of adventure. Beyond that, his generosity in sharing his writing lectures on YouTube gave me crucial tools and helped better my craft.

PROLOGUE

They stalked him from the shadows. The man could hear their careful footsteps in the leaves and twigs, disturbing the otherwise peaceful night. Stars sparkled brilliantly overhead, illuminating the dusty, well-traveled path on which the man walked. A gentle summer breeze playfully kissed the back of his neck, as though Mother Nature was flirting with him. He chuckled quietly to himself as he casually strode through the forest, not minding the shuffling that followed him just out of sight. The moon above was bright enough, and after years of traveling through this same beaten path at night, the man had grown used to walking by its pale light. Even the shadows that stirred in the darkness were like his constant companions. Though they never stepped out onto the path, their constant presence just out of the moonlight's reach was a strange comfort to him. Not that he desired for them to come any closer, but he also knew they never would. They knew who he was, and what he carried.

No one in their right mind would have dared to venture out in the night as he did, which meant that loneliness was part of the burden of responsibility he carried. The man hummed quietly to himself, his pack bouncing lightly against his back as he strolled.

Suddenly, the slow, methodical crackling of the forest undergrowth stopped. The man paused his midnight stroll and cocked his head to the side, listening to his companions. In a frenzied rush, the shadows in the woods turned and darted away, their footsteps fading into the dark.

The man raised his eyebrow, curiosity heightening his senses. He shut his eyes and listened to the regular sounds of the nocturnal nightlife just out of sight. Opening his eyes again, he scanned ahead, looking for whatever it was that scared the shadows away. There. Off in the distance small orbs of light floated as if in formation. They were headed his direction. The man crossed his arms and furrowed his brows, planting his feet firmly in place.

Bobbing in the sea of darkness, the orbs floated closer, growing larger and more vibrant with every passing second.

"Oh, hurry up already, wouldya?" the man called out. "I haven't got all night!"

Within moments, a group of men burst from the forest, their orbs of light illuminating their angry, rugged faces. They surrounded a young woman, whose hands were tied and mouth was gagged. Wet streaks smeared the dirt underneath her pleading eyes that said what she herself couldn't.

"What'cha doin' there, friend? Walkin' 'round here at night like this?" the man standing at the front said. He swayed back and forth, the crazy look in his eye making it clear that his intentions were about as crooked as his teeth.

"I might ask you the same question ... friend." He met the man's eyes with total confidence. He knew the type of person that stood in front of him. Desperate and yet overly confident he would walk away from this "chance" meeting.

Crooked Teeth stepped forward. "We're out here lookin' for someone. Middle aged. 'Bout mid-thirties. Light brown hair. Kinda like you, matter fact. Heard they might have somethin' reeeeal special. Know where I might find someone like that?" He cocked his head to the side, his eyes never blinking.

"Well, ya know ... friend. Matter of fact, I think *I'm* lookin' at someone who's got somethin' real special... and my guess is she doesn't belong to you. Is that right?" He gazed over at the woman, her watery eyes meeting his. She nodded furiously before one of the other men shoved her to the ground, silencing her.

The man kept his arms crossed, but clenched his fists as he watched the woman struggle on the ground. Still, he remained motionless. For now.

Crooked Teeth took another step forward, anger flashing across his face. "She ain't none of yer business! Now ... my gut tells me that you're exactly who we're after. All by yourself in the middle of the night. Not a single nightstalker scratch on that pearly white skin of yours. Why is that?"

The man rolled his eyes. "Listen. You want gold? Take some gold." He tossed a couple of coins in the dirt in front of Crooked Teeth.

"Oh, no, friend. We're not here for gold." He spastically shook his head from side to side. "We're here for somethin' so much more than gold. Now, you'll give us what we want, or we'll *take* it from ya."

He took a few more steps forward, stopping just a foot away from the young man. His crooked teeth jutted out from his maniacal smile, but he said not a word. The summer sounds of the crickets chirping were the only noises that could be heard. It was as if everyone had held their breath and were waiting to see who could hold it the longest.

I am protector and defender.

Words passed down from his master echoed in the back of his mind.

I wield my magic; it does not wield me.

I brandish my power with wisdom and resolve.

The young man eyed the group before him. His arms still crossed, his feet still firmly planted, and his eyes never leaving Crooked Teeth's.

I do not strike first, but I strike true.

"GIVE IT TO ME NOW!" Crooked Teeth shrieked, leaping forward toward the man. "I want it! I want it! Give me!"

The man dodged to the left, just in time, as the deranged leader flailed past him. In one swift motion, he kicked the man's knee with his boot, sending him barreling to the dusty ground.

I do not seek battle, but I will end it.

He swirled his hand and hurled a giant wave of fire at the man fumbling on the ground. Crooked Teeth's shrill screams echoed through the night. Then they stopped. The man turned toward the rest of the group, who had fanned out and was inching toward him. Their leader may be gone, but their objective was not.

"Last chance," the man said. "Leave the young lady here, unharmed, with me, and turn back towards town, and you won't end up like your ... friend here."

Their eyes narrowed at him, and they inched even closer. The man sighed. It was going to be a long night. Lightning crackled from his fingertips. With a single jab in the air, he arced it across several men, who crashed to the dirt upon impact, their orbs of light diminishing as they fell. One of the men still standing grabbed at his arm and received a kick to the ribs. Another went for his feet. The man swirled his hands and flung a large boulder that smashed into his attacker's side. Whether by his fists, his feet, or his spells, the assailants all eventually succumbed to the man's abilities. With each person that fell, their orbs of light disappeared, darkened by their own foolishness. When every single body lay motionless on the dark forest floor, the man approached the woman, and gently removed her gag and ties.

"You okay?" he asked quietly.

She rubbed her tender jaw before slowly nodding in response. He sat next to her, not minding the dust that he knew would collect on the back of his otherwise clean linen trousers. She looked to be a couple of years younger than him: late-twenties, maybe early thirties. Even though dirt covered her face, it would be impossible for it to cover her beauty. Her kind brown eyes no longer showed fear but gratitude. It was too dark to tell if she wore a wedding band, but the man tossed that thought aside. No woman would ever want to live the life he lived.

"Thank you," she finally said. Her voice cracked with the trauma of the night.

"Here, drink some water, m'lady." He pulled a large stagmoose skin canteen from his pack and handed it to her, which she avidly accepted.

After a rather long and greedy drink, she lowered the waterskin, and heaved gulps of air in satisfaction.

"Ugh," she sighed, and leaned back against a tree trunk. "Thank you. I was ... so thirsty ..." Her eyes started to close.

"Oh, no ma'am. Now's not the time to fall asleep, I'm afraid." The man glanced at the floating white eyes that had come back to stare at him again. He cast an orb of light that hovered around the two of them and shook her awake. He knew the beasts in the shadows would never attack him. In some ways, he could always guarantee his own safety. His new, temporary traveling companion, though, was a different story.

"Don't worry, you'll sleep soon enough, but we've still got a ways to go before you're safe."

He reached down and helped her up. After dusting herself off, and wiping the dirt from her face, she looked up at him.

"What's your name, sir?"

He smiled at her. No wedding band. "The name's Einar Falkenburg." He bowed low. "At your service."

She smiled back and did a slight curtsy. "Fedelma."

They gathered their supplies and continued on the path, doing their best to ignore the snarls and sounds of his traveling companions feasting in the dark behind them.

CHAPTER 1

Small pebbles tumbled down the steep incline with each strained step. Sweat poured down Griff's back and it wasn't just from the climb. The intense heat from the summer sun beat at the back of his neck as though it were angry with him. But he hadn't done anything wrong. King's crown, he didn't even know how he'd gotten here. Or where *here* even was. As though the wind thought the sun was being unfair to the poor young mage, she blew gently and steadily across the rippling waters below, rising up to wick the moisture from his body.

He reached the top of the steep, stony slope, brushed the dirt off his trousers, and allowed his eyes to feast on the breathtaking surroundings. The island on which he stood was like a lush, grassy oasis protruding from a never-ending desert of blue. As far as the eye could see, deep waters surrounded him in every direction, save for the tiny sliver of land to the north.

Griff plopped onto the soft, grassy floor and allowed himself to catch his breath and enjoy the moment, knowing that it wouldn't last long. There was a mystery that lay before him, some small thing that was tugging at the edges of his consciousness like a word almost remembered, but still forgotten. Where was he? And why was he here? Considering his previous year, and the dreams in the lava caverns, he assumed that this was another dream. He was at least thankful he wasn't underground with the bats and Korrun's pet again.

Once his ragged breathing had returned to normal, it was time to investigate the rest of the island. It was going to be difficult to find answers to questions he didn't even know to ask. Tall grass playfully swiped at his legs as the salty ocean breeze drifted around him. Happy birds chirped with delight from the trees above, and the steady rippling of the surrounding waters threatened to lull Griff into a deeper sleep, if that was even possible. This would have been a restful, almost even luxurious place to be, had it not been for the unnerving feeling at the edges of his consciousness.

He cautiously approached a wall of shrubs and trees. The bushes almost seemed smashed together, and the trees towered over Griff, standing tall and proud. It was as though they were the guardians of the shadows within the tiny forest atop the island. That small, lingering pull at the edges of his mind egged him forward. There was no sound, no words, nothing. Just this ... knowing feeling that something called to him. This mystery that begged to be solved. And not just by anybody, but by him, and him alone. Like a personal invitation to a party where he was the only guest.

With every step closer, it was as though the trees bent lower, investigating the tiny ant that dared to tread on the guardians' hallowed ground. Though this was just an illusion brought on by the height of the trees and the shadows they cast, Griff still half-expected them to place their branch-like hands on their hips and say, "And where do you think you're going, boy?"

There was no opening in the shrubbery, just tightly packed leaves with thorns — yet another sign of unwelcome. And yet, that feeling that he was supposed to go beyond these guardians continued to beckon him forward, like the smell of fresh bread from the baker's window. Griff cleared his throat and was about to say, "Excuse me," but realized how dumb it would be talking to inanimate objects like these thorn bushes.

Suddenly, there was a rustling sound coming from within. At first, he thought there might have been a rabbit who'd just realized his presence, but the rustling sounds grew louder, and the shrubs trembled. He leaned in closer and noticed the intertwining branches were moving. Sliding across one another, like tangled snakes. They unwound themselves from one another until an opening appeared right in front of him

Though the shrubs had unraveled themselves, Griff's stomach did the opposite. As he took his first steps forward into the shadows of the guardian trees, a knot formed in the pit of his stomach.

It's just a dream. It's just a dream. He thought to himself. *Nothing can hurt you here. You need to do this. You're safe.* The words felt empty and hollow. Leaves and twigs crunched under his feet with every step. Their sounds, the only sounds Griff could hear, echoed in the shadows. It seemed that not even the wind dared to follow him here.

Were the trees watching him? Griff slowed as a shiver raced up his spine. It felt like eyes tracked his movements, but when he glanced around, he only saw shadows. The eerie illusion made him feel like a foreigner, a trespasser.

Ahead, Griff saw light trying to break through the shadows; a clearing. The still, small voice in the back of his mind, that mysterious presence that lured him into the shadows in the first place, jumped with excitement. The young mage accelerated, his once slow and careful steps replaced with quick, agile strides. As he ran, small plants with large leaves slapped at his torso and legs, as though they were trying to stop him. Leaves swirled around him, blocking his view. Vines snaked across the ground, inches from his feet. It was as though the entire forest was sparing no effort to keep Griff from reaching the clearing.

Griff sprinted faster. His feet pounded against the forest floor. Strange mixtures of opposing emotions flooded his mind: Fear—which was his own—and excitement—which was not. Finally, just as Griff was beginning to think the entire forest would cave in on him, he broke through the darkness and was swallowed whole by the light of the sun. Thankful for its endearing light, Griff laid on the ground and closed his eyes, allowing the golden orb in the sky to welcome him into the clearing.

He heaved huge, desperate gulps of air. Knowing he was in a dream did nothing to still the fear he had felt in the shadows. Finally, his beating heart started to slow, and that inkling in his mind urged him to continue. He was so close. He could feel it. Well, he could feel *something* telling him he was close.

Griff sat up and reached his hands behind him to steady himself. Just then, the ground rumbled. It was faint at first and came in small, consistent bursts. But with every second that passed, the tremors grew in intensity. Something was coming. Something big. His heart sank, and he felt as though he was glued to the ground. The overwhelming fear inside him grew, but the other mysterious presence in him felt excitement.

His hands were shaking, and not because of his fear, but because the tremors had intensified to the point that he could visibly seem them shake. Loud booms and crashes echoed from the woods, as though trees were snapping in two. Whatever it was, it was getting closer. Griff tried to scoot away from the edge of the forest, but his hands and feet wouldn't cooperate. They were at the mercy of his own fear and the quaking of the ground.

As suddenly as the tremors started, they stopped, and the forest was still and quiet. Griff's eyes zipped back and forth, scanning the edge of the woods. There was no sign of life. No sign that anything had been there at all. He wiped the sweat from his forehead. Then the wind, which was absent in the shadows, cast a gentle breeze that teased his messy black hair. He quickly regained control of his limbs and stood. Eyes still scanning for life, he turned and faced the forest.

Without warning, the world behind him erupted in a flurry of activity and sound. The ground convulsed, and it sounded like lightning had struck at his back.

His heart seized. He twisted and fell to the ground. Pure terror gripped his every thought and emotion when he found the source of the commotion. Beady, red eyes stared into his soul. Long, deadly talons gripped the dirt in hatred. Smoky, gray scales seemed to almost absorb the sunlight instead of reflect it. Large, elegant wings gracefully extended and blocked out the sun. Pitch black smoke billowed from its snout.

Griff sat frozen. His heart beat loudly against his chest, and his pulse thumped in his ears. And yet strangely enough, the presence at the edges of his consciousness leaped for joy. Towering over Griff stood the final guardian of the forest—and the last clue to his location: a Nightflame dragon.

The monster's eyes narrowed at him, and it leaned its head closer. Griff stared at the jagged teeth that looked as though they had been dipped in a bucket of red paint. Teeth that were so close, he could smell the overwhelming metallic odor that came from the blood. It sniffed him, going up one side of his body and down the other. Its shoulders rose as it inhaled deeply, lifted its head to the sky, and erupted in a ferocious roar that chilled Griff to his very core.

Then, the dragon stumbled backward and fell on its side. It lay motionless in an awkward position, not breathing. It was dead.

"Griff!" A dirty pillow thumped against his head before falling to the tent floor.

He sat up and groaned from the pangs of waking from his deep slumber. The cot underneath him creaked from the years of use.

"You were muttering in your sleep again last night," Leena Driscoll said from the other side of the tent.

"Yeah?" Griff said, flinging his feet to the side and sliding on his dirty socks. "Sorry if I kept you up."

Leena shook her head and rolled her eyes. "That's not why I'm telling you that." She gave him that mother's stare that demanded more information.

"I dunno why I was mutterin' in my sleep."

"You sure about that? No strange dreams or anything? No lava caves or nightstalkers or Korrun Aldamund?"

Griff paused and pretended to look for his shoe, knowing full well he had placed it under his cot the night before.

"No," he finally said, realizing he had been quiet for far too long. "Not that I remember, anyways."

"Remember that the king said if you have any more dreams about Korrun, you're to tell Professor Coen ri—"

"I will, mom! I promise! Now, can I *please* go get some breakfast? I'm starving."

Leena paused as though she was wrestling with how to handle her son's outburst. She sighed and said, "O-okay, honey. Go get you some breakfast." Then she walked out of the tent.

Griff sighed. He knew he hadn't been fair to her. But after telling the king his recent dream about Korrun in the catacombs not long after Cordelia had fallen, he was tired of people treating him differently. Whether it was his parents watching his every moment, especially as he slept, or whether it was other Cordelians staring at him like he was a human nightstalker, he just wished things could go back to normal. Griff promised himself he would make amends with his mom once he got some breakfast in him. He may have lied about his dreams, but he hadn't lied about being hungry.

"Hey Griff!" Sylva said as soon as Griff drew back the tent flap. "Sleep well?"

"Literally, Sylva, I can't even take a single step outside my tent before somebody comes barging at me."

"Oh … sorry, Griff. I'll just … I'll go." The look of hurt on Sylva's face was like a dagger to Griff's heart.

"Sylva, wait. I'm sorry. I-I just … I'm hungry and I'm tired."

They walked through the ruins of Cordelia, down cobblestone streets that were no longer familiar. Ash-covered debris littered the ground, and the smell of the fire still lingered. It was strange to be at the heart of the town and still see all four walls of Cordelia. Only two weeks ago, shops and houses used to block those views, and now there were only plots of land with rubble and maybe a fence at best. Some yards housed humble tents that the king had provided, but they weren't as tall as the buildings they had replaced.

"Yeah, you must be tired and hungry," Sylva finally said after walking beside Griff in silence. "Let's get you some food."

"…That's … that's what I was about to do."

"Oh. Right." Sylva shifted uncomfortably and continued walking in silence, periodically looking at Griff, then back to the ground. It was like he didn't know how to talk to his childhood friend anymore.

Finally, Griff halted and looked at his friend. "Sylva. I need you to do something for me."

"Yeah? What's that?"

"Treat me normal."

"Normal?"

"Yes." He put a hand on Sylva's shoulder. "Everyone here looks at me all crazy like. Some treat me like I'm carryin' some sort of disease that'll spread to them if they get too close, and others treat me like I'm some sort of celebrity or that I'm famous or something. And I'm neither of those things!"

"Well … you are apparently a really, really, *really* strong mage or whatever. And you have had those dreams that interest the king…"

"Yeah, but nobody else knows that." Suddenly, a thought occurred to Griff. One he hoped wasn't true. "They *don't* know that ... right, Sylva?"

"...right," he said and continued walking toward the food tent.

Griff raced to catch up to him, grabbed him by the shoulder, and turned him around. "What did you say?"

"I didn't say anything!" he said, holding his hands in the air.

"Then how does everyone know about my dreams?"

"I-I dunno. Maybe your parents told them?"

"My parents know better than to go spoutin' off important information like that. I guarantee you it wasn't them. And you're lookin' awfully guilty."

"Fine!" Sylva said, looking like a terrified mouse. "I ... I was just so proud that *my* best friend is important ... you know? And – and he's strong! Crazy strong! And that he saved my life! So ... yeah, maybe I said a little too much about you, Griff, but nightstalker's fury, I'm thankful you're my best friend, okay?"

Griff sighed deeply. It was one of frustration, but it was also one of contemplation. He calmed himself before he spoke again.

"I'm thankful you're my best friend as well. But ... Sylva ... this is *important*. We don't know what these dreams mean or why exactly I'm having them. And we're at *war*. That means if any important information gets into the wrong hands, it could be bad. And last but not least ... I, as your best friend, am *begging* you not to tell anyone else about this stuff, ya hear? Please."

"Okay, Griff, I promise. No more. My lips are sealed shut."

"Good," Griff said. "Because I got something really important to share with you. And I need your help ..."

CHAPTER 2

Wave after wave pummeled the stone wall below. Tyrell closed his eyes and listened to the soothing song of the ocean, but it did no good. For some, this would be as close to paradise as you could get on this side of life. Not for him. For him, sitting on the edge of the cliff watching the sun sparkle across the top of the water was a waste of time. He hadn't forgotten his reason for being here, and waiting for Korrun to run his little errands wasn't helping him achieve his goal.

"What'cha doin' all the way out here away from everyone?"

Tyrell turned to face the dark-skinned girl who plopped down beside him on the hard, stony ground.

"Nothin'," Tyrell said, fixing his eyes back on the ocean.

"That sounds boring. I bet you're bored, aren't you."

"You could say that."

"Wow, and you don't talk much do you? My parents say I talk too much and it gets me into trouble."

"Well, your parents might be on to something."

"Yeah. They tend to be right about a lot of things. Well ... but not everything."

"Yeah, well sometimes parents can be wrong about things," Tyrell said, hoping that was enough to end the conversation. Maybe agreeing with her would shut her up. Plus, he couldn't agree more with her on that last point. From where he sat, he'd watched his father walk proudly alongside Korrun as they marched down the steep, wet steps along the side of another cliff. He didn't know what they were doing or why, but anger burned inside him as he was forced to stay behind with the rest of the black cloaks.

"Yeah..." The girl kicked her legs back and forth over the cliff wall and drew in the dirt with her finger.

She may not have left, but at least she was quiet now. Tyrell was too comfortable to move, anyway. After the long march here, his legs yearned for rest. Plus, where else would he go? Stand in the middle of the rowdy gang of black cloaks and nightstalkers? Not a chance. He knew better.

"I'm Ava, by the way," the girl said, reaching out her dirty hand. "Ava Adebayo."

Tyrell stared at her for a moment. The look he was trying to give her was one that demanded she put that hand back on the dirt instead of in his face, but he could feel his resolve dwindle under her kind and innocent eyes. They were hazel. Just like his mom's.

He sighed and reached his hand out and grasped hers in welcome. "Tyrell."

She smiled and daintily shook his hand. "Nice to meet you, Tyrell No-Last-Name."

She finally released his hand and fell backward into the dirt, allowing the midday sun to cover her face entirely. She shielded her eyes from the sun with a hand and watched the seagulls with fascination. And silence.

Finally, all too soon, she spoke again. "You know, this would be a perfect day if it weren't for the whole 'following Korrun on his path of death and destruction' bit."

"That's *Master* Korrun."

"He's not my master," she snapped.

"Maybe not, but if you wanna survive out here, then you better get used to saying it."

"What about you?" She leaned up on her elbows and squinted at him. "Are you just surviving out here?"

Tyrell snorted. "I'm on a mission. Survival is only half of it."

"What's the other half?"

He shook his head. "Doesn't matter. Not to you, anyway."

He turned his back toward Ava and stared at the entrance to the cave. They had been in there for so long … what were they doing?

"You know what I think, Tyrell No-Last-Name?" Ava said.

"No, and no offense, but I don't really care what you think. You or anyone else here at this camp."

Ava chuckled. "You say 'no offense,' then you say something offensive. I don't think that's how that works. You put up quite the strong front! But even though you don't care what I think, I'll tell you what I think anyway, 'cause that's what I do."

Tyrell refused to look at her, but he could feel her eyes on him, boring into his back.

"I don't think you're here for *Master* Korrun. You're here for some other reason."

"Yeah? What's that?"

"I dunno yet … but I'll figure it out."

"Good luck with that. Maybe I'm just here like all the other black cloaks. Maybe I buy into Master Korrun's ideology that he can save the world from the Corruption, no matter the cost."

"There! Right there. See, the way you say that leads me to believe you *don't* buy into it."

Tyrell sighed. "You're frustrating me."

"Well, get used to it, because now I'm along for the ride too."

Just then, Korrun and his entourage appeared in the opening of the cave and Tyrell perked up. The leader of the black cloaks looked furious, and Randolph matched his quick strides, words tumbling out of his mouth just as quickly.

Ava cocked her head to the side at the sight. "What do you think *they* were do—"

"Shh! I'm trying to listen." Tyrell tilted his head toward Randolph and closed his eyes.

"Sir, I'm telling you, it's in one of these caves. I know it. They may have been careful, but I'm certain it's here."

Korrun stared ahead and didn't speak a word. For the first time since joining the black cloaks, Tyrell watched his father's calm, confident, and stern demeanor falter under his master's irritation.

"Hey, who's that guy?" Ava asked. "He looks a lot like you. You two related?"

Tyrell never took his eyes off the man he'd called "Father" his entire life. This man, whom he'd share a home with. Watched him laugh and play with his family. Sat at his feet as he roasted meat over their firepit on the back porch and told the best campfire stories. He stared at the man who had just now paused, took a deep breath, and regained his stoicism, before matching his master's strides yet again.

"No," Tyrell whispered somberly. "We're not related. Not even close."

Tyrell stood, slapped the dust off the backside of his pants, and walked away. He'd seen enough.

CHAPTER 3

"Are you sure this is a good idea?" Sylva asked for what felt like the one hundredth time. He stomped behind Griff, trying to keep up.

"We have to, Sylva. I'm not doing this because I think it'll be *fun*. We're at war, remember? And sometimes you gotta do things you don't wanna do when you're at war."

"Yeah, but shouldn't we at least have told your parents or that one professor where we're going?"

Griff sighed and remained silent, his mind a blur of thoughts and justifications. None of the reasons that popped into his head seemed to make sense now that they were already an hour outside Cordelia. Or ... what was left of Cordelia, anyway.

"We could have. But I don't think they would have let me go. And I *need* to go. I need to be there to see it for myself."

"But don't you think that if the king had given you this quest to find the shards, that he'd, I dunno, make some sort of decree that allowed you to be part of the search party or somethin'?

Griff didn't say anything.

"... Griff, did the king actually give you this quest to find the shards?"

"Well ... no."

"Griff! Seriousl–"

"But I *know* that's what he's doing, Sylva! I know it. He's looking for the shards so Korrun doesn't get to them first. He may not have *told* me that's what he's doing, but he might as well have. And if – if I am somehow connected to these things, then I *need* to use it for the king's mission. It's not a mission he gave me, but it's one I can help with. I'm going to find the next shard. If you wanna go back now, that's fine, but I gotta keep going."

They walked in silence together for a while before Sylva finally said, "You really think it's there, don't you?"

Griff turned to look behind them, checking to make sure they weren't being followed. They'd used a lesser-known path through the Cordelian forest for the first hour, hoping no one would see them leave. Still, he felt like they needed to be careful. From his large pack, he snatched out one of the many muffins he'd stolen from breakfast and took a large bite. After wiping his mouth on his sleeve, he slowed his pace just enough so he and Sylva were side-by-side.

"Aye. I do. I really do. All last year I had dreams that Korrun was searching for a shard, and he eventually found it. I don't want to make that mistake again. If he gets all those shards ..." Griff paused. "Well, I don't know exactly what'll happen, but the king and the headmaster made it seem like it wouldn't be any good. And I don't want to waste time trying to convince everyone what I already know."

Griff dusted off his hands from any remaining muffin crumbs, pulled out his handle, and crafted his magical blue blade. With one swift motion, he sliced a thin, dead tree that was blocking the narrow path.

Sylva chuckled. "I literally could have pushed that thing over."

"I know, I know, but it feels so good to do magic without a huge audience." Griff let out a sigh and stretched his hands out, his blue blade effortlessly trimming the hanging branches as he walked. "I just feel so *free* right now!"

After a few minutes of pointlessly chopping through more branches, he extinguished his blade and sheathed it as they stepped onto the main path. The midday sunlight poured in from the cloudless blue sky, and he turned his face up to readily greet it.

He turned to face north toward Cordelia, and scanned the wide concrete path, making sure there was no one trailing them. When he was convinced they were safe from any followers, he relaxed his pace and Sylva followed. They walked along the faded double-yellow lines that had been painted on this path many years ago. They laughed as they placed one foot in front of the other to see how far they could make it before they lost their balance and their foot touched the unpainted, weathered concrete.

Although they laughed and joked, Griff was fighting an internal battle. He was trying to force a sense of adventure in place of the feelings of guilt and fear he felt at leaving with no notice. The two boys sauntered along, and Griff shared story after story of all the things he had experienced in the last year. Stories of the king and his son. Of Bergots Castle. Of the epic Altar Storm matches. He shared his terrifying experience within the Corruption storm and the horrific scenes within. Sylva hung on to every last word.

"Once we make it to Solastran, you'll get to see more magic. You'll love it. The shops, the park, the people. Everything."

For once, Sylva didn't speak. His eyes dropped to the ground and glazed over.

"Sylva?"

"Sounds like Solastran is way better than Cordelia ..."

"I—uh, it's, well ..." Griff paused. His heart sank. How could he have been so calloused? He was so excited that Sylva and his family were moving to Solastran, that he hadn't stopped to think about the change that would be for his friend. Not only that, but Sylva was still mourning the loss of his home. It was all he had ever known. While the loss of his hometown still stung, Griff had at least experienced what life was like outside the four stone and metal walls. He had friends who were waiting for him. He had a ... a girlfriend? He shook the thought from his mind. *I'll figure that one out later.*

"Sorry, Sylva," Griff said. "I know you're hurting. I know it's a lot of change. And ... and I'm gonna miss home. A lot."

A tear slid down Sylva's cheek, and as quickly as it appeared, he wiped it away. Griff picked at his fingernails while they walked and pretended not to notice.

"Listen, you have every right to feel this way. And I don't want to rush you and the healing process. But ... but just know that you have something good to look forward to. And you won't have to experience it alone. I'll be there with you!"

"But what about your school? And homework? And your other friends?"

"Well ..." Griff paused. "Well, I want to introduce you to my friends. Then they'll be *our* friends, okay? And yeah, classes can get kinda busy, but I promise I'll come visit. And I think there's a school in Solastran too. I think they teach younger kids—"

Sylva shot him a look.

"—*and* teach non-magical folk too!" Griff held his hands up as though they showed his innocence.

"Do they teach about animals and magical creatures there? Y'know, like wargs and nightstalkers and dragons and stuff?" Sylva asked.

"Maybe? Why, you interested?"

"I dunno. Maybe. Just trying to figure out what life out there looks like for me."

"Well," Griff said, scratching his chin. "Trust me, I know we'll both miss Cordelia. But just know it's not all bad where we're going. You'll find your place there, too. I just know it."

The journey ahead was long and uneventful. Conversations sparked and died. It didn't help that the scenery stayed the same: tall trees with wide branches, faded signs with shaggy, unkempt grass that swayed at its base, and never-ending chirping coming from the birds that sang from the branches shadowing the sides of the road. When he could bear it no more, Griff used his spells and abilities to keep things interesting. Eventually, Griff shielded his eyes and gazed toward the sun, being careful not to look directly at it.

"It's about two. We should be getting close. Another hour or so and we'll be there, I think?"

A thunderous roar from behind shredded through the quiet setting. Strong gusts of wind at their backs sought to push the two boys to the ground. Griff turned and took a step back, but the scene before him made his knees weak and he fell.

A warg dove in his direction and landed only a few feet away. Griff scooted backward on the ground, fear keeping him low, and his desire to live keeping him moving. A few seconds later, a second warg landed with matching ferocity.

"There you are!" a familiar voice barked.

Griff's eyes grew wide as he watched Gale Driscoll and Professor Coen dismount from their wargs. Gale gave Kindra an absent-minded pat on the head before walking toward Griff. Griff's heart sank into the pit of his stomach and he thought he might get sick.

"Where ... have ... you ... been?" Griff's dad said through gritted teeth. The professor stood silent next to Magnus with his arms crossed as Gale marched forward and picked Griff off the ground with one arm.

"I—I—" Griff stuttered, suddenly unable to form words.

"We have been worried *sick* about you, Griff! Leavin' right after breakfast without so much as a single note!" Gale released his son and took a step back and folded his arms. "Answers. Now."

"I've seen it!" Griff burst out. "I—I had another dream and I think I know where a shard is!"

"Another shard?" Professor Coen suddenly stepped forward. "You've seen another shard, Griff?"

"Well..." Griff gulped. "Not exactly. You see, I had another dream. One like before with Korrun. I–I didn't see the shard, exactly, but it was the same type of dream as before."

"You didn't see the shard?" the professor asked. "Then how do you know it's there?"

"I just ... I just know, okay? I can feel it."

"Why didn't you tell us?" Gale asked.

"Because I didn't think you would believe me. And I didn't think you would let me come. And I just didn't want to waste time and then Korrun get another shard. If I have this ability to see the shards, well, then, I want to use it! We've got to find the rest of them before Korrun does!" Words tumbled out of Griff like small loaves of bread falling from an overturned basket.

Everyone paused, all eyes on Griff. Sylva had quietly shuffled behind the men, one hand now busy rubbing the top of Kindra's head, doing his best to remain unnoticed. Gale scratched his chin, a custom Griff was all too familiar with. His dad was now in deep thought, wrestling to soothe his anger and seek the best response. Usually following a silent moment such as this, his dad would, in one sentence, relay Griff's punishment and offer profound wisdom. Gale walked over to Griff, placed a firm arm around his shoulders, and pushed him toward Kindra.

"Get on." Gale turned his attention to Sylva. "You. With him," he said, thumbing over his shoulder in the direction of the professor and Magnus.

There had been no words of wisdom. Only the punishment of returning to camp empty handed. "We can't go back! We have to go get the shard!" Griff argued. He wouldn't physically fight his dad, but he had to try and stand his ground.

"Who says we're going home? You say there's a shard nearby, I say let's go check it out."

Griff halted. "Really? You believe me? You're ... you're not mad?"

"Yes, really. Yes, I believe you. And no, I'm not mad. I'm *furious*." Gale narrowed his eyes at Griff and said, "Trust me, you're not getting off that easy. But this little adventure of ours will give me time to find the proper way to deal with you when we get back home."

He climbed on top of Kindra and offered a helping hand to Griff. "Until then, I guess we're off to find this ... this shard of yours."

"Which is where, by the way?" Professor Coen called from Magnus' back.

Griff paused, then said with a crooked smile that showcased his guilt, "Umm ... the ... uh ... the Dracorian Sea?"

Gale stood at the cliff's edge, leaning against a palm tree and gazing out over the Dracorian Sea. He remained silent the whole ride over, but Griff could tell he was still wrestling with a hard, simmering anger.

Thankfully the trip to the island in the middle of the sea had been quick. They had crossed over the deep blue water and scanned the sea for any island that Griff deemed familiar. Flying from island to island, it didn't take long before he spotted the right one. The one from his dreams. Thankfully, having Kindra and Magnus with them meant they didn't have to make the steep climb that would have otherwise been unavoidable. While the last time he had been "here" had been a dream, the danger he felt climbing the cliff had felt all too real. It was a feeling he was thankful he could avoid in his awakened state.

"And how exactly did you expect to get here without our help, huh?" Gale finally asked, pushing off the palm tree and turning to face Griff. Kindra, as if sensing Gale's fury, walked over, rumbled affectionately at him and rubbed the top of her head across his shoulder. Never taking his eyes off Griff, he gave her a loving pat then asked, "Were you just gonna swim here?"

"Yeah ... uh ... I hadn't thought that far out."

"'Course not." Gale responded flatly.

"Well, you picked a beautiful spot at least," Professor Coen said. He placed his hands on his hips and inspected the beauty before him, allowing the salty, warm summer breeze to ruffle his wavy brown hair.

"That's just it," Griff answered. "I didn't pick this place. I think it picked *me*." He was avoiding trying to explain the feeling at the edges of his consciousness. That somehow it was as though someone or something had invaded his mind and was trying to lure him here.

The professor untied his pack from Magnus' saddle, walked to the edge of the cliff, and looked down. "You were really gonna climb this, huh, Griff?"

Griff wrestled with his own pack and pretended not to hear, knowing there wasn't a good answer. Sylva walked past Griff and breathlessly whispered to no one in particular, "This place is amazing!"

Even though they had landed in the same place that Griff, in his dream, had rested following his ascent, he still examined the area, trying to gather his bearings and remember where he entered the forest.

Gale sighed, long and slow, which was usually a sign of him shaking off his anger. "Where to, Miracle Boy?"

Griff scanned the length of the forest. All the tightly packed bushes full of thorns looked the same. He didn't know if he could find the exact spot at which he entered from his dream. Maybe it didn't matter? There was only one way to find out.

"Into the dark, creepy forest we go."

They marched to the entrance, the thorn bushes and the towering trees behind them doing nothing to ease Griff's anxious mind. He thought that perhaps in his dream, his perceptions might be off. Distorted by his sleep. As he gazed into the shadows, the same feeling that the forest was watching, waiting, loomed over him once again. The still, small presence in the back of his mind grew excited.

They stared at the thick, almost impenetrable wall, before Professor Coen stepped forward and snatched a handle from its holster and ignited a long, blue blade.

"Wellp, let's get this over with," he said.

"Wait!" Griff stepped between the professor and the wall.

The professor cocked his head.

"I don't think … that's necessary."

"So what do you suggest?" the professor asked, extinguishing his blade.

"I … I don't think the forest would like that very much. Just … watch."

Griff took a deep breath and held it as he stepped closer to the bushes. He didn't know if it was all part of the dream, or if the bushes were actually somehow alive. But if they were, it would probably be best not to anger the forest.

Nothing happened. Griff let out a whoosh of air. He was thankful he was wrong. Now they didn't have to worry about some sort of guardian forest trying to keep them from the shard. Or maybe it had been a test? Maybe the forest in his dream was making sure he was the right one for the job. Either way, he was glad that—

Suddenly, a sharp rustling filled the silence. The bushes trembled and shook as branches unwound themselves. Everyone took a step back except for Griff, whose heart sank. So, it *was* a guardian forest.

Gale unsheathed his sword and readied himself. Sylva stumbled backward behind the group. Professor Coen reignited his blade and spread his feet.

"Wait!" Griff called, holding out his hand toward the others. "Just give it a second."

"This happen in your dream, too?" the professor asked.

"Yeah."

The group complied, but Gale and Professor Coen didn't sheathe their weapons.

The bushes continued their shuffling until they created a large opening. Thorned branches were tightly woven together, reaching up and over the new hole in the barrier to create an arched entryway. The trembling stopped. It was quiet again. Another gentle breeze fluttered the leaves on the bushes, generating a shushing noise, as though it was telling the whole island to be silent.

Griff wiped the sweat from his forehead and turned to the rest of the group.

"See?"

"King's crown! That was ... that was something else!" Sylva exclaimed but maintained his position in the back of the group.

Gale and Professor Coen exchanged looks, then lowered their weapons and allowed their muscles to relax. Griff took another deep breath and let it out slowly. "All right, everyone, let's do this."

He cautiously stepped forward through the entryway, careful not to touch any of the thorns. The presence in the back of his mind urged him to run, to sprint through the opening, but he swatted the feelings away like an annoying fly. He looked to the branches hanging over him and said, "Uh ... thank you!"

After he had crossed the threshold and was covered in the shadows from the forest, the quiet island erupted in noise as the barbed entryway collapsed on itself. Thorny branches reached across the opening and snatched at one another, drowning out the panicked cries of the group. Within seconds, the sunlight vanished as the bushes returned to their position so they could do what they do best—keep people out. Realization turned Griff's blood cold. He was now alone with the dark forest at his back.

CHAPTER 4

"Griff! Griff! Are you okay?" Gale called from the other side of the bushes.

Griff could hear Professor Coen ignite his handle before yelling, "Stand back!"

"No!" Griff hollered back, hoping it wasn't too late. He paused and listened to the other side. "Don't do it! Don't make the forest angry, okay!"

"We're gonna find a way in, Griff. Just stay there!" Gale said.

"I'm fine. I promise! I think this is something the forest wants me to do alone. But I've got my handle and I've got my pack of supplies, okay? I'll be fine! Just stay here and wait. I'll be back in less than an hour. If I'm not ... well, then ... then you can hack and slash your way in here."

Nobody from the other side spoke a word.

"Deal? Give me an hour, please? I can do this!"

"Deal." Gale said with a defeated tone. Griff imagined Sylva and the professor were both staring at him. This was his son, after all, and anyone who knew Gale Driscoll knew not to get between him and the safety of his son.

"One hour. Not a second longer, ya hear?" Gale called.

"One hour!"

"Please be careful, Griff."

"I will, Dad, I promise."

"Love you, son." Gale's voice cracked.

Griff paused. His dad was plenty in touch with his emotions, but he almost never let them slip like this. Not unless he thought Griff was in real danger. It was a warning sign Griff hadn't expected. "Love you too, Dad. See you soon."

Griff turned and sprinted into the darkness. Since the bushes surrounding the forest had come alive like they had in the dream, he was now operating on the assumption that the rest of the forest would do the same as well. But why would the bushes allow him through, and the forest try to stop him? He assumed this had to be a test of some sort. Either way, that presence in the back of his mind seemed to swell in excitement with every step forward.

The dense forest canopy smothered any possible sunlight. Darkness—thick, unending darkness—covered Griff like a thick wool blanket. Nothing moved. All was quiet. Not even the wind ventured inside this dangerous labyrinth. His senses were on high alert. His head swiveled from side to side. Things felt … off. It was like the forest was holding its breath, waiting to see what Griff would do.

He tiptoed forward, hoping he was moving in the right direction. A bright flash of white shredded through the darkness and temporarily blinded him. *Why did I have to stare right at my own light spell? King's crown, you're smarter than this.* The light was brighter than it needed to be. Griff demanded that it diminish, but his adrenaline, not to mention the shard from the Orb of Essence inside him, disobeyed. He held out his hand, facing his palm away from him so the blinding orb of light wasn't directly in his eyes.

There was no clear path in front of him. No convenient separation between the thick plants. No dirt trail for him to walk on. Instead, he shuffled ahead, pushing through overgrown ferns with sharp leaves and tall plants covered in flowers with long white petals. With every movement, the shadows from the vegetation danced along the dirt floor.

It as was though there were a thousand tiny, shadowy demons prancing at his feet, waiting for a chance to overtake him.

After twenty minutes of tiptoeing through the woods, Griff spotted a tiny glimpse of sunlight deeper in the forest. His heart jumped with relief, but the presence in his mind rejoiced even more. Griff's steps were now less careful. Faster. He trotted forward and watched as the tiny pinprick of light ahead grew.

Two ferns with large fronds and sharp edges came to life and flung their branches to the side, closing a gap in front of Griff, forcing him to the left. He picked up his pace. Another set of ferns sealed off another path. A tall plant with purple flowers growing along its vines slapped at his legs as he passed by. Suddenly, the rest of the forest was alive and against him.

He sprinted forward, ignoring the branches from the trees that seemed to reach for him. More plants slapped at his knees and legs, leaving shallow cuts that started to bleed. Griff's eyes stung from the sweat that poured down his face. His breath was quick and shallow. His heart pounded against his chest.

He heard a crack from above and dove just in time to miss the large branch that fell where he had just stood seconds before. He scrambled to his feet and scanned the forest canopy. The upper branches of the trees surrounding him shook violently. It was as though they were shaking their wooden fists in anger, sending a steady rain of branches on him.

Keeping his light steady in one hand, he swirled his other and cast a powerful gust of wind in all directions, flinging the falling branches away. He unsheathed his handle and ignited his blade. He had tried to be kind to the forest, not wanting to make it angry, but it was too late for that. He sprinted toward the beacon of sunlight ahead. Another group of ferns pushed their sharp leaves together, but Griff sliced through them with ease. A sense of satisfaction flowed over him as he watched their branches recoil in pain.

Thick branches reached down like fierce, wooden claws, but Griff quickly cut those away. Now that he didn't care about the forest's feelings, his pace quickened. He carved a path forward and steadily moved closer to the opening ahead. As its light grew, he diminished the white orb in front of him and used that hand to cast protective wind spells against the raining branches around him. The presence in the back of his mind urged him forward, cheering him on. His panic slowly diminished and confidence started to grow in him with every slice of his blade and with every wind spell cast.

Suddenly, he felt a stabbing pain in both his legs. A scream erupted from his throat and his body jolted forward. He slammed to the ground and his handle slipped from his grip and skidded across the dirty forest floor. The blue blade extinguished, covering Griff once again in the dark shadows of the forest. Thick, thorny vines slid across Griff's makeshift path and wrapped around his legs, squeezing their thorns deep into him.

Griff howled in pain as the vines became taut and started dragging him deeper into the shadows. He gritted his teeth and reached for his handle, but it was too far away. He tried to bury his fingers into the ground and claw his way forward, but the vines were too strong and their thorns were too deep. He groaned as he was pulled further into the forest, the vines not caring if there were rocks or sharp branches along their path. White hot pain threatened to knock him unconscious, but he squeezed his eyes shut and forced himself to stay awake.

He sucked in lungfuls of air, then swirled his trembling arms in front of him and sent bursts of fire toward the vines, away from his body. They clenched tighter around his legs, penetrating their thorns even deeper. The world went black for a moment and Griff's anguished scream echoed through the forest. He teetered on the edge of consciousness. He sucked in short, shallow breaths and sent another burst of fire in the same place. This time, the vines trembled, then went limp. The fire had burned right through the vines, severing them.

His shaking hands tenderly pulled the vines away, extracting the thorns from his legs. They had shredded his pant legs and blood was seeping out of the holes. He hissed in pain, but knew that it was only a matter of time before something else would attack. When he had freed himself, he took off his shirt, wiped the blood from his legs, and tore two wide strips to bandage them. Pain pulsed up and down his lower body, but he was able to walk. He limped over to his handle, ignited the blade, and pressed on.

Anger burned in his heart, and fear invaded his mind. He sliced his way forward, taking extra care to watch his back for any more vines. Every second felt like minutes. Every step felt like miles, but slowly, the light in front of him grew. He quickened his pace, his legs screaming out in pain with every lumbering step, but he gritted his teeth and did his best to ignore it. He wearily slashed ahead, barely able to control his movements. With a final burst of energy, he crashed into the clearing and fell on soft, green grass.

He dropped his handle beside him, snuffing the bright blue blade. He closed his eyes and smiled at the wonderful sunlight that bathed his face. The plush grass caressed his aching body as if congratulating him on making it through the trials.

When he had caught his breath and his hands were no longer shaking, Griff pushed himself into an upright position and examined his legs. The makeshift bandages were soaked in blood, but he pulled an edge away from his skin and peeked at the wounds. He was no medical expert and wished that Sylva was at least beside him. While his friend was no doctor, he'd learned enough from his mother to be of use right now. The wounds trickled blood, but Griff imagined he would be all right. He might be slow, but he was still mobile.

Just then, Griff remembered the rest of his dream. A shot of adrenaline coursed through his body. *The dragon.* He groaned and forced himself to stand, but quickly ignored the pain and spun to face the rest of the clearing. Large boulders covered in moss were scattered in every direction. Swaying gently with the breeze stood a few palm trees. The presence in Griff's mind urged him to walk closer. The intense throbbing in his legs begged for rest. He stumbled further into the clearing, using boulders for support when he passed them by.

In his dream, the dragon had come crashing from the forest, so he kept quiet and strained his ears for any sounds that could alert him in case it happened again. He rounded the corner of a large boulder and stopped. His heart jumped to his throat. His hand instinctively reached for his handle, but he paused. He scanned the large mass of scales, teeth, and claws. The body in front of him wasn't moving. Wasn't breathing.

Frozen by fear, Griff stood and stared at the dragon. Though on its side, with its back facing him, he estimated it to be as large as a one-story house. Wings that were awkwardly folded in on themselves looked as though each could span the width of two houses. Its smoky gray scales were covered with dried mud. And though he couldn't see them, Griff imagined if he circled around to the front and its eyes were open, they would be the color of blazing fire.

He set his jaw in place and staggered forward. Time was of the essence. If he didn't find the shard and make it back through the forest soon, the rest of the group would make the trek to find him. After how the guardian forest treated him, he shuddered to think of how it would respond to the others. As he stumbled forward, he felt a new sensation coming from the presence at the edges of his consciousness. This whole time, it had projected feelings of urgency and excitement. Now, all Griff felt was sadness.

Sorrow that was not his own washed over him. He reached a trembling hand forward and gently touched the beast's hard scales. They were warm. Not from the life inside—there was none—but from the amount of time this body had spent in the sun. Strangely, though, there was only a faint scent of decay. This body was fresh. Could it be that he had witnessed this dragon's demise in his dream just the night before? Another salty breeze gently caressed Griff, as though comforting him. No longer did this quiet, peaceful clearing feel like a welcome relief from the deadly forest surrounding it. Now, it felt as though he were witnessing a silent funeral. One where he was the only attendant.

It didn't feel right to use the Nightflame's body for support as he walked around it, so he sucked in his breath and made do without. He staggered to the front side of the beast and stood merely feet from its face. Long, jagged fangs protruded from its large snout. Spikes the length of Griff's arm jutted out from the sides of its chin and jaw. Two long, deadly horns protruded from the top of its head. He ran a tender hand along a deep scar. One of many, all which had healed and were probably very old. He didn't know how old dragons lived to be. After all, they were so rare that their very existence had been relegated to nothing more than old wives' tales. Considering its size, the time-worn scars, and the lack of any noticeable wound that would have caused this creature's demise, he wondered if this dragon had died from old age.

Griff felt a solemn nudge within his mind. There was nothing he could do, and he needed to find that shard. He took one last look at the creature of legends and stumbled ahead. He didn't know what to look for, but thought that perhaps the presence within him would help. Slowly making his way past more boulders and palm trees, he noticed something ahead that piqued not only his interest, but the interest of the presence inside him. Smaller boulders that reached about the height of his knees had been assembled together in a perfect circle. Inside that circle was a collection of large sticks and leaves: a nest. Yes! A nest! Of course! All the legends told of dragons guarding a treasure. What if this dragon had been the guardian of a different kind of treasure? One of immense value? A shard of the Orb of Essence.

Excitement filled Griff, and this time it was his own. He jogged ahead, adrenaline fueling his steps and allowing him to push past the pain coursing through his legs. He was about to do it. He was actually going to find a shard and be one step closer to stopping Korrun. Thick layers of sticks and dried leaves covered the floor of the nest, and for a moment, Griff's heart jumped to his throat in excitement when he saw a shape radiating bright light. He peered closer and realized it was an eggshell. Scattered throughout the nest were several pieces of eggshell left behind by baby dragons that had hatched. They were deep black, smooth, and reflected the sun when angled just right. Griff's heart sank. No shard here. He scooted some leaves to the side and pulled out half an egg. It was much smaller than he expected a dragon egg to be. He would have thought that a full-size egg would be the size of his torso, but the half shell he held in his hands indicated a whole one was probably half that size.

Clenching his teeth, he reached down and dug through the bottom of the nest. It had to be here. He knew it. This was the place he had dreamed about. This was where he was led. He had dragged Sylva here. Disappointed his family and the professor. And fought through the forest. It couldn't all be for nothing. Sweat dripped from his forehead onto the leaves and disappeared in between the layers of nest. The heat from the sun beat against his aching body as though it were angry at him. Sharp tips from the dried twigs scratched his hands as he continued to dig.

His feelings of excitement were long gone and raging frustration took its place. *Where is it? Don't tell me you're going to lead me here only to get beat up and walk away with nothing!* He wanted to shout at the presence in his mind. His frustrated sigh broke the calm silence of the clearing and he stood with hands on his hips. Hanging off the other side of the nest was a large tree branch yet to be broken and assembled with the rest of the nest. Griff walked around the large circle of stones to investigate.

The sea breeze caressed the dead leaves along the large branch, which fluttered at her touch and sounded like gentle rain. The branch hung over the side, creating a sloping cover. Griff hobbled closer and peered through the leaves to discover another black egg. This one was whole, unbroken, and protected from the intense afternoon sun. He scooted the branch to the side and held the egg with both hands. It was heavy. And it was warm. He was holding an actual Nightflame dragon egg in his hands.

Griff looked past the nest and stared at the boulders ahead, remembering the body that lay on the other side. That must have been the mother. Sadness flooded his mind again. If the egg hatched—and that was a big if—but if it hatched and had no mother, the creature would surely die. He limped cautiously as he carried the egg toward the body of its mother and stood near the dragon's face.

"I ... uh ... I found your baby." He felt so strange talking to the corpse of a dragon, but something inside him told him it was the right thing to do. "I don't know if it'll hatch or ... or not, but I'll protect it until it's ready to be on its own. Maybe I'm crazy for doing that, but I'll give it a try."

He paused as if waiting for the dragon to respond, but there was nothing. Just silence. He held the egg close to his face and said, "Just please don't eat me, okay?"

Resting a gentle hand on the side of the dragon's snout, he scanned up and down its body, wondering how in the world he would hatch and raise a baby dragon. Something sparkled in the mother's claw. Her talons had been tightly closed, so Griff hadn't noticed it before, but something shimmered within. He carefully set the egg down and pried two talons apart just far enough so he could reach his hand in. Something jagged brushed against his skin, and as carefully as he could, pulled it from the grip of the Nightflame.

Shining from the center of Griff's palm, not from the light of the sun but by its own light, was a shard of the Orb of Essence.

CHAPTER 5

"Seriously? Why are you following me? I prefer to fish alone." Tyrell marched past the last tent in the camp, training his eyes forward as he passed a group of black cloaks. One of them, Theo, glared at him, but he pretended not to notice. Ever since he had accused Tyrell of killing that boy during the night of the invasion, he did his best to steer clear. Not because he was afraid of him. And not because he was trying to generally steer clear of the entire camp. It was because Theo was on to him. He was suspicious, and Tyrell didn't want to give him any more reasons to call him out.

"And I prefer to stick with you, is that a problem?" Ava said.

"Yes. Yes, that is a problem. That's what I'm trying to say."

"Well, too bad. I'm not staying in that camp with those people. And you're different than all of 'em, so I'm coming with you whether you like it or not."

Tyrell huffed but said nothing. Instead, he repositioned his grip on the fishing net he had borrowed from the supply captain and strode toward the cliffs ahead, taking care to stomp on the tiny flowers in his path.

"Plus, I've never been fishing," Ava continued, rushing to Tyrell's side. She eyed the large net slung over his shoulder. "Ought to be fun watching you try."

Tyrell eyed her but remained silent. After they passed the last tents that were set atop the cliffside overlooking the ocean, he stopped and peered over the small drop off at the sandy beach that met the turquoise waters below. He breathed deeply through his nose. The air smelled of salt water and fish. It was the scent of fresh possibilities.

"Perfect spot," he said to nobody.

"Perfect? What do you mean perfect?" Ava glanced nervously over the cliff's edge at the water.

"It's a short, easy climb down, and then there's the shore. Nice sand, plenty of space to cast, and plenty of space to ..." he eyed her before continuing, "spread out."

She scooted away from the edge. "Nice try, there Tyrell, but that's not happening."

"Fine. Stay here, then." He planted a confident foot down on a stone that jutted out, giving him an easy first step.

"Wait, wait. Just ... wait, okay? I ... I'm afraid of the ocean, okay? But I'm still coming with you!"

The confident, talks-too-much Ava crossed her arms as if hugging herself. She gazed at the ground, and her hands slowly ran up and down her arms. Her dark skin glistened with sweat, but Tyrell imagined it wasn't all from the intense heat. He smirked. Maybe some of it was from the nerves. Had he broken her confidence already? He raised an eyebrow at this new demeanor.

"I'm afraid of the ocean," she repeated, giving herself a tight squeeze. "Rivers ... streams ... that's all fine. But ... the ocean is just something different to me, ya know? You just never know what's under those waves." Her head remained lowered, but she glanced at Tyrell to see his reaction.

"Fine. Stick with me. Just keep the annoyances to a minimum, you hear?"

It didn't take long for them to climb down. The ledges were more like wide steps that sanctioned their request to fish on the shore. Ava was surprisingly agile, hopping from ledge to ledge and creating her own path down. It seemed as though her confession had released a heavy weight off her shoulders … and her mood. A happy-go-lucky Ava was the last thing Tyrell wished for on a fishing trip meant to be spent alone.

She kicked the sand in the air as she ran on the beach. Two cartwheels and a loud yell in excitement later, she ran back to Tyrell who had carefully rolled his pant legs above his knees and was untwisting the net. He waded into the ocean until he was knee deep, keeping his eyes trained on the water, looking for fast moving shadows.

"You'll pull me out if things start to get crazy, right, Tyrell?" Ava called from the shore.

Without a glance back, Tyrell muttered just loud enough for her to hear, "They won't get crazy. It's just fishing. But yes, I got your back."

"Okay! Here I come!" She squealed and dashed into the water. She yelped and splashed the entire way until she reached Tyrell and clamped both hands on his shoulder, forcing a hiss of pain out of him.

He wheeled around and glared at her. "You're scaring the fish."

"Scaring the fish?" she said, out of breath. "I'm more scared than they are!"

"Well, I'm about to leave you out here by yourself unless you let go of me."

She relaxed her grip, but didn't let go. She bit her lip and for the first time since Tyrell had met her, he saw pain behind her eyes.

"Look." Tyrell sighed. "I'm sorry, it's just … you're scaring the fish. If we don't come back with something, then they won't let us come back here, okay?" He placed a hand on hers and gently removed it from his shoulder. "I won't let anything happen to you, but you gotta give me some space to work, all right?"

For a moment, Ava said nothing, then she nodded and said, "You're right. Sorry …"

"All right, just … stand over there, okay? And let me know if you see any fish." He pointed about ten feet away, off to the side and behind him.

She slowly waded to the spot, then placed her fingertips in the cool water and closed her eyes.

Tyrell resumed his position, net at the ready, eyes scanning the water. A few stray baitfish swam by, but they were too small. A net like the one he carried wasn't meant for fish that size. They could easily squeeze through the holes. But where there was bait fish, there might be something chasing them worth catching.

A few uneventful minutes went by in silence, before Ava's squeal pierced through the quiet.

"There! Right there! Hurry!" She pointed ahead and her finger followed the mass of shadows in the water. "There's so many!"

Tyrell took two large but careful steps, then with a twisting motion, flung the net in the direction of the fish. The net spread wide and splashed in the water, perfectly on top of the shadows. Tyrell began yanking the slack line of the net, closing the bottom and trapping the fish inside. Ava dashed to the net, all expressions of hurt eliminated by excitement and curiosity.

Suddenly, the clump of shadows separated, and the school of tiny fish wriggled the holes in the net. *Bait fish.* Tyrell huffed and turned to Ava, doing his best to maintain an even tone.

"Those are bait fish. As you can *see*, they're too small for this net. We want to catch what *eats* these fish."

"Oh, I see!" she said in wonder. She was like a distracted child shadowing her parents as they worked. Curious about the work, but not enough focus to really learn anything.

Tyrell continued to pull the net toward him. "Well, there's enough bait fish in there, we might can snag a few and use them as chum," he said.

Suddenly, the net jerked and disappeared in a cloud of sand and water. Ava screamed and pointed.

"A shark! A shark just went after the fish!"

The line jerked out of Tyrell's hands before he could tighten his grip or plant his feet. About ten feet away, a large fin with Tyrell's net tangled around it rose out of the water. Tyrell yelled, "Stand back!" as he desperately searched for the remaining slack line.

Ava shuffled her feet, trying to back away from the spot where the net once was. Suddenly, she screamed and fell in the water, her body fully submerged. Tyrell sprinted, screaming her name. She resurfaced for a breath and spluttered for help. He reached down to grasp her extended hand, but then it was gone. Her foot was caught in the slack line of the net. It was dragging her under. Her struggling body fought viciously against the force pulling her away from Tyrell, but it was no use. This wasn't her territory. It was the shark's.

But ... it wasn't a shark. Not really. At first glance, that's exactly what it looked like: a long flat head in the shape of a hammer, and following it was a tall fin that sliced through the water. But where the tail was supposed to be, a giant bony crab claw flailed about, fighting the tangled net.

Tyrell's heart pounded against his chest, and he chased after Ava. He dove into the water and swam as fast and as hard as he could, keeping his eyes on her, who had just resurfaced again for another quick breath of air. It was no use. Even with Ava in tow, the monster was too fast.

Quickly, Tyrell stood and swirled his hands around. A thick wall of ice formed in front of the monster. It slammed into the icy barrier, and that's when Tyrell saw its legs. Giant, plated lobster-like limbs flailed about as it whirled the beast's body around, forcing it back the way it came. Its razor-sharp lobster-like claws dug in the sand and propelled it forward, thrusting Ava back underneath the waves.

Tyrell worked furiously, casting more ice spells. This was his one chance to save her. Each time the beast turned, it faced another wall of ice. Each barrier grew wider until they all connected with each other. Tyrell shuffled forward as quickly as he could, refusing to take his eyes off Ava.

Every time her head resurfaced, a small wave of relief hit Tyrell. But the time between each surface was getting longer and longer. The shark-like creature thrashed about in the water. The walls of ice now completely connected, forming a watery prison.

When he was close enough, Tyrell slammed one hand against the surface of the water, and with the other, froze the connected trail of water droplets from the splash. He snatched the jagged, icy spear from the air and thrust it deep into the eye of the beast. Immediately, the water turned crimson. While the monster writhed in pain, its deadly tail thrashing wildly about, Tyrell reached down and pulled Ava from the water. She was unconscious. Dodging the monster's tail, he quickly untangled her foot from the rope, then without looking back, dashed to the shore by the cliff's wall and gently lay his friend on her back. She wasn't breathing.

"Ava? Ava, can you hear me? Wake up!" He gently slapped at her cheeks, but she didn't respond.

Tyrell pressed his lips to hers and began to breathe, forcing his air into her.

"C'mon, Ava, breathe. Breathe!" He counted out the chest compressions, then resumed his breaths.

Each second felt like an eternity as he worked on her lifeless body. Suddenly, her chest heaved, and she spewed saltwater all over Tyrell.

"Ava?" he screamed, helping her to a sitting position and pounding her back as she coughed and spluttered.

"Y-you're alive!"

She turned to face the sand, supporting herself on her shaking arms and knees. She retched and coughed, heaving gulps of air in between each one. Finally, she slowed, turned around, and sat next to Tyrell. He tried to slow his own breathing once he knew she would be okay, but was still finding it difficult. Ava placed her head on his shoulder—a sentiment that would normally make him fuming mad—but one that was welcome in this case. He kept his hands behind him on the sand, doing his best to support both their weight.

"Th—" She coughed again. "Thank you." Her voice was raspy and weak. "Thank you, Tyrell."

"Told ya I'd keep you safe."

"Just ... barely."

He nodded. "Yeah. Barely."

They sat on the shore underneath the shade of the cliffs in silence and watched the dying creature's thrashing grow weaker until it grew still and floated on top of the crimson water, its plated legs stretched in awkward angles.

Tyrell leaned back against the cliff, closed his eyes, and said, "Well, at least we'll bring *something* back to camp."

"What, that thing?" Ava pointed at the corpse.

Tyrell shook his head. "Yep. Which, as you can see, is *not* a shark."

"Hmph. Well, I'm not going to get it." Ava crossed her arms and leaned against the cliff.

Tyrell chuckled, but said nothing. He took long deep breaths to try and still his racing heart. The wind ruffled his long, wet hair that felt stiff from the salt. It was a strange experience. One he'd never had before as he had always tried to keep his hair cut short, like a soldier. Like his father. He ran his fingers through his hair. He wasn't like his father. Not anymore.

Sitting in the shade of the cliff, listening to the crashing of the waves in the distance, and welcoming the ocean breeze almost made the moment feel like a vacation. Something he hadn't had in a long time. With Ava now safe and Tyrell enjoying the moment, he realized he hadn't felt this relaxed in a long time. The call of sleep beckoned him in the quiet moment and he eagerly welcomed it. But it was all interrupted by the sound of Ava's gentle voice.

"Can I ask you a question?"

Tyrell kept his eyes closed, trying to stay in the moment, but he could already feel the tides of sleep slipping away.

"Mm-hm," he grunted.

She hadn't moved from her spot, her head still on his shoulder. He could feel her fiddling with her hands, as though gaining the courage to ask her question.

"Go on with it," he said, repositioning himself against the wall, still refusing to open his eyes.

Her fidgeting stopped. "Why are you here, Tyrell? Really?"

The question caught him off guard. While she pestered him about his mission the first few days of her arrival, he had made it abundantly clear that such conversation was off-limits. She pulled away and angled toward him.

"You stay away from the other black cloaks. You sleep outside of camp every single night. You're constantly trying to hear every word the second-in-command is saying. I don't think you're here because you want to follow Korrun."

"*Master* Korrun."

"Yeah, yeah, I get it. *Master* Korrun."

"It's for your own safety," Tyrell said.

"Okay, fine. Anyways, I don't think you actually buy into what it is he's doing. If you were, you'd be like all the other black cloaks. Fighting for his attention. Constantly sharpening your sword. Talking about the glorious battles you've been a part of. Dreaming of the day when Korrun sits on the throne. But that's not you. Why?"

Tyrell took a deep breath and let it out slowly. It was probably a mistake to trust her, but strangely enough, he did. Also, he had just saved her life. She owed him, if nothing else, her discretion.

"The second-in-command is my father."

"I *knew* it!" Ava hollered.

"*Was* my father."

Ava cocked her head to the side.

"He's not the same. Something's ... different about him. I think he's under the influence of the Corruption."

"Hmm ... I've heard of that before. One of the mages in our village used to talk about it all the time. Said nightstalkers weren't the only form of Corruption. Water sources, grass, trees, all of nature is affected by it. Even humans. He said it would come for all of us one day. We just thought he was a little ..." she whistled and circled her finger around her ear.

"Yeah, well he may not have been as loony as you think. My dad used to tell me all the time that the more you're exposed to the Corruption, the more it affects you. Drives you crazy. Turns your morals inside out. Leaves you with little to no love in your heart."

Tyrell glanced in the direction of camp, though the stony cliffs overlooking the sea blocked his view.

"That's what I see in my dad right now. He was gone for so long, then he shows up and barely acknowledges my existence."

He turned to face Ava, their eyes locking. "I came here to bring him back. Pull him away from the Corruption."

Ava placed a gentle hand on Tyrell's shoulder. "I'm so sorry, Tyrell. I didn't know. That's got to be horrible to see your dad like that."

"Yeah. It is."

He huffed and faced the waves, which was Ava's cue to remove her hand.

"I don't know what else to do. I've tried talking to him, but he's more loyal to Master Korrun than his own family. I'm afraid if I keep going, I'll be seen as an enemy. I ... I don't think he's at the point of saving anymore." His lower lip trembled at the last word, but he fought to still it.

Ava remained silent, a feat which was rare for her in Tyrell's presence. They stared at the floating beast in the distance, watching its body bob up and down in the waves, the final segments of the ice walls having melted back into the ocean.

Tyrell stood and dusted the sand off his trousers. "It's getting late. We better head back or they'll come looking for us. Oh," he turned to face Ava so he could communicate the seriousness of his next words. "Do everything you can to keep you and your family away from camp. I don't want to see you all turn like my father did."

She nodded. "We will. My dad's a fair hunter; we could probably stay away from camp that way."

"Hmm. Good. You know ... you're ... you're always welcome to come fish with me too, ya know."

"Tyrell Falkenburg, I will never fish with you again."

CHAPTER 6

"We're coming, Griff!" Gale Driscoll screamed at the top of his lungs. He reared his sword back, taking aim at the thorny bushes in front of him.

"No need, Dad." Griff hobbled out of the forest a few yards away, a weak smile on his face.

"Griff!" Gale said, rushing to his son and wrapping him in his arms. "You made it! Are you okay? What happened? Why are you limping? Where's the other half of your shirt?"

"Easy … Dad …" Griff said through pained breaths. "You're squeezing a little too tight."

"Oh … right," Gale gently set him back down, but his eyes grew wide as he stared at Griff's bloody half-shirt that was used to wipe and bind his legs after the vine's attack.

Professor Coen eyed Griff's tattered form, slowly looking him up and down before he asked, "What happened in there?"

"Yeah, are you okay, Griff?" Sylva said from behind the professor.

Griff sucked in a lungful of air and let it out slowly. "Yeah, I'm okay, I think. And the rest is a long story …"

The long shadows of the forest grew longer with the setting sun as he shared as much detail as he could about his journey into the forest. How it seemed as though the entire forest was testing him. He described the surprise attack from the vines, the dragon's corpse, and its nest, but he was careful to avoid mentioning the egg that was now safely tucked away in his large pack. Then he carefully reached into his pocket, and said,

"And then, tucked away in the dragon's fist, was ... this." He opened his hand and the shard of essence glowed from his palm.

The three men gathered around him, leaning in close to see the shard.

"Real dragon treasure, I guess," Griff said.

"King's crown, Griff," Sylva breathed. "That's amazing."

Gale laid his arm on top of Griff's back and pulled his head into his muscular chest. "I'm so proud of you, Griff. You did it, m'boy. You really did it."

When they all backed away, Griff held the shard out toward the professor. "Here you go, sir. All yours."

"Much appreciated, Griff. Good work." He tucked it away in an inner pocket of his vest. "I'll make sure it gets to the king straightaway. In the meantime, let's get you all back. It's getting dark and you've got quite the journey ahead of you. And I don't mean our flight to Cordelia."

Griff groaned. He was talking about the move to Solastran. As much as he was looking forward to being back there and eventually seeing his friends and Mira again, there was so much left to do before they made that journey. So much to do in the next three days, and yet every inch of his body pulsed with pain. He gritted his teeth and limped forward. "Yeah, I guess so."

"Where are you going, Griff?" the professor asked.

Puzzled, Griff turned to face him. "Back to the wargs? Back to Cordelia?"

"Not in that condition, you're not. Here, lie down for a sec and take off your bandages."

Griff complied and laid in the soft, green grass, appreciating the moment of rest.

"Now, I'm no field medic, but I did learn a few healing tricks for the battlefield. Stay still." The professor closed his eyes and waved his hands.

Faint blue light illuminated Griff's legs, and they began to tingle. At first it was a gentle massaging kind of sensation, but it grew more intense, as did the blue light. Pins and needles shot up and down his legs as he watched the penetration points from the thorns close. The regular pulsing of pain that he had felt since the attack dampened but didn't completely disappear. It was as though Professor Coen's magic took everything intense about the injury and pain, and reduced it. Immediately, the group was plunged back into the almost darkness of dusk as the professor's light disappeared.

"Well, how's that?" he asked.

"Better!" Griff said, surprised. "Much better."

"So, I'd say it's a good thing we came with you after all, huh?" Professor Coen said, crossing his arms.

The truth of his words stung. How could he have been so foolish to think he could find a shard guarded by a dragon with just himself and Sylva? Griff nodded in acknowledgement. "Yeah, guess so."

With a strong pat on the shoulder, the professor said, "Well, learn from this today, and we'll call it even." He looked at Gale. "...At least, from my end."

"Deal."

The pins and needles feeling pestered Griff, so he tried to scratch them away, but it did nothing. "I see what you mean, Dad. Healing magic does itch."

By the light of Griff and the professor's magic, they walked back to the place where Magnus and Kindra laid. They did a once-over to make sure they had all their supplies, and while Griff tightened his pack against Kindra's saddle, a shirt landed on his head.

"Here." Gale said. Griff held the shirt out and recognized it as one of his dad's regulars. "Because I'm not explaining that bloody half-shirt of yours to your mother."

Once Griff had changed, they saddled up and traveled across the dark sky back to the ruins of Cordelia where Griff was sure to meet his doom once he came face to face with his mother. Considering he hadn't seen her since his bold—or was it stupid? —quest to find another shard, he imagined she had been planning his punishment should he ever come home alive. His stomach twisted at the thought, but the egg tucked safely inside his pack slightly eased his troubled mind and gave him something exciting to think about.

Griff's predictions about his mother were more accurate than his dad's arrow shots, which was saying something. He had never seen his mother's emotions shift from one extreme to the other in such a short amount of time. She cried tears of joy for his well-being, and she cried tears of rage for his stupidity. She seized him and hugged him tightly and wouldn't let go, her tears—of joy or rage, he wasn't sure—soaked the top of his dad's shirt that he wore.

After his quest to retrieve the shard, his chore load increased a hundred-fold. He was forced to work alongside Talley as his assistant the next three mornings, where they would provide any remaining citizens with breakfast. Afterwards, he would saunter off back to the crumbled ruins of his home and dig through the stones and charred wood for any supplies they could take with them in the move to Solastran.

It seemed as though there were always eyes on him. He could never venture out of his parents' sights without hearing, "Where are you going?" or "Stay close." As annoying as this would have been in normal circumstances, it was worse knowing he had a dragon egg tucked away just outside of town, stowed behind some bushes that caught sunlight most of the day.

Once Sylva learned of Griff's secret, he was more than excited to help him any way he could with the egg. Though he may have been Griff's accomplice on his quest, he wasn't a prisoner in his own home like Griff was. It also helped that his mother was the town doctor, so whenever Sylva stepped into the forest, most thought it was to find more herbs for his mother's medicinal remedies.

After serving the final breakfast in Cordelia on the third morning, Griff, Sylva, and their families packed what little supplies they had found and began the trek to Solastran. Having waited for other families to salvage their belongings and move on to other towns, they were the last ones to leave the ruins of their hometown. As they strode onto the dirt path, past the bent, metal gates, Griff's heart sank deep into the pit of his stomach. He was leaving home. And while an exciting adventure awaited him, he couldn't help but feel as though he were at another funeral, taking his final look at the casket before leaving.

He gazed at the charred remains of buildings and houses. Talley's Tavern. His friend's house. His house. Reduced to nothing more than rubble. The screams of Cordelians fleeing for their lives haunted Griff, like a distant echo that wouldn't leave him. Those screams of his friends and neighbors fighting to protect their home. Thankfully, the body count was low. After gathering reports of what happened that night, it seemed as though Korrun had sent a message earlier that day: "Join me or die." He didn't give the people much time to make up their mind, but most were ready to leave as the first wave of black cloaks appeared. Others were ready to fight and either died trying or fled once they realize defeat was inevitable.

Griff clenched his fists. His hometown reduced to ashes because of Korrun. He would do whatever he could to take that man down. No matter what. Using the sleeve of his shirt, he wiped a single tear from his cheek and turned to leave, knowing he would never come back.

While the trip to Solastran took several hours on the back of a warg, a journey by foot with lots of supplies stacked in a wagon that was pulled by the men of the group would last about a week. Griff was happy to see Talley throw his belongings into the wagon and join them for the trip.

As it turned out, Talley was offered a position as head chef at Solastran Inn. Griff knew better than to think that his position would last too long, as Talley was a man who liked to work alone. Regardless, it was a pleasant surprise, knowing he would see Talley on his trips back and forth from the castle.

The journey to Solastran was long, arduous, and boring. Other than seeing new towns along the way and setting up camp inside their walls at night, Griff thought he might die on the road from sheer boredom. Professor Coen did his best to entertain the group with stories from his time as commander of the battlemages, some of which Griff had heard during his first trip to Solastran almost one year ago. Still, after so many hours of storytelling, Griff's mind wandered, and he found it drifting toward thoughts of Mira.

The last time he'd seen her was in the study room ... *Come back to me, Griff Driscoll.* Well, he hadn't exactly done that. He had assumed someone from the school had notified his battlegroup about what had happened in Cordelia. What was Mira's reaction when she heard? Would she consider him brave for fighting against the black cloaks and Korrun? Would she consider him stupid? Would she be angry that he didn't make it back before the end of the semester? That they would be forced to withdraw from the final Altar Storm match, putting that much more pressure on their future matches? Or would she understand? These questions plagued Griff throughout the trip, forcing his stomach to do flips as he thought about seeing her again after all that had happened.

On the last two days of travel, the mountain on which Bergots Academy stood could be seen. Slowly, ever so painfully slowly, the mountain on the horizon grew, and the beautiful city at its base became visible. Griff no longer wanted to stop for rest breaks. He wanted to be done with traveling and finally settle down into something normal again. To sleep in a bed instead of on the ground. To take a bath at the end of the day. To wake up and not have to pack all their belongings back up and walk for hours on end.

Finally, after what seemed like an eternity, the weathered group trudged onto the cobblestone streets of Solastran. Gale, Leena, Sylva, Lilly, and Nessa all stared with wide eyes and open mouths at the bustling town, while Griff, Talley, and Professor Coen casually strolled in.

It seemed like an entire lifetime had passed since he and his friends last visited—with only the final Altar Storm match of the semester looming over them. The town was exactly as Griff remembered it. The shops had their doors open to display their wares. Children at the park played under the supervision of parents or grandparents. Some of the adults present were using their magic to levitate a ball as part of a game. Another parent swirled their hands, using a wind spell to push their three kids on swings while talking to another parent who must not have been magical, as they manually pushed their swinging child. Griff's parents paused to admire the statue of the Solastran founders and the words of hope written underneath. *Solastran: where real magic is found not in our humanity, but our human-unity.*

"Up ahead is Solastran Inn, where Mr. Colm has graciously agreed to allow you to stay for free, while your homes are built," Professor Coen called back.

"Good ol' Mr. Colm." Talley cackled. "Been years since I seen that old man!"

"You know him?" Sylva asked, running up beside Talley.

"Aye, we grew up together. Well, ya know, until he went off to Bergots since he was all *magical* and what-have-you."

"You grew up here, in Solastran?" Griff asked.

"Aye. Till I signed on to be in the king's army. Might not have been a mage, but I could swing a sword all right. I served my king well, traveled the world and saw the good and bad of it. I knew my time was comin' to an end in the army, and decided to settle somewhere ... a little lesser known."

"Well, ya did just that when you moved to Cordelia!" Gale called from the back.

Talley chuckled and scratched at his mutton chops. "Aye. That I did, Driscoll, that I did."

Griff fell in beside him. "Talley ... thanks, by the way."

"For what, boy?"

"For watching me all those years. Knowing..." Griff touched his heart, where the shard lay hidden. "Knowing there was something different about me. Thank you for keeping an eye on me."

Talley smiled and gave a nod. "Aye, lad. Happy to 'ave done it. Gave me purpose outside me tavern while I lived in Cordelia all those years." Suddenly, Talley's eyes glazed over, as though he were reminiscing on his past. "All those years ago..."

The burly man continued his march in silence through the streets, eyeing the buildings on either side of him before he quietly said, "But now I'm back home."

They strode through the large double doors into Solastran Inn, where a beaming Mr. Colm awaited them. Talley grasped the old, thin man in a giant bear hug and together they laughed in their embrace.

"Welcome back home, Talley."

"Aye, been a long time, but it's good to be back."

"Well, I suppose you can start calling me boss, then, eh?"

Tally cackled. "You know I'd saw my right foot off and feed it to the nightstalkers 'fore I start callin' you that, old man!"

CHAPTER 7

Beads of sweat poured down Griff's face, stinging his eyes. Forgetting what he was doing, he immediately grunted and furiously wiped his eyes with his sleeve.

"OUCH!" Gale called from inside the halfway-assembled stone house.

Griff blinked the burning sensation away and looked over at his dad who limped over to a nearby tree stump and sat down. He wrenched off his shoe and sock and inspected his foot, which was now bright red and already swelling.

Griff grimaced. "Sorry, Dad!"

"Thought you had the hang of this magic thing, son? What happened?" Looking closer, Griff could see his dad's big toe was split and bleeding.

"Sorry ... some sweat got in my eyes and, well, yeah I'm just sorry."

Gale stared at the blood on his toe, then smiled up at his son. "All's forgiven."

Over the last couple of weeks, Griff and his dad had helped the two builders assigned with the construction of their new home on the outskirts of Solastran. He was supposed to float the large stones over to his dad, who would then carefully place it on the newly-applied mortar. It was fast and efficient. Well, so long as he maintained his concentration.

There hadn't been much time to wander about the familiar streets and show his parents the town. Prior to their arrival, half-acre plots of land had been secured by Mayor Gregory Scholz—"Mr. Gregg"—as he preferred it, for all those who had traveled to Solastran in search of refuge from Korrun's rampage. He had personally visited each site to welcome the families—not as refugees, but as new neighbors. At each site, piles of stone and wood sat next to buckets of mortar. Simple materials that, when combined, wouldn't just build a building, but rebuild a life.

Every morning, Griff snuck his dragon egg into his pack and then the Driscolls, along with Sylva's family, marched the same twenty-minute stretch from the inn to their plot of land and began work. He'd quickly find an excuse to leave, like needing a bathroom break and his privacy, so he could take his egg to a safe spot out of eyeshot and into the sun. Then, after a full day's work, he'd sneak the egg back into his pack, and the Driscolls and Karlsons marched back as the sun set. Other than a few breaks for food and water, Griff had no reprieve.

The sun beat down against his worn body, painfully reminding him that summer had truly only just begun. Time had slowed to a baby's crawl thanks to the monotonous, never-ending construction process. It didn't help that all he wanted to do was see his friends again. He'd hardly seen much of Sylva either. Other than the quiet walks to and from the inn, Sylva and his family had their own house to build just down the road. Thankfully, in addition to the workers assigned to their home, some of the locals had offered to help the Karlsons. In true neighboring fashion, some of the Solastran ladies played with Lilly as her mother and brother worked. The only one not exhausted from the day's labor, Lilly would bounce and skip alongside the Driscolls and her family, telling stories of the new magic tricks the ladies showed her that day.

After about a month of grueling labor, and only a week after the Karlson's house was completed, the Driscolls had a new home. While similar to the other homes nearby—two stories of stone and wood, set in an "L" shape with a tiny front porch jutting out at an angle from the middle—the Driscolls did their best to put their personal touches on their home to distinguish it from the others. After building some beds, a kitchen table and chairs, and securing a wood-fire stove, Gale proudly displayed the few forged art pieces he retrieved from their barn back in Cordelia and was already in the process of building a small shop in the back yard.

Leena hammered in fence posts along their property in preparation for a scaled down version of their barn back home. Their plan, she said, was to raise chickens and pigs. Excited, Griff knew that meant a steady supply of eggs and bacon. When she was done building the fence, she tilled small strips underneath the front windows, where she planned to plant her favorite flowers. Griff made a mental note to be on the lookout for twilight roses, or at least some of their seeds. Even though he was a traitor, it seemed that Marth's old friend Tyrell knew how to give his mother good gifts. Considering his return to Bergots was only two weeks away, though, he wasn't sure how he could earn enough money to buy some even if he were to find them.

As he worked on the furniture with his dad and helped hammer in the fence posts with his mom, something in the back of Griff's mind pestered him. A small thought at first, like a black fly in the summertime—something he merely shooed away, refusing to deal with it at the time. But as persistent as a fly, it kept coming back and wouldn't leave him alone. This quest to find all the shards of the Orb of Essence had taken over his mind. Other than a few lingering thoughts about he and Mira, finding the shards was all he could think about. But what would happen after all the *other* shards were found? What about the shard inside *himself*? Once all the other shards were in the king's possession, would he find a way to take back the shard inside him? Would that require Griff to die?

The annoying swarm of questions about his shard had pestered him for weeks. He wanted so badly to talk to someone about these things, but between the move from Cordelia and settling into a new life in Solastran, there wasn't any time. His parents each had their own projects that they were intensely focused on. And now that they had moved into their own homes, even the little time he spent with Sylva each day was gone. For now, it seemed, he was left to deal with the pesky questions alone. Save for his Nightflame egg, who was an excellent listener.

Griff's eyes sprang open. The sounds of the ocean waves faded fast, along with the details of his dream. Frustration replaced his grogginess. It was the call of another shard. It must have been. And yet, he couldn't remember anything other than it was near an ocean. He clenched his eyes shut, trying to hold onto any small detail that might help him remember. Nothing. Just ... wind and waves.

The bright morning sun streamed through the thin curtains. *Nine o'clock already?* Why did his parents let him sleep in? They still had lots of projects for him, especially since his departure to Bergots was nearing.

Griff flung the covers over to the side and placed his bare feet on the wooden floor. He hadn't become accustomed to the absence of his old iron bed's creaks just yet. The wooden bed his dad had built was strong, sturdy and didn't make a sound.

He threw on his shirt and snagged the first pair of trousers he could find off the floor, hoping it was clean enough. Rubbing his eyes, he sauntered down the stairs until a familiar smell hit his nostrils. *Bacon? Pancakes!* He had totally forgotten! Before he could even make it off the stairs, his dad hollered, "Is that you, birthday boy?"

"Mornin'," Griff replied with a sleepy smile. He strode across the living room and glanced over at his dad in acknowledgement, then immediately scanned the table and countertops, looking for his food.

"Mornin' Mom," he said, giving her a quick side hug with one arm, and sneaking a slice of bacon off the plate next to her with the other.

"I saw that," Leena said, her eyes narrowing on him. Then she smiled. "And I'll let you be. This time."

"So, *birthday boy* here gets to steal a slice but I, the one who went into town and bargained left and right for some bacon, have to wait, eh?"

Gale ruffled Griff's hair before returning to his work. Pen scratching across the parchment with careful, meticulous strokes. They may have been in a different town in a different house, but Gale Driscoll kept his work habits the same: sitting at the kitchen table drawing out his next project.

"How goes the forge?" Griff asked.

"Aye, not bad, not bad. Without the same amount of space, I'm going to have to be more intentional with how I use it."

"What your dad's trying to say, Griff, is that he can't be a slob anymore," Leena added.

Gale smiled, not looking up from his parchment, and replied with a simple, "Aye."

After setting a plate down in front of Griff—pancakes, eggs, and bacon—Leena sat down and smoothed out her dress.

"Honey, I know it's your birthday, and we would normally give you some coin to call your own, but … we just don't have any to give you right now."

She stared at Griff, trying to read his expression. He hadn't expected anything. King's crown, he'd forgotten it was his birthday in the first place.

"It's okay, Mom. I understand. We need to worry about starting a new life right now, anyways."

"But don't worry, 'kay? We're … we're still gonna go to that treat shop next to the park, and we'll get you a nice birthday dinner too." She spoke quickly, like trying to squeeze the "but here's the good news" out as quickly as possible. A tear welled up in each eye. The features on her face were scrunched with worry, and she bit her lip.

"Mom, seriously. It's no big deal. I can … I can get a job around here, if that's what you need?"

She let out the air she'd been holding and laughed. "No, no, sweet boy. No. You just focus on doing your best at Bergots and figuring out what you want to do after you've graduated. We'll be fine, I promise. We're just saving what we can until your dad gets the forge up and going. That's all."

She reached over and squeezed his hand. "We're so proud of you, Griff. I hope you always know that."

A strong hand fell on Griff's shoulder. "Aye. So proud, Miracle Boy," Gale said. "Now, it's time for the story, I think, isn't it?"

Griff's head fell forward, and he sighed. "Every. Year."

Griff's senses exploded in pure delight upon the first lick of his ice cream cone. As they left Mage's Magical Treats, and stepped out into the hot sun, the cold, freshly churned dessert was a welcome relief. His parents, who hadn't seen much magic up close, stared in wonder as the mage had used ice magic, freshly drawn milk, and flavored syrups to create the delicacy. While his parents had marveled at the magic, Griff studied it. He watched the mage's every move so he might gain insight. He would do whatever he could to learn as much about essence manipulation as possible, even if he was still on his summer break. After all, there was a war to fight, and he needed every advantage possible.

Shooing thoughts of Korrun and the shards from his mind, Griff took another lick of his ice cream and joined his parents on the bench just outside the park. He closed his eyes and relished the moment: the sweet vanilla flavor on his tongue, the warm sun on his face, the laughter of the kids as they slid down the slides, the rhythmic, almost jingling sounds of the metal swings.

"Griff!" He hadn't heard that voice since he'd left Bergots. It was one he was familiar with, as the owner of that voice used it often. He smiled before he even opened his eyes, knowing he'd find a goofy-grinned, blond-haired Marth staring at him.

"Hey!" Griff jumped off the bench and wrapped his arms around his friend, splashing melted ice cream bits on some passersby. They glared, but otherwise, wiped their sleeves and kept walking.

"We were just about to search for you, mate!" Marth said.

"We?"

Marth thumbed behind him, and said, "Got the whole gang back together again. Just missing you!"

Griff looked over Marth's shoulder. Vincent, a head taller than all the other people walking past him, flashed him a smile. Standing just to the side of him, and really ... *just* to the side of him, was the scowling ginger, Sadie. But she didn't scowl at Griff this time, which meant she was smiling.

And then, there she was. Mira. She stood back, hands in her pockets, green eyes barely able to meet his own. She shifted her weight from one leg to the other and then back. Probably because of the work she did on her family's farm, her tan skin was even darker since he'd last seen her. Since ... *Come back to me, Griff Driscoll.*

His heart plummeted into his stomach. He'd thought about her all summer. So much so that he was beginning to think it had all been a dream. That maybe the battle in Cordelia did something to his mind, and Mira had only been a part of his imagination. And now, here she was, standing right in front of him. Not a dream. Real. And was she ... *nervous?* He'd never seen her like this before. She was usually confident. Overly confident, if anything. And now she couldn't make eye contact with him? Or maybe she wasn't nervous. Maybe she was ... angry? Frustrated that he hadn't come back and finished the semester? The whirlwind of thoughts, emotions, and questions swirled inside Griff stronger than any corruption storm.

All he was able to say was a simple, "H-hey, guys!" He awkwardly tossed up his hand in greeting, though for some reason, suddenly the concept of waving one's hand felt foreign.

Awkward. He knew it. He felt it. Griff did his best to shrug it off, sectioning those questions and emotions about Mira to a deeper part of his brain for a future visit. He heard someone clear their throat from behind him.

"Oh yeah! Hey, uh, so these are my parents. Uh, parents, this is my team from last year."

"Gale Driscoll!" Griff's dad said, cheerily snatching Marth's hand in his own, then working his way through the rest of the group.

"And I'm Leena," his mom said, waving at the group. Sadie did her best to smile, but Griff could tell it was forced.

"Say, son, you've spent quite a bit of time with us lately. Your mom and I'll head out and meet you back at the house for dinner." Gale turned his attention to the rest of the battlegroup. "You're all welcome to join us if you'd like! I mean to brag when I say my wife here makes the best stagmoose steaks in all of Oriel. We could probably snag a few more on our way home." He quickly eyed his wife, who gave him a permissible nod.

"Count us in!" Marth said, patting his stomach with both hands. "I'll put that to the test!"

After Griff's parents had left, the battlegroup found an empty table at the edge of Mage's Magical Treats. The shade from an overhanging tree branch was a welcome respite from the hot sun now that Griff's ice cream cone had been completely consumed.

"Your parents seem really nice," Vincent said, taking a seat next to Sadie.

"Yeah, mate! From afar, I thought your dad was *you* for a moment! Till I saw him put his arm around your mom. Then I *knew* ..." He eyed Mira, who had sat in between Marth and Griff, "uh ... that he wasn't you."

Mira leaned back in her chair, smiled at Griff and said, "Glad to see you alive."

Was the smile forced? Did she really mean what she said, or was it a reminder that he failed to keep his promise to her? He couldn't tell. *You're over thinking it. Again. Just stop already!*

Marth slammed his fist onto the table, the noise startling Sadie who wasn't paying attention, and said, "King's crown, Griff. You need to start talking, and I mean right now." Marth missed Sadie's scowl pointing in his direction, but it faded quickly as she turned her attention toward Griff. Everyone stared, but no one said a word. They wanted to know about Cordelia.

Griff scanned the group, gathered his thoughts, took a deep breath, and began his story.

CHAPTER 8

"You are going to be in so much trouble if anyone finds out about this. And there's no way you can hide it forever."

Mira's eyes never left the egg as she spoke. The warm breeze fluttered her dark brown hair that had fallen over her face. She tucked it behind her ear.

"But still ... what are you going to name it?" she asked in an almost hushed tone.

Griff smiled. It was good to be with her again. The two of them sat under a shady tree a stone's throw away from the house, staring at the obsidian-colored egg as it reflected the setting sun. His parents readied dinner for him, his battlegroup, and Sylva. In Cordelia, the evenings would have been cooler, and perhaps Mira would have snuggled in close for warmth. Here, farther south, the air held its heat, and so the distance between them lingered.

Not only did Mira's presence ease the parade of shard-related questions bouncing around his mind, but it felt so freeing to share his secret of the egg with another person besides Sylva. As part of his story at Mage's Magical Treats, Griff shared with his friends about the discovery. And while Marth was itching to see it for himself, Griff had only invited Mira for the first viewing. Marth, on the verge of exploding from his silence, seemed to understand the sentiment. Even though the veins bulging in his neck told Griff that didn't still his anticipation.

"A name? No idea." Griff finally said as he trailed the tips of his fingers along the smooth shell. His tanned face reflected in the dark, almost mirror sheen. "I don't even know if it's a boy or a girl. Or what to feed it if it hatches." He turned to Mira. "Am I crazy for doing this?"

"Yes."

He sighed, closed his eyes, and laid his head back against the tree. "I know."

"But ... in a way, it's very sweet."

He opened one eye and gazed at her. Her smile flushed him with confidence. Her bright green eyes never leaving his made him feel as though he could take on a whole army of nightstalkers. And win.

Mira gently touched the egg while she spoke. "This dragon would have probably died out there without a guardian. And I'm not the kind to see animals die needlessly. You're a rare breed, you know that? You're the caring kinda sort, Griff. You don't just fend for yourself. You *see* others. You care what happens to them. Even those who'd otherwise be invisible." She squeezed his arm. "It's one of the many things I like about you."

She reached over with her other hand, carefully picked up the egg, and cradled it in the nook of her elbow.

"It's heavy! And ..." she held up the egg to her ear and listened intently. "Do I feel movement?"

Griff laughed. "Yeah. Baby dragon's started to stir the last week or so. I don't know if that means it can hatch any day now or what. I don't even know how fast dragons grow, either. It's not like I've had the time to find any books on raising dragons, if any of those books even exist."

"I bet Bergots has something on it," she said, tucking the egg back in the nook of her arm. "I'll help you find it."

Mira cradled the egg in silence while Griff tried to find the right words to ask her what had been on his mind all summer. For some reason, in this moment, words didn't seem to come. This was his chance to finally talk one on one with her about what happened last semester, and yet, his mind was a muddled mess. He shouldn't have been nervous. She smiled at him. Told him what she liked about him. And yet, the words that floated around his brain were like multiple puzzles spilled onto a table——he couldn't piece them together. When he could bear the silence no more, he finally stumbled out, "Hey ... s ... so, we're okay, yeah?"

She stopped rocking the egg and stared at him. "Yeah, of course. Why?"

"Well, I left before the year was up. You guys didn't get to go to the final Altar Storm match. I ..." His face started to flush. Saying it all out loud made him realize how silly all his worries had been up until now. "I guess I thought you'd be mad at me for leaving and not coming back."

Mira paused her rocking, carefully calculating her words. "I was for a bit. But, Griff, you were saving your family. Your home. And it sounds like you played a big part in saving lives back there too. I can't be mad at that. If anything, that makes you a hero." She leaned over and kissed his cheek.

Butterflies magically appeared in his stomach, fluttering wildly. He reached over and placed his hand in hers, intertwining their fingers together. All those fears throughout the summer melted away in that moment. She gave him another squeeze, released his hand, and began rocking the egg again, this time giving it a little bounce and cooing at it.

"Plus," she said, "Now that your family's safe and you have a new home here in Solastran, we can get back to Bergots and really show off in the arena. After all, Headmaster Aldamund told us that they would be watching us more closely this year. So, we'll just have to hit the books that much harder!"

"You say that like it's a good thing," Griff teased, flashing her a smile.

She turned to him with a look so serious it melted his smile. "It *is* a good thing."

"That was so dumb!" came the giddy whisper from behind them.

"Seriously, Marth, are you spying on us right now?" Griff called out, not trying to hide his annoyance.

Marth stepped out from behind a nearby tree, wearing the biggest, dumbest, goofiest smile.

"Aw, I'm just messin' with you guys. We just got here to tell you, Miracle Boy, that your birthday dinner's ready!"

Griff looked behind him to see Sylva, Vincent, and Sadie walking through the knee-high grass. Vincent was shaking his head at Marth in disproval.

Griff sighed and carefully took the egg from Mira. "They told you the story, did they?"

"Yeah, *Miracle Boy*, they sure did! Hey! Is that the egg? Lemme see, lemme see!"

"Later," Griff grumbled, tucking the egg into an inconspicuous bundle of leaves he had planted at the base of the tree. "I'm hungry," he said. Then, hand in hand with Mira, they sauntered off toward the house, listening to Marth's constant blabbering to Sylva along the way.

CHAPTER 9

This is his final chance, Tyrell thought, using his fingers to comb back his long hair that had been ruffled by the ocean breeze. He gritted his teeth. *Last chance, or I'm out.*

Nothing was going to change his mind. Not only had he grown bored staying in the same location for so long, but with each passing day, the realization that he had failed in his mission was becoming clearer. He wasn't going to bring his dad back. Randolph Falkenburg was too far gone. The Corruption had warped his mind beyond all repair.

He gave a nod as he passed some black cloaks that were training in essence crafting. They took turns drawing their handles from their sheathes and crafting different weapons with their magical energy. Some of the younger mages produced short blades of yellow from their nervousness or red from frustration. Those not of magical origin sat at a distance and watched in wonder or envy.

He passed a series of large, dark tents set underneath shady trees where Korrun's pets slumbered. One of the smaller nightstalkers, looking like an oversized black badger with long, black barbs instead of whiskers, perked its head and let out a soft, high-pitched growl before returning to its resting position. Its beady white eyes followed Tyrell until he was past the tent.

Strong, savory scents overpowered the usual salty seaweed smells. Lunch was almost ready and based on the aromas coming from the multiple fire pits in the middle of camp, venison was on the menu. Tyrell ignored his rumbling stomach, an untamable beast who had woken the moment the smells reached Tyrell's nostrils. Food would have to come later.

There was no door to the tent, so Tyrell stood at the entrance until his eyes adjusted to the darkness within. The tent looked empty, but the rustling sounds coming from behind a series of wooden dressing panels told him Randolph was present.

"It's me," he called, taking a confident step forward. He placed his hands behind his back and waited for his father to respond.

"Tyrell!" Randolph called. "One moment, please."

As he waited for his father to finish changing clothes, Tyrell once again recited his opening remarks in his head. Words he'd repeated in his mind over and over again every night for the past three nights. *I'm leaving. Come with me if you're still my father. I'm leaving. Come with me if you're still my father.*

"I was hoping to see you sometime today." Randolph emerged from behind the dressing screen wearing his usual black trousers, shirt, and cloak with a white stripe. His outfit was pristine, unlike the muddied set Tyrell knew was carefully folded and placed on a table behind the screen. One of the newest recruits to the black cloaks, one who could offer no magical or combat experience, would come by in the evening to wash and later return the set to Korrun's second in command. It was a routine Tyrell had seen many times in their stay next to the ocean. His dad had been very busy exploring the numerous caves along the coastline. And as each day passed without success, Randolph came back to his tent dirtier than the day before. Perhaps he was getting desperate because they weren't finding what they were looking for?

"You were?" Tyrell asked, maintaining his respectful posture, keeping his hands behind his back. He was still a soldier. For now.

"It's time we had a talk."

"Talk?" Where was this going? His father had been completely silent, ignoring him since their conversation the morning after his initiation into the black cloaks. Where, on the outskirts of a smoldering town, Tyrell had tried and failed to get answers from Randolph. He'd been too emotional. He'd let his father's lack of care get the best of him. So, he attacked. Well, tried anyway. Since then, Randolph hadn't spoken to him. Tyrell figured his attack meant the end of their relationship as father and son.

"Yes. It's time you learned something very important about our family."

Randolph sat at a small, round, wooden table toward the side of the tent and offered his son the extra chair. Tyrell sat awkwardly, unable to get comfortable. Suddenly, his clothes felt too heavy. He could feel every bunch of material behind his knees. He desperately wanted to roll up his sleeves to give his forearms freedom. He felt trapped in his own clothes, and any shifting of his body did nothing to ease the anxious sensations he had.

"Do you remember your Great Grandpa?"

"Great Grandpa? ... No. I mean, not really. I can kind of picture his face and ... and beard, but ... that's really it. He was really old, is all I remember."

"Well, he passed when you were five years old. I would be surprised if you remembered him at all."

Randolph tapped his fingers on the table and stared out through the tent flaps, though his mind was clearly elsewhere.

"William Falkenburg—your great grandfather—was as pleasant as salt on a fresh war wound. Even to his own family. He was not a good man, let alone father or grandfather."

Tyrell did his best not to scoff. How dare this man claim to know who was good and who wasn't after all that he'd put his own family through.

He'd left them to join a corrupt man's corrupt cause. And here he sat, bringing judgment on these other men.

"From what you told me, it sounds like he and your dad had a lot in common," Tyrell said, his eyes never leaving his father's. "It must run in the family." He hoped Randolph felt the sting of those words. It was intended.

Randolph only paused the drumming of his fingers for a moment before saying, "Actually, that's exactly right. It *does* run in the family."

"What do you mean?"

"My father and grandfather didn't come from a line of virtuous men. Save for one that we know of. Generations ago, there was a man from our family tree named Einar Falkenburg. *He* was a good man."

"Einar Falkenburg? If he was so good, then why haven't I heard of him?"

"Because to tell the story of Einar, is to tell the secrets of Einar. Rumors, legends, stories that have been heavily guarded and passed down from generation to generation. From one Falkenburg to the next."

Randolph pulled his chair back and walked toward the opening of the tent. After checking to make sure no one was around, he closed the flaps and tied them together. Not the most secure way to keep passersby from listening in, Tyrell thought, but better than nothing.

After returning to his seat and resuming his drumming, Randolph continued in a low voice.

"Einar Falkenburg was assigned an incredibly important task. It was dangerous and could cost him his life should he fail."

"What was the task?"

"Well, it was really more than just a task. It was a way of life. Einar Falkenburg was a Guardian of the Shards."

"Okay ... you say that as though I'm supposed to be amazed or something. I don't even know what '*The Shards*' are, let alone why they would need to be guarded, or whatever."

"I don't have time to go into the complex history of the shards and the Guardians, but suffice it to say, the shards are a part of a powerful magical artifact. Long ago, the artifact shattered into nine pieces——the shards. Master Korrun believes that with the nine shards, he will have the power to restore the artifact. Rumor has it that this artifact has unimaginable power. Power to destroy. Power to create. Master Korrun seeks to use this power to destroy the Corruption, and bring healing and peace to the world."

At those words, Tyrell sat back in his chair and crossed his arms. He wasn't going to be sold so easily.

"Einar Falkenburg was part of a group of elite mages who sought to protect the shards that had been discovered from getting into the wrong hands. From the moment Einar took on this responsibility until the day he retired from old age, he risked his life for the shards. Now, he fathered two children, a boy and a girl. The girl, Freya, took after her father——righteous, upright, pure of heart. The boy, Arthur, well, he did not. He was evil. When Einar passed the secrets of the Guardians onto his daughter and not his son, the boy went on a magical rampage, nearly destroying their town. Nobody knew where he went after his tantrum. But he became obsessed with learning the secrets of the Guardians. Once or twice, he was caught stalking his own sister, and even tried to pin her down and force her to tell him about the shards. But every time, he was bested."

For the first time since he started his story, Randolph actually looked at Tyrell. Excitement in his eyes.

"Freya never told her brother a single thing about the shards. But Arthur didn't need her information any longer. He had something *better*."

Randolph stood and reached in his cloak pocket and retrieved a worn leather book and carefully set it on the table in front of him. "Einar Falkenburg's journal," he said proudly as he sat back down. "He guarded that with as much care as the shard in his possession. At first, he just wrote about the journeys he experienced. However, toward the end of his writings, when he was clearly close to retirement, knowing his old age would become a liability to the safety of the shards, his writings became more cryptic. But Arthur knew that his father was talking about the locations of the shards. Possibilities of where each one could be hidden if there ever came a need."

Randolph proudly tapped the leather cover with his finger. "That information has been handed down from one Falkenburg to the next ever since. We Falkenburgs have spent generations trying to decipher our ancestor's clues. I have notes written in the margins here from many different Falkenburgs. Some had no clue what they were talking about, while others wrote insightful ideas. Regardless, this priceless family artifact has been handed over to me, now. I am its protector."

Tyrell's mind was reeling with the new information. His ancestors were guardians. Protectors. Righteous and gifted mages. They had purpose. They had a strong, weighty responsibility placed on their shoulders. And it sounded as though they carried it with great pride. These were all the things that Tyrell had been looking for—and thought he'd found in his mission to rescue his father. To have been a Guardian of the Shards sounded like just the kind of responsibility Tyrell would have cherished.

"Wait, so if this information has been passed down for generations, why has no other Falkenburg tried to find the shards?" Tyrell asked.

"Well, early on, some of them tried. Only to find themselves face to face with a guardian. And those guardians take their jobs seriously." Randolph scratched his clean-shaven chin as he thought. "Then, some of them were too lazy. Didn't think it was really worth the effort. As time and generations passed, the stories turned more into rumors and legends. Many thought that if there were any guardians left, they would have moved the shards. They continued the tradition of passing the family stories on, but after such a long time, us Falkenburgs stopped trying to find them."

"Until you."

"Until me." Randolph smiled in such a gross, self-righteous manner that it made Tyrell's stomach churn.

"What happened to the sister? Did she have any kids? Did they go on to be guardians as well?"

"Now, see, this is where things get interesting. Einar's daughter never married. Never mothered any children. It is said that she died of old age, and the shard she protected was lost. But I told Master Korrun that I had a sneaking suspicion of what she did with the shard. And I was right!" Randolph banged his fist on the table in excitement. "The family legacy of being Guardians of the Shards was to be short-lived since she never had any children. So, I believed that she took the shard to the tomb of her father, Einar, and buried his remains elsewhere. It was a way to honor him, and protect the shards at the same time. And I was right!"

"So, you were the one who told Korrun—"

"—*Master* Korrun."

"Uh, right. Master Korrun. You told him where a shard was?"

"Yes. I led him right to the one in Einar's casket. And we're here at these ocean cliffs because of another Falkenburg family legend. After all, Master Korrun is trying to use these shards for good."

"And how many people will he kill ... how many innocent men, women, and children will die so that Korrun can get to play hero? Huh?"

Tyrell's heart was pumping furiously. Not out of fear for his father, but out of anger that Randolph Falkenburg had been sold such an outrageous lie, and shared treasured family secrets with this corrupt man.

"How many towns will he burn to the ground in search for these shards? Huh? He commands the *darkness,* Father," Tyrell held his hand out in the direction of the nightstalker tent. "He commands the darkness. And not to do his biddings of light, no matter the verbal juggling he may do to convince you otherwise."

"You're still not sold, are you, Tyrell?" His father said calmly.

This only infuriated him even more.

Tyrell stood in defiant anger. "Nor will I ever be." He clenched his shaking hands into a fist.

"I'm leaving," he said. "And ... I don't want you to follow me."

CHAPTER 10

Tyrell would only have to bear with the smells of salt water and the constant nagging sound of the ocean waves a little longer. From the moment they'd set camp here two months ago until tonight, they had always been there. Never ceasing. Every breath in was salty. Pervasive. And the sounds of the waves would either grow or shrink in volume depending on the tides, but they were never quiet. Soon, it would all be behind him, and he didn't believe he would ever miss them.

Tyrell turned on the dark beach and looked back toward the camp on top of the cliffs. It could easily be seen at night with the many campfires the black cloaks lit. Though he might not miss the ever-present ocean sounds, there was one thing he would miss from his time here. One person. And that person was not his father. His father might as well be dead.

He didn't have the heart to tell Ava of his plan to leave. He knew she would stay with her family. He knew she would try to convince him to stay with her. But it was time to go home. He'd held onto one single fine strand of hope that perhaps Randolph would listen. And yet, that strand had been broken. His mission had been a complete failure. It was time to scrap his plan and salvage what he could. Perhaps they would let Tyrell back into school if he provided them intel. He imagined everyone would have a hard time trusting him again. But that was a burden he would have to bear. He was still a soldier, and he would fight. He'd find another way to bring honor back to his family name.

He turned away from camp and trudged along the beach. His feet were damp already, and the tiny little grains of sand rubbed against his skin with every step. Never again would Tyrell find himself on a beach. Never. Again. But he knew it was the right call. The nightstalkers would be out hunting in the forest like they did every night. He didn't dare try to escape through there. That would mean either certain death or capture.

Suddenly, pain exploded in the back of Tyrell's head and blurred his vision.

"OW!" he yelled, hand racing to cover the back of his head. He turned and dipped low, a red fireball already hovering in his palm. Another large seashell flew where his head had once been. But before he hurled the fireball at his opponent, he stopped. There, reflected in the moonlight, Tyrell could see tear streaks on the cheeks of a beautiful girl. The one he'd left behind.

"You're leaving ..." she whimpered.

Tyrell stood and quickly extinguished the fireball before anyone from camp noticed. "Yeah," was all he could muster.

Arms crossed and hands gripping her elbows tight, Ava said, "You're leaving ... *me*."

Tyrell took a step forward. "N-no, Ava, I wasn't—"

"—Why? Huh? Why would you leave me now? Why are you leaving us?"

"Listen, Ava ..." But he knew there was nothing that could prevent her tears. They flowed freely down her cheek before falling and getting lost in the damp sand.

Tyrell's heart ached in a way he didn't know was possible. Why did he care so much that he'd hurt her? Deep inside he knew the answer, but squashed the thought before it could rise to the surface.

"I've failed, Ava. I ... I can't get my dad back. He's too far gone. The Corruption ... Korrun ... they've taken him to a place beyond help. That's not my dad anymore, Ava. He's gone."

"Yeah, well ..." she said, and for the first time since he'd seen her out here on the beach, she wiped her wet cheeks with the sleeve of her shirt. She took a defiant step forward. "Well, *I'm* here. And so is my family. We are *prisoners* here, Tyrell. We leave, we die. And we're not the only ones."

"I'm sorry, Ava. I really am. But I came here on a mission. A mission that I failed."

"Oh yeah? Well, boo-hoo! Cry me a big, fat, shark-creature-infested ocean about it, why don't ya? You failed. Big Daddy Randolph isn't coming home. Well, you know what? Neither are any of us, Tyrell. You came for just one person who needed rescuing, and what you found was a whole group of people in the same predicament."

"What are you talking about?"

"It's what I've been trying to tell you. It's not just me and my family who have been manipulated into joining this psychotic man's mission. Nobody says it outright, but there are whispers of people just looking for a chance out. A chance to escape. Or even a chance to fight our captors. But we're all scared, Tyrell. We're all scared, and we need someone who can lead us."

Tyrell turned and continued walking down the beach away from camp.

"Then why don't you lead them, Ava."

It wasn't so much a question; it was meant to be his final farewell. A last thought for her to mull over and walk back to camp with. And yet, he could hear her loud, quick footsteps squishing in the wet sand behind him. She clamped her hand on his shoulders. Her grip was surprisingly strong and her nails dug into his skin.

"Don't. Turn. From. Me. Tyrell," she said, like a mother scolding her son. He grunted in pain and turned to face her. Only then did she release her vise-like grip on him. The moonlight overhead cast dark, eerie shadows across her scrunched face. He'd never seen her so angry. So … forceful, before.

"You have such narrow sight," Ava continued.

"Hey, my eyesight is just fine, thank you," Tyrell argued.

"No. Not your *eye*sight. Your *mind*sight. You only care about one thing in this world. You and your family. You are so selfish you can't see that there are others here you *can* help. I'm sorry about your father. I really am. But he's one person. And you have the potential to save more."

"You keep saying that, but what does that mean? You saying I need to lead a whole bunch of people to escape Korrun's camp of black cloaks and night stalkers? That's insane! There's no way we could sneak a group of people away from here."

"Who said anything about sneaking away from here?" she asked. "*You're* the son of Korrun's second in command. Your father was one of the king's very own battlemages. The combat training you must have. The military strategy he must've taught you. I'm not talking about you leading people to escape. I'm talking about you leading people to *battle*."

"To battle?" Tyrell asked incredulously. It sounded so ridiculous coming from someone as innocent as Ava.

"Think about it, Tyrell!" She stomped her foot in the sand and clenched her fists. "This is one of Korrun's biggest mistakes! He's brought tons of people into his ranks, people that didn't want to be there. There are people—families—that are only here because they want to live. But these same people, I'm willing to bet my life, that they would fight if given the chance. If given the hope. And *you* can bring that hope."

A single tear dropped into the sand. But this time, Tyrell could tell it wasn't a tear of pain. It was a tear of passion. She believed in him in a way that he hadn't felt in a long time. Ava actually believed that Tyrell could lead a group of rag-tag people, some mages, some not, into a battle against Korrun's army. As completely ridiculous as it was, Tyrell couldn't help but feel honored by her belief in him. Even if it was misplaced.

Ava placed a tender hand on his cheek. Her hand was wet from the tears she had wiped away, but it was warm. A welcome feeling against the chilly ocean breeze. Shivers crawled down Tyrell's neck and into his back.

"You saved me once. Here. On this very beach. Now I'm asking you to save me again. And when you do, you'll save a whole lot more people than just me."

She searched his eyes as though she was scanning his very soul. Pleading without words. Speaking to more than just his logical side. It was as if she was communicating with the very essence of himself. Her warm, comforting hand never left his cheek. He never removed it.

The ocean breeze ruffled Tyrell's long hair, but he didn't try to fix it. The tide rose with every new wave that crashed on the shore. Their feet were getting soaked, but they didn't move. After what felt like forever—a forever that wasn't entirely uncomfortable—Tyrell gently took her hand off his cheek, kissed her fingers, and said, "I'll stay."

She squealed with glee and wrapped her arms around Tyrell. He immediately tried to shush her, but her excitement could barely be contained. He gave her a squeeze back before pulling her off so he could finish.

"I said I'll *stay*. That doesn't mean I'm going to lead a revolution. That doesn't mean we're going to lead half of camp in a daring escape from here, okay? I'll stay a little while longer so I can think about what you said. If I can at least get you and your family to safety, then *maybe* that's what I'll do. Ava, I make you no promises other than my presence right now, deal?"

"Sure, Tyrell. Whatever you say," she hugged him tight. This time, under the moon and stars, amidst the pervasive, salty air and the ever-present crashing of the ocean waves, Tyrell held on tight. And he had no intention of letting go.

CHAPTER II

Chaos had overtaken Solastran Inn. During the summer, its tavern had been quiet. Because Solastran was one of the biggest cities in Oriel, save for Lightstone Grove—where the king's castle resided—there were other places to eat and drink. Now, however, it was once again filled with the raucous sounds of new and returning students, mothers and fathers giving last-minute advice about hygiene and studying, and the clinking of forks and knives against their plates. Savory smells of bacon and stag-moose sausage filled the air as much as the noise. In some ways, things were just the same as last year the day Griff entered Bergots. However, in other ways, they were very different.

"There ya go, Nyall! Let's keep 'em coming! Woo!" Talley's shouts of encouragement could be heard every time the kitchen door opened and the tired, blonde waitress emerged. Griff wasn't sure if she was exhausted from the amount of customers she had to wait on, or putting up with Talley's inexhaustible enthusiasm.

With all the movement in the tavern, Griff had carefully positioned his large pack underneath the table and placed his feet on either side. Inside the pack was his dragon egg and some clothes to act as padding and a warmer. Scared someone might bump into it, or worse, trample it underfoot, he thought this was the safest place. Strangely, his pack felt warmer than it should be. He wondered if perhaps the egg was absorbing the incredible amount of body heat from the room.

Vincent leaned back in his chair and placed his hand on his belly. Three empty plates and three empty cups were stacked in front of him. "Mmm," he grumbled in delight. "Doesn't get much better than that. You were right about that Dragon's Beard drink, Griff."

"So good!" Marth cut in before Griff had a chance to respond.

"Yep. Talley's been makin' that special drink of his since before Griff was born," Gale Driscoll added.

Knowing that finding enough seating for Griff, his family and his battlegroup was going to be an issue, they were one of the first to arrive at the inn that morning. They had squeezed two tables together, and now that everyone had their fill of breakfast, every inch of the wooden table was covered in dishes.

"Hey guys!" Sylva squeezed past a mother who was hugging her son way too tightly, then quickly ducked under a floating trunk, narrowly missing one of its bottom corners.

"Sylva!" Griff said, waving him over.

Gale stood. "Here, take my seat."

"Thanks," Sylva said. He took his large pack off his back and hung it from the back of his chair. Gale stood awkwardly behind Sylva's chair, trying his best to stay out of the way of the families squeezing between tables.

"What are you doing here?" Griff asked.

"Well ... I'm coming with you!" Sylva grinned sheepishly. "Just found out they've accepted me as a stable hand at Bergots! I'm going to learn how to take care of magical creatures!"

"That's wonderful!" Leena said, squeezing his hand. "I thought you would have taken after your mother and gone into medicine. But this sounds like a fantastic opportunity for you."

"Yeah, I thought about it. Mom's taught me lots over the years, but after being with those wargs back in Cordelia and feeling a connection to them, I just felt like I had to learn more."

"Awesome, Sylva!" Marth clapped him on the back. "Watch out for the male wargs, though. They'll eat ya for lunch if you don't bring enough meat with you. My sisters told me about this one time ..."

Suddenly, Griff's left leg jolted to the side. Had his bag fallen? He looked under the table to see it on its side. *Strange*, he thought to himself. The bag had felt secure between his legs. He carefully positioned it upright, making sure it was evenly balanced, giving it one less excuse to fall over again. Was it the constant movement around the room, his imagination, or was his pack *vibrating*?

He turned to look at Mira, who was already bored with Marth's supposed "true" story. She had been watching Griff with curious eyes half-squinted in interest. Griff looked around before meeting her gaze and shrugging his shoulders.

Dragon's egg? She mouthed.

Griff gently nodded, trying not to draw attention. Mira ducked under the table, pretending to tie her shoes, then popped back up. She shrugged her shoulders at him as if to say, *Looks fine to me*.

"So will you stay in the dormitories like everyone else?" Vincent asked, snapping Griff back to the present.

"Yeah, I think I'll be with the first years, but I'm not sure. They just told me the basics of what to pack and more will be explained when I get there."

"That's ... that's so great, Sylva!" Griff could feel the pack jittering between his legs. Something was happening, but he was unable to look inside to find out.

"We'll *definitely* cross paths while we're there," Griff added, giving him a knowing look. Being at the stables would be very helpful in trying to raise a dragon.

Sylva returned it with a nod.

"Okay everyone, it's time!" Professor Coen's voice boomed across the tavern. "Please make your way to the basement with all of your belongings. Say your final farewells and please watch all of your trunks! No need for injuries before we even make it to school!"

He clapped his hands together in excitement and shouted, "Bergots awaits!"

"Well!" Griff snatched his bag as quickly as he could without making a scene, then said, "Time to go! Love you, Mom and Dad!"

"What's the rush, son?" Gale said after receiving a half-hearted hug from Griff. "We're all the way in the back of the room. You're not scooting past all those people to the front, are you? And you're *definitely* not leaving here with that pathetic hug. No, no. That just won't do. You need to give your big man somethin' better than that!" He grabbed his son and squeezed him tight, much to Griff's embarrassment.

"Dad!" All Griff could think about was keeping the egg safe and getting inside the dorms so he could see what was happening.

"Love ... you ... Dad," he said through pained breaths.

After bidding farewell to his parents, he summoned his trunk to his side, grabbed Mira's hand, and together with his battlegroup and Sylva, they followed the slow-moving crowd.

"Oh!" Marth suddenly said, his voice bright with pleasant surprise. "Hi Kara!" His eyes were wide like a lunatic's, and he waved overenthusiastically at a tall, skinny girl with long, wavy black hair that spilled over her shoulders and bounced effortlessly with each step. She turned to greet Marth. Her eyes were sharp with intellect, but soon turned warm and friendly at seeing her friend.

"What's going on, Griff?" Mira half-whispered, snapping Griff out of his focused observation of Marth making a fool of himself with the girl.

The commotion of the crowd was so loud, Mira's words were almost lost to the noise. They could have screamed an entire conversation about joining Korrun's cause and nobody would be the wiser.

"I ... I dunno. I think ..." Griff huffed in frustration as someone stepped on his toes, their floating trunk narrowly missing his head. "I think something's happening with the egg, but I can't tell. I need to get to the dorms. Now."

Griff tried to push past some energetic first year students, silently praying his own trunk didn't knock the enthusiasm out of them.

"Did you see her, Griff?" Marth said, squeezing past the same first years.

"See who?" Griff responded half-heartedly. Normally, he would have been very interested to hear Marth's story. But right now, he really didn't care. He just wanted to get to the dorms. He also didn't want to push away one of his best friends either.

"Kara Thorson!" he said, as if Griff was supposed to echo his enthusiasm. "She never came back after the holidays last year, remember? Apparently, her parents didn't think it would be safe for her. Now that Korrun seems to be busy elsewhere, and after *tons* of begging, her parents finally agreed she could come back!" Marth rubbed his hands together, glancing back toward Kara. "And I *think* she's still single..."

Griff let Marth's words fade into the background. The crowd moved painfully slowly, and his pack vibrated and shifted with ever increasing intensity. Looking for a way of escape, and realizing there was none, Griff suddenly felt trapped.

"Hey, I know that guy!"

Griff sighed in frustration at the realization someone else wanted to chat, yet that frustration melted away when he saw a friendly face emerge from the jumbled mess of other faces: Milo Ofner. Proudly holding one of his hands was a second-year girl, with black curls that were pulled back in a tight ponytail. Erian Fairweather, known for her strong magical abilities, waved politely to Griff with her free hand, and with the other, held another boy's hand.

"Ready for your second year?" Milo asked, shaking Griff's hand with his own free one.

"Oh yeah, I've been r— Oh!" The boy holding Erian's hand let go and wrapped Griff in a bear hug as tight as his father had.

"Uh ... hi," Griff said.

"Mm-hmm, you too!" the boy said with a gigantic smile. Then, without hesitation, he hugged everyone in the near vicinity.

Realizing he was next to receive a hug after Mira, Marth greeted the boy with his arms held wide. "Me too, right?"

"Yep!" the boy replied.

Sadie tried to escape into the crowd, but there was nowhere to go. She stepped behind Vincent, but was exposed when he bent down low to return the hug. The boy pushed Vincent to the side, and before Sadie could threaten the boy with violence, he wrapped his arms around her tightly, pinning her arms to her sides.

"You smell like echium vulgare, ficus benjamina, and wild carrots," he said before letting her go.

"Um ... what?"

The boy didn't answer, but returned to Erian's side and grasped her hand once more. Vincent leaned toward Sadie and sniffed, which earned him a hard punch to the side.

"Ha, sorry Griff," Milo said, laughing as Vincent grunted and doubled over in pain. "This is my brother, Connor. He's a first year. He's a big hugger and loves nature—especially plants. Mom says in most ways he's normal like you and me. In other ways, he's very unique and special."

Connor looked similar to Milo in some ways: spiky brown hair and blue eyes. Yet, there was much that was different. Though he shared Milo's eye color, they were more almond shaped and had lighter-colored spots that almost made his irises look like gemstones. Milo was tall, but this boy was shorter than Erian. Unlike Milo's larger ears that almost seemed to stick out, Connor's ears were smaller and almost the shape of circles.

"Nice to meet you, Connor," Mira smiled genuinely at him. He returned her smile, then scanned the commotion around them. While everyone else seemed eager to leave the tightly packed tavern, Connor smiled and waved at everyone who passed by.

The flow of the crowd naturally ceased the group's conversation and pushed them out into the hallway. They eventually walked through what was once an ordinary door that led to the basement, but now had expanded in size and was highly decorative. The ornate sign next to the door with the words BERGOTS AWAITS greeted them as it had the year before.

Professor Coen was almost through with his speech that was probably the same as last year's. Something about it being a privilege to come to Bergots and to make wise decisions while they attended. Mr. Colm, the owner of Solastran Inn, stepped up to the blank stone wall the crowd faced and waited for the professor's cue.

A loud voice cut through the quiet chatter. "Hey Griff, why's your bag moving around like that?"

Griff spun to face Connor. His heart leaped in his chest, but he did his best to look cool. "Uh ... it's not." Griff turned to face the front, watching as the two men placed their hands on the stone wall and began generating the portal to Bergots.

"Yes, it is. I just saw it move again."

Several nearby students turned to look and Griff could feel his cheeks flush.

"I ... uh ... must be my stuff jostling around in there. I'm not a very good packer."

"Nuh-uh, there's something moving like it's alive or something." Connor reached a hand out to touch Griff's bag, but Griff quickly took it off and held it low to the ground so no one would see. Connor was right, though. The sides of Griff's bag swelled and shrank and odd intervals. It was as if the egg inside was slowly swiveling.

"No, it's probably nothing."

"It is, it is, it *is* something. I saw it. I wanna see."

"Connor, let's pause." Milo placed his free hand on Connor's forearm and rubbed it gently. Milo eyed Griff's bag with curiosity, but then said, "That bag belongs to Griff. It's not ours, and we should be polite and respect his privacy."

Connor huffed and his lower lip pooched out. "'Kay."

Griff did his best to smile amidst the overwhelming stress. "Thanks, Connor."

Blue light emitted from the swirling vortex and the two men stepped to the side. A loud but pleasant song radiated from the portal and bounced off the walls, distracting everyone, except for Griff, from the conversation he'd just had with Connor.

"Remember!" Professor Coen spoke over the music. "When you step into the portal, keep walking. I'll see you on the other side!"

Professor Coen disappeared into the song and light, followed by a jumbled line of students and their floating trunks. Griff could tell there were some students who, like he was last year, were nervous to step through. He remembered all the fears he'd had as he stared at the vortex for the first time. Now, however, he wasn't afraid of the blue vortex. But that wasn't to say he was without fear. This time it wasn't the portal—or what lay beyond it—that sent his heart racing. It was the loud *CRACK* from within his bag.

CHAPTER 12

"What was *that*?" Connor asked, looking around. Eyes wide, he stared at Griff's shifting bag. By that time, they had made it to the stone wall and the swirling blue portal. Mira and Griff exchanged a quick glance, then before anyone could say another word, he stepped through to the other side.

Music, flying colored confetti, and chaos greeted him as soon as his feet landed in the grand foyer of Bergots. He didn't wait for Mira, Sylva, or the rest of his battlegroup, but walked as quickly from the portal as he dared without drawing attention. An unusually loud, but familiar voice echoed over the sounds of the floating, musicianless instruments. Professor Strickland, an attractive blonde woman whose classes Griff had yet to attend, cycled through the usual announcements. New students were to drop their belongings by the bowler-hatted gentleman with the extravagant mustache, and returning students were to head to their dormitories and prepare for lunch.

Taking two steps at a time, Griff quickly climbed the stone staircase. He ignored the fact that his trunk kept bumping into other trunks as he squeezed past their owners. Suddenly, a slap on his shoulder made Griff jump.

"Hey, whoa!" Marth called, yanking his hand back. "Nightstalker's fury, Griff. What's going on? Why are you acting so weird?"

"The egg," he huffed back quietly, not slowing his pace.

"Really? It's happening?" Marth answered way too loudly.

Griff snapped around and gave Marth a scowl to communicate what he chose not to say aloud.

His friend put his hands up defensively. "All right, all right. Let's get you upstairs, then."

They turned toward the dormitories as soon as they reached the top of the stairs, but just before they reached the hallway, someone called his name. Griff's head dropped. He knew that voice and knew he couldn't ignore it.

"Over here!" Professor Coen waved Griff over.

"Meet you back at the rooms," Griff mumbled to Marth.

After a heavy sigh, he turned away from the dormitories and trudged toward his professor. How could he dash away and not look suspicious?

By that point, Mira, Sadie, and Vincent had climbed the stairs and were walking toward the dorms. Mira gave Griff a questioning look as he passed them, but he didn't bother trying to explain.

"Hey!" Griff did his best to look excited, but found it challenging.

The professor who had just finished high-fiving some of the students nearby—including Sylva, who had just made his way to the front of the group—pulled Griff away from the crowd.

"Any more dreams?" he asked, looking around.

"Sorry, no." Something from his bag jabbed him in the spine and he twisted uncomfortably.

"Keep me updated, yeah? Pull me outta class if you need to. You're one of our best bets for finding these shards."

"You'll be the first to know. I ... promise." Griff gritted his teeth against the pain of another jab.

"Also, I'll stay in touch about using the practice room. Let's just get through the first week alive, eh?" The professor chuckled, as if it was an ongoing joke between the two of them.

"Sure, sure. Sounds great."

Just then, Professor Strickland joined Professor Coen at his side, her hand clasping his, their fingers intertwining. Griff pretended not to notice, but took note to ask the professor about this interaction later. Two sudden bursts of high-pitched sounds emitted from his pack. It was like a loud creak of an old wooden door or the prolonged squeak of a mouse.

"What was that?" Professor Strickland asked, looking around. Thankfully it seemed as though the chaos of the room cloaked the direction of the sound.

"Uh ... I dunno. But I gotta go!" Griff said, spinning on his heels and dashing toward the dormitories. He glanced back at a baffled Professor Coen and called out, "I'll let you know if something comes up, I promise!"

Not caring where his trunk flew or whom it hit, Griff sprinted through the halls of Bergots and dashed up flights of stairs until he finally reached the second-year boys' dormitories. He flung open the door, climbed the stairs to the top of the common room, and entered the farthest room possible. Checking to make sure there was no one around, he sat on a bunk in the back corner of the room, away from the door, and set his pack on the ground. He quickly severed his connection to his floating trunk and it *thumped* on the ground.

Slowly Griff reached for the zipper on his bag. It jolted to the side and fell over without him touching it. He already knew what he was going to find as soon as he opened it. But was he ready? What would happen? Would this baby dragon fly around and breathe fire all over the room? Everything, save for the stone walls, was flammable. Either way, he had brought it this far. It was time to meet the baby Nightflame dragon.

Carefully, he unzipped his pack and was immediately met with obsidian-colored egg fragments and a thick, slimy substance. Opening his pack wider, there amid the mess, licking itself clean, laid a dazzling onyx-black baby Nightflame. Once the light from the room hit the dragon's eyes, it jerked its head toward the opening and let out another long shrill protest. When it did, a line of bright white light radiated from the tip of its nose to the end of its tail.

"Whoa," Griff whispered.

Stunned, all he could do in that moment was stare into the brilliant ruby eyes of the baby Nightflame, who stared back with as much curiosity. Griff guessed that when this dragon stretched out, it would probably be about as long as his forearm. And when it was ready to stand, it would probably be about as tall as the mugs of Dragon's Beard Talley would serve. Its smaller, pointed ears resembled a bat's, covered in fuzzy, black fur. In between them stood two small horns that were almost indistinguishable from the other ridges on the dragon's head and body.

Hands shaking, Griff held out a single finger and slowly inched it toward the baby. The dragon cocked its head, but otherwise remained still. He stopped his finger half an inch away from the dragon and wondered if it had teeth. Would it bite him? Gum his finger raw? Could it breathe fire?

Suddenly the baby Nightflame closed its eyes, let out a pleasant trilling sound, and stretched its head towards Griff's hand. Surprisingly warm, slimy scales and ridges slid across his finger.

"Umm ... hi, baby dragon," Griff said. He ran his finger along the middle of its head and down its spine. The dragon arched its back in response and let out a soft, high-pitched rumble. As it did, its scales lit up as before, but the light was much softer, not as brilliant.

"Here, let's get you out of this bag." Wading through the obsidian egg fragments and slime, he carefully reached into his pack and wrapped his hands around the dragon's waist. As soon as it was free from the bag, it stretched its wings as far out as it could, let out a long, soft trill, then fluttered its wings before settling them back to its sides. It didn't wiggle or try to escape Griff's grasp, which he took as a good sign.

He placed the dragon on his lap and started picking off bits of egg fragments. It shook a few of the bits off its body, laid on its belly, and placed its head on Griff's thigh. It wasn't sleeping, but staring pleasantly at him as he worked.

Suddenly, the door to the room creaked open and Marth yelled, "Found him!"

The dragon's head shot up and stared in the direction of Marth's voice and it let out a hiss of warning.

"Shh," Griff said, petting it gently. "It's just Marth. He may be loud and obnoxious sometimes, but he's good people."

The dragon didn't move, but stopped its rumbling and focused its attention on the blond boy, who at this point had tiptoed across the room, carefully set his trunk on the floor, and gingerly sat on the bunk across from Griff.

Marth stared in disbelief at the dragon laying on Griff's lap. Without taking his eyes off the creature, he whispered, "I'm gonna ignore the loud and obnoxious comment because you actually have an actual dragon sitting on your actual lap right now. Nightstalker's fury. How. Awesome. Is. This."

"Very," Vincent said as he walked up beside Marth's bunk.

"So ... what now?" Marth asked as Griff resumed picking off the last bits of eggshell.

"Well," Griff said, "at some point I'll need to get a new pack, as this one's ruined. Maybe we can build a crate to put it in when we're gone? We'll just need to make sure we're the only ones who use this room. But I guess I need to find out what dragons eat. And quickly."

"You're in luck there, mate." Marth said. "Your girlfriend's probably already headed to the library to find some books on dragons. Said she was going to drop off her stuff and make her way down there."

"Perfect," Griff said.

"You think of a name yet?" Vincent asked, sitting at the foot of Marth's bunk.

"I can't tell if it's a boy or girl, so I'm not sure what to name it."

"Marth Jr., if it's a boy, of course." Marth said. "After all, this dragon is bound to be brave and strong, so it would need a proper name to match."

"Hmm..." Griff scratched his chin. "Sounds like a good girl's name to me. I'll keep that in mind, thanks."

Marth chuckled, opened his trunk, pulled out his pillow, and flung it at Griff's head. Griff easily dodged it, but the dragon immediately stood up and hissed at Marth, the line of scales lighting up brilliantly.

"King's crown, mate!" Marth exclaimed, eyes wide. "That's the coolest thing I have ever seen!"

"Hmm!" Vincent nodded, eyes wide in excitement.

"Once that dragon is off your lap, though, you'll pay for your foolishness. Marth as a girl's name? Seriously?"

"Clearly this dragon is already loyal to me. So, by the time you notice it's off my lap, it'll be too late. I imagine you'll be alone, questioning your choices while applying burn cream to your backside. So, I welcome your challenge, friend," Griff said with a smirk.

Much of the stress of making it to the room without anyone noticing a dragon hatching in his pack had worn off, and Griff was finally able to relax. He knew it wouldn't last. He needed to find a place for it to stay, figure out what kind of food it needed, and how to continue keeping this living, breathing, noisy creature from being seen.

"Here," Marth said, reaching back into his opened trunk. He tossed a towel and an empty leather pack at Griff. "You can use this for now. I don't imagine you plan on keeping that thing up here while we go to the dining hall, do you? You'll need a way to transport it."

"Thanks, Marth." Griff opened the pack. It was slightly larger than the one he'd brought. The dragon still wouldn't be able to spread its wings, so it would have to be a temporary solution. But if the dragon could sleep in it ... suddenly a thought occurred to Griff.

"Hey, where's the closest place we can find a bunch of twigs and leaves? Maybe even some hay?"

"Well, sticks and leaves you can find on the way to the Altar Storm pitch. For hay..." Marth trailed off deep in thought.

"Stables, probably," Vincent answered. He had gotten on his knees and was inching closer to the dragon, who had settled back down onto Griff's lap and was watching Vincent's every move.

Vincent held out his hand and allowed the dragon to smell him from afar, before he reached over and gently scratched its chin. The dragon rumbled in pleasure and closed its eyes.

"Seriously, Vincent?" Marth said. "You must have the magic touch or something."

"Hmm," he answered.

"So, the dragon's nest I found on that island was made out of sticks and leaves," Griff continued. "If I can make a nest inside this pack—with your permission, of course, Marth—then maybe it'll sleep in there. At least until we can figure out what to do with it. Maybe bring it to Sylva at the stables."

"Well, then." Marth stood from his bed. "Let's go to the stables, sneak you out some hay, and show the girls your cool, new pet. Plus ..." Marth rubbed his belly. "I think it's almost lunch time anyways."

CHAPTER 13

A large, heavy book slammed on the table, making Griff flinch and silencing the other tables in the Dining Hall. The current owner of the book placed her hands on her hips and stared at the rest of the battlegroup.

"Found it," Mira said proudly. "Didn't take me long at all, either."

"'Course not," Marth said, "you know that library better than Mrs. Finnegan does. She may have been around when Bergots was founded, but that mind of hers is a steel trap."

"Bergots was founded in 180 D.Z., she is *not* four hundred seven years old, Marth." Mira plopped into her seat next to Griff and took a small bite of sweet potato.

"Yeah, well, I'm not so sure about that. If she's not over four hundred years old, she's gotta be close," Marth answered.

Having sneaked hay and wood chips from the stables on the way to lunch, Griff, Sylva, Marth and Vincent made a cozy nest for the dragon inside Marth's pack. Having spent enough energy hatching from the egg, it seemed as though the nest was good enough for the tired beast. It had tucked its wings to its sides, curled into a tight ball, and fell fast asleep. As long as Griff walked slowly and carefully, the dragon stayed silent. Once or twice, he stumbled on an uneven space between the stone tiles and received a high-pitched grump from within the bag. Otherwise, the trip to the Dining Hall was smooth. It seemed that this plan—having the dragon in Marth's pack—would work. For now.

"Okay, it says here …" Mira paused, quickly scanning the pages of her new book. "Mm-hmm, yep. Just as I thought …" She continued reading silently to herself.

"Uh … care to share with the rest of us?" Griff gently elbowed her side.

No one, not even Vincent, had taken another bite of their lunch since she started reading. Instead, they had leaned forward, eyes focused on the book.

"Oh, right. Sorry," Mira said. "So, while dragons do eat meat—and a lot of it as they get bigger—they also have been known to enjoy soft fruit as babies."

"Griff, you're gonna have to play mama bird and give this pet of yours some chewed-up food, I think," Marth chuckled.

"May I?" Sylva asked Mira, pointing to the book as he settled in beside Griff and the others. She slid it over, then snatched a small piece of ground stagmoose meat from Griff's plate.

"Can I pretty please be the first one to feed it something?" Mira cooed, batting her eyelashes furiously at Griff.

Griff looked down at his pack. From the movements within, he guessed the dragon was beginning to stir. Probably feeding time anyway.

"Sure, I guess. But remember, *I'm* its mama. Or … papa … or whatever."

"Oh, trust me. I'm only putting the food *in*. When the food comes *out* … I'll remember you're its mama. Promise."

Mira winked and quickly ducked under the table. Everyone else followed.

"Guys! You're going to look suspicious! Heads up!" Griff said, though he was just as guilty as the others. However, he felt justified considering this was *his* dragon that was being fed.

The rest of the group pulled their heads up from under the table, though they still sat awkwardly, cocking their heads at weird angles, trying to see the dragon's first meal.

Gently, Mira untied the rope that cinched the opening of the pack and waved the meat in front of the dozing dragon's face. One eye peeked open and followed the swaying food. Then the second eye opened and did the same. Without moving any other part of its body, the baby dragon's head lurched forward and snatched the food from Mira's hand, causing her to squeal in surprise. The stagmoose meat was gone in a single chomp. Then the dragon let out a pleasant trilling sound in the back of its throat. It stretched its head high, eagerly swaying from side to side, looking for more food.

"Aww, it liked the food!" Mira squealed.

Even Sadie had let out a small "Aww ..." before realizing she had said it aloud. She straightened back up and glared at everyone. "What? A girl can't think an animal's cute?"

Marth held his hands up defensively, but Vincent couldn't stifle his chuckle.

"Here, Griff, it wants more," Mira said, apparently oblivious to the tensions at the table. Before Griff could say anything, she snatched his plate and placed it in her lap.

"Hey!" Griff protested.

"Want some more, you wittle pumpkin?" she cooed, ignoring Griff's objections. Within only a few minutes, every morsel of food on Griff's plate was given to the dragon: stagmoose meat, mashed sweet potato, pumpkin slices, and buttered toast. Mira even allowed the dragon to lick the plate completely clean.

"Well, now *I* don't have anything to eat!" Griff complained, holding his empty plate. Sadie laughed at this, but Mira barely seemed to notice. She was too busy petting the fur behind the dragon's bat-like ears.

"Oh please," she said. "It's called parenting, Griff. *You're* its daddy, which means you're going to have to learn to sacrifice for the sake of your new family member. Plus, you can always get seconds, you know."

"Yeah, yeah," Griff replied, "I'm getting a new plate too. But this time, *I'm* feeding *my* dragon."

A few moments later, Griff returned to the table, shuffling between people, his eyes glued to the wobbly towers of food that threatened to slide off his plate. As he lowered his dish on the table, Sylva suddenly popped his head up from underneath, almost knocking the whole thing to the ground.

Completely ignoring Griff's glare, Sylva flipped through the pages of the book, then snatched another piece of food off Griff's plate before disappearing back under the table.

"Seriously?" Griff asked. "Am I ever gonna eat?"

The dragon had seemingly warmed up to Sylva, rolling onto its back and exposing its belly while Sylva examined it, giving it small bites to keep it in place. Finally, once he had finished his examination, Sylva surfaced, fed the dragon another bite from Griff's plate, and said, "That's a good *girl!*"

The dragon tucked itself into a tight ball and closed its eyes as Sylva cinched the bag shut.

"Girl?!" Griff asked, ducking under the table and pulling at the strings of the bag.

"Hi Griff, what's going on?" a girl's voice made Griff jump and bang his head on the underside of the table.

"Nightstalker's *fury*," Griff said through gritted teeth. He pulled himself back into his seat and rubbed the top of his head with his hand.

"H-hi, Kara." Griff tried to force a smile.

Kara Thorson held an empty plate in one hand while the other was planted firmly on her hip.

"What were you doing under the table?" she asked teasingly.

"Just, uh ... tying my shoe." Griff glanced under the table, but there was hardly any movement inside the bag.

"Mm-hmm." Kara eyed Griff but didn't say another word. Instead, her eyes trailed to the underside of the table.

"Well, hey! We're glad you're back at school!" Griff said way too loudly, scooting his seat to block her view.

She raised her eyebrows in surprise. "You are, are you?" Then she smiled. Her eyes locked onto his. "I'm glad to be back at school too. Maybe you can help me catch up on what I missed from last semester?"

She took a step closer, the faint smell of jasmine tickling Griff's nose. Trapped in his chair, he was unable to move as she placed her free hand gently on his shoulder.

"Let me know, okay?"

And just as quickly as she had placed her hand, it was now gone as she turned and walked toward the trash cans by the door. She took one last glance at Griff's group and said, "Oh, and Mira! I hope it's okay that I put my stuff next to yours! We can be roomies!"

Griff turned to Mira, her eyes narrowed in on him. He held up his hands. "I—I—I barely know her! I just didn't want her to see the egg! Promise!"

"Yeah, uh, I don't think she knows you two are a thing, Mira," Marth said, coming to Kara's defense. "She wasn't *here* last semester, remember?"

"Well, you make sure she knows without a doubt that we *are* a thing," Mira demanded.

"Yeah, well. Happy to do it. Ya know … for *your* sake of course…" Marth's eyes followed Kara all the way back to her seat. There was a pitiful longing in his look that Griff could only chuckle at. It was the same type of look Vincent would give to his first plate of food before any given meal.

Sylva glanced at the first years leaving their table and walking toward Professors Coen and Strickland. He wiped his hands with his napkin and smiled at Griff. "Well, it looks like I don't have much time, but congratulations, Griff. You have a baby *girl* dragon."

Both Mira and Sadie let out an uncontrollable squeal that they must have been holding in since they first learned of the news. Clearly the tension in the air that Kara brought with her had subsided.

"Aww! A baby *girl* dragon, Griff!" Mira said, her voice reaching new octaves.

Sadie squeezed Vincent's arm so tight, the bulky giant winced in pain.

"Hmm ... okay. It's a girl," Griff said. He looked to Sylva. "You're sure?"

"Please don't make me go into the details, but yes. I'm sure."

"I have so many suggestions for names already!" Mira squealed. "Elizabeth. Alexandra. Victoria."

"No way," Marth said. "This is a *dragon* we're talking about here, Mira. It needs a name that instills fear in Griff's enemies. Something that communicates power. Like ... Deathwing: Destroyer of Evil."

As the battlegroup and Sylva discussed names, Griff looked around the Dining Hall to make sure no one was watching, then ducked under the table. He loosened the drawstring of the pack and stared at his sleeping dragon. Her eyes were shut tight and her chest was already slowly rising and falling. *Doesn't take her long to fall asleep.*

He thought back to the dragon's mother. She had been the protector of more than just the shard. She was the protector of her children as well. While Griff didn't know what happened to the other eggs, whether they had hatched or were destroyed by predators, this one was her last child. And now, as Griff had promised the mother, he was its protector. Using one finger, he stroked it down the dragon's snout, which caused her to yawn and stretch out her legs. He cinched the bag shut and joined the ongoing conversation about different names for the dragon.

"How about ... Runa?" Griff said, interrupting Marth.

"Runa?" Mira asked.

"Yeah. Runa."

Everyone mulled it over as though they had a say in this decision, though Griff knew better.

"Destroyer of Evil?" Marth asked.

Griff smiled. "Sure, Marth. Runa: Destroyer of Evil."

"Yes!" Marth pumped his fist in the air. "Then, I like it!"

"Well, she's your dragon, Griff. If that's the name you want to give her, then I like it too." Mira rubbed her hand on his arm. "But you're still cleaning up after it. I'm not picking up any messes that dragon makes."

"Yeah, I think I'm in for more than I realized ..." Griff said.

"Yup," Marth said. "But I wasn't going to tell you that. I've always wanted a friend who had a dragon. That way, I could pet it, ride it, and feed it, but I could always give it back."

Vincent, who had three cleaned plates in front of him, chuckled. "Seems like a good deal to me."

"Actually, we need to talk about how we're going to care for her, Griff," Sylva said, closing the book and gathering his trash. Professor Coen was waving him over to join the other first years.

"You won't be able to keep it hidden in your room for very long. According to the book, these things grow wicked fast! This first meal was only three plates, but in the weeks to come it'll be more. She needs lots of food and space to grow. I've only just met the stablemaster, Mr. Dingmann, and he seems nice enough. But I don't know if he's someone you can trust with your dragon just yet."

"Yeah. I mean, I haven't even told Professor Coen yet," Griff admitted.

"As much as I would love to help you hide the cute little draggy-wag-gy," Mira said, cooing her last words, "I am *not* about to lose good standing with the school or the king. If you get caught, I had absolutely nothing to do with it. Got it?"

"Got it," Griff answered. "I brought it here, it's my responsibility. I just felt like ... like I owed its mother somehow. And this was a way I could fulfill that."

"Well," Sylva said, "Mr. Dingmann's resting from warg training. It sounded like he had a tough time with the new pups. If we hurry, I think we could get a good weight on the dragon and check its health. This book is full of good information on baby dragons. I think I can use it to help track its growth and health. I'll stop by the dorms, then we can go to the stables together. Mira, can I take this book with me?"

Mira paused, searching for the right words. "Well, um, I have really good standing at the library, and I don't want to lose that. Can we stop by, and I'll check the book in and you check it back out? That way it's under your name and I won't be accused of subleasing books. Library rules, not mine!" she said defensively after seeing everyone gawking at her.

"Fine," Griff answered. "Sylva, go do your thing with the first years. We'll stop by the library, then meet you at the stables."

CHAPTER 14

Sunlight danced along the forest floor as the canopy above Tyrell swayed with the wind, letting the sun's beams in at different intervals. The shade was a welcome relief from the brutal heat they had experienced the past few days. And even though Tyrell had spent most of those days in the water with his fishing net and shirt off, his bright red skin told him he needed a break from the sun.

As promised, Ava had stayed far away whenever Tyrell went fishing. For him, having just the ocean waves and the seagulls above for company was plenty. Staring at the water with only a singular mission of bringing back fish soothed his restless mind.

He was a good fisherman, and he knew it. And it worked in his favor. Because he consistently brought back a net full of fish, the supply captain allowed him access to a net anytime he pleased. It was a sanction he took full advantage of. Whatever it took, he would find a way to keep himself busy and stay away from camp. And the Corruption.

His father was happy that Tyrell had decided to stay, but the man hardly spoke to him at all. Tyrell thought that perhaps Randolph would take extra time to try and convince him that Korrun's mission was good. That he just needed to trust that what he was doing was all for the right reasons. Instead, other than the half-hearted, "I'm glad you decided to stay," all Tyrell had from his father was his silence. Which suited him just fine.

Tyrell stared at the skinny man in front of him. The man hacked away with his machete at some underbrush that was blocking his way. He was older. The white goatee gave away his age and stood in stark contrast to his dark skin that matched his daughter's. Most notably, though, was the object he wore on the bridge of his nose. An object that Tyrell had only seen a few times, and only from a distance. The man, Kwame Adebayo, called them "glasses." It was a technology before Day Zero. Something he had discovered in his studies that salvaged his failing eyesight and allowed him to see with new clarity.

Kwame was a quiet soul, though when he spoke, it was with well-earned confidence. The man was clearly intelligent. But unlike his daughter who was always full of words, whether necessary or not, he only used them as he had need.

While Kwame was a man of few words, his wife, Amina, had no trouble filling the silence. Still, she paled in comparison to her daughter, who didn't just fill in the void of silence with her words. She drowned it. Amina was slightly taller than her daughter, her skin darker. Tyrell guessed Ava's parents were a few years older than his own father. Amina's long, braided hair hid light streaks of gray. The thin wrinkles on the sides of her eyes only confirmed what Tyrell had already witnessed about her: she smiled. A lot. And not just with her lips, but with her entire face. Laughter came easily for her, bubbling up almost incessantly in every conversation. She was a joyful woman who never let anything stand in the way of that.

After creating an opening in the brush, the man silently gestured for Tyrell to lead the way. Tyrell was followed by Amina, who tightened a grip on her bow as she walked through, then Ava, who carelessly carried her spear on her shoulder. The Adebayo family moved through the forest as one silent unit. While Tyrell was skilled in the art of fishing, he was learning quickly that Ava's family knew the art of the hunt well.

Kwame held up a fist and the group paused. He pushed the glasses higher up his nose, then knelt and pointed to a broken branch on a nearby bush. He searched the ground and found a fresh hoofprint. He stared at Tyrell and made a "shushing" gesture, before tiptoeing farther into the underbrush.

"I think I know what it is!" Ava whispered excitedly, grasping Tyrell's arm. Immediately, he shrugged her off before her parents saw and made assumptions. Amina had already disappeared into the brush after her husband, but Tyrell didn't want to risk being labeled by them.

"Shh!" Tyrell motioned with his hand, directing Ava ahead of him through the brush so he could guard their backs. And so he wouldn't have to talk.

Thankfully, they marched in silence, following Kwame's lead, pausing only to check for fresh signs. Kwame's pace quickened. They were getting closer. A few minutes later, Tyrell heard a loud snort. Kwame held up another fist, halting his family and Tyrell a few yards behind a large fallen tree. Grasping his machete tighter, Kwame tiptoed the rest of the way to the trunk. He was silent. Meticulous. Careful. He signaled for the family and Tyrell to stay where they were. Amina nocked an arrow into the bow, but kept it lowered.

Kwame's knuckles paled as he clenched his machete tight. Deep breath in. Long breath out. He pushed his glasses up higher, then gritted his teeth and dashed over the fallen tree.

A loud squeal pierced the silence of the forest.

Tyrell could only see the top of Kwame's head bob up and down as he chased whatever was on the other side. Tyrell itched to join the fight but maintained his position.

"NOW!" Kwame screamed.

Without another thought, Tyrell and the rest of Kwame's family bolted over the obstacle and into the chaos. Tyrell paused as soon as he landed. Kwame stood on the opposite side of the clearing, blood splattered on his left leg. It wasn't his. Facing Kwame, with its back to Tyrell, stood a large boar-like creature Tyrell had never seen before.

The beast resembled a stockier version of the boars Tyrell hunted back home, however, this one was about a foot taller. There was no snout. Instead, the top of its mouth was like a deadly spaded shovel turned upside down. As scary of a weapon as its non-snout looked, it was probably used mostly for digging up roots. The three deadly sharp horns shaped like a trident on top of its head, however, was another matter.

Not noticing the others had joined the fray, it stared at the man who had sliced its front shoulder and grunted in pure hatred. The beast lowered its head and sprinted, pointing its trident-like horns at Kwame. Amina took a step forward and launched an arrow at its hindside. Another angry squeal. It snapped around and charged at Amina. Ava readied her spear, looking comfortable in the motion. Amina stood motionless. Confident. Tyrell's heart leapt to his throat. She wasn't going to move. The boar lowered its head. Tyrell held out his hands, ready to cast his first spell.

Suddenly, with reflexes that seemed contrary to her age, Amina stepped to the side. The creature dashed past her, only to be met with Ava's spear. It shrieked and fell to its side. Dead before it even hit the ground.

Wide-eyed, Tyrell stared at Amina. If he had known her better, he would have screamed at her. Told her how stupid her plan was. That she could have gotten killed. But he kept those thoughts to himself. A skill he wished Ava would learn.

She gave Tyrell a kind smile. "You were worried 'bout me, weren't you?"

Tyrell blushed and nodded. Had he been so obvious?

"Well, honey, you don't have to worry 'bout me. We been doin' this a lot longer than you been alive." Amina walked over to her daughter and kissed her cheek.

"Just like we taught you. Good work, Ava."

Kwame walked over, nodded to Tyrell, then stood next to his daughter.

"Good size," he said, rubbing his goatee. He cocked his head to the side. "Two hundred pounds or so, I believe." He looked to Tyrell and pushed his glasses up his nose. "You want first or second shift?"

"First or second shift?"

"Hmph!" Kwame laughed. "We got to get it back to camp somehow!"

Tyrell sighed, then nodded. "First."

Sweat soaked through every stitch of Tyrell's clothing. It poured down the back of his neck and the sides of his face. But he was too stubborn to acknowledge he needed help. Thankfully, Kwame didn't dishonor him with asking either. The man led the way, holding his wife's hand the whole time. On one hand, it was disgusting. On the other, it reminded him of a time before all of this, when his parents used to do the same. He and his younger brother, Alex, used to make gagging noises at their parents with every small act of affection, which would only encourage them more.

He wondered how his brother was doing without him. Though the temperature at this location was still warm, he knew winter was coming. Which meant he would miss his brother's ninth birthday. Overwhelming guilt sank his heart. He tried to shake the thoughts out of his head and decided to keep his eyes on the path instead of on the romance ahead. He focused on his breathing, trying to keep it steady with every step, but it was getting harder to do.

Ava didn't seem to notice. She half-skipped beside him, spear slung over her shoulder, chatting about the first thing that came to her mind. Though normally this would annoy him to the point of anger, he didn't mind it as much, now. He was getting used to Ava's need for conversation, and he learned a lot about her family as well. For example, the Adebayo family have been hunters for generations. Legacy was incredibly important to them. So, whatever they learned, whatever material possessions they gained, it was passed on to the next generation.

Kwame, though, picked up new skills not seen throughout his family. He was an artifician. He studied old world technology before Day Zero to restore it. Apparently, he was the best. While he wasn't the most gifted socially—something Tyrell had already noticed early on—his natural curiosity and the way his mind worked allowed him to see complex objects differently. His curiosity was like a blazing fire that had been lit early on in his childhood when he had stumbled across the very glasses he wore now. Realizing there was so much from the past—from before Day Zero— that could benefit the present, he set off on a journey of discovery that led him to create all types of new gadgets.

"So I've gotten to travel all over the place while Dad does his research. I've been to big, big, big cities. I've been to the mountains. Did you know they had cities on mountaintops? Who would wanna live all the way up there anyways? It snows a lot on mountains, you know. And just so you know, this isn't the first time I've been to the beach, either. But, ya know, I still stay away from the water." Ava chuckled shyly.

Sweat stung Tyrell's eyes, and he paused to wipe it away.

"Hey, you've been carrying that thing for awhile now. Is your shift about over? Want some help?"

Tyrell blinked the sweat away. "No. I'm fine."

"Hey Dad!" Ava called. "Isn't it your turn?"

Kwame and Amina turned and locked hands.

"Ready for a change in shift?" Kwame asked.

"Sure."

Tyrell slumped the beast off his shoulders and heaved a heavy sigh of relief. He arched his back and felt multiple cracks along his spine.

Kwame knelt, and with a strength contrary to his stature, lifted the boar onto his own shoulders.

"Ava, why don't you walk with your mother for a while." He locked eyes with Tyrell. "I want to get to know your friend better."

Great, Tyrell thought. *More conversation.* So that he didn't look weak—because he wasn't—Tyrell returned the look and nodded.

Ava's father fumbled with the boar's body for only a moment before it was on his shoulders and he carried it effortlessly. Tyrell assumed it was more of a show, though. Kwame, though a skilled hunter, was still leaner than Tyrell, and from recent, personal experience, Tyrell knew that boar was heavy.

"So, Tyrell, what is your plan here?" Kwame asked gruffly.

"Sir?"

"What are you doing here?"

"Here as in this hunt? Ava invited me." He knew that wasn't Kwame's question, but he was not one to volunteer too much information too quickly. People, especially people he didn't trust, had to earn it.

Kwame grunted. "Here as in Korrun's camp."

"*Master* Korrun, Daddy!" Ava called from ahead.

"Master. Hmph. Far from it," he more or less whispered to himself. Just loud enough for Tyrell to hear him.

Tyrell didn't know how to answer the man. He didn't have a full grasp on why he was here either. Not since that night on the beach with Ava. Before then, things were clear. He had a mission: bring his dad home. He'd failed that mission. Now, every day was a blur. He spoke with his father less every day. Sure, he paid attention to the conversations around him to gather as much intel as he could. He did his best to play the role of a black cloak. But other than that, he was stuck in survival mode.

"I don't really know, sir," Tyrell answered honestly.

"Hmph," Kwame grunted again. Then he paused and turned to Tyrell. "Is Korrun *your* master?"

Tyrell locked eyes with the man. "Far from it."

That earned a smile from Kwame. And a gentler tone as well.

"Korrun wants me for my artifician skills."

"Hmm. Ava told me about some of the work that you did, restoring old world things."

Kwame nodded. "And more than that. Before Korrun showed up, I was on the brink of finding ways to infuse magic into old world technology. I've heard of you mages already doing some of that. Sending letters through old typewriters, printing books. Astounding inventions. But there is so much more potential that exists out there."

"What do you mean?" Tyrell asked.

"You ever been to one of the big cities?"

Tyrell shook his head. Whisperspell was the biggest town he knew, its population sitting around a thousand people at most. He'd heard of the bigger cities from his dad's stories. Once upon a time, before they all turned to rubble, the big cities boasted shops and restaurants so numerous, a single person would not have the time or money to visit them all. Between the fallout from Day Zero and the Corruption it left behind, almost all large cities were rendered inhabitable.

"Well, if you ever do go, you'd be amazed at what you can find in the destruction. I found these small, cylindrical items called 'batteries.' Most people thought they were junk. I knew better. After further investigation, I discovered that they store *energy*."

"Store energy?"

Kwame paused and pushed his glasses up higher on his nose—an almost comical event given the fact that he was carrying a dead animal that weighed more than he did.

"Indeed. Think about those lightning spells you mages cast. It's a lot like that, but the energy is stored, controlled, and released as needed. Much of the old world technology was powered by those small things. Well, anyways, I saw them in every city I went to, so I knew they had to be important. Well, what if we could somehow use them? What if a mage could inject it with lightning magic? Could we use it to power other old world machines and start to get back to where we were before Day Zero?"

Kwame grunted and shifted the boar on his back. Tyrell could see that, physically, Kwame was already getting tired. Emotionally, though, he was just getting started.

"Or how about *better* water filtration systems? Or even *portable* water filtration systems? Right now, any city with running water has to have people at the pumping generators. And those cities with mages? Well they're lucky enough that they can use their magic to keep the machines running. But even then, not every city has people who can manipulate essence. So then, you have people doing it manually. But when there's no people, there's no running water."

Kwame's voice trailed off and he remained silent for a moment, as though lost in a memory. Tyrell, never a fan of talking, decided to allow him as much time as he needed. He remained silent and watched ahead as Ava and her mother played a game of nicknaming the foliage around them with absurd names.

Finally, Kwame continued. "Can you imagine the quality of life change our world could see if we could reinvigorate old technology and make it better with magic? More people with cleaner water. We could light the dark streets at night to keep the nightstalkers away. Kids could feel safe again. The way the world is supposed to be."

It was all above Tyrell's head. But he got the picture. Kwame wanted to make the world a better place using his new gadgets. Well. Old gadgets made new.

"I think Korrun, however, sees my skillset as a way to build instruments of war. Explosives imbued with magical energy. Gauntlets that can fire spells without the mage. I think that's why he forced me and my family to join him."

Kwame awkwardly pushed his glasses back up his nose and then looked at Tyrell. There was a fire behind those eyes. A fire, he could see, burning deep within Kwame's very soul.

"But I will *not* use my gifts for such wretched schemes."

Tyrell didn't know what to say. Kwame had just poured out his soul to him—something Tyrell imagined wasn't a normal occurrence for him. Tyrell wasn't used to having such deep conversations with anyone besides Ava. And even then, he only dug so deep.

They walked in silence for a few moments before Tyrell could find any words. "I like your vision for the future." It was all he knew to say.

"Vision is only the start, Tyrell. I don't want this to stay a vision. A vision is the starting point. I want to make my vision a reality."

Tyrell sighed. He'd hoped his words were just the final word and that they could continue to walk in silence.

"And that's not the kind of reality Korrun intends to create ... *if* he's not stopped. Ahead and to the right, dear!" Kwame called ahead to his wife. Tyrell looked around and realized they were no longer on the trail. Frustrated he hadn't been paying more attention, he grit his teeth and determined to do better. Amina nodded at her husband's words and pulled Ava forward between two trees. Kwame stopped and turned toward Tyrell, which he took that as a signal to follow suit.

"I'll cut to the chase, Tyrell. I know who your father is. I know what he used to do and what he's doing now."

Tyrell sighed. "Ava told you, didn't she?"

"Of course." Kwame pushed his glasses higher. "She also warned us about the effects of the Corruption—something I've theorized myself, but never had confirmation—and that we should stay away from it as much as possible. And so we have. That's all thanks to you."

Tyrell nodded, deciding to remain silent. He knew there was more coming.

"I asked what your plan was here because I believe—as does my daughter—that there's something more you can do. I believe your father was ... once ... a good man. And a good father. I believe that he told you stories. Taught you to fight—to protect. I believe he shared strategies and insights with you that could be extremely useful right now."

"What do you mean?"

"I mean, I want to get my family out of here, Tyrell. But I also don't want to leave behind the others that are here that want the same thing."

"Ava mentioned there were others who felt the same way," Tyrell said.

"Hmph. It's not hard to see past Korrun's empty words. Sadly, many still buy them. But there are still those who are smart enough to catch the lies. All we need is someone who can lead us."

"Who am I to lead a rebellion within Korrun's army?"

"That's what I intend to find out," Kwame said. "It's why you're here."

"I thought Ava invited me?"

"Who do you think planted that idea in her head?" Kwame smiled, adjusted his glasses once more, then continued marching forward.

Tyrell followed silently, staying a few feet behind Kwame. His mind swirled with their previous conversation. Him? Lead a rebellion? There was no way. Sure, everything he said about his upbringing was true. In addition to his father's teaching and training, he'd also read many military books. Not that he considered himself a "bookworm," only that he found such books interesting. It was like it gave him a chance to live the life his dad did. And to prepare him for a life like his dad led. Everyone believed Tyrell would follow in his father's footsteps. And he was proud to agree. Until the day his dad left.

"Here we are," Kwame said, tossing the boar's body on the ground with a groan of relief.

"Where are we?" Tyrell asked.

Ava rushed over and grabbed his arm. She pointed ahead to a set of cliffs. "There. See it?"

Tyrell covered the rays of sun with his hand, and strained his eyes forward. He leaned closer to Ava so he could better see where she was pointing. At least, that's what he told himself.

"A ... cave?"

"That's right, hon," Amina responded. "A big one too. Much bigger than it looks from the outside."

"What about it?" Tyrell asked.

Kwame stepped forward and wrapped his arm around his daughter. Tyrell immediately stepped away from Ava, his cheeks suddenly feeling hot.

"Well, for now, let's just call it the 'safe place.'"

"Safe place?"

"Mm-hm. Should things start to go sideways around camp, or should we ever get separated, this is where you go."

"It'll be our secret little hideaway!" Ava chimed, as she danced up and down.

"So we didn't really come out here to hunt, did we?" Tyrell asked Kwame.

The man shrugged his shoulders. "I am a man of efficiency. Who says we can't accomplish multiple things within the same trip?"

Kwame accompanied his daughter back down the trail to where the body of the boar lay. Amina grabbed Ava's other arm as they passed by.

"Speaking of efficiency," Kwame called back. "I think it's your turn to carry the beast."

CHAPTER 15

Crash! Griff's eyes popped open. He wasn't in his bed. Runa wasn't sleeping on his chest anymore. *Where am I?*

Although his eyes were open, he couldn't see a thing. It was pitch black all around him. Pervasive. Unending. It was as if he was back in the caves with the lava pit all over again. Only this time, instead of the smell of sulfur, he sensed another fragrance: mold and salt water. Another loud noise came from behind him. It sounded like rolling thunder, and at the same time, like a long, drawn-out roar. Griff stood to his feet and found a wall. Keeping his hand on it, he carefully followed the sounds until he could see a pale light. Once he could see the crescent moon from the opening of the tunnel, he sprinted forward. In trying to stop, Griff slipped on the downward-sloping slick stone ground.

He was no longer in control of his own body. He tried to grab hold of any surface. Something, anything to stop his slide or slow him down. Gravity, however, had him in its grasp. His heart leapt into his throat as he slid out of the entrance to the cave.

He was falling. Screaming. And then, a few feet later, his body hit the hard, unforgiving bottom of another stone ledge.

He knew this was a dream, but the pain felt very real. Griff groaned as he rolled onto his belly. Tiny pebbles were lodged into his back. All the air from his lungs had been forced out from the landing. He laid on his belly until he was able to breathe normally again, though with each breath he was painfully reminded of his fall. He pushed himself up to his knees and looked over the ledge. At least a hundred feet below him was the ocean. The waters were dark in the cover of night, and its waves were angry, crashing violently into the stony cliffs. They sounded their furious roars with each attack. But every time, they were beaten back by the immovable walls.

He'd known there was a shard near the ocean, but with only one dream that he could barely even remember, he was completely clueless as to its location. He searched the stars for clues. Looking for the pictures in the sky that his father had taught him over the years. He drew in the dirt at his knees, wanting to recreate the night sky as best as possible. He needed to practice, because as soon as he woke up, he would head to Headmaster Aldamund's office and try to draw this map of stars again in hopes that it would help them find this place. Then, he scanned the cliffs along the ocean for landmarks. To his left, the cliffs seemed to have no end. But to his right, there was a wide channel of water that led to a beach. Across that channel were a shorter set of cliffs. Set atop them, breaking the darkness of night, was a large camp with hundreds of tents, some large, some small. Campfires were scattered among the tents with a large bonfire in the middle of the site.

"Korrun?" Griff asked no one. With a campsite as large as this, and so close to a shard, it had to be, right? The campsite was just far enough away that the shadows passing back and forth in front of the fires were fuzzy. It wasn't until he saw the blurry outline of a feline creature that he was sure the camp belonged to the king's brother.

Should he be afraid of nightstalkers prowling around here? Would they find him? And if they did, could they see him? Hurt him? As Griff sat and pondered these things, he saw a small light materialize on the beach. It didn't come from a torch, but from a hand.

Soon after, three other lights appeared behind the first. It was a line of black cloaks and a few nightstalkers walking on the beach away from camp. A few of the black cloaks who didn't generate light carried swords or axes on their backs. The crashing of the waves made it impossible to hear anything they were saying. The lights slowly bounced through the darkness as the group trudged in the sand toward the cliffs that Griff stood on.

Glad he hadn't given his own position away with a light spell, he retreated to the back wall of the cliff and looked up. He had only fallen a few feet. The opening to the cave was just too high for him to jump and grab the ledge. He looked around him to see if there was any help: a large rock to climb on, or a vine along the wall to pull himself up. Nothing.

Then he remembered his first Altar Storm battle.

"Vincent, you clever giant," he whispered to himself. There wasn't much room for him to back up, so he placed his heels on the edge of the cliff, forcing himself not to look down. Then, in a burst of speed and energy, he sprinted to the wall, angled his hands down, and cast a wind spell toward the ground. He knew he'd made a mistake as soon as the energy left his hands. It was too strong. His body flung through the air, passing the opening in the cliff. He sailed higher and higher until he landed with a loud *thud* on top of the cliffs. Sadly, the soft grass did nothing to ease the landing on his already aching back.

Griff grunted and pushed himself to his feet. Adrenaline dulled his pain and heightened his senses. There was a group from Korrun's army coming this way. He didn't know if he could be seen, but more importantly, they were close to finding the next shard. He peeked over the ledge that he had flown over with his wild wind spell. There was no real way back down. No rocks jutting out to place his hands and feet. Not to mention the entire side was wet from the ocean spray. If he wanted to enter the caves now, it would have to be from the other side. Where the black cloaks were headed.

He crept along the top of the cliff, hoping no one from the camp would spot him. When he got to the other side, he could see the group of black cloaks nearing his location. He climbed down the short slope to the beach and ducked behind a bush.

"We're close. I can feel it." Griff dared to peek out from behind the bushes. The voice sounded distant and distorted amidst the crashing waves and wind at Griff's back, but there was no mistaking its owner. This was the king's brother. Even if he hadn't heard Korrun's voice, the six-legged, three-tailed alligator-like nightstalker gave him away. Korrun's pet. What Griff wouldn't do to have a chance to run his sword through such a monstrosity. Or watch it burn. Anything to destroy that permanent crocodile smile.

"I knew it," another man spoke out. "I *knew* there was one here. All the clues pointed to this place."

Was that ... Tyrell's father? It felt like a century had passed since the attack on Bergots, but that man looked like the one Tyrell had spoken to in the grand foyer.

"All the clues pointed to *this* place?" A familiar, cocky, better-than-you voice responded. A less large, though still stocky, Kaden Horter pushed past two black cloaks. "This place, here? In the middle of nowhere, hidden in some unknown caves? What makes this place so special?"

"Mind your tone, boy," Tyrell's father responded.

Korrun laughed. "You have no patience, do you? What's your name?"

"Horter. Kaden Horter, Master Korrun."

"Right. Well, *Mr. Horter*, this place is more special than you realize. These last couple of months searching in this location may have made you impatient, but we will all soon be rewarded." Korrun gestured to the cliffs and ocean beyond them.

"Many years ago, before Day Zero, a group of people discovered something that would change the course of history forever. Their discovery shaped the world as we know it now. They didn't discover it in these caves, no. They had technology that allowed them to swim deep down into the depths of the ocean. These people believed that there was so much more to learn about our world beneath these very waves. After a long time, they found an underwater cave that housed something very special."

Korrun spat on the ground. "These people did not treasure this discovery as they should have. And now, we find ourselves living in a broken, corrupted world."

"Sir," Kaden said, almost in awe, "What is this treasure? Gold? Silver? New, uh, tech ... tech-a-knowledge?"

"Ha!" Korrun laughed. "You mean technology. It's not for you to know. You have your place. I have mine. But it is far greater than any gold, silver, or *technology*. But what better place to hide a piece of it than where it stayed hidden for centuries?" He gestured to the ocean again.

"Sir? You don't mean to find a way underneath the ocean, do you?"

"I do."

"How? That seems impossible!" Kaden said, bewildered.

"Hmph. Hidden somewhere in these caves is a map that will tell us exactly where it is. Then, we'll use something that the people long before us didn't have. Magic." Even from this distance, Korrun's evil smile reflecting in the moonlight made Griff shudder.

"Well, sir. I ... uh ... I don't have any magic," Kaden said. "I don't know why you brought me along."

Korrun casually flicked his hand in dismissal. "You won't need magic." He smiled at Kaden, making the overconfident boy shrink back from his master. "Once we find that map, you're going to be our little test run."

CHAPTER 16

Griff bolted up from his bed. Well, he *tried* to bolt up from his bed. In only the two weeks since he'd been at school, Runa had already gained at least ten pounds. She had snuggled what parts of her she could on top of his chest, and the rest fell off the side in an awkward position. The dragon was not impressed when Griff scooped her in his arms and placed her on the sheets. She let out a low grunt of disapproval, then curled up against his pillow and fell back to sleep.

He rummaged in the dark through his disorganized trunk at the foot of his bed and found some paper and a pencil. He needed a light, but dared not conjure one. Every now and again, apparently even in his dreams, he still had a hard time controlling his power. Heart still hammering against his chest, he decided to draw by the window instead of risking his magic.

He gazed up at the night sky. The moon and stars shone brightly, but they looked different than the picture Griff was drawing. He could see the same pictures in the sky, but everything was skewed in a different direction. While he felt like he knew so little about the moon and stars, he believed at the very least that this meant Korrun and his army were nowhere near Bergots.

As fast and as quietly as he could, Griff sketched out the same starry map as in his dream, tucked it in his pocket, then creeped over to Marth's bunk. He slapped him on the shoulder.

"Psst!" Griff leaned down low when Marth's eyes popped opened, ignoring the sleepy glare from his friend. "Can you watch over Runa for a bit? I need to talk to Headmaster Aldamund."

Marth put his glare away. "A dream?"

"Yeah. A big one, too. They're getting close."

Marth nodded his head. "Go on. I'll take care of her."

Griff nodded his thanks, then slipped out the door, past the empty common room, then out to the rest of the castle. Last time he had snuck around the castle at night, he was quiet and cautious, not wanting to get caught. He had been on a secret mission to leave and save his family. This time, however, he wanted to be caught. He needed to see the first available professor who could take him to see Headmaster Aldamund. His footsteps pounded against the hard stone floor and echoed down the long hallways. The light from his hand cast long, eerie shadows along the walls that warped and moved with every step he took. Every few minutes, Griff checked to make sure the drawing was still in his pocket.

He didn't know where the professors slept, but perhaps there was one still in their office? He'd been to that wing of the castle numerous times in his visits with Professor Coen, and no matter the time of day, there was always at least one professor in their office, going over homework assignments, preparing for a lesson, or Griff suspected, even trying to take advantage of some quiet time away from students.

He turned down the hallway that led to the offices and immediately noticed a light on in one of the rooms. Not Professor Coen's, but a few doors past his. He sprinted to the door, unsure who he would find inside. Just as he approached the opening, he heard Professor Coen tell the punchline of a joke, and he, along with another woman, chuckled together. Griff didn't bother to stop and process what he'd just heard. Instead, he barged in on Professor Coen and Professor Strickland, sitting next to each other on top of her desk laughing.

"Griff!" Professor Coen hopped off the desk quickly and awkwardly. "Uh ... wha-what are you doing? You're supposed to be in bed!"

He could barely meet Griff's eyes. Professor Strickland on the other hand, casually placed a hand on his back.

"Everything okay, dear?" she asked Griff.

"I know where Korrun is," Griff blurted out. Professor Coen's eyes got wide.

"Well, okay. I-I have some clues about where he's at. And ... and he's close." Griff hinted. He didn't know how much he was allowed to say in front of the other professor. "He's close, sir."

All the awkwardness drained from the professor's face. He stared into Griff's eyes before saying, "Come with me." He turned to Professor Strickland. "Sorry, my dear. I must handle this now."

She flashed him a smile. "All good. I've got papers to grade. See you soon."

Without another word, the two stepped into the hallway, leaving Professor Strickland to finish her task.

"Are you taking me to Headmaster Aldamund's, sir? I've got something to show him that might help. And what were you doing in Professor Strickland's office this late at night? Why did she call you darling? And you called her dear? Are you two—"

Questions spilled out from Griff's mouth. All the adrenaline from his dream and the sense of urgency to find a shard before Korrun did overwhelmed his mind. He felt like he was vomiting words uncontrollably. Now he seemed to understand Marth on a whole new level.

"Shh!" Professor Coen cut Griff off, then eyed the dark corridors. He picked up his pace and Griff matched it. Several turns later, the professor finally said, "We're ... trying something out..."

"I knew it!" Griff exclaimed quietly, though dared not to say any more. A crooked smile appeared on the professor's face that stayed with him for several minutes until they rounded a corner, and he suddenly halted.

Griff, lost in his own thoughts about the dream he'd had, almost ran into him.

"What in the—why did you stop?"

The professor put his finger to his lips, and pointed at the eerie orange light that spilled across the stone floor several yards in front of them. The mail room. The door was open and someone was inside. They could hear papers ruffling and the eerie creaking of wood.

Griff conjured a small flame, showing he was ready to fight, but quickly extinguished it when Professor Coen held out his hand.

"Probably just another professor sending a late-night letter to family or something," he barely whispered.

"Does that happen often?" Griff asked, matching Professor Coen's volume.

The professor set his jaw in place, and shook his head slowly, which explained why he had been so quiet.

Together, the two mages crept along the side of the wall. The professor looked calm and in control—the exact opposite of how Griff felt. It was strange to feel such a heightened sense of alarm in a place he considered to be his second home. However, after Korrun's attack on the school last year, anything seemed possible.

Professor Coen held out a hand, signaling Griff to stop. He peered around the corner and stared at the intruder. Griff tried to read the expression on his face to give him any sort of clue as to what he was seeing. But he was emotionless. He just held a calm stare as if gathering intel. Then, the corner of his mouth turned up, he shook his head and let out a silent chuckle. The professor stepped fully into the light and waved Griff to join him.

"Little bit of late night reading, eh, son?" the professor asked lightly.

"Did you know that the Selaginella lepidophylla is a plant that can survive dehydration for *years*?" Connor Ofner said excitedly. Milo's younger brother sat on the table closest to the typewriter used to send and receive letters. Next to him was his lantern and a small, potted plant with green and purple leaves.

"You know, Connor, once the postman leaves and closes up the mail room, you're not supposed to break in here for some private reading time," Professor Coen said.

"I know, I know, I know," Connor answered, closing his book and hopping off the table. "But my book went missing and I was told it was here. I just wanted to finish this chapter on the flora of arid landscapes. It's so good!"

"How did you even break in here?" the professor asked, examining the door handle, tugging at its elongated, ornate structure.

Connor pulled a tiny twig from his pocket and sheepishly held it up for Griff and Professor Coen to see. "Hawthorn twig! They were used around cities to protect 'em since they're so thorny and tough. *But* I learned in *another* plant book that people have used its thorns for all sorts of tools. Lockpicking included!" Connor smiled up at Professor Coen, unaware that, impressive as his skills were, it was not something he should have admitted with such pride.

"Hm. I see." The professor scratched his goatee in thought. "Well, son, lockpicking is strictly prohibited here on campus. And, well, everywhere really. So, how about next time, just wait until the door is unlocked, eh?"

"Aye, aye!" Connor tucked his book under his arm and saluted the professor with enthusiasm. A folded piece of paper slipped out of the pages of his book and fluttered to the ground at Griff's feet.

"Here ya are, Connor," Griff said, pulling it off the floor and extending it out to the boy.

"Hold on there," the professor said with a sense of urgency. He quickly snatched the paper from Griff, but not before he could see who the letter was addressed to: The Deceiver.

"Who's The Deceiver?" the professor asked, his eyes scanning the contents of the letter.

Connor shrugged his shoulders. "I dunno. The letter printed while I was reading my book. Makes for a good bookmark though! I was gonna bring it back and see who it belonged to. The Deceiver sounds like a really cool name!"

"Did you read this letter, Connor?"

Connor raised his eyebrows as far as he could and shook his head vigorously. "No, no, no. I don't read letters not for me. That is *not* okay."

"Good." The professor locked eyes with Connor and said, "Hurry straight to Professor Strickland's office. Have her escort you back to your room, okay?"

Connor saluted him again with a big smile, completely missing the urgency in the professor's voice. He adjusted the book under his arm, grabbed his plant and lantern, and dashed off into the dark hallway.

Once Griff was sure they were alone, he turned to Professor Coen, who was locking the door behind them. "What's going on? Who's The Deceiver?"

"I dunno," he mumbled before turning on his heel and walking with purpose. "But whoever this deceiver is works for Korrun."

"What!" Griff called in shock, receiving a sharp "Shh!" from the professor. Just then, he heard a shuffling sound coming from behind them.

"Did you hear that?" he asked.

They stood in silence, Griff's ear turned toward the mail room. Nothing.

"Connor?" he risked calling out. No response. The hairs on the back of his neck stood tall.

"Hmm. No, I don't hear anything. Let's go."

The two mages were silent the rest of the trip, each probably thinking the same thing: Who was The Deceiver? What was their plan? What did Korrun hope to accomplish by having someone stationed in the school? Griff desperately wanted to know what was written in that letter, but knew better than to ask. Now wasn't the best time. Plus, while The

Deceiver remained a mystery to which Griff had no answers, there was something else to which he *did* have answers: the location of the next shard. He tried to extinguish the burning questions about the letter Professor Coen held and instead focused on remembering what had happened in his dream.

Together they wound through the castle, up tall, spiraling staircases to the very topmost part. Griff knew exactly where they were. Not because he had ever been here, but because he had seen it from the outside. It was the largest tower of Bergots, with windows on all sides that overlooked the courtyard and Altar Storm pitch, as well as the city of Solastran. Every time he walked back from Altar Storm matches, he would gaze up at the tower and wonder what was inside. He was about to find out.

Two short raps on the door, a pause, then one loud bang with Professor Coen's fist was all it took for the headmaster to answer. Griff didn't know what to expect. Maybe a frazzle-haired, sleepy-eyed headmaster who, without a morning shave and wash, would have looked about ten years older. However, Headmaster Aldamund appeared almost as he always did: not a single strand of his long brown hair was out of place, his brown and speckled gray beard neatly trimmed, and not a bit of sleep crust in the corner of his eyes. The only noticeable difference were the reading glasses on top of his head and an old heavy book tucked carefully in his arm that was marked halfway through with a gold ribbon.

"Ah, Professor Coen. Griff. Pleasant surprise."

"Sorry, sir," Professor Coen said. "Griff here would like to have a word with you. Said it was important."

"Mmm." The headmaster nodded and stepped to the side, allowing the professor and his student entry. Griff did his best not to make a scene when he stepped inside. He'd been inside the headmaster's office before, just after the holidays to tell him the dreams he'd been having about Korrun, but that room was located at the end of the corridor of offices he'd just come from. This was the headmaster's living quarters. He was walking into what he thought would be his bedroom. Yet it was so much more than what Griff could have imagined.

The room he now stood in was as big as the common rooms in the dorms. Though instead of stairs that led to a loft area on a second story, the back wall was filled with shelves of leatherbound books from floor to ceiling with a ladder that slid from side to side.

Hung meticulously on the walls were large, detailed paintings of Oriel's cities and rich tapestries depicting ancient legends, many involving different breeds of nightstalkers.

In the center of the room, dark purple velvet couches etched with gold symbols circled a long, ornate mahogany coffee table.

And perched atop of one of the couches, staring right at Griff with its large, curious, silver eyes was a large feline.

Whether it was a large cat or small snow leopard, he wasn't sure, but its beautiful, pristine, white fur also stood in stark contrast to the deep purple velvet. Its long, narrow ears that were the length of Griff's forearm stood at alert. The creature never moved, and its eyes never left Griff's.

"Ah, I see you've met Oberon," the headmaster said.

"Oberon?" Griff asked, not moving.

"Aww, don't be shy, buddy." Professor Coen walked across the room toward the creature. Its ears lowered and it began a low purr that sounded more like the distant rumble of thunder. The professor squished his face against Oberon's and started baby-talking as he scratched the beast's neck.

"C'mon Griff, he won't bite," Professor Coen, whose hair was now a tangled mess, said.

"Unless I order him to," the headmaster said with a wink.

Oberon's fur was softer than the most royal of blankets. Thick as it was, the silky fur moved with ease between his fingers. Oberon's purr grew louder, as though the thunderstorm moved closer, and the vibrations reverberated through Griff's hand.

He shifted, trying to roll on his side for a belly rub, then promptly fell off the couch. He bounced off the cushion before landing on his feet, dazed but right-side up.

"Clumsy beast," the headmaster chuckled, "but he always lands on his feet."

Oberon shook violently, and Griff noticed the absence of hair being flung through the air. Then the professor's pet gingerly hopped to the top the couch where it had once rested.

"Why did you two need to see me?" the headmaster asked, taking a seat on the couch across from Oberon.

"This, for one," Professor Coen said, handing Connor's letter to the headmaster. "But also, sir, Griff has something important he'd like to share with you."

As Griff fetched the map he had drawn by his bedroom window from his pocket, he recounted to the professor every single detail he could remember from his dream.

"... and I hope that helps," Griff said at last. "That is the layout of the stars from where I was."

The headmaster quietly studied the rough map of stars before finally saying, "Thank you, Griff, for your service to the kingdom. I will pass this on to my father and his experts to see if they can get a location based on your map."

Griff stood. "Sir, will you please let me know when the king is ready to move? I would like to be with that group when they leave. I can be ready at a moment's notice."

Professor Coen's eyes were wide at the request, but he didn't say a word. Together, the teacher and student stared at the headmaster as he scratched his chin, deep in thought.

"Your request in noble, Griff. I can see the desire in your heart to be of help to your land. Oriel needs more sincere, brave men and women such as yourself. However, I cannot acquiesce to your request. You will stay here and learn."

"Sir!" Griff tried to argue, but the headmaster held up a hand.

"This is but one battle in a war. Not just against my uncle and his army, but against the Corruption as well. This mission is only one piece of a very complicated and dangerous puzzle. You have already served your kingdom. And you will have your opportunity to serve again, but for now, the best thing you can do is prepare for what is to come."

"But ... I-I've *been* there! In my dreams, maybe, but I've seen it. Not only that, but I can *feel* it, sir! I know when we're close! Please, you have to let me go. You *have* to!" Griff was on the verge of tears. He could feel his blood pumping through his veins. He clenched his fists so tightly, his fingernails dug into the palm of his hands.

After a long breath, Griff said, "At least ask the king."

"My father and I are of one mind. Your participation in future missions has already been discussed. You performed brilliantly in defense against your hometown, but you have no official warfare training. There are strategies, ways of communication, and defensive skills to protect yourself and your allies on the battlefield. You have none of those, Griff."

The headmaster stood from the couch and suddenly he looked much taller. "This is my decision, and it is final. You will not go on this mission."

Tears of frustration appeared in the corners of Griff's eyes. He gritted his teeth, turned on his heels, and flung open the door. Without another word, Griff stormed back into the dark castle, hoping neither man would follow.

CHAPTER 17

An elbow jabbed Tyrell in the side. He grunted awake, but was quickly quieted by a hand on his mouth.

"Shh!" Ava glared at him. Tyrell nodded his understanding before she pulled her hand back. She was getting good at this reconnaissance business.

He repositioned himself and peered through the patch of beachgrass they had been hiding behind. The barely visible rising sun sparkled off the choppy ocean waves. Seagulls glided against the gentle breeze and their calls echoed over the waters. Ava scooched closer to Tyrell to peer through the opening he had created in the grass. Her hair, loose in the breeze, tickled his nose, but he didn't mind. The faint smell of roses wafted toward him, and he wondered how, after these past few months of camping in this rugged, nightmarish place, she could still smell so good. It would have been the most perfect sunrise, save for the silhouettes standing on the shore watching the waters.

The silhouettes weren't admiring the sunrise. They were waiting. After tracking them to this same stretch of coast for the past two days, Tyrell had his suspicions as to what they were waiting for, but he hadn't dared risk getting too close to eavesdrop. Even under the cover of night. With Ava right beside him, it was that much more important he didn't get caught.

Suddenly there was a disturbance in the water that scared the seagulls from their peaceful flight. About the length of an Altar Storm pitch away from the shore, the water began to churn and splash. The activity slowly moved closer to the beach until a spherical wind spell broke through the depths and three black cloaks surfaced, completely dry. Two of the black cloaks swirled their hands about, keeping the spell alive, while the other black cloak, a taller, blond boy, stood between them, hands in his pockets and a triumphant, mischievous smile plastered on his face. Tyrell had watched that boy and the two black cloaks disappear in about the same way a couple of hours earlier. Wading in the water, with a wind spell pushing the ocean away from them. But this wasn't the first time Tyrell had seen this boy. He had been around camp since the attack on Cordelia, and each time that boy opened his mouth, it made Tyrell shudder with the amount of arrogance and stupidity within each sentence. As Tyrell hunkered behind the grass, watching that smug boy, he dreamt of all the ways he would love to wipe that smile off his face.

Korrun stepped forward to meet the squad, leaving Tyrell's father and the rest of the small team of black cloaks standing at attention. Randolph stood motionless, save for his cloak, which whipped backward in the wind, exposing the guns on his hips. The ocean breeze, which somehow seemed stronger, more aggressive now, muffled the words of each man as they spoke. But no words were needed when the blond boy pulled a hand out of his pocket and revealed a shimmering object to his audience.

Tyrell's heart sank into his stomach. They'd found a shard. Anger welled up inside him. He should have stopped them. Should have found a way to get to it first. But he'd failed. He clenched his jaw as the blond boy's victorious laughter reached his ears. Seeing his father give a nod of approval to the boy only made Tyrell clench his teeth harder.

A calm, gentle hand on his back broke him from his fury.

"It's okay, Tyrell," Ava whispered, her lips barely an inch from his ear. He didn't realize his anger had been so obvious, but Ava's words somehow pierced through the raging storm inside him. He took slow, calm, deliberate breaths, then turned to catch her staring. Not with fear or hesitation, but with genuine care in her eyes. Her hand hadn't left his back, and he didn't want it to.

"They found it." He sighed.

"They were bound to eventually," she said, shrugging, though he could tell she felt defeated as well.

He didn't want to watch the boy hand the shard over to Korrun, but knew he needed to watch every moment, save every tiny detail in his mind. This was a reconnaissance mission, after all. That was the whole point. If he couldn't stop them from finding a shard, having as much information as possible might be the next best weapon.

Tyrell peered through the grass again, eyes focused on the shard, but his mind was on the hand still on his back. He worried the immense sweat dripping off his ever-lengthening hair and down his well-tanned neck would have deterred her show of affection, yet she never removed it. If anything, it ventured closer and closer to his other shoulder, as though she were on the verge of a hug. Had any other human being tried such a stunt, his fist would have immediately met their face. Not her, though. Never her. Finally she laid her head on his shoulder.

"I could go to sleep right now," she said groggily.

Tyrell half-grinned. "We might be on the move soon, but go ahead and close your eyes. I'll keep watch."

Before he had finished his statement, he could feel her slow, steady, rhythmic breathing, her whole body expanding and contracting as she sank deeper into sleep. He wrapped an arm around her waist to keep her from falling. Her breath was like little puffs of air on his neck, cooling it from the hot sun.

Suddenly, there was screaming from camp. An explosion. Ava jumped off Tyrell and tried to stand in her rush of adrenaline, nearly exposing the two of them from behind the grass. Tyrell yanked her back down, though he realized it wouldn't matter. Everyone on the beach was staring in the direction of camp, not at the bushes. Black billowing smoke from the far edge of camp began filling the sky. More screaming. Another explosion. More smoke.

Tyrell looked to Ava, her eyes wide with confusion and fear. He put a finger up to his mouth to remind her to be quiet. She nodded, then he whispered, "We have to wait." She nodded again.

Korrun looked at the black cloaks and pointed to those who had come out of the water. Tyrell didn't need to hear the words to know what he said.

"Go. Now."

The black cloaks nodded and ran toward camp. The leader of the black cloaks then turned to Randolph and the others. He spoke briefly before they all turned and started walking toward the edge of the forest. Toward Tyrell and Ava.

Tyrell's heart leaped into his throat. They were going to be spotted. Ava clenched Tyrell's hand. They were behind a small set of seagrass with nothing to either side. Getting to this patch was easy with the cover of night in their favor. Now, though, there was nowhere to run. Nowhere else to hide. The forest was at least fifty yards behind them with nothing in between.

Suddenly, Korrun's pet nightstalker stopped and lifted its snout to the wind and sniffed deeply. Its eyes locked onto the grass covering Tyrell and Ava.

Tyrell's heart sank into his stomach. The sounds of the screaming and explosions faded into the background as Tyrell's mind spun in a thousand directions, trying desperately to come up with a plan. Korrun's pet could smell them. And though nobody else seemed to notice, the group still moved closer. Close enough to where they could hear Randolph Falkenburg speak.

"Do you think they've found us, sir?"

Korrun stopped, but didn't answer. Instead, he quickly turned in the direction of the ocean, covered the bright rays of the sun with one hand so he could see, and launched a powerful lightning spell toward the sky.

Tyrell hadn't seen them before. They had used the brightness of the sun to conceal their attack. But it was clear what was happening when a warg and its rider, covered in magical battle armor, fell from the sky and landed at the water's edge.

The king's battlemages were here.

"In the sky!" Korrun called, launching another lightning spell. Tyrell shielded his eyes against the sun just in time to watch another mage on a warg dodge to the left before sending their own spells in response. The mage's spell barely missed, hitting the ground and sending an explosion of sand upward. Korrun and his black cloaks were fast, already running back toward the water for the fight.

Six more warriors and their wargs landed on the beach close to the water and surrounded their fallen comrade, who was struggling to get back to his feet after being hit by Korrun's spell.

Randolph unfastened his guns from their holsters and aimed. He was calm. His fingers rested just beside each trigger. Tyrell had seen his father's mastery over these weapons and knew that Randolph's old comrades were in serious trouble. The two other black cloaks that stood on either side of him pulled the bows off their chests. Together, they stood as a wall in front of Korrun. As if he needed their protection.

Just as the black cloaks launched the first of their magical arrows, one of the battlemages rolled to the side, arrows narrowly missing his shoulder. The man jumped to his feet, quickly waved his hands, and sent a powerful gust of wind at the ground, generating a barrier of sand between his team and the black cloaks.

Before the dusty barrier was even fully formed, a volley of magical arrows came from behind it. One arrow grazed the side of a black cloak. The mage shouted in pain and grasped at his side. The rest of the arrows missed wildly and were extinguished in the sand only a few yards away from the grass Tyrell and Ava were crouched behind. Each impact hurled small bursts of sand into the air, showering them with the grit from the shore.

A guttural growl tore Tyrell from his daze. He wiped the sand from his eyes and watched as Korrun's pet charged toward the diminishing sand barrier. The monster's jaws were wide open, readying itself for a feast. Or was it just smiling at the thought of its enemy's demise? The beast launched itself at the nearest battlemage, knocking him on his back into the shallow water.

Randolph moved along the sand with confidence and ease. His hands a blur as they moved from one target to the next. Brilliant blue bullets of magic streaked through the air, bouncing off his old comrade's magical shields. Randolph was so fast, the mages were forced to focus their efforts on keeping their shields up. Their old friend had put them on the defensive.

Tyrell imagined that the only upper hand these battlemages had was knowing full well who they were facing. They had trained with him. Seen him in action. Stood alongside him in battle. Tyrell had seen enough of his father's abilities to know they stood no chance. He couldn't watch anymore. He knew where this battle was headed.

"Now's our chance," he said, grabbing Ava's hand and pulling her toward the forest. Together they sprinted as fast as they could into the thick cover of trees and shadow.

"What about my parents?" Ava screamed. "We can't just leave here! We have to get to camp!"

"Nightstalker's fury, Ava! That's what we're doing! But we have to go the long way around; we can't be spotted. That was way too close."

Tyrell had known for some time now that there were black cloaks who had their eyes on him. Watching his every move. As if being the son of Randolph wasn't enough, the rumor that he had killed Liam a few months back only drew more attention. He couldn't just show up from out of nowhere while the battle raged on at camp. Some might think he led the king's battlemages to their location. Which he hadn't. No, he and Ava needed to sneak in somehow, and make it seem like they had been there all along. He just didn't know how.

Neither one of them had the breath to continue their conversation. Their hearts beat hard against their chests, the muscles in their legs burned and ached for them to stop their sprinting. Pushing past the pain, they fled deeper into the forest, where its dense foliage drowned out the sounds of the battle on the beach. When Tyrell felt they were far enough away, he pulled Ava the direction of camp.

"Finally!" She huffed. Even though she clutched her side, she didn't slow down.

"Let's go find your parents," Tyrell said, squeezing her hand.

"You think ... they're ... okay?" Ava wheezed.

Knowing this pace wasn't sustainable for her, Tyrell slowed a little.

"Well, if they're as tough as you are, then they'll be just fine," he called back. She let out a pained laugh and then the two were quiet.

Hand in hand they fought their way off one path and found another that led them to the back of camp. As they got closer, the sounds of battle intensified. Sunlight assaulted their eyes as they broke out of the forest, momentarily blinding them. Tyrell fiercely blinked against its bright beams, and when the battle came into focus, he avidly searched the mingled bodies for Ava's parents.

Nearby, a battlemage sliced a small tree with a bright blue axe blade and, in one swift motion with a wind spell, sent it hurtling at a tall black cloak. The black cloak let out a loud grunt before being flung into the air, landing at the feet of Tyrell.

Tyrell stooped to help the black cloak up, but paused when he realized he was staring at the blond boy from the beach. The one who had found the shard.

The boy growled with rage, snapping Tyrell out of his thoughts. Begrudgingly—and only to preserve his cover as a black cloak—Tyrell extended a helping hand, but the boy scowled and righted himself up instead.

"What are you doing?" he screamed, eyeing Tyrell and Ava. "For king's sake! This is no time for *romance*! Fight, you two!" The boy shoved Tyrell in the chest. "Man up, son of Randolph! You got big shoes to fill!"

Before Tyrell could respond, the boy turned and sprinted back into battle without a glance back. Tyrell and Ava exchanged awkward looks.

"You wish," Ava said, a somber smile on her face. She squeezed his hand. There was no time. No time to tell her what he'd hoped had been obvious. They needed to find her parents. He squeezed her hand in response, and only said what he needed to: "It'll need to be our cover if anyone asks. Let's go."

He let go of her hand, trusting she'd follow him. As quickly as they could, they wove through the chaos. Tyrell ducked under a deflected fire spell. They passed by a tent with two black cloaks Tyrell recognized as the stocky blond boy's parents. The father covered his ears with his hands and screamed to block out the noises of the battle. The wife sobbed into a lace handkerchief.

A few steps later, a king's battlemage bumped into Tyrell as he fought with another black cloak. Tyrell shoved him toward a group of greedy nightstalkers, who pounced the second the man lost his footing. He heard Ava gasp in horror, but hoped she would forgive him for what he needed to do.

"Look out!" cried a female black cloak from behind them. She pointed urgently to the sky above. Rows of deadly sharp icicles crackling with blue electricity rained down from above.

"Down!" Tyrell called. Ava immediately obeyed and dropped to the clay ground. Tyrell barely had enough time to levitate a large, flat boulder over them as the icicles struck. The ice shattered against the rock, causing it to shudder above them. The electricity, however, made its way around to the underside, where Ava lay and Tyrell crouched. It took all his focus to keep the boulder afloat. He grunted with effort as the ominous energy arced across the surface. The hairs on his neck stood as it danced dangerously close to his skin. With a burst of adrenaline, he flung the boulder to the side before the spell could connect.

Tyrell offered a hand up for Ava, but the two were flung into the air by powerful wind magic. Tyrell landed on his left shoulder and felt a surge of fiery pain down his arm. He screamed in response, but couldn't move. The soldier who had cast the wind spell sprinted forward, closing the gap. His hands were lightning fast. Tyrell couldn't respond even if he'd wanted to. The searing pain in his arm wouldn't let up. He writhed on the ground as the man conjured more razor-sharp ice shards that circled menacingly over Tyrell.

There was no grunt of effort from the man. No emotion on his face. Only a hint of determination. The man flicked his hands toward Tyrell's direction. Tyrell tried to curl. Tried to move. But he couldn't.

With utmost precision, the ice shards punctured the edges of his sprawled-out cloak, not even touching his pants or shirt. The man leaned in so close to Tyrell's face, he could smell his sweat and the blood that stained his clothes.

"I served with your dad. He saved my life on more than one account. My debt's been repaid. If someone's to kill you, be it someone else. If you survive this day, maybe you'll think again about fightin' on Korrun's side. And if you don't, then you'll answer to me." The man glanced over at Ava, whose teary eyes were wide with fear. "Same goes for you, lass. You're fightin' on the wrong side. Leave while you can."

He scanned the horizon, looking for his next victim. Seeing a fellow soldier fighting off a family of porcupine nightstalkers, he sprinted off to help.

Dust flew into Tyrell's eyes as Ava slid to his side in a panic.

"Tyrell! Are you okay? Can you move? What hurts? How can I help?"

Tyrell could only scream in pain and hold his elbow.

"I—I—I don't know what to do!" Ava screamed. She grasped at an ice shard buried deep in the ground and began pulling. It didn't budge. She sat on the ground and kicked it as hard as she could. It took several hard kicks, but finally the long, icy spike dislodged from the ground.

"Ava! Tyrell!" The Adebayos rushed over. Amina clutched her daughter tight while Kwame kicked the remaining ice spikes out from the ground. Ava and her mother were lost in their reunion and Tyrell was still unable to move due to the pain. Only Kwame was able to keep his eyes on the surrounding battle. Thankfully, all the battlemages around them were too busy with other black cloaks and nightstalkers to give them a second thought.

"What's going on, son?" Kwame asked kindly.

Tears streamed down Tyrell's face. He didn't have the energy to hold them back. "My—my—" he tried to hold his arm up to show the man, and screamed as another rush of pain flooded his body.

"Mmm ... I see." The artifician scratched his white goatee. He grabbed Tyrell's cloak sleeve and yanked on it. Tyrell screamed in agony. His vision blurred, and he could barely hold on to consciousness.

"What are you doing to him?" Amina yelled at her husband.

"I believe Tyrell, here, has a dislocated shoulder. I need to pull his arm out of his cloak to get a better look."

"Well, be gentle, Daddy!" Ava said.

"Do you want gentle or do you want efficient?" He huffed, turning back to examine Tyrell. "Sorry. We need to get you—and us—out of here and to the safe place."

"Here, let me," Amina said, rushing to Tyrell's side. Gently, she slipped a knife under his sleeve and cut a slit. Then she made another cut on the shoulder of his shirt. Even with her gentle, caring movements, Tyrell couldn't help but yelp in pain.

"Aha," Kwame said, almost a little too proudly of himself. "Thought so. Dislocated."

"You sure?" Ava asked, eyeing a nearby skirmish in which a black cloak was losing to two battlemages.

"Pretty sure," Kwame said, scratching at his goatee again.

Just then, the battlemage felled the nearby black cloak and turned toward them, only to be stopped by a large spider-like nightstalker.

"It's our best bet," Kwame said in a panic, and before anyone could say another word, he snatched Tyrell's left arm, placed a foot into his armpit, and leaned back, pulling Tyrell's arm tight. Pain flooded his every thought and feeling. He writhed and screamed, not caring who heard. Suddenly, he felt a *pop* in his shoulder and relief flooded him. Kwame let go of his arm and removed his foot from Tyrell's armpit. Tyrell's vision blurred again as relief immediately left him and a deeper pain set in. Overcome with nausea from the pain, Tyrell turned to the side and vomited. Then, his world went black.

CHAPTER 18

"We'll talk about it later!" Professor Coen hissed as he hurried along the path. He looked behind him to make sure none of the other students or teachers could hear his conversation.

Griff had to hustle to stay next to the professor, who walked with purpose toward the Altar Storm pitch. From the moment Griff woke from his dream that morning, the rage inside him had been boiling. Now, it was almost to the point of explosion. Though his body felt like an oven with too much coal, he jerked his cloak tighter around himself out of frustration. He opened his mouth to argue, but the professor continued.

"There's nothing we can do about it now, anyways," he said.

"Nothing we can do about it? How about send more men! How about send me! How about next time you and the headmaster actually let me go on a raid to find the shard!"

Griff was nearly shouting, but he didn't care. It had only been two days since the headmaster refused Griff's help to find the shard. Korrun had found another shard, and Griff had been stuck watching it from the comfort of his dreams again. He saw the king's battlemages arrive too late. Witnessed the battle. Witnessed Korrun disappear into the trees, shard in hand. It wasn't right. If only they'd let him go with the king's battlemages, they could have gotten there sooner. Griff could have led the way.

King's crown, he'd *been* there! He'd seen where the shard had been calling from. Sure, he didn't know *exactly* where it was, but he had no doubt that had he gotten closer, it would have called to him. Well, maybe not to *him*. It would have called to the shard *inside* him. Griff gently touched his hand to his heart, where the shard that saved his life had found its home. He still didn't know exactly what would happen if the king gained possession of every shard except this one. Or worse, if *Korrun* found out where this shard was.

"Watch yourself, Griff. Remember who you're talking to." The professor's voice snapped him from his thoughts.

To Griff's surprise, the professor didn't sound angry. It was like he was a parent telling their child to be careful next to a cliff.

"Be mad. Don't be stupid."

Griff took a deep breath, held it for a moment, and let it out slowly, sending a light, warm puff of cloud into the chilly morning air. He was right. Though they had spent a lot of time together in the training room and enjoyed each other's company, this was still his teacher. And even though they fought alongside each other, defended each other, Griff was still his student. And he still respected him. He was just so ... *angry*.

"Sorry. I just ... I feel so out of control."

"Mm..." The professor smiled. "Welcome to the wonderful world of adulthood, Mr. Driscoll. The older you get, the more you realize how much is outside your control." He slapped Griff on the back. "Control what you can, when you can, and let the rest be. You'll sleep better that way, I promise."

"Yeah, I think I'll sleep better when those shards stop calling to me," Griff mumbled.

Professor Coen forged ahead without Griff, signaling the end of the conversation, so Griff trailed back to find his battlegroup. Together, the five of them marched in silence the rest of the way. Griff knew his anger was so palpable that they knew not to ask any questions. Even Marth, normally oblivious to such obvious social cues, knew to steer clear. Only

Mira made any attempt toward Griff and that was a gentle scratch on the back, as if to say, "I'm here. It's okay."

Today was the Altar Storm games for the second-year mages, so needless to say Mira was aggressively focused. Griff could tell she was working diligently to keep the level of her tenacity down, knowing he was struggling with the news of Korrun's recent shard capture. But even then, she could only do so much. He was just thankful she was quiet, rather than her usual hyper-focused conversations around theories or strategies for the coming match. Or even worse, barking orders at the team, making sure they're getting in a full meal or quizzing them during breakfast.

Quiet was what he needed. He wanted to focus. Focus on the shard that was stolen. The shards called him when someone was close to their hiding spot. Like a plea for help. He wondered if maybe he could still hear their calls, even now. He placed a hand on his heart as he walked, his eyes on the path to the field, but his mind a million miles away.

Please. Griff called out to the cosmos. *Please! Can you hear me? Where are you? Show me! I'll come find you! I'll ... I'll come rescue you! Just show me where you're at!*

No response. Griff kicked a pinecone on the ground, sending it flying off the path. Sadie and Vincent exchanged looks but said nothing.

It had to be the noise. The raucous symphony of cheering and singing behind him made it impossible to hear anything, let alone think clearly.

Bright morning sunlight spilled across the path, catching the cold dew clinging to the grass and making it shimmer. Griff let the warmth from the sun sink in while he could, his eyes drifting to the dark clouds gathering in the distance. He had a feeling that soon enough, he would battle under their shadow.

They approached the arena, and while the rest of the school began filling the bleachers, Griff, his battlegroup, and the rest of the second-year students circled around to the other side, where a large tent with thick cloth siding blocked their view from their coming challenge.

After giving a polite nod to Finn, the small, mousy boy who always seemed to be nervous about everything, Griff stepped inside the tent and plopped down onto one of the cold wooden benches along the side, thoughts of the shard still swirling about.

Mira quietly sat next to him and gingerly placed a gloved hand on his arm. For a long time, she said nothing, only watched the other battle-groups and listened to their quiet conversations as they all tried to figure out what their challenges would be.

Finally, she reached down and squeezed Griff's hand. "So ... I know you have a lot going on through your mind right now, but..." She paused and waited for him to look at her. "But ... there's nothing you can do about it *right now*. Maybe later. But right now, we have a match in front of us. A match that will ultimately play a major role in our future. In *my* future. So, Griff, can you be with me, with ... with us right now? Can you focus on the match?"

Griff gritted his teeth in frustration. Not at Mira. Only at the fact that she was right. There was nothing he could do about the shard. It was gone. For now.

He nodded slowly and looked into her eyes. "I'll do my best."

"'Kay," Mira said. She turned and nodded to the others who had been close by. They all huddled together and kept their voices low.

"So," Mira continued. All that energy she'd held back the entire morning exploded out of her like a pent-up bull. "We've been building our elemental magic, right? Ice spells, lightning, fire. I'm thinking they'll pick one of those and really make sure we know how to use it. For ice, I think we might see something like we did last year, with some sort of pool of water that we have to freeze or something. Lightning? Well, I'm thinking maybe some sort of box from before Day Zero that only opens with lightning magic. Then there's fire. Maybe with the cooler weather, they already have ice down on the field, and we have to melt it."

"Yeah, and don't forget archery from Essence Crafting class," Marth chimed in.

"Oh, don't worry," Mira said confidently. "If archery is the challenge, then it'll be a quick match."

"Yeah, but I'm guessing you won't be able to use regular arrows ... you'd have to conjure some up for yourself..." Marth added, though he realized he'd gone too far and took a step away from Mira and toward Vincent.

"I've gotten better!" Mira growled. "Plus, once I get an arrow conjured, it's game over and you know it."

It was true. While she may have struggled conjuring arrows, Griff had never seen a better shot than Mira. One of her regular responsibilities back home had been to hunt for their family while they took care of their small farm. Duskhaven was not kind to farmers. Rain was slim. The Corruption crept closer each year, so even the game numbers were falling. It was Mira's job to fill in the gaps so her family had enough to eat. And as Griff knew all too well, whatever she set her mind to, she succeeded at worst and overachieved at best.

"We haven't seen much Essence Crafting in the games so far," Griff said. "Sure would be nice to use that skill today."

"Yes, but according to *Bergots Altar Storm History*, the unabridged version, there is an unusually low number of Essence Crafting challenges," Mira said. "They want all students to know Essence Manipulation, while they only provide Essence *Crafting* to create a more robust education and spot those who would do well in military service."

"What even *is* an unabridged version..." Marth mumbled from behind Vincent. Mira ignored him.

"How about something from Professor Strickland's class?" Sadie interjected.

"Oh! Good thought, Sadie!" Mira said. "Everyone talks about the importance of ethics in magic ... there's ... yeah ... there's a good chance they could do something with that. Maybe we're faced with some difficult decisions and we have to make the ethical choice to move forward?"

Just then, the crowd beyond the tent exploded in cheering. Professor Coen must have stepped out onto the battlefield. His muffled voice echoed through the air, but even with Griff straining to hear, his words were incomprehensible. They had probably positioned this tent in such a way to avoid spoiling the challenge to those who waited within.

After what felt like an eternity, the professor stopped talking and the crowd resumed their cheering and singing.

"Okay, okay everyone!" Professor Coen stepped through the tent flaps. "We've got a good one for you today!" He smiled cheerily at the groups, though no one returned his sentiment. Finn looked like he was ready to lose his breakfast.

"Well, all right then," he said, looking at the different groups. "You five are first." He pointed to Tyrell's old battlegroup who had found a strong replacement: Fredrik Burns. Standing a head taller than everyone, other than Vincent, Fredrik was one of the most desirable battlegroup choices after Korrun's attack on the school. Though not particularly strong with his essence manipulation, his skill with swords and spears made him a formidable ally on the Altar Storm pitch. Griff was thankful he didn't have to worry about that guy today. He had too much on his mind.

"...along with ... you five," Professor Coen continued, pointing to Katrine Penderson's group. Her blue eyes widened in surprise, but then she frowned and pulled her curly blonde hair back into a tight ponytail. She nodded to her group and the two groups followed the professor out of the tent.

The match lasted about twenty minutes by Mira's count—a count Griff trusted as much as any time piece. Everyone in the tent was silent, straining to hear anything from the match that might give them some clue as to what they might have to face next. But it was useless. The cheering and outcries of shock from the crowd were too loud to catch any useful information. Griff finally gave up and sat back down on the wooden bench and blew warm air into his gloved hands. Vincent and Sadie huddled together in the far corner of the tent, deep in inaudible conversation. Mira paced back and forth, whispering ideas about the match to herself, while Marth kicked around a pinecone that had found its way into the tent.

Everyone else in the tent nervously fiddled about as well, periodically huddling with their group to discuss possible strategies. Finn tried to strike up a conversation with Griff, but Griff could only offer him half-hearted responses. He had too much on his mind. The shard, Ko-rrun, the king. It was all too much. The match ahead seemed so trivial compared to what was happening out there in the real world. Not some safe sport carefully crafted and monitored by professors. There was real chaos out there that needed to be dealt with. And sooner rather than later.

Finn seemed to receive Griff's message that he wasn't really in a talking mood and joined back up with his battlegroup.

Finally, after what felt like an eternity, the crowd, which Griff didn't think could get any louder, erupted in applause. Someone had won.

"I think it was Tyrell's old group!" Marth said, his ear to the tent wall. "Yeah! They won! Poor Katrine, she's gonna be so mad they lost. I am *not* letting her live that one down." Marth chuckled.

The professor popped his head in through the tent flaps. "Griff! Finn! Grab your groups, it's your turn now!"

Griff looked over to see Finn wide-eyed and staring at his opponents.

"Oh boy…" he moaned aloud.

A taller boy with short, curly black hair by the name of Patrick playfully shoved Finn's shoulder. "Hey now, we got this."

"Yeah," Caitlin, a short, squat brunette added. She eyed Griff and his group, sparks crackling from her clenched fists. "We *definitely* got this."

Sadie glared at her from across the tent. It was a glare that would have frozen Griff's blood, but Caitlin seemed to enjoy it.

"Well, good luck, guys," Finn said without a shred of confidence in his voice.

"Good luck to you too, Finn. See you out there on the battlefield," Marth said, giving him a warm smile.

Vincent walked over and shook Finn's hand. "You'll do great."

The two groups fought against the cold breeze that continued to grow colder and stronger as the day wore on. The overcast skies that had come in since the first match did nothing to dampen the mood of those in the stands. Everyone exploded into cheers as the two groups strode onto each side of the field.

Standing on top of a single tall stone pillar at the center of the field that overlooked the crowd was a brilliant statue of a winged creature with three heads: a lion, a goat, and a snake. It sat proudly atop the thin tower, all three heads staring up, its brilliant sheen shining almost in defiance of the dark sky. Its wings were tucked in, leaving just enough room for two smaller pillars, where each team's storm orbs sat.

"How in the king's crown are we gonna get up *there*?" Marth exclaimed. He turned to Vincent. "Think you can chuck me up that high?"

Vincent didn't respond. Griff and the rest of the group gathered around the empty altar where the storm orb normally sat on their side of the field. Somehow, they were going to have to find a way up to the creature, steal the other team's orb, and bring it back. All while keeping the other team from capturing theirs. But how? Griff looked around the rest of the arena for clues. There was hardly any grass this time. Instead, it looked like ... wood planks? No. Not planks. Squares. Giant wooden squares surrounded the stone pillar. And there were markings in the center of each one. Griff couldn't tell what they were from where he stood, but it didn't matter as Professor Coen's voice boomed across the field.

"Welcome, teams, to your next Altar Storm Challenge: The Opal Chimera!" He held his hands out and waited for the inevitable cheers. Griff shook his head. As tough as this man was, he was clearly just as much of a showman. As the applause died, the professor turned his attention to the two teams.

"The Chimera: a creature of legend. Myth. Yet rumors swirl about that some claim to have seen it. Three heads united under one body. In many ways, essence manipulation is the same way. There are a lot of different aspects of it, yet it must be united in harmony within the mage if it is to be mastered.

"Magic has many different elements. Fire, water, ice, lightning, and so on. Today, second-years, you will be tested on your elemental essence manipulations. To reach the other team's storm orb, you will need to master the elements. Work with your teams, and as always, defend yourself against the other team if you stand a chance at victory."

The professor leaned over the guardrail from the stands and pointed at Finn's team. "Ready?"

Patrick, Caitlin, and everyone else other than Finn, viciously shouted their response. The professor smiled and turned toward Griff, locking eyes. "Ready?"

Together, his battlegroup shouted their own reply. Sadie glared ahead at the competition, conjured a flame around a closed fist, then punched her open palm. The fireball detonated and disappeared, though the violent intent remained. She was ready to take this team down.

"Oh my!" Professor Coen said. "Well... Ready? Set? Go!" Brilliantly colored sparks filled the air around the Opal Chimera as Headmaster Aldamund signaled the start of the match. Screams and cheers and singing filled the air once more as each team huddled quickly together to formulate a plan.

"I told you! Elements!" Mira shouted.

"Fine, fine, you were right, Mira. Now, what're we going to *do*?" Marth said.

"Symbols," Vincent said, pointing to the wooden squares on the ground.

"Can you use more than two words here, pal? We don't have a lot of time," Marth said.

"There's symbols on the ground up ahead," Griff said. "Probably will give us clues as to what elements to use."

"Okay, so we cast the elements, and then what?" Mira asked.

"I don't know and I don't care. They're coming," Sadie said, pointing across the field.

"Okay, so ... so—" Mira said.

"I got this," Sadie answered, not waiting for a reply. Caitlin sprinted across the field, green electricity crackling in her hands. She smiled when she saw Sadie break away from the group and march confidently toward her with red flames engulfing her fists.

At twenty yards, Caitlin fired first, her lightning bolt narrowly missing her opponent's legs. Sadie dove to the side and rolled, the fire in her fists extinguishing in the maneuver. She growled and jumped to her feet, reigniting the flames. Her fire burned a deeper, darker red this time. Without hesitation, Sadie sent rapid bursts of fireballs toward the girl. She marched forward, sending wave after wave of fire in front of her. Each of which was blocked. Their talents clashed in a mesmerizing display of spell power, each one equal in strength and spectacle. It seemed as though they were locked in a battle where neither could win.

Griff's mind flashed back to the battle in Cordelia. The headmaster and Korrun had been an almost equal match for each other as well. They had exchanged blow for blow. Spell for spell. Had it not been for Professor Coen's arrow to Korrun's side, who knows what the outcome of that battle would have been. As powerful as Griff knew Headmaster Aldamund to be, he couldn't help but wonder what would happen if

Korrun got the rest of the shards. If it came to that point, he didn't think even the king himself could defeat his brother. Korrun would be unstoppable. Griff needed to find those other missing shards.

"We're running out of time, here!" Marth called, snapping Griff's attention back to the arena. Sadie and Caitlin continued to fight, each just as strong as the other.

"I bet those symbols tell us what spells to use. And I'll bet that when we use it, something happens that will help us get closer to the orb," Mira said.

"Hmm. Let's go, then," Vincent said.

He and Mira rushed to Sadie, who had just dived to the ground to avoid yet another bolt of green lightning. Vincent pulled her up to her feet while Mira sent a gust of wind toward Caitlin. The gust dislodged dust and dirt from the ground and sent it careening toward the girl. Caitlin took a deep breath in, ready to send more bolts of lightning. Then she sneezed. And coughed. Caitlin extinguished her lightning as her coughing fit overtook her.

"She's allergic!" Mira called behind her. "Griff! Hurry! Get over here and help us!"

"Oh! Right." Yet again, he found himself buried deep in his mind, thinking—no, *obsessing*—about the shards. He tried to push the invasive thoughts away—at least for now.

Sadie chased a coughing, sneezing Caitlin back toward her group, while Mira, Vincent, and Griff caught up to Marth, who was kneeling on top of a wooden square with a symbol. Finn and the rest of his team were doing the same thing on their side of the field. Sadie was closing the gap fast. Griff didn't know what Sadie's plan was, but hoped she would be smart. As angry as she looked, and as deep red as her spells had been, he knew she couldn't take on the whole battlegroup.

Marth's finger ran over the engraved symbol that looked like a teardrop. But it wasn't smooth. Hanging from the bottom of the drop were long, jagged spikes.

"Frozen water? Ice?" Marth guessed.

"I think you're right," Mira said. "Here, stand back!" She didn't even wait for the others to respond. She stepped on to the square, spread her feet to the textbook length of shoulder-width apart, held out her hands, and closed her eyes. Blue energy pulsed in her palms, then danced playfully around her fingers, before she sent a perfect ice spell onto the wooden square. As soon as the spell hit, the ground trembled and the tile grew, shooting three feet into the air and sending Mira flying off it and onto her back. Her squeal of surprise echoed through the arena.

Griff raced over and immediately pulled her off the ground and dusted her back. He held his breath as he waited for her to say something.

"It worked!" she screamed victoriously.

"But maybe we just don't stand on them when we cast the spell..." Marth said quietly.

Mira's glare said all that she needed to say.

Just then, Sadie, completely out of breath, joined the group. Her red hair was frazzled and smoldering at the ends. Her battle armor had tears on the shoulders and legs. And her face was covered in dust and dirt.

"Five ... five on one. Bad idea," was all she could muster. She licked her fingers and pinched a burning tip of her hair to put it out.

Griff looked over Sadie's shoulder and saw Caitlin nursing her left elbow, and Patrick limping over to Finn.

Finn, for once, wore a look of pride as he had also discovered the secret of the wooden tiles. He was now standing tall on one that had grown to the same length as Mira's. Although it now meant any advantage Griff's group had was gone, he was happy that Finn had gained a win for himself.

"Here we go!" Marth called as he summoned a blue lightning bolt on the adjacent tile. It was a good thing no one was standing on this one, as it grew even taller, yet with the same explosive force. Three feet taller than the one next to it. He jumped from the first to the second tile.

"Vince!" he called. "Hit that one up!" He pointed to the next tile with an engraved flame symbol.

The giant nodded and immediately sent a ball of flame where Marth had pointed. The tile grew, shooting up another three feet taller than its predecessor and again, Marth climbed on.

"C'mon, guys! Catch up!" Marth said. He glanced at the other group, who had now spread out and were spawning tiles all over their side of the field for Finn to climb. Griff's battlegroup was falling behind quickly.

Light sprinkles fell from the dark sky overhead. The temperature dropped and the wind shifted as the dark clouds, once far away, had moved above them.

Griff maneuvered to the far right, allowing himself some space from the group, while still finding a way to be helpful. He cast spell after spell onto the wooden tiles, ignoring the red colorations in his magic. Knowing that his inward frustration was on display for all to see only made him angrier. At least he knew the professor was watching. He hoped, at least, that it would display his frustration to the professor in a way he couldn't with words.

The wooden tiles were becoming slippery, and the team slowed their pace of casting and climbing to accommodate the new conditions. The rain grew heavier with each level of tiles they climbed. Between the two teams and their newly generated stairs, the battlefield was turning into a makeshift pyramid around the opal chimera. Finn was only two levels ahead of Marth, who was a little more careless in his ascent as he tried to catch up.

A flash of green lit Griff's vision. A lightning bolt had whizzed right past Griff's ear. His mind had been miles away as he quietly worked by himself. Distracted and frustrated, he'd barely paid attention to his team on the left and had completely missed the danger flanking him on his right. He glared over at Caitlin, who had a mischievous grin that he desperately wanted to wipe away.

"Just barely missed ya!" she called.

"Aww, come off it, Caitlin!" he called back. "I'm not in the mood!"

"Doesn't matter to me! I'm just here to win!"

Griff shook his head. He quickly cast a wind spell down at the ground with a tile that had a matching symbol and watched it shoot up beside his. He shuffled around the corner to where Caitlin couldn't hit him with another spell and sat down. He thought about Mira's words before the match.

Can you be with me, with ... with us right now?

Griff hoped she didn't see him tagging out of the match right now. Because deep down, he knew that's exactly what he was doing.

Even bigger raindrops spilled from the sky. He pushed his guilt to the side and ran his hands through his drenched hair. The wind was making it hard to hear anything, and he just needed a moment. Some time to pause and try to care about this match that felt so trivial.

He took some time to assess the battlefield. He'd been so intentionally slow in his climb that the rest of the group were several levels above him. He needed to catch up. But Caitlin was going to be a problem. Not just for him, but if he didn't stop her, she could take the group from behind. Where was she, anyway?

Near the top, Sadie and Vincent battled against Finn, Patrick, and another girl named Dakarai. Finn mostly tried to stay out of harm's way, casting half-hearted spells as he climbed. Patrick and Dakarai, on the other hand, fiercely stood their ground. At least, they tried to. They sent wind spells to knock Sadie and Vincent off their platforms, but Griff's teammates deftly dodged and retaliated with their own spells.

Griff looked up. Marth and Mira had caught up to Aiko, the last of Finn's group. Even more shy than Finn, she kept to herself, and clearly didn't want to fight. Marth and Mira didn't seem to care.

Aiko's panicked shriek pierced through the sounds of the rain as she dodged Mira's perfect lightning spell. The fiery focus in Mira's eyes while she barked orders to Marth scared Griff. He was now glad he was lower on the makeshift pyramid where he couldn't be on the receiving end of that intensity.

"GRIFF! Get up here!" Mira screamed.

Never mind.

WHAM! Griff's vision went black. He felt his body lift off the platform. His side exploded in pain as he landed on the tile below his, its sharp edge digging into his ribs. His vision came back, but he felt powerless against the force of gravity. It yanked him unmercifully down the pyramid. Each platform he struck on the way down sent shockwaves of pain across his body. He pulled out his hand to try and stop himself, but it slipped against the wet tiles.

He finally landed on the muddy arena floor. He groaned and gripped his aching side. Sharp ringing filled his ears. Every part of him hurt. Every movement sent fresh, biting pains like lightning across his body. Not wanting to sit up, he allowed the large raindrops to pound against his face. He was ready to give up. His heart had never been in this battle in the first place. Now he had an excuse to remove himself from it. Even then, he still had to see what was happening.

He growled with exertion and pulled himself into an upright position, which was tricky considering the mud was trying to suck him back down. Mira and Marth were at the top of the pyramid. Aiko was nowhere in sight. Griff had only hoped they didn't send her down the pyramid like him. Surely from that height, one of the professors observing the match would have at least slowed her fall. As skinny as she was, Griff didn't think Aiko's little body could handle it like his had.

Marth pointed ahead and mouthed something, but Griff couldn't hear. Climbing down on the opposite side of the pyramid were Sadie and Vincent. They were still battling Patrick and Dakarai, but this time ... it looked like they were retreating!

No. Not retreating. Griff scanned further to see Finn carrying *both* storm orbs, one under each arm. And he was getting closer to their altar! *Genius, Finn*! Griff thought to himself. He was frustrated and proud at the same time. Now if Griff's team wanted to win, they'd have to chase him down and steal one of those orbs back.

Sadie and Vincent were gaining on the other team. Dakarai tumbled under the force of a fire spell from Sadie that exploded at her feet. Patrick stopped to help her, but slipped in the mud. Vincent took the opportunity and cast an ice spell that froze Patrick's hands to the mud.

Hearing Patrick's grunt of pain, Finn turned to see what had happened, fear plastered all over his face. He was so close to the altar, but it was now two against one: Sadie and Vincent against Finn. The two sprinted ahead, their spells whizzing past Finn as he weaved through the chaos. He may not have been the bravest or the most skilled at Essence Manipulation, but nightstalker's fury, he was a hard target to hit.

Sadie screamed with effort, and sent a wild, spiraling wind spell toward Finn that finally connected, sending him sprawling to the ground, the two orbs rolling just out of reach. Griff sighed a breath of relief. *Here we go.*

His pain had dulled. His team needed him. He wiped his muddy hands on his pant legs. It was time to set his emotions to the side and, for once this entire match, show some effort.

Suddenly, his heart sank into his stomach. He watched in horror, seeing the events before him unfold as if in slow motion. The worst part was knowing he was unable to do anything about it. He was too far away.

Caitlin slammed into Sadie's back with her shoulder. Sadie yelped in pain and crashed to the ground next to Finn. Before Vincent had a chance to respond, she placed a hand on his chest and fired a lightning spell. Though Griff knew his armor took the brunt of the damage, the power of the spell flung Vincent back several feet.

Caitlin marched over and picked Finn off the ground. The two of them dashed to the storm orbs before Vincent or Sadie could recover, and before Marth and Mira could catch up.

Together, Finn and Caitlin scrambled over to their altar and placed one of the orbs on it. Together, they held the other one up for all to see. The match was over and there was a clear winner. Multicolored sparks whizzed through the air and the cheers from the crowd were deafening.

Griff dared himself to look over at Mira. Her mouth hung open in disbelief. Then she turned to stare back at him. The look of disappointment in her eyes was like a punch to the gut. He'd let her down. He hadn't shown up for the match the way she needed him to. After giving him the space to deal with his emotions, she'd politely asked him to focus on the match, and he couldn't do it. Because of him, Caitlin was able to sneak in behind Vincent and Sadie and take them out of the match long enough for them to win. Griff hated losing—but he hated the looks his friends gave him even more.

CHAPTER 19

Griff's stomach rumbled. He pretended not to notice. The meat he'd snuck out of the castle during dinner wasn't for him. He let out a long sigh, his breath like a fog curling in the cold air that faded like it had never been there at all. The lake beside the castle was still. Calm. Something he wished he could be right now.

From where he stood, Griff could see all of Solastran. Beyond the lake's edge, the land sloped downward in rolling hills and jagged cliffs before leveling into the town, where buildings stacked together like pieces on a game board. Tiny figures moved between them, too small to tell apart. Tiny lights flickered against the darkness cast from the mountain's shadow that loomed over the town.

Though the sun hadn't fully set, merchants and citizens alike were beginning their nightly routine of lighting their lamps. Not to keep the nightstalkers at bay. Not as a signal for the kids to make their way home so the city could lock up against the monsters. The lamps weren't for survival. No, they were for staying awake. So the students from Bergots who chose to visit following the Altar Storm matches could continue to eat, shop, and enjoy their weekend. Something he wouldn't allow himself to do.

Deep down, he knew he was punishing himself. The distance he felt from his friends—and especially from Mira—didn't seem like punishment enough. He *deserved* the gnawing hunger. Sure, he would eat eventually. He wasn't going to literally starve to the point of death. But for now, he needed to physically *feel* the punishment.

They'd lost the match. To Mira, it was like consigning her to shoveling warg poo for the rest of her life rather than working for the king. And while Griff didn't think it had to be that drastic, he knew better than to say anything. After all, it was still his fault they had lost, and everyone knew it.

Milo Ofner had found Griff walking back to the castle alone and clapped a hand on his back.

"Tough luck there, Griff. I dunno what was going on with you back there, but just remember: there's more matches to come." He cupped his hands around his mouth, breathing on them to keep warm. "Plus, they don't look at *just* wins and losses, ya know? They look at individual performances as well. Overall, your team didn't look that bad..." He stopped himself, but Griff knew what he was trying to say.

"Just me..." He finished for Milo.

"Well ... okay, yeah. But everyone has their bad days!"

Everyone has their bad days. Griff reiterated Milo's words to himself as he picked up a smooth, flat stone on the edge of the lake and tossed it across the calm waters. The ripples from each skip of the rock spread outward, then disappeared.

As if losing the Altar Storm match and disappointing his friends and girlfriend hadn't been enough, when Griff returned to his room to sulk, he found his entire trunk emptied onto his bunk. All his belongings scattered on top of the sheets, some of it spilling onto the floor. At first, Griff thought maybe his friends had taken their anger out on him, until he saw the message. A message that had been carved on the underside of the top bunk. A message left for Griff to read every night whenever he laid down and stared above him:

I KNOW YOUR SECRET

Thankfully, Runa had been tucked in for a nap in the furthest corner of the room, around the corner from Griff's bunk. She seemed to like the makeshift crate he and the guys had built for her using thick branches from the forest. Whenever they left, they would toss their dirty laundry and blankets around the crate—a guaranteed way to keep any lurkers from getting too close. Nobody would have dared move closer to that mound of dirty, stinky teenage boy clothes.

But *had* the intruder seen Runa? Did she make a noise and the intruder heard her? Is that what the note alluded to? Or was it the fact that he had a shard inside him? That he drew his power from it. That he was connected to the king and Korrun's quest more than most realized. Who had invaded his room? Was it the same person Korrun's letter was written to? The Deceiver?

A curious growl snapped him from his thoughts. Runa had swallowed the last bite of meat and now turned her attention toward Griff. She sat on her hind legs and cocked her head, which was almost comically larger than the rest of her body. She was now about the size of a large dog, though the growth of her head looked like it was outpacing the rest of her body.

Fitting into Griff's trunk had been unpleasant for her *and* for him. She was clearly outgrowing it, showing her discomfort with a sassy snort as soon as she was free. Today would probably be the last day he could fit her in there. Once she tucked her wings and tail in, then—and only then—could the lid close properly, and Griff would levitate the trunk through the castle as quickly as he could. Most thought he was like the others whose families lived in Solastran, that he was merely bringing some belongings to and from his home. Though that only worked on the weekends, Griff's lies were becoming more and more intricate as Runa needed more and more outside time.

"I'm fine, Ru," Griff lied to Runa. He walked over to the small pile of bones she had left next to the trunk. They had been picked completely clean. He reached under her chin and lovingly ran his hand along her rugged jawline. She closed her eyes and leaned into his touch, her long rumble showing her appreciation.

"Are those your horns coming in?" he asked, gently rubbing over two small bumps on her forehead. In response, she leaned in even farther, relishing the attention.

For a moment, Griff allowed himself to feel at peace. He was standing next to a pristine lake overlooking Solastran, enjoying the cooler weather and a beautiful sunset with his pet dragon.

Pet. Dragon. How cool was that? How many people could say they had one of those? He continued stroking Runa's head, and the longer he did so, the harder she leaned into the gesture. She rumbled even louder and leaned in with what felt like all her might, knocking Griff onto the grass with surprising force.

Stunned to find himself pinned under her weight, Griff just accepted the moment and laughed. Her head was on his lap and his bum ached, but nonetheless, he didn't want to the moment to end. His laughter echoed across the lake, then trailed into nonexistence, leaving only the sound of Runa's continued rumble. He looked into her curious ruby eyes that stared back at his own. She had gotten stronger. Bigger. Too big.

"You know..." he said, patting her head, "we've been really lucky that we've had the bedroom to ourselves this year. Otherwise, I dunno how we could have hidden you for so long. But..."

She looked up at him and trilled before standing and ruffling her adolescent wings. He groaned in relief to have her weight removed from his body.

"But," he continued, "you're getting so big, Ru-Ru! I don't know how we can keep hiding you! I dunno if Sylva can hide you in the stables or not. I mean, Mr. Dingmann is nice and all. I just don't know how he would feel about having a dragon around."

Runa walked over to the pile of bones and nudged at them with her nose, almost as if she was ignoring what he had just said. She sat next to the bones and stared at Griff.

"All right, all right, fine. But we're not done having this conversation yet, okay?"

He jumped up from the ground, dusted his backside off, and picked up one of the bones. She stood on all four legs, crouched, ready for the throw. Griff waved the bone in front of her, and only her eyes followed.

"Now, remember. Don't go off too far. You're supposed to be a secret, okay? Ready? Go!"

Griff threw the bone with all his might, sending it several yards across the grassy terrain. Runa ran with a speed and agility he had not seen from her, catching the bone easily in her mouth before it could hit the ground. She pranced back to her owner, proudly placing the bone at his feet.

"Wow," Griff muttered. "That was impressive!"

She snorted in response and small puffs of smoke blew out her nose.

"That's new too! You gonna start breathing fire now? I thought we still had some time before I had to worry about that! Okay. You want a real challenge, huh?"

He picked up the bone, and Runa readied herself again.

"Challenge accepted, huh girl? All right, betcha can't get this one!"

Griff launched the bone high into the air, aimed his hand, and sent an overly powerful wind spell that connected with the bone, sending it across the grassy field and into the thick woods.

Griff sighed as Runa bolted with purpose after the bone, disappearing into the thick foliage.

"Oh boy." He rubbed his forehead in frustration. "Please come back."

Though he couldn't see Runa, Griff listened intently and could hear her stomps through the forest, eagerly searching for her prize.

"I was told I might find you out here."

Griff's heart leaped to his throat. He spun to meet the voice, already unholstering his handle and crafting a bright blue blade.

"Whoa, whoa, easy there, son." Gale Driscoll held his hands up innocently.

"Dad?" Griff's heart continued to pound against his chest, even after recognizing his own father. "But … but how?"

"Well, Sylva came home to visit, and your mother and I asked if we would get to see you this weekend. So … well, he told us about your day today…"

He trailed off, though Griff was able to decipher the silence.

"Yeah … it was … not a good one."

"Well, we try not to embarrass you with any parent visits to the castle, but I thought I might give it a shot and see you anyway."

Suddenly, Gale's eyes widened, and he took a step back and pointed behind Griff.

"D-D-Dragon!" He screamed.

Griff's heart sank. *King's crown. Runa!*

She was barreling out of the thicket toward Griff, eyes bright and bone in mouth.

Gale yanked at Griff's arm and tried to pull him away, back toward the castle.

"Dad! Dad! I can explain! Let go!"

His grip was tight, and he was still stronger than Griff. He became more aggressive the closer Runa got. And she was quickly closing the gap.

"Get behind me, Griff!" Gale stepped in front of his son, planted his feet firmly on the ground, and pulled out a small dagger from the lining of his pants.

Runa was merely yards away. Gale's hand tightened on the dagger. His other reached behind him, keeping Griff out of harm's way.

"Runa!" Griff shouted from behind his dad. "Sit!"

The dragon froze, skidding to a stop. Understanding replaced the playful gleam in her eyes. Several feet from Gale Driscoll, Runa the Destroyer plopped her backside onto the ground as she had been told. She gingerly placed the bone she had finally found in the forest onto the grass, then cocked her head, waiting for Griff to speak.

Breathless, Griff said, "Dad ... meet Runa. Runa ... meet my dad."

CHAPTER 20

Gale didn't move. Didn't speak. Didn't even blink. Griff could tell he was having an internal battle, trying to come to grips with everything that had just happened. His knuckles were white as he continued to grip the handle of his dagger—keeping it out as though he thought Runa might lunge at him at any moment. His other hand remained behind him, trying to keep Griff in place.

Runa, however, merely continued to stare. Her tail swished back and forth, caressing the grass. As the sun continued to set, her brilliant ruby eyes almost seemed to glow in the dark, which only made her look more menacing. Which is not what Griff wanted right now, given the state of things.

"Dad?" No response. Griff sighed and gently grasped Gale's hand that had been holding him away from the dragon. "Dad. It's okay. She's *my* dragon. She's safe."

Griff delicately pushed his father's hand to the side and stepped in front of him, facing Runa.

"Good girl." Griff smiled at her. He took a step forward.

"Griff!"

"Dad!" Griff pleaded. "Please. Just watch."

Griff smiled at Runa, to show her everything was okay. She seemed to understand. Her tailed swished faster as Griff walked closer. He reached down, picked up the bone she had fetched, and held it out for her. She rumbled her approval, gingerly picked the bone up with her front teeth, and proudly showed it to Gale. Griff rubbed the side of her head, and she closed her eyes, giving another grumble of affection.

Griff looked to his dad, who stood wide-eyed and slack-jawed, the dagger still in his hand. But not in a defensive grip. The blade drooped toward the ground, forgotten by its owner. From what Griff could tell, his father wasn't scared. Not really. It seemed like he was caught between disbelief and acceptance at the sight of seeing his son command a dragon. His shaky breath sent small puffs of air whirling into the air as the evening grew colder.

"R-Runa, you say?" Gale said, trying to gather himself.

Griff nodded. "Runa."

"Mm-hmm." Gale lowered the dagger, but didn't move. He straightened out his cloak and tugged at the sleeves. He took a deep breath, letting it out slowly. "Where, uh, where did you *find* this dragon? I don't think they give you dragon pets here, do they? Surely, they would have mentioned that to the parents."

Griff sighed. *Time to come clean.* "I found her egg when I found the shard. Remember the dead dragon I saw on the other side of the forest? That was her mother."

Gale stood silent, gathering himself, searching for the right words, as he usually did in serious moments like this. The silence between them felt like an eternity. He sheathed his dagger and finally spoke.

"Can I pet her?"

"What?" Now it was Griff's turn to be shocked.

"Is she safe? Can I pet her?"

"Y-Yeah. Yeah, she's *really* safe. Come on over. I'll show you."

He turned to Runa and whispered, "Don't mess this up, girl. He's good people. You'll see." She rumbled her understanding.

Gale stopped just in front of Runa and Griff, for once looking like he didn't know what to do with his own body.

"Okay," Griff said. "Okay, just, uh place your open hand under her chin, and stroke along the side of her jaw. That's her favorite."

Gale's hand was shaky, but he didn't hesitate. He did as he was instructed. Runa dropped her bone to the grass and leaned in, making Gale jerk his hand back with a nervous laugh.

"Sorry, there, uh, Runa." Gale coughed, embarrassed.

Griff chuckled. "She liked it. You're okay, Dad."

Gale took a step closer and stroked the side of her head again. She rumbled her approval and leaned in for more. The wide smile on his father's face eased Griff's heart. He knew their conversation wasn't over, but at least getting to pet a real-life dragon might relieve some of the tension between them. But he knew more questions were coming. Might as well get it over with.

"Dad, I ... I couldn't just leave her there. I felt some ... some connection with her mother. I can't really explain it, but it was like ... like because of who I am—the fact that I have a shard inside me—I feel like I'm supposed to guard these shards with my life. Just like Runa's mother. She was protecting the shard and now it's my turn. And ... and when I saw Runa's egg, I just felt like I needed to protect it. Like I owed that to her mother somehow."

Words tumbled out of Griff's mouth like water spilling out from a broken dam. He didn't know if any of it made sense, but it felt nice to finally come clean.

His dad didn't say a word, only continued to stroke Runa's head. Something she enjoyed thoroughly.

"What ... and how," Gale stated. "That's where we have the issue."

"Huh?"

"You know, Griff. You're a really good kid. Well, you're not a kid anymore, are you? But you're a really good guy. You want to do the right things. *What* you did was good. *How* you handled it, though, wasn't."

Griff nodded with understanding and stuck his hands in his pockets.

"You lied. You hid. You snuck around. That's not how to handle things. Your mom and I have always been on your side, son. We want what's best for you—when are you going to see that? I thought you would have seen that earlier when I came *with you* to retrieve that shard."

Guilt dragged Griff's heart down to his stomach. His dad was right.

"You're your own man, now. I get it. But as your father, let me help you. Let's work together. We can figure things out so we can not only do the good 'whats,' but also with the right 'hows.'"

"I'm just so afraid if anyone finds out that they'll take her from me," Griff said. "And she needs me. And I think I need her too."

Gale nodded. "I get that. You have a right to be afraid of that. I mean, it *is* dangerous keeping a dragon at school. What was your plan? How were you going to keep hiding her? King's crown, she's already pretty big! And just wait till she starts breathing fire! Then what?"

Griff kicked at the dirt. "Yeah, I know. I was ... tryin' to figure something out. Sylva works at the stables now, so ... I dunno. I was thinking about seeing if we could hide Runa out there."

"And you don't think she'd be found there by someone?"

"That's the problem. Mr. Dingmann, the stable master, is there all the time. He loves animals. Sylva thinks probably more than people."

"Is he friendly?" Gale asked.

Griff paused. "You know, I haven't talked to him much myself, but Sylva says he's really nice. Reminds him of Talley, actually."

"Hmm." Gale scratched at his chin. "You know, if I needed help with raising a dragon, I think I could trust Talley. Talk with Sylva and see if you think this Mr. Dingmann can be trusted. If not him, I bet you could talk to Professor Coen." He placed a hand on Griff's shoulder. "I don't want you to lose Runa either. It seems like you two have a good connection. But I also want you to do the right thing, even when it's hard." He removed his hand and crossed his arms and laughed. "Plus! Now you have a dragon to match your Nightflame sword handle I made you! You've come a long way in the ways of fashion. I couldn't get you to match trousers and shirt. Now, here you are, matching weapon and pet!"

Griff chuckled, letting some—but not all—of his fears and frustrations melt at his dad's line.

Gale knelt and picked up Runa's bone. Her ears perked and she stood tall, eyes following every small movement of Gale's hand. He looked to his son and asked, "May I?"

"She would love that," Griff answered. It was strange seeing his dad asking *him* for permission for anything. It had always been the other way around. Maybe his dad really did see him as a man now. If only the headmaster could see him that way...

Whatever frustrations he'd allowed to escape were back now, and swelling with force.

Gale threw the bone as hard as he could, and Runa sprinted after it with all her might.

"Dad. Korrun found another shard."

Gale's smile disappeared, and he searched his son's eyes. Griff knew what he would find in them: pain.

"You're sure?"

Griff nodded. "I might as well have been there. I saw the whole thing. It was like the shard was calling for me, asking for my help. And the headmaster ... well ... he wouldn't let me go so I could help them find it."

Runa returned with her prize and dropped it at Gale's feet. He threw it again, this time without as much enthusiasm.

"I see," was all Gale could seem to muster. The silence that followed told Griff he was searching for the right words.

"Remember the night you discovered your abilities?" he finally said.

"Yeah, No Moon Night, how could I forget?"

Gale rubbed his right pant leg in remembrance. Underneath, Griff knew, was a scar from the nightstalkers who had attacked his dad that night.

"I didn't let you go that night, knowing the risks. Even now, I still don't know if it was the right call."

"What do you mean?"

"Well, I mean, I had just talked to you that morning about how you were turning into a man. And that meant new freedoms and responsibilities. Yet, I held you back from those—keeping you from joining the nightly guard that evening. Why do you think I made that decision?"

Griff sighed. "Because you love me," he answered reluctantly, feeling slightly embarrassed to be talking about feelings.

"Exactly. My love for you fueled my desire to keep you safe. But since you're becoming a man, now, I can't keep getting in the way of giving you the opportunity to make your own decisions. And ... letting you live with the consequences of them."

Runa proudly pranced back to Gale with the bone in her mouth, dropping it at his feet yet again. He grinned, patted her head, then picked up the bone and flung it toward the forest once more.

"It seems to me that Headmaster Aldamund probably faces a similar battle. It's clear he cares for you, and he's been given the major responsibility of your protection while here at Bergots. Maybe he was wrong to keep you here. But I get it. He's responsible for you just like I am. But he doesn't have the advantage of being your father."

"I think it's more than just that he cares for me," Griff responded, his mind taking him back to that night in the headmaster's quarters. The feelings of rejection stung once again. "I don't think he trusts me. I think he still sees me as a new mage, a ... a ... child incapable of standing strong and winning battles. After all, he *did* have to come to my rescue in Cordelia. He probably thinks I can't even look out for myself."

Once Runa had dropped the bone in front of Griff's father's feet, Griff took a step forward, snatched the bone off the ground, clenched his jaw tight, and threw the bone high into the air. Instead of a wind spell like before, Griff shouted then launched an angry-red fire spell toward the twirling bone. The fire consumed it. Ash rained from the sky, falling on a very disappointed Runa. She shook the ash off and cocked her head at Griff.

Griff huffed. "Sorry, girl. Shouldn't have done that." He looked to the place where she had previously eaten her dinner and nodded his head toward the pile of bones left over. "Go grab another."

Her ears perked up and she pranced happily over to the pile, gingerly nosing through until she found the largest bone. She walked right past Griff, almost with a glare, and placed the bone at Gale's feet, before plopping down on her backside. Griff understood the gesture. And decided to stay out of their game.

After throwing the bone for her, Gale turned back to Griff. "Remember how Grandpa Driscoll used to tell us stories around the campfire in the backyard?"

"I do." Griff sighed. "Barely. He died when I was, what, seven or eight?"

"Yeah..." Gale said sadly. "You were eight."

He paused for a moment of reflection, then smiled and faked throwing the bone toward the forest, sending Runa sprinting in the wrong direction. That forced a laugh out of both father and son before Gale then tossed the bone in the opposite direction.

"Your grandpa loved telling stories. But one of the biggest problems of storytelling, is we like to place ourselves in the stories. And what character do we like to pretend to be? The random side character? No. We like to pretend *we're* the heroes. We're the guys who rescue the princess and save the kingdom. We like to pretend we're the main characters.

"And you know what, Griff? You are the main character of your story. And I know you'll write a great story out of your life. But you've also been invited into an even greater story than you could ever write yourself. The *king's* story. He's out there trying to stop Korrun and rid the world of the Corruption. And you've been invited to play a part of that story."

When Gale tried to grab the bone that had been dropped at his feet, Runa dashed forward and grabbed the other end of the bone, initiating a tug-of-war that Gale was bound to lose.

"Oh no you don't." He laughed, pulling with all his might. Runa trilled loudly, tugging and shaking her head from side to side. Finally, Gale let go and tried to shake the pain from his hands. "There was no way, but I had to try." He laughed.

"Anyways," he continued. "You can fight to be the hero of your own story, alone. Or you can step into something greater and make a real difference. But you've got to work *with* the king and his son. The decision is up to you."

Griff wanted to argue. To tell his dad that he was more than some side-character in someone else's story. But deep down, he knew his dad's words to be true. He slowly walked over to Runa, who was holding her bone playfully, trying to provoke Gale into another tug-of-war game. Griff gently held out his hand and she hesitantly placed the bone into his palm. It was then he noticed there were still fragments of ash on her back that hadn't been shaken off. He held out his hand and cast a soft wind spell that cleaned her.

"Sorry about earlier," he said. He opened his palm, and with a thought, gradually levitated the bone. It spun slowly in circles. Runa's eyes widened, and she cocked her head.

Griff smiled softly and said to his pet dragon, "I'm ready to be a part of the game again."

CHAPTER 21

"I want to come with you," she pleaded, holding Einar's hand. Tears formed in the corners of her eyes, and Einar wanted nothing more than to wipe them away.

"Fedelma, you can't. It's too dangerous," Einar responded, secretly hating himself. He glanced out the window of the small inn they had stayed at for the past few weeks. The sun was getting lower. It was almost sunset.

Einar let out a slow breath. Having her join him as he moved the shard to its next location would be a dream come true. But he knew better.

He folded the last of his shirts and tucked them neatly in his pack before gently placing his journal on top and cinching it closed. "I'll come back for you after this assignment."

"And when will that be, exactly?" She crossed her arms, pouting. On one hand, it was adorable. On the other, she was pouting because of *him*. Guilt seeped into his heart.

He sighed. "I dunno." He grasped her hands in his. "I wish I knew. I just can't risk you getting hurt. It's too dangerous," he repeated.

"I'm safer with you than anywhere else in the world." She squeezed his hand and looked deep into his eyes. "You're not just a guardian to … I don't know what … but you're also *my* guardian, Einar. Please. Please! Take me with you. You can teach me how to control my powers. You can protect me from the shadows. And … and … I just can't stand the thought of being without you. These last few weeks have been … amazing. Please, Einar." The tears finally fell down her cheeks.

He let go of her hands and broke her gaze. Carefully, he tied his canister of fresh water to the side of his pack, his mind and heart racing. Would it be selfish of him? To bring her along? He had always been told not to "carry too much baggage." He knew that meant more than items in his pack. This "baggage" would only slow him down and make him more vulnerable to the enemy. Master Lochlainn made it clear to keep any and all ties short.

Einar sighed heavily. Not out of frustration. But because for the first time in his life as a Guardian of the Shards, he was going to ignore his master's rules. "Okay," he said.

Fedelma squealed in excitement and squeezed him tight. "I'll go pack my things!" She nearly danced out of Einar's room and into the hallway before disappearing.

Einar let out another long sigh. *What have you gotten yourself into, Einar?*

He shook his head, then chuckled with excitement. The life of a Guardian was often lonely. Any relationships began and ended in weeks. More than the constant threat of attacks, the lack of company was the worst part of his job. That was all about to change now. Einar fiddled with the object he kept hidden in his pocket. It was all about to change. And maybe for good.

The shrill squeal of the heavy iron gate closing behind Einar and Fedelma made him wince. Not just because of the sound of the gate, horrible as it was, but because he was leaving one of the nicest towns he'd ever visited.

The people were friendly. The food was delicious. The fall weather had been mild. Children played in the street while their parents worked. It was a small enough town that most people knew each other. *And* trusted each other. But large enough that they had everything they needed.

After reassuring the gate guard that they would be fine at night, the guard sent his best wishes to Einar and Fedelma as he closed the gate behind them. The man was ready for another night of protecting the town from nightstalkers.

Einar had offered to guard the gate while he was in town. He had nothing better to do and knew that his friends in the shadows would stay away from his post. But they kindly refused, saying he was a guest in their town and that they had plenty of men willing and able to take up arms. Whisperspell had been such a lovely town. Einar took note of the lovely experience he'd had, and knew that any chance he got, he would come back if possible. For now, though, he had another assignment. A message from his master told him to visit Thornwood Peak, a town in the mountains a week or so away from Whisperspell. When Fedelma had been told that the journey would be arduous due to the terrain, she merely laughed in response.

"I'm *still* coming with you."

Normally, when leaving a nice town like Whisperspell behind, Einar's heart would ache, as if he were leaving home. He took one last glance behind them as the guard's torches faded into the distance. For the first time, though, his heart was full of joy. He grasped Fedelma's hand in his right, while his left skimmed the top of the tall wheat heads at the edge of the path, their soft, feathery heads tickling his palm. The setting sun cast an orange glow over the expansive field, creating the illusion that the two travelers were casting off into a sea of gold.

Einar imagined they still had an hour before they would be visited by his friends. Ever near. Ever dangerous. Never seen. Yet he knew, as always, they would stay out of sight from the guardian. They were drawn to the shard's power like a moth to the light, yet repelled by its power and the righteous wielder of it.

An hour later, like clockwork, they heard the sounds of distant crackling of leaves and twigs. Footsteps in the night. His friends had found him once again. He believed they were different ones than the previous journeys, yet to him their glowing white eyes all looked the same. So he pretended they were.

To him, these monsters might as well have been his traveling buddies. Sometimes he would tell them stories. Stories from his travels. Stories he made up in his head. This time, though, he didn't need them for company. He fidgeted with the object in his pocket and looked to the woman whose hand he held.

At first, they had walked close together simply to stay warm as the sun set. They had even clasped hands as a sign of affection. Over the course of the walk, though, Fedelma's grip changed. She held on as though at any moment something might snatch her and drag her off into the shadows. Without him, something would have. So, she held onto Einar not out of affection, but out of fear. As though he were a floating log on a rushing river.

Einar squeezed her hand and smiled. "Don't worry, Fedelma. They're not going to get you."

She forced a smile and tried to laugh. "That obvious, huh?"

"Yep. Pretty obvious. But you know, under normal circumstances, you would be right to be afraid. My friends in the shadows are merciless."

She raised a brow. "I still can't believe you call those nightstalkers your *friends*," she teased.

Einar chuckled, but said nothing.

"But as you were saying, I'm not under normal circumstances, then, Mr. Falkenburg?"

He smiled and looked to the ground. "No ma'am. You're not. There's nothing normal about what I do." *Not yet*, he thought, still playing with the object in his pocket. *Not yet.*

"Then, please, for king's sake, tell me. What is it that you do? What are you guarding? Why do the monsters not attack, yet seem to follow your every movement?"

The sweat from his hand made the object in his pocket slippery. Still, he continued to fidget. If she was willing to go with him to Thornwood Peak, to travel by night, without even knowing what he did, then she could be trusted with his secret. It would mean breaking yet another rule of his. Another rule of the Guardians.

"I am ... a Guardian of the Shard," he said at last.

"The ... Shard? What's a shard?"

"Well, now, you *know* what a shard is. It's a piece of something else, broken off from the whole." Einar released the object in his pocket, then fidgeted with the lining of his trousers. He pulled out a shining sliver from the hidden compartment inside the waistline and held it out for her to see. He could hear the monsters in the shadows recoil from the shard's power and light. They scurried deeper into the woods. Twigs snapped. Leaves dislodged into the air. And an angry hiss echoed between the trees. Fedelma jumped at the sudden, unseen chaos.

"It's all right, it's all right. They ... well, they don't like the shards. Yet, for some reason, they're still drawn to it. This," Einar held the shard closer to Fedelma, "is a shard from the Orb of Essence."

"Or ... Orb of Essence? What is that?"

"A powerful artifact. We don't know a lot about it, but what has been passed down from Guardian to Guardian is that this orb was responsible for Day Zero."

Fedelma's eyes widened. She took a step back. It was understandable, Einar thought, that she would be afraid. He held a piece of the world's end in his hand.

"You can imagine the power that the orb must have had to reshape our world the way it has. This here is one of nine pieces." With a thought, he levitated the shard just above his open palm, letting it dance and twirl in the darkness. "Many years after Day Zero, the Guardians of the Shard recovered all nine shards and have kept them separate from each other. Lest we plunge the world into something far worse."

"So ... you just, stick it in your pocket and walk around, going from town to town? Never settling down? Never finding a home?"

His heart sunk with each question. "Doesn't sound like a very family friendly life, huh?"

"Oh! No, no. Sorry, I didn't mean it—what I meant was ... that it sounds very lonely." She placed a gentle hand on his chest and looked deep into his eyes. "I'm glad I can be here with you. You shouldn't have to do this alone."

Her eyes turned to the shard, still hovering, still dancing. It was a mesmerizing sight. Even Einar—who'd carried the shard for years—never stopped marveling at it. How could something so beautiful be so terrifying? It was both exquisite and powerful. Delightful, yet dangerous. And here it was, dancing the night away, parting the curtains of darkness with its glorious, radiant white light.

"You can't just bury it somewhere?" Fedelma asked, breaking the silence and removing her hand from his chest.

"Hmph. I wish it were that easy. The Council—elders of the Guardians—have opted for unpredictability as part of the safety of the shards. We receive our tasks from them, and we do not sway until we hear otherwise. One time, for three years, I traveled the same path between two towns every other night."

"The path you and I met on? Where you saved me?" she asked. She stepped to Einar's side and wrapped her arm around his waist. Together they stared at the shard still floating in mid-air.

"Mm-hmm. The same one."

He didn't move. He didn't want to. Instead, he closed his eyes and allowed the sounds of the night to wash over him. The evening breeze blew a few strands of Fedelma's hair onto his face, but he didn't mind at all. Instead, her signature honeysuckle scent was even stronger, now, and it was intoxicating. Fedelma continued to stare at the shard, struck by its beauty. Time meant nothing to him in this moment. To him, the world was standing still. It seemed as if moon, the stars, even the wind itself leaned into this intimate moment and didn't want to let it go. Finally, after what felt both as slow as eternity and as brief as a heartbeat, he lowered the shard and closed his fist over it before stuffing it back into his waistline.

"Think you got another hour or so in you?" he asked.

As if that triggered something in her, Fedelma yawned and wiped away the accompanying tears that always seemed to follow.

"Maybe. But you're gonna have to keep me awake. Got any good stories?"

Einar smiled. "Aye. I've got enough to get us all the way to Thornwood Peak and back. Some will excite enough to keep you awake. Others might make the hairs on your neck stand on end. And then some might make you laugh till your stomach can't stand it anymore."

"That's what's on the menu, then, huh? Then in that case let's start with a fresh, exciting one. Then I'll probably order a couple funny ones to top it off. You can leave the horror ones to yourself for now. I don't think I'm quite ready for those just yet."

They continued walking hand in hand. Her grip was loose, casual. Not like before.

"Once upon a time, I wasn't either. But I understand. In time there will be a need to share those with you, as those stories serve as a dire warning. Those are the kind of stories that bring wisdom."

He squeezed her hand and gave her a wink. As he did so, the chirping of crickets dimmed and the sounds of leaves crackling and twigs snapping returned. Einar was proud that even though his friends from the shadows were back, Fedelma's grip remained relaxed the rest of their walk.

She lasted about three more hours. Two and a half more than Einar expected out of her. But with every hour, her pace slowed. As physically adept as she seemed, she wasn't used to this much traveling. There was no real rush to get to Thornwood Peak. It would be several days before they got there anyway. He was told where to go but never told how to get there or when to get there. That, the Council left up to him.

"Here," he said, pulling her off the path and into the woods. She shrank into him before stepping into the forest, her grip on him tight. Her long nails painfully dug into his skin.

"They won't come for you, I promise," Einar whispered into her ear. "Remember who you're with."

She nodded and loosened her grip. They walked about five minutes into the forest, the footsteps of the creatures from the dark following them the entire way. As expected, they stayed just out of sight. Einar finally paused next to a large oak tree with a base as wide as a room. He pulled out a blanket and folded it neatly before placing it on the dirt floor. He gathered a couple of thick branches and with a flick of his hand, had a warm fire for the two of them.

"Lesson number 247: there's no need for kindlin' when you're a mage." Einar laughed.

"Clearly," she said, motioning to the fire. "Or do you just prefer to play with your fire spells?"

"Why can't it be both?" he said, dusting off his hands and taking a seat next to her. He leaned back against the base of the oak tree and wiggled in to get comfortable. She leaned against him, that sweet honeysuckle scent washing over him once again. He stuck his hand in his pocket. *Still there.*

"Thank you," he said.

"Thank you? Thank you for what?" she asked, pulling back off him. "I had to *beg* you to allow me to come. I should be thanking you."

"Well, you were right. Being a Guardian ... well, it does get lonely. This is the first time since traveling with Master Lochlainn that I've had company. It's been years. And it's really nice. And there's no one else I would rather have by my side than you."

"And even if it meant walking miles and miles in the dark with those nightstalkers following me, I would have it no other way as long as I'm with you."

"I ... I was hoping you'd say something like that." He reached in his pocket, but fear kept him from pulling the object out. "I know it hasn't been long since we've been ... together. But I just—"

"—Two months and ... ten days to be exact."

Einar laughed. His face felt warm, now. And not because of the fire. He pulled the worn-out ring from his pocket and twirled it between his fingers. He had purchased it from an older woman in Whisperspell whose husband had long since passed. Seeing his and Fedelma's relationship blossom, she tried to give it to him. Instead, he took it and hid some money under a flower pot she kept outside her kitchen window that overlooked the front yard.

As Einar fiddled with the ring, he dared not look at Fedelma's reaction. As soon as she saw it, though, she gasped, yet didn't speak a word.

He continued playing with it while he spoke. "I've met a lot of people on my travels. Some nice. Some ... not. But I've never met anyone like you, Fedelma. You're kind. Gentle. Humble. And really, really, *really* easy to look at, too."

The firelight reflected off the tears welling up in her eyes. She laughed and wiped them away before they could fall.

"Since I left home and became a Guardian of the Shards, I've lost that sense of 'home.' Every town I travel to, I see husbands and wives. Fathers and sons. Mothers and daughters. I see 'home' in other people's lives. It's always felt like something distant, unattainable for myself. Until I met you. You are my home, Fedelma. You're what I've been missing so dearly this whole time, and I see that now. I lost a home once upon a time. I can't do that again."

Einar shifted to where he was on a single knee. He looked deeply into Fedelma's tear-filled eyes and held the worn ring out for her.

"Will you be my home now and forever, Fedelma? Will you marry me?"

She didn't answer. Tears streamed down her face. She didn't bother to wipe them this time. He couldn't tell if she was sobbing or laughing. His heart sunk. It had been too soon. They had only known each other for a few months. He should have waited.

Suddenly, she grabbed him and pulled him toward her. There, in the black of night, with only the moon, stars, and nightstalkers as their witness, she gave him his answer. She didn't need words. Her kiss was enough. But what she said after that kiss would follow him for the rest of his life.

"I'd love nothing more."

CHAPTER 22

Griff barely managed to cover his yawn as Mira dragged him and the rest of the battlegroup toward their next class. Griff could barely stand on two feet. And it was all thanks to Runa.

Runa's tossing and turning in her crate and constant whining for snuggles kept Griff awake most of the night. Multiple times, he thought about giving in and allowing her a spot on the bed. Considering her size, though, that would have meant him sleeping on the floor.

Looking back now, getting a full night's sleep on the floor sounded much better than what he'd actually experienced.

The hallways were bursting with the sounds of laughter, students chatting about next month's holiday plans, and the echo of scurrying footsteps on the stone tiles. First year girls gathered and giggled at boys passing by. Fredrik Burns was helping Finn, who had just tripped over his own shoelaces and spilled his books all over the floor. Connor Ofner stepped over Finn's books, shifted his plant to his other arm, and gave Griff a big, one-armed hug before continuing his way to another class.

It seemed like life as usual to most people. Griff imagined none of them felt the weight that he did. Trying to hide a growing dragon in his room. Feeling the desire to find the next shard. Wondering what would happen if someone finally did have all the shards and only needed the last one ... inside him. And then there was the threatening note he'd received: *I know your secret.*

Someone had been watching him here at school. And his best guess was The Deceiver. The one who was spying for Korrun. Right now, though, he was too tired to care about any of those things. He just needed to get through the next two classes before he could skip lunch and take a well-deserved nap.

"Here we go!" Fredrik shouted, snapping Griff from his dark thoughts. Having helped Finn with his books, he had returned to his previous activities. He and several other guys were levitating a laughing first year, and Fredrik had just shoved the boy's legs, forcing him to spin in the air. Nearby students cheered and laughed loudly as Fredrik spun him faster.

"Okay! I'm ... going ... to ... hurl!" the boy said.

Mira rolled her eyes as they passed the rowdy group, muttering to herself about getting to class on time.

"Hi, Griff!"

Griff turned to see Kara Thorson leaning against the wall, books tucked neatly in her arm. Her smile widened when he looked at her. He stood straighter and tightened his grip on Mira's hand, hopefully showing Kara where his loyalty lay.

"Hi, Kara." Griff sighed, making sure to express a lack of excitement.

"Getting colder out there, huh?" she said casually, stepping to Griff's other side and matching his and Mira's pace.

"Mm-hmm," he answered. Griff eyed Marth, who had immediately stopped talking about something his sisters had taught him, and ogled Kara without a hint of shame.

"I hope we get a lot of snow this winter. I love playing in the snow. What about you, Griff?"

"Uh, yeah. It's all right." He didn't really know what to say. He'd seen enough of it to last a lifetime. Cordelia's winters started early and ended late. But in an effort to cut the conversation short, he skipped all those details. Sadly, it was all in vain.

"Hey, Griff, let me borrow you for just a second, please. Thanks!" Kara snatched Griff's free hand and pulled him away from an open-mouthed Mira.

"Hey! What're you—Kara!" Griff grunted as she dragged him to the side, next to a large stone column. Away from the crowd but not invisible to them either.

"What's the deal, Kara?" Griff huffed. He was too tired for games.

She flipped her wavy black hair out of her face. "So ... listen. I know *now* that you're with Mira. I get it. She's pretty. She's smart ..." Kara glanced over at Griff's battlegroup, who had slowed to watch. Mira stood among them, arms crossed and eyes narrowed. She maintained her position, but looked ready to pounce if needed. "... But ... I just need to know. How serious are you two?"

"Uh ... what? What do you mean?"

"How serious are you two? Are you, like, in *love* or whatever? Are things good between you? I just need to know."

"Well ... they're ..." He paused. Mira had been more distant since the last Altar Storm match. It had been almost two weeks and the loss still hung between them unspoken.

But he wasn't about to explain that to some girl he barely knew. He still wanted to be with Mira more than anything.

"They're ... serious enough, Kara. I'm very happy to be with Mira. So ... please, just ... just ... let us be. Okay?"

Kara sighed, looking disappointed. She glanced back over at Griff's group, at Mira, then eyed him once more. Her blue eyes bored into his own, as if looking into his very soul.

"Okay," she said finally. "Well ... you just let me know if something changes, okay?" She leaned over and kissed his cheek before he knew what had happened. She turned and walked down the hallway, opposite Griff's group.

Stunned at her boldness, Griff stood still and waited for Mira to come stomping over.

"What. Was. That?" she demanded.

"Whoa, whoa, whoa," Griff said, pulled out of his stupor. "She asked if I was happy with you and if we were serious."

"What!"

"But! But I told her I was *very* happy with you, Mira, and that she needed to look elsewhere. I promise."

"Then why did she kiss you?"

"That came out of *nowhere*! She just … just … kissed me all the sudden! I dunno why! I had just told her that we were serious!"

"Hmph! Well, she *better* look elsewhere. And you, Griff Driscoll, you stay away from her."

He held up his hands. "You don't have to tell me twice. King's crown, you didn't have to tell me once! She was never a threat anyways."

"Good." Mira stomped away, past the group, and marched toward their next class.

Marth, Vincent, and Sadie tried to hide their surprised expressions, but Griff could tell they were having a hard time. As Griff rejoined his group, he continued to try and wipe away the feeling of Kara's kiss on his cheek. But it was like trying to wipe away soot that had accidentally gotten on your arm. The more you try to rub it off, the deeper you rubbed it in.

"So … Kara's still single, then?" Marth finally asked.

Sadie turned with a disgusted look and punched Marth in the shoulder. Hard.

"OW!" he cried, turning the heads of several students nearby.

"Seriously, Marth!" Sadie said, before she grabbed Vincent's hand and pulled him toward the classroom.

Griff chuckled wearily and shook his head.

"Go for it, Marth, I don't even care."

Professor Nyra Venn was already hunched over a large, rectangular device at the front of the classroom when Griff half walked, half stumbled into his seat beside Mira and pulled out his *Magic and Machines: An Introduction into Technomagical Applications* book.

"Made it just in time, dearies," she said to Griff and Marth. She glanced up from her machine with a grin. A dark streak of grease lined her left jaw, and her wild, curly, white hair was pinned at the top with what looked like a leftover spring. It was as if she had stretched the coils to jam her frizzy hair through then let it snap shut, cinching it all together. Knowing the professor's quirkiness, Griff imagined she had forgotten what a bow was and just grabbed the nearest tool instead.

As much as he loved Professor Venn's class, today was more about survival than gearshifts or thermocouples. So, Griff propped his book upright on the table and hid his face behind it so he could try and catch a quick nap without being noticed. It was a lazy effort, almost guaranteed to be thwarted, but he had to try. And if he was caught, he knew Professor Venn would at least be nice enough about it.

Just then, he heard a metallic *thwang* and Professor Venn mutter, "*Nightstalker's fury!*" When the rest of the class chuckled at her misfortune, Griff's curiosity got the best of him. He set his book back down to see the professor sucking on her thumb and sliding metal pieces to the side of the table to make room for her textbook.

"Well now, let's get started, then I guess, shall we?" she said, thumb still in her mouth. "Hopefully your essays on energy applications pre-Day Zero are going well. Remember, you can always stop by my shop to talk if you need help. For now, though, I want you to take a look at what I have here!"

Griff sighed and wiped his forehead in frustration. *That essay...* He made a serious mental note to absolutely start right after his lunch time nap.

Professor Venn gestured at the large, white machine. "From my studies on old world technology, this is what they called a *portable air conditioning unit.*" With every word of the name, she pointed in the air to emphasize each part of the name.

"Most scholars I've been in contact with believe that this machine was used to cool rooms which were too hot. People before Day Zero didn't need to open their windows or fan themselves off with a wind spell. Instead, they kept their windows and doors shut and turned this device on instead.

"As you now know through our time together, as is the case with most machines, this too requires electricity. I myself have tinkered for many hours with this, and have gotten it to work on occasion. However ... I seem to overload the cooling mechanism, and it becomes more of a widespread ice spell than a room cooling machine ... Still have to work on that."

She thumbed through the pages of her textbook, going back and forth, muttering to herself as though she had forgotten which chapter they were on. "Ah! Here we go. Now, class, please turn to chapter nineteen of your books, and we will discuss how this device was used."

Students shuffled through their bags, pulled out their books and eagerly flipped to the page. Griff, less than eager today, thumbed through the book, page by page, until something made him stop abruptly. Scribbled in dark, black ink was a message Griff knew was just for him.

HE'S COMING FOR YOU

Griff's heart thudded hard against his chest. There was no denying who the "He" was in this threat. The message was in the same handwriting as what had been carved above his bed. Hands shaking, Griff continued flipping through his book. More messages had been scrawled on the pages. *You're not good enough. Watch your back. Join Korrun's army.* And the original message was back: *I know your secret.*

Mira looked up for the first time in minutes from her furious scribbling and peeked over to see what Griff was staring at. He slammed the book closed before she could see, causing Professor Venn to stop mid-sentence.

"Everything all right, there, Griff?" she asked kindly.

"Sorry..." he muttered. "I ... I don't think I feel well. I need to go lie down."

"Mmm, it is that time of year again, where you young ones can't seem to stay well. Take care of yourself, deary, and come see me if you need anything."

Griff nodded, packed up his things, and tried to ignore the questioning look Mira and the rest of the group gave him. She was too worried about classes and Altar Storm matches to have to help him with his own junk. He just needed a breath of fresh air and a nap.

Lost in his own thoughts, Griff stormed down the hallway. He turned the corner and yelped as he crashed into Connor Ofner and his plant, sending them sprawling to the ground.

"Sorry! So sorry, Connor!" Griff said, scrambling to his feet and helping Connor up.

"Rooty!" He screamed, diving back to the ground to pick up his purple and green leafed plant and brush as much spilled dirt back into the pot as possible.

"Is it okay?" Griff asked, knowing next to nothing about plants.

Connor placed his nose into the leaves and took a deep breath in. "Yeah. I think she'll be okay. Thanks."

"What are you doing out here, by the way? Aren't you supposed to be in class?" Griff asked, slightly annoyed. It had been his fault that he wasn't paying attention, but he was also not expecting anyone else to be around.

"Um ... nothing. Just taking Rooty for a walk. Gotta go!" He reached up and gave Griff a giant squeeze before dashing off.

Griff took a deep breath in, held it, then slowly let it out. He rubbed his face in both frustration and exhaustion.

"I really need that nap."

CHAPTER 23

Hushed whispers and groans of pain awoke Tyrell. His vision blurred when he opened his eyes, but it wouldn't have mattered much anyway. It was dark wherever he was. Only the flickering of a few torches pierced the surrounding darkness. He moved, then grunted as pain surged down his left arm.

Tyrell clenched his teeth. *Oh. Right.* His shoulder throbbed in complaint as he laid his head back down on the stone floor. *Where am I?* he thought to himself. He blinked a few times and carefully turned his head to gather his surroundings.

"Oh good! You're awake!" Ava half-whispered, leaning over to move the hair away from his eyes. She touched his cheek. "How're you feeling?"

"Like I just battled against the king's battlemages." Tyrell grunted.

"Well, you're back to your old self, at least." Ava laughed.

Kwame walked over, smiled down at Tyrell, then offered a hand up. Tyrell took a deep breath in and held it with his good hand, refusing to show weakness as he lifted himself off the ground. Still, to his frustration, a small grunt of pain escaped anyway. He nursed his left arm, careful not to move it too quickly.

"Where are we?" he asked Ava. She didn't answer. Not with words anyway. She looked all around the stone room. At her family and the small group of black cloaks huddled within it.

Tyrell nodded in understanding. *The safe place.*

"Stay right here," Ava said, before stepping over another passed out black cloak and walking over to an older woman at the entrance of the cave. The darkness of night seemed to almost invade the cave, seeping through the opening and smothering the light from the few torches that were lit.

The older lady that Ava had spoken with was having a conversation with an injured black cloak, one Tyrell recognized as Ivar. The man leaned against the opening of the cave, his eyes squeezed shut, hand clenched on his side, and he answered the lady's questions through short, pained breaths.

He was maybe a few years older than Kwame. His long, straight, gray hair had been pulled back into a tight ponytail. Tyrell remembered seeing him training with other non-magical black cloaks. He was a talented swordsman, but his training in spears had impressed not only Tyrell, but Ivar's training chief as well.

As talented as the man was with weapons, the gash on his side and the burn marks on the surrounding hole in his shirt told the story that Ivar could not. While Ava talked with the lady tending to the man, Tyrell looked around the rest of the room. There were people of all ages and backgrounds. There were some that were barely teenagers, others as old as the king. Ignoring their own wounds, parents fussed over their teens, tending to minor scratches and bruises as none were gravely injured.

Tyrell suspected that was intentional—the king's battlemages had saved the worst for the adults, sparing the younger ones as a mercy and a warning of what happens when you choose the side of evil.

Everyone well enough to help did so. Some bandaged nasty looking gashes, while others just tried to take attention off the pain with polite conversation. Short, whispered exchanges and pained moans continued to fill the space. Tyrell's eyes bounced from one person to the next, keeping count in his head. Not including himself, there were forty-two people packed together in this cramped room.

"I hear you need some help, love?" the older woman escorted by Ava said. She smiled kindly at Tyrell, her eyes affirming what he could already read about her: she was a genuine soul who wanted to help. She held out a hand covered in age spots. Tyrell, always taught to respect his elders, let go of his right shoulder and awkwardly grasped her hand in return.

"Veyla Vexley," she said, her eyes turning to his shoulder.

"Hi ... uh ... Tyrell," he answered through shallow breaths. "I ... uh ... I don't know how you can help."

"Well, trust me dear," she said confidently, letting go of Ava's arm and taking a step even closer to him. She smelled of dirt, sweat, and blood. None of it hers, though. "I *can* help. Do you trust me?"

"Uh, sure," he answered.

The old woman raised an eyebrow.

"Okay, yes. Yes, I do trust you."

Satisfied, she smiled and nodded, then hovered her hand over his shoulder and closed her eyes. He flinched when she reached for him, afraid she might try some quick move like Kwame had earlier when he set his shoulder back into place. The sudden movement sent a spike of pain through his injured arm, and he yelped. Ava tried to stifle a laugh, but received a quick glare from Tyrell.

"Hold still, now. As you can tell, I'm old enough to know what I'm doing." The old lady waved her hand slowly back and forth over his shoulder and about a minute later, he began feeling relief. The throbbing pain began to dull. Rather than a forceful hammer pounding pain down his arm, it was more like a gentle pat. Tyrell sighed as the relief, both physical and emotional, flooded him.

"There," she said at last. "It's not perfect, and you still need to take care of that thing." She pointed to his arm. "The inflammation is mostly gone, but it's still weak and needs time, now, more than magic. At this age, every day's a blessin', so don't go hurtin' yourself again, boy, as there's no guarantee I'll still be around!" She cackled to herself as she delicately ambled over to her next patient.

"*Now*, how are you feeling?" Ava asked.

Tyrell took a deep breath in, then released it. "Better. *Much* better. So, what is this? Why are we here?"

"What do you think, Tyrell? We needed a safe place to go, and this is *the* safe place we mentioned before. After you passed out, my dad carried you all the way out and we met up with the others who share their hate for Korrun."

"*All* these people here? They all hate him too?"

Ava nodded. "My parents have talked to everyone here at one point or another. Remember, for everyone, it was either join Korrun or die. They didn't choose *him*, they chose life. This is the first time we've all been together in one location. They're the only ones who knew of this place."

"You're the son of Randolph, aren'tcha?" a man called from the corner of the room. He pointed at Tyrell, and all eyes turned to face him. Suddenly the room quieted. Tyrell's cheeks felt hot; heat flooded the back of his neck. He didn't like attention on him, ever. Even when he'd done something good. Now, though, a group of unwilling black cloaks whose lives and homes had been threatened by Korrun were calling him out as the son of the second in command. There were no loyalists here. No one to stop them if they decided the son of Randolph Falkenburg didn't belong.

Tyrell stood tall and looked from one staring face to the next. Silent. Refusing to give in to their gaze. Refusing to back down and show weakness. Because he wasn't weak. He'd left his home, infiltrated Korrun's army, gathered intel, and had yet to be caught. He wasn't weak.

"Not anymore," Tyrell said finally. "That man you call Randolph Falkenburg is not the Randolph Falkenburg that raised me. That's who I came to save, but that man is dead."

Tyrell stared at the man accusing him. The man nodded with a look of acceptance. Something Tyrell didn't really want or need. He'd spoken the truth. Whether they liked it or not didn't matter to him.

"So what are you still doing here if the man you came to save is dead?" a mother holding a whimpering teen asked.

Tyrell looked to Ava as he tried to find words. He just didn't have any.

"I ... I don't know."

The room grew still again, save for the small groans of pain coming from the wounded.

"Tyrell may not have been able to save his dad—the Corruption is too deeply rooted in him now—but he *can* save us. And maybe more." Ava said, stepping forward.

Relief flooded Tyrell as attention moved to Ava, but he bristled at the way she seemed to make promises about him and what he could do.

"I've seen the good in him. I've seen the power. He's saved me more than once already. Tyrell is ... was ... the son of Randolph Falkenburg. A high-ranking soldier from the king's battlemages. Randolph taught Tyrell how to fight, *when* to fight. He taught him military strategy, survival skills. Tyrell might be too young to be a battlemage, but king's crown, he might as well could be."

Kwame proudly stepped beside his daughter and addressed the crowd. "What she says is true. We believe that this young man can help us work together to bring an end to this gruesome chaos."

Tyrell's cheeks flushed with heat. His heart pounded hard against his chest. He'd told Ava he would *think* about it. *Think!* He made no commitments, and now here she and her dad were, addressing a crowd of rebels and making him out to be some sort of leader that he wasn't. All those things they said were true. He knew he was a good fighter. Yes, he had *some* military training. But it's one thing to be a good soldier. It's another to be a *leader* of soldiers.

"So, what? Are you suggesting that this young bird lead us to take out Korrun? *And* his whole army?" another older man spoke up.

"I'm saying," Kwame said politely enough, but also didn't bother to hide his frustration, "that he has the capabilities to help us band together and do what each one of us has *thought* but never been able to *accomplish* alone."

"I wanna hear from the boy," an older lady said. "Are you willing to help us stop this madness and bring about peace?"

Tyrell ignored everyone else's stares and looked only to Ava. She had always seen the best in him. Gave him more credit than he ever deserved. It was both exhilarating and frustrating at the same time. She believed in him more than he believed in himself. But she was always pushing him to be better than he allowed himself to be. This was a clear moment where she thrust him into a place of having to step up. To lead. To save. He didn't care so much for the other people in the room. But he did care about her. And he didn't want to disappoint her. He may not be able to save his father, but if somehow this saved her? Then it would all be worth it.

He stepped forward, steadying his voice, forcing every trace of weakness away before he spoke. "Listen. I'm no leader, okay? Let's just get that out of the way. I didn't come here to be some leader of a rebellion. I just wanted my father back. But ... that's not going to happen. So. I can share what I know. I can teach what I've learned. But I'm not here to lead a group of people to their deaths. I came to save and that's exactly what I plan to do."

A warm but humid breeze washed over the town of Crystora Bay, ruffling Tyrell's longer black hair. Set atop a small hill and tucked into dense forest, the town overlooked the sparkling ocean—some twenty miles south of where Korrun's army had been secretly stationed. Crystora Bay had likely been built back from the coast to shield it from ocean storms, while still maintaining access to sea trade. The tall wooden walls at the back of town told Tyrell something else: nightstalkers were still a problem here. Perhaps they didn't have enough mages to protect them, like Solastran or Whisperspell.

He entered through the seaside gate, blending in with the crowds coming and going from the docks. The walk to Crystora Bay had been long and grueling. After waiting two more days in the cave to make sure it was all clear, and to give the wounded a little more time to recover, they made the trek to the nearest town. Some of the Forty-Two limped their way through the forest; others had to be levitated on makeshift wooden mats tied together with tree branches and rope. For now, they remained hidden just outside of town, waiting for the signal from Tyrell, Ava, and Kwame.

After nearly six months in the same encampment, Tyrell was more than ready for a taste of civilization. Not the people, but for the simple comforts a town could bring. The smell of spicy chicken and smoked sausages drifted through the streets. Palm trees swayed above cobblestone roads where shopkeepers called out to passersby, trying to draw them in. Mages and non-mages alike haggled in tight circles, arguing over prices and portions.

Together, Tyrell, Ava, and Kwame stepped up to a large shop off to the side of the town square. The worn, crooked wooden sign hanging above the door read: SEASIDE SHACK. Nailed to the door hung another sign with carved letters that read:

We don't care who ye are. Just pay yer tab. Also not responsible for lost limbs or coin. – Mgmt

Kwame cocked his head to the side as he read with a curious and questioning look.

"Hmph, sounds like there's some stories here," he said as he pulled the door open and waved Tyrell and Ava inside. On the outside, the Seaside Shack hadn't been much to look at. It was almost as if it had been put together by driftwood and rusty nails, but the inside told a different story. The walls were highly decorated with colorful paintings of pirate ships and fish, while from the ceiling hung the bones of an array of sea creatures. Some, were familiar, like the sea turtle or a shark. Others, he had never seen before, and didn't care to. Some had jagged bony spikes where fins should have been, others had multiple tails, and one even had a saw for a nose.

Tyrell paused under a large, menacing, shark-like creature with not one, but two lower jaws, each lined with razor-sharp rows of teeth. The larger lower jaw hinged beneath the smaller one, wide enough to fold completely over it—hiding the creature's inner grin, an unsettling sight for any ill-fated soul unlucky enough to witness it. Tyrell shuddered at the thought of seeing such a beast in the ocean waters. He imagined swimming next to it, its size already more than intimidating, then it pulled open its mouth to reveal a wicked smile underneath. He imagined Ava, of all people, would see this creature as one more reason not to swim in the ocean.

"Table for three, eh?" an older man with a scraggly red beard and a smile as wide as his face said. He carried two trays as he passed by the door. The aroma of steamed fish and buttered bread tickled Tyrell's nose, tempting him to snatch the tray for himself.

"We're looking for someone," Tyrell said flatly, choosing not to match the man's friendly tone.

"Well, someone's always lookin' for someone 'round here." He nodded toward the direction of the tables. "Have after it, then!" The man bounded toward a table off to the side, where a man and woman were holding hands and whispering sweet nothings to each other.

"Who are we looking for again, Tyrell?" Ava called, raising her voice over the rowdy patrons.

"Dunno. I'll know 'em when I see 'em," he responded. "This was the last known rendezvous location should we ever get separated, remember? They said someone would be here to direct us."

Suddenly a hand clenched Tyrell's shoulder tight. It wasn't Ava or Kwame, and it didn't feel like a friendly gesture. Tyrell whirled about, fists tightened, ready to face whoever had the gall to touch him like that. Then he stopped. He unclenched his fist and sighed in frustration.

"Theo."

"Yeah, well I'm not too happy to see you either, Tyrell. Was hoping the king's battlemages had gotten to you, just like you got to Liam."

"Nightstalker's *fury*, would you let it go? I didn't kill your friend, okay?"

Theo shook his head. "Not buyin' it. Anyways, Master Korrun left me here for any of you stragglers who couldn't keep up. He said follow the coast for another twenty miles, and you'll see them tucked away in the trees."

Tyrell groaned. "*Another* twenty miles?"

"You questioning Master Korrun, Tyrell?" Theo leaned in, his rancid breath as much of a weapon as his magic.

Tyrell sighed. "You know I'm not, Theo. I'm just ... we're *all* just tired, okay? I've got some injured with me, and they need their rest. We all do."

Theo shrugged his shoulders. "Not my problem. You do what you got to, but in three days' time, Master Korrun is setting off to his next location. We've got *much* farther to go this time. Apparently, we're not done seeing sand just yet. Master Korrun's got a lead on ... whatever it is he's after. He's dead set on finding it fast, too. At least we'll get to travel by nightstalker, though. We'll see if you can keep up."

Without waiting for Tyrell's response, Theo strolled over to his table in a dark corner of the room and pounded on it to get the waiter's attention. Tyrell imagined this had been his post the last few days as he waited for more black cloaks looking for direction.

Tyrell turned to face Kwame and his daughter. "We can't ask them all to travel another twenty miles right now. Some of them won't make it."

"And we can't just keep camping under the stars, either. We need something better than that," Ava chimed in. She clutched her stomach. "And we need food. Like ... now."

Kwame smiled and patted his pocket. The quiet sound of coins clinking together were barely audible over the noise. "Maybe we could all use a vacation here in Crystora Bay."

Ava gasped. "Daddy, really? We can stay here?"

"What about the rest of our people?" Tyrell asked. "There's no way you can put everyone up for a night ... can you?"

Kwame smiled, trying to be humble, yet Tyrell could see he stood a little taller. "Being an artifician has its benefits."

CHAPTER 24

"We good to go?" Griff asked Marth as soon as he returned from the common room.

"Think so. Pretty sure everyone's asleep," he responded, peeking through the cracked door as if he hadn't just come from that room. "Griff, are you sure we can trust Mr. Dingmann? I've never met the guy, and my sisters never spoke of him, either."

Griff shrugged his shoulders. "Sylva says we can. I may not trust this Dingmann guy, but I trust Sylva."

"Yeah … me too," Marth said, almost sounding defeated.

Vincent walked up and put a large hand on Marth's shoulder. "I'm gonna miss her being here, too."

Marth didn't say anything, only nodded and continued to look out through the cracked door into the common room.

Griff was glad that Marth and Vincent had finally come around after their disappointing loss in the Altar Storm arena. The loss they had taken because of him. It had taken some time, but after enough apologizing and doing their share of the chores around the dorm, they had finally forgiven him.

Mira, on the other hand, still had to be convinced.

Griff turned to Runa and got down on his knees. She had been fed, cleaned with some towels, and smothered with affection from Griff and the guys. It was time. She was too big to hide in the trunk now. It was impossible to sneak her outside any longer, and guilt tugged at Griff every time she had an accident in the room. It would be cruel to keep her here any longer, and Sylva had been working up to getting Mr. Dingmann's approval to house Runa in the stables.

"I'm going to visit you every day. Multiple times! You hear me, girl? Every. Day. You'll *love* being in the stables. You'll see Sylva"—her head perked up at the sound of his name—"and you'll get to have much more outside time too. But..." Griff held her head in his hands and brought his cheek to hers. "I'm still going to miss you."

She rumbled her affection and gazed into his eyes. Her big slobbery tongue slid up his cheek and over his left eye.

"Ugh! Gee, thanks girl." It took the entirety of his sleeve to get all the slobber off his cheek, but he appreciated the sentiment.

Vincent walked over and patted Runa's head. She closed her eyes, stretched out her neck, and nuzzled Vincent's chest.

"It's time," he said. "Better now than never."

Griff nodded and stood. "Okay, here we go. Marth, you're up front, Vincent in the back. We know the best way to go to get to the stables without running into someone. Especially professors. Marth, you got your papers?"

Marth turned and smiled mischievously before patting his back pocket. "Got 'em!"

"Vincent? Got your book?"

Vincent reached over to his bunk and pulled his library book off the neatly-made bed. "Hmm."

Finally, Griff turned to Runa. "You have the hardest job of all. *Don't. Get. Caught.* All right? Just be really quiet, stick to the shadows, and don't make a single sound. Can you do that?"

He took her excited body wiggle and slobbery kiss as a "yes."

Griff sighed. "All right guys, let's do this."

Together, the four of them crept through the dark common room. Griff made sure Runa didn't accidentally bump into one of the side tables or shove a chair to the side. Any screeching sounds coming from the sliding furniture was bound to send a few curious students their direction. Marth slowly and quietly opened the door to the hallway and peeked out. He turned and nodded to them before disappearing into the darkness. Griff started to follow, but noticed Runa wasn't immediately behind him. She had turned toward a side table where someone had left remnants of a spiced apple loaf from the evening's dessert. She gobbled it up, almost knocking over a marble statue of a lion. Griff caught it just before it *thumped* to the ground.

He put his fingers to his lips. "Shh!" She lowered her head in apology, then obediently followed Griff out the door.

Marth waited at the end of the hallway, just by the stairwell. He held out his hands as if to say, "What were you doing?"

Griff shook his head in frustration and pointed to Runa, who was still delightfully licking her chops. Vincent had to put a hand over his mouth to conceal his quiet laughter.

Marth peeked down the stairwell before waving the group to follow him. Runa's nails clicked against the stone steps, sending echoes in all directions. They paused at the base of the steps so Marth could scout ahead. While they waited, Runa opened her mouth and let out a big, loud yawn. Griff whirled around and tried to clamp her mouth shut, but the damage had been done.

"Girl, you gotta be quiet, okay?" Griff whispered. She shook the yawn off and nuzzled his side. "Okay, okay. I'm not mad at you, just... I don't want you to get caught."

At Marth's signal, they continued their movement throughout the castle. Runa had finally seemed to understand what it was they were trying to do, and didn't make a peep the whole time. It was her first time seeing the castle for herself. Ever since she had been nothing more than an egg, she had always been escorted in *something*. And the larger she grew, the larger whatever carried her had to be. So, naturally, curiosity tried to steal her attention, but Griff was always there to steer her back on mission.

They only had to pause once to allow the librarian to pass. Old Mrs. Finnegan clearly had nowhere important to be. She took her time, walking slower than they'd ever seen her, which only wore Griff's already diminishing patience. They were closing in on the courtyard, which meant they were close to the stables. Marth disappeared around a corner, and before Griff had a chance to follow, he heard Marth's voice echo loudly in every direction.

"Oh hi, Professor Burke!"

"Mr. Hayes? What are you doing out of bed?" she asked.

Griff pulled Runa to him and together they leaned against the wall, trying to blend in with the shadows. He could hear Marth rustling his papers.

"Well, I haven't been in bed, yet. I was just headed to see if Professor Venn was in her shop. I was working on her essay on energy applications before Day Zero and I had some questions. But, hey! Since you're here, maybe I could talk to you about it instead? You are the professor over Essence Corruption. I'm sure you know lots about stuff from the Old World too, right?"

Griff smiled. *Smooth, Marth. Real smooth.* He often gave Marth a hard time about most everything, but if there was one thing he was good at, it was talking himself out of situations. Granted, most of the situations he got himself into was *from* his talking, but if he could talk himself into something, he could talk himself out.

"Well..." Professor Burke hesitated. "Number one, you're headed in the wrong direction. Professor Venn's shop is *that* way. And number two, it's way too late for you to be out and about. You need to head back to bed."

"I know, I *know*, Professor. It's just that I want this essay to be *perfect*. I love talking about this kind of stuff and I really want to impress Professor

Venn. I'm learning so much. Like: did you know that there were these things called *fuses* that acted like a safety mechanism in electrical devices? They kept machines from using too much electricity and damaging the device or causing it to malfunction!"

"Yes, yes, Mr. Hayes. I'm fully aware of what a fuse is and how it works. Here. Let me show you to Professor Venn's shop. If she's there, great. If not, then it's straight to bed with you."

They passed by the opening to the hallway in which Griff, Runa, and Vincent were hiding, but Marth continued to talk, placing his paper in such a way that it blocked the professor's view of them. Griff knew that he owed Marth in a big way after this. Perhaps he would even talk to Kara on his behalf and get him a first date.

After they could no longer hear Marth's constant chatter, Vincent took the lead, passing through the courtyard and out to the back field with no issues.

Subtle firelight from the stables broke against the blackness of the night. Sylva sat at the entrance, waiting for his friends, and jumped at the sight of them.

"Where's Marth?" he questioned, a look of worry on his face.

Vincent chuckled. "Doing homework."

Griff laughed. "Yeah, he had to distract a teacher for us. He took one for the team."

"I think he enjoyed having a chance to talk," Vincent said. "He was probably about to bust with all the silence."

"So," Griff said, turning to Sylva. "Mr. Dingmann is in there? He's good with watching over Runa?"

Sylva nodded. "He said he was willing to meet with you. I think you're safe, Griff. I think Mr. Dingmann will take her and take good care of her."

"Wait, 'willing to meet' and 'agreeing to take her in' are two very different things. I've never met this man before. We've only ever snuck in here and used his stuff. Is he going to take her or not?"

"I *think* he will. I'm almost sure of it. He just wants to meet her first. That's all I know. But he's a good guy. Let's just go in there and see what he has to say."

Griff's heart pounded against his chest. Would Mr. Dingmann take Runa away from him and never let him see her again? Would he send her away to some … cage? Locked away forever? Doubt crept into Griff's mind and fear stole his courage.

"It'll be okay, I promise," Sylva said.

Griff could only nod in response.

Together, they all walked into the dimly lit stables. Magnus and Kindra laid next to each other on some hay. They raised their heads when Sylva and Griff entered, but they stood when Runa stepped in. They didn't snarl or bark at her. They had seen her many times before, whenever Griff came to weigh or measure her. The wargs stood to greet a friend they hadn't seen in awhile. Runa pranced over to her friends and nuzzled her head against their soft coats, which they returned happily.

"What a beautiful creature you have there, Mr. Driscoll."

A burly man with a thick horseshoe mustache that hung over a thick beard stepped into the light. His cheeks were rosy and his smile was warm. He wore simple cloth garments and held in his hand a young warg pup, who was trying to wriggle loose from his grip.

"Hello, Mr. Dingmann, I'm … my … my name is Griff, sir." Griff scooted past Runa and the wargs and shook Mr. Dingmann's free hand.

"Aye, I know who ya are, Griff. Sylva's talked you up quite a bit. Here ya go, why don't you hold this one, so I can meet Runa." He handed Griff the pup, who whimpered loudly at the exchange of hands. It took more focus than he realized to keep the warg pup from playfully biting his fingers, but eventually he got it calm enough that he could watch Mr. Dingmann's interaction with Runa.

He walked carefully but confidently toward her and gently called her name. She stopped playing with Magnus and Kindra and cocked her head at the man. She lifted up her nose in the air and gathered his scent. This wasn't the first time Runa had been here, and Griff realized that she must have picked up Mr. Dingmann's scent from her previous visits here. So, while she had never met him, she recognized something familiar. She took a few guarded steps forward, curiosity overriding caution. Mr. Dingmann held out his hand. The whole room, even the wriggling warg pup, paused to watch. Would she flinch? Would she bite? Would she lunge?

Gently, ever so gently, the burly stablemaster placed his open palm under her chin and called her name. Runa's body relaxed and her eyes closed. She rumbled her approval and leaned into the affection even further.

"Ah ha!" Mr. Dingman said victoriously. "You're a good girl, aren'tcha, Runa?"

She wiggled in response. After a few moments of bonding, Mr. Dingmann stood and placed his hands on his hips and smiled down at the dragon.

"You got yourself a cute dragon, Griff. I don't know how you hid her for so long, but I'd be happy to take her in and care for her."

Griff heaved a heavy sigh of relief. "I'd really like that, sir. She needs something more than I can offer her right now, but ... but I still want to be able to see her as much as possible."

"Aye, don't you worry about that. You might as well be her mother. She's bonded to you, it's clear to see that."

As if on cue, she pranced over to Griff and sat next to him, leaning her weight into his legs.

"Sir, um ... there's just one thing you need to know. The, uh ... the headmaster doesn't know about Runa."

Mr. Dingmann laughed. "Well, now, I figured as much. You wouldn't be meeting me here in the middle of the night if he did, now would ya?" He placed a hand on Griff's shoulders and looked him right in the eye. "You let me worry about Headmaster Aldamund, yeah? I got your back. You have nothing to fear."

CHAPTER 25

An explosion of light and fire blinded Griff. He shielded his face not just from the light, but from the fragments of the wooden box that had just exploded.

"See?" Professor Coen said. "Adding that light spell *into* the fire spell really adds an extra layer of danger and tactics to the battlefield. Hit your enemy *and* blind his comrades."

With a flick of his wrist, Professor Coen used a wind spell to push the charred remains to the corner of the practice room, where the other debris had been piled from their lessons so far.

"Your wind and fire spell that you cast at Korrun was impressive, but that was pure emotion. Now you gotta learn to *control* it; master it. Make it yours. You can do a light spell. You can do a fire spell. Now we need to combine them together, just like you did in your hometown ... just ... without all the teenage emotions."

Griff snickered at the professor's jab. Although these practice sessions were meant to be a punishment for sneaking off to save his family last year, he was quite enjoying learning how to fight. And if he was forced to do these training sessions, he was glad it was with Professor Coen. He was a good teacher. And friend. And Griff liked to think as much as he enjoyed having the professor's company, the professor liked it just as much.

Nodding at the professor's instructions, he grit his teeth and visualized the spell. *Fire. Light. Put them together.* He easily conjured a brilliant white light in his left hand, and in the other, he held a blazing ball of fire. Professor Coen stepped to the side and crossed his arms to watch, a proud smile forming. The fireball needed to be bigger. So, Griff focused his efforts and felt the energy shifting toward his right hand. He watched as the fireball grew to the size of a watermelon.

"You know what to do next!" the professor called. Griff nodded in response, refusing to lose focus.

He slowly, carefully brought the two spells together, trying not to burn his hands with the fire spell while still merging the two. With a thought, he sent the ball of light into the ball of fire, and as it entered, the light was snuffed out. Frustrated, Griff flung the fireball at the wooden box across the room anyway, watching it explode, sending fiery embers to either side of the room. At least *that* was still satisfying.

"Argh! I know, I know," Griff said, trying to beat the professor to the punch. "I lost focus as I was moving the light spell."

The professor closed his mouth, thought for a moment, then nodded. "Yeah. You pretty much nailed it." He stood next to his student. "But also, I think you're trying to be a little too careful."

"Too careful? Never thought I'd hear a professor say that to me."

"Yeah." He laughed. "And normally you would be right. But ... here ... watch."

As fast as lightning, Professor Coen conjured light and fire in each hand. In the blink of an eye, he'd slapped his hands together and pushed the newly merged spell forward, sending a brilliant, blazing ball of flame and light at a half-charred box in the corner of the room. Griff barely had time to close his eyes before the spell made contact, filling the room with the roar of the explosion and the blinding light that followed.

"That was so fast!" Griff exclaimed as he used his wind spell to clear the debris. The smokey smell of burning wood had filled the room, and Griff decided it was time to put an end to the smoldering splinters. He felt the moisture in the air and with a swift clenching of his fist, he pulled it all together and sent the water over the burning fragments.

The professor coughed and waved his hand around his face. "Yeah, I guess it was getting a little smokey in here. Nice water spell, too, Griff."

"Speaking of water." Griff walked to his chair next to the door and grabbed the canteen off it and took a massive swig. The cool water did much in bringing his internal temperature down. In addition to the fire and smoldering wood, the amount of energy he had spent practicing his spells was making him feel overheated. He wiped the sweat from his brow, took another big swig, then sat down—signaling his break to the professor.

"Good idea." Professor Coen sat next to Griff in his own chair and took a sip from his own canteen.

"So, I've been thinking about what you told me the other day. The messages you've been receiving? I think it *is* The Deceiver."

"I mean, who else could it be?" Griff answered. "Clearly, they're big fans of Korrun. They have it out for me, saying they know my secret."

"Which could be the shard inside you, or the baby dragon I've just now learned about," Professor Coen said, elbowing Griff's side.

"Yeah ... not my greatest moment. Sorry again." Griff took another swig and enjoyed the cool water that spilled down his chin and neck before making its way into his shirt.

"All is forgiven," the professor answered. "Anyway, I think it's time you read the letter we intercepted that one night. Well, the letter *Connor* intercepted that *we* then intercepted. Here." Professor Coen pulled out the carefully folded page from his pocket and handed it to Griff.

Griff wiped his hands and unfolded the letter. He had always wondered what the letter said, but was always too afraid to ask. He was learning to trust that if Professor Coen thought Griff needed to know something, he would tell him. This was one of those moments that confirmed that truth for Griff. The letter was much shorter than he had anticipated, and it didn't take him long to read it.

The Deceiver,

Your information is weak. Your tactics are sloppy. Keep a low profile. Keep an eye on everything you see. Especially the boy. He's critical to our success. Do better. Be better. You know whose lives are at stake here. Report back with better intel soon.

—K

"Especially the boy?" Griff asked. "Is he referencing me?"

"Aye, I think so. You said it yourself, you think Korrun knows you have a shard. I don't know what other boy in this entire school would be more important to keep tabs on than you."

"Well, yeah. But all I'm doing is going to class and learning about thermocouples. I'm not out conspiring against Korrun or anything like that."

"Who knows what he's after. I don't think he's in his right mind anyway. He's losing it. He's paranoid. But he's still dangerous. Any idea who this Deceiver character might be? You notice anyone following you or acting suspicious at all?"

"Hmph. Ever since my disaster of an Altar Storm match, everyone close to me has been acting off. I dunno. Nothing comes to mi—wait. You know what? Actually, the other day when I saw those messages written in my textbook, I *did* see Connor out in the hallway. He acted a little off. Distracted. But ... *Connor*? There's no way he'd be The Deceiver. Sure, he's a little quirky, but he's too innocent. Right?"

"You're probably right. But we did see him in the mail room late at night, too. *With* that very letter in hand, I might add. But it was probably just a 'wrong place at the wrong time' kind of thing."

"Yeah, I agree."

"But *still*, keep your eyes open and pay attention to your surroundings. I've danced this dance before, and you'd be surprised what people are willing to do to save their own skin."

The professor's words stung Griff more than he'd probably realized. It made him think about Kaden Horter. A name he hadn't thought of in what felt like an eternity. And though he never liked Kaden—after all, he was prideful, rambunctious, and always looking for any excuse to bully Griff growing up—he couldn't believe he and his family would side with Korrun. Just to save their own skin. He hoped that the Horters would survive their stupidity and come to the right side of things.

Professor Coen slapped Griff's shoulder as he stood. "Ready to get back at it?"

"Yeah, yeah. I guess," Griff mumbled, trying to shake his thoughts.

He cracked his knuckles and shook the tiredness from his bones. What he was doing here was important. No longer was this just a lesson on cool magic tricks. He needed to be ready for anything. *You know whose lives are at stake here.* Griff didn't know who Korrun was talking about, but he was right. There were lives on the line. And as much as was possible within him, Griff had lives he needed to protect.

He rolled up his sleeves, narrowed in his focus, and said, "Okay. Let's do this."

CHAPTER 26

For the first time ever, Vincent hadn't touched a single item on his plate. Stacked like a tower were several cinnamon flatcakes with a side of stagmoose sausage patties and a few over-easy speckled bramblehen eggs. While the rest of the school fueled up for the day's Altar Storm matches, Griff's battlegroup sat frozen, eyes locked in disgust on Marth and his new girlfriend: Kara Thorson.

Several days after Kara had pulled Griff to the side and asked about his relationship with Mira, Marth had decided to take his shot. He invited Kara to walk the streets of Solastran one Saturday evening and was delighted when she enthusiastically accepted. At first, Griff was happy for him, that he'd finally found someone. Griff had Mira, Vincent had Sadie—not that they'd ever admit it—and Griff knew Marth had always felt a little left out.

But the way Marth made it seem like no one else in the world mattered except for Kara, the way they kept giving each other googly eyes and ignoring everyone else in the room was getting annoying.

"Well." Griff coughed, trying to get Marth's attention, but he was too busy cutting Kara's cinnamon cakes for her. "Shall we talk some strategy? What do you think this match will be about?"

"Okay, well, we've had more *active* matches lately, right?" Mira said, leaning forward and pulling out her Altar Storm notebook. "But remember last year? We had a puzzle that needed to be solved. It was less ... build a pyramid with your magic spells and magic tiles, and it was more knowledge-based. So, I'm thinking it's about time for another one of those types of challenges. It's the end of the semester, we've been hit with a lot of information that we'll need to compile and use."

"Hmm, that's true," Griff answered. "But you know, Professor Coen's been really hammering in Essence Merging in our practice sessions. So, what if we—"

"—Or another idea I had was we haven't seen much Essence Crafting, either. Last year, the second years were given an essence crafting handle to use. Maybe we'll have to do something with that as well. What do you think, Sadie?"

Griff furrowed his brows in frustration. *Did she choose to ignore me? Or was she just so deep in thought she didn't realize that was what she was doing?*

Sadie shrugged her shoulders. "I'm up for anything, really. So long as I get a good fight in, I'll be happy."

Griff chuckled and said, "Well, we know we can always count on you for that!"

Sadie and Mira stared at him as though he'd picked a booger right in front of them. What was going on with them today? Mira sighed and turned back to the rest of the table.

"Vincent? You got any ideas?"

"Hmm." He pointed to his mouth, which was finally full of flatcakes. *At least* he *is acting normal now*, Griff thought.

"I'd love to see something from our Technomagical Applications class," Marth said at last, joining in with the rest of the group. "As the son of a well-known *literarian*," he eyed Kara to see if perhaps that impressed her somehow, "I'm very familiar with magic and machines."

"Hmm, that's a good thought," Griff answered. "What kind of challenge do you think that coul—"

"—You think it could be a simple all-out brawl?" Sadie asked, hopeful. "Like just two teams and the field and that's it?"

"Now, hold on a second." Griff huffed. "Why is everyone interrupting me or ignoring everything I say?"

Everyone silently stared at him. Vincent took another bite of stag-moose sausage. Nobody answered.

"Maybe they're just being more cautious, you know?" Kara said. "I think after your last match, tensions are still a little high..."

Everyone turned to look at her as though she had just shared their deepest secret. Marth gently elbowed her side.

"What? Sorry, I'm just reading the room, here," Kara said, clearly realizing she had just crossed a line. She stood and turned to Marth. "I'm going to throw my trash away. Can I get you something while I'm up, sweetums?" He shook his head and gave a cheesy smile before turning back to the group.

"Is it true?" Griff asked. "You don't want to include me because I messed things up last time? I said I was sorry! I thought we were over this by now. I've shown that you can trust me. I'm focused. I want us to win."

"Yeah ... I-I believe you, Griff." Mira placed a hand on his. "We just ... we just need a good win under our belts to close out the semester. Okay? Can you just ... listen and be present this time?"

Griff huffed loudly, regained control of his hand, leaned back in his chair, and folded his arms. "Fine."

Kara returned and as soon as she sat down, she scooted her chair as close as physically possible to Marth's and whispered loudly, "What did I miss?"

Griff rolled his eyes, snatched up his plate, and walked away. The holidays couldn't come soon enough.

Griff flexed his hands to try and bring feeling back into them. The blue sky and bright sun betrayed him. It looked like such a beautiful day outside, yet, it was freezing cold. Great. The first really cold day of winter and he had to spend it outside. He pulled his cloak tighter around him.

The sounds of excited students filled the air around him. It was a sentiment he couldn't share. He was left to walk several steps behind his tightly bundled battlegroup onto the Altar Storm pitch. Not once did anyone look back to see if he was keeping up.

His feelings of abandonment suddenly faded into the background when he noticed the dark metal wall halfway down the field. It stood about as tall as a two-story house—matching the height of the stands perfectly. Griff couldn't see the top of the wall, but it looked thick. Thick enough for someone to walk across it once they were on top.

To the far right of the wall, looking as though it were somehow attached to it, was a tiny room made of metal and glass. A tall rectangular box of windows. It looked like it could fit at most four or five people in it.

As if that wasn't strange enough, Griff and his group had now made their way next to the empty altar and stood around a table that held another contraption he had never seen before: two boxes connected by a string of cords. One box was large, bulky, and made entirely out of metal. The other one was shorter, but square and had a reflective surface that felt like glass, except Griff couldn't see through it. Sitting just next to the second box was the one thing Griff was slightly familiar with: a typewriter.

Griff sighed. Marth was right. This was going to be a technomagical applications kind of test.

"Welcome, welcome, students!" Professor Coen's excited voice echoed throughout the field. He hopped over the barrier between the stands and the field and landed on top of the metal wall. As Griff suspected, it was at least wide enough to walk across.

"Today, you won't get much instruction from me. You'll have to put your knowledge and your skills to the test to solve the puzzles before you today. The only thing I'll say is that you must retrieve your storm orb from the other side of the field and bring it back to your team's altar. It is locked away in a safe that cannot be forced open."

A safe? Griff thought, as he looked at the larger, bulkier box. *So that's where the storm orb is?* Griff's thoughts turned to the team on the other side. *This is what they're coming for.*

Professor Coen thumped on the side of his head with his forefinger. "Use your noggin. Think about what you've learned over the last several weeks and put it to good use. Rely on your teammates. Build a proper strategy. And remember: your professors are watching and protecting. Don't try any lethal tricks or you're *out of here.*"

He pointed to Griff. "Your team ready?" Griff huffed. As if they would tell him even if they were. He gave a half-hearted nod. The professor pointed across to the other team Griff couldn't see but knew to be Katrine Penderson's battlegroup. "Ready?"

Griff heard excited shouts in response.

"Okay, then. Let the match ... BEGIN!" At the professor's cue, colorful sparks filled the air in true Headmaster Aldamund style.

"Okay, okay!" Marth shouted to his team. "I know what that is over there!" He pointed to the tiny room of metal and glass. "It's called ... like ... a ... an el ... ele ... va ... elevator!" He screamed at last. "An elevator! It's old world technology that people used to get to higher places. So that's how we get up on top of the wall."

"Nice work, Marth," Griff said, though nobody acknowledged he said anything.

"Well, we need someone to go with Marth—'cause you definitely have to come help us with the machines—and I'm *down* to be protector," Sadie said confidently.

"Hmm," Vincent said.

"You'll come too, big guy," Marth said, reaching up and slapping his shoulder.

"I can come," Griff offered.

Marth looked to Mira.

"Well, Marth's got Vincent and Sadie. That's a pretty solid setup. Maybe you and I can stay back and guard this side."

"But! But I …" Griff grit his teeth. "Okay, fine. It's not like I haven't seen actual battle or whatever, but fine. We do need someone to stay back."

He stomped away from the group and pretended to examine the metal boxes on the table. He didn't know what to look for but needed to find something to do.

Marth, Sadie, and Vincent hustled over to the elevator. Marth barked some orders to them, but Griff couldn't hear what he said. Marth stepped in the room and Vincent and Sadie swirled their hands together in sync. The elevator shuddered violently, sending metallic screeching sounds across the field, but it did nothing.

Levitation spell, huh? Good idea, Marth, Griff thought, silently cheering them on. They needed this win.

After a few minutes, and more ear-piercing screeches, they gave up. Marth stepped out and they huddled back together. Finally, they pulled away and Marth walked over to the side of the elevator. He pulled open a small hatch and directed a string of lightning into the opening. Suddenly, lights appeared on the elevator and Marth ordered everyone inside. He mashed a button and the elevator lifted them to the top of the wall.

"Looks like a lightning spell is what powered that elevator thing," Griff said to Mira. He pushed his morning frustrations to the side. Time to earn their trust again.

With new purpose, Griff turned his attention away from the wall, where now he could see his team casting spells down toward the other team, and focused more on the object housing the orb.

"If a lightning spell powered the elevator..." Griff said aloud to nobody. "Then maybe we need to do the same thing here."

"Yeah, but Griff, this isn't our orb here. We just need to guard it."

"I know, I know. But if we can figure this part out, maybe we can help them over there."

Sounds of the battle ahead were escalating. Marth and Vincent were still atop the wall, but Sadie had made her way down to Katrine's side.

He examined every inch of the contraption in front of him. The metal safe was hooked to a typewriter and a box with a glass side. He didn't know what the box was, but imagined that the safe wouldn't open unless he did something to the typewriter and box. He looked behind the box and saw a tangle of cords and connectors.

"Here we go," he said, pointing to one of the cords and turning to Mira, almost as if he were asking permission to exist on his own team. Ridiculous as it was, he did *not* want to mess things up again. She nodded hesitantly, but that was all he needed. With a thought, he sent a small and controlled burst of lightning into one of the connectors. Nothing happened. He moved to the next, then the next. One by one, he directed lightning into each connector, until finally, he heard a soft *pop* and the glass on the front of the box flickered to life, displaying a message.

"Oh!" Mira exclaimed, staring at the screen. "I can't believe I didn't recognize this until now! I *know* what this is! Of course! This is a computer! People used this to gather information, kind of like libraries. But also, they could send messages from one computer to another. It was like having a library, teacher, historian, and messenger all in a single box! How could I have missed that?"

Griff placed a hand on her shoulder to calm her down, before she beat herself up too much. "It's all good, Mira. We all make mistakes sometimes." He tried to make it sound genuine and not sassy. He didn't know if he achieved that goal or not, but she seemed to take it well.

By now, Vincent and Marth had disappeared on the other side of the wall, their battle cries joining in with the other sounds of chaos.

"What's the message say?" Griff asked.

Mira read aloud:

I awaken at the intersection of fire and ice,

Measuring something specific sounds really nice.

If that's not enough, then let me say,

I can take that fire and make it play.

"King's crown," Mira whispered. "That tells us *nothing*!"

"Wait ... hold on." Griff reread the riddle line by line. Finally, he chuckled. He turned to Mira with a goofy grin painted on his face.

"What? What is it?"

"This whole time, I've been complaining about learning about these things and thinking it was completely useless. The answer is *thermocouples*!"

"Wait, what?" Mira almost flattened her nose against the computer screen as she read it again.

"Listen, thermocouples *measure* something specific: temperature differences between two metals. One hot and one cold."

"Fire and ice," she whispered.

"But I was reading recently in our textbook that it can also take heat and generate small amounts of electricity too."

"Take the fire and make it play," Mira repeated.

Griff crossed his arms in triumph. "Exactly."

Suddenly, Mira straightened from the screen and whipped her head toward him, eyes wide with surprise. She seized him by the shoulders and shook him hard. "Genius!"

She took a step backward.

"There's no *way* the others are going to get that, Griff!" Mira said in a sharp whisper, eyes wide at the sudden realization.

"Well, we need to give them that information, then."

"Um, okay. Well, you figured it out, you should go. I know you want to be in the action. They would probably appreciate you being there."

"No," Griff said, eyeing the wall. Katrine Penderson and another teammate, looking worse for wear, had made it to the top. "I'm staying here to defend the orb."

"But—"

"No, Mira!" He pulled her in close. So close he could smell the mint leaves she always chewed after breakfast. "It's time you trusted me. I can do this. You go play hero and give the others what they need. I got this."

"O ... Okay."

Griff didn't hesitate. "Let's go."

He escorted Mira to the other side of the field where the elevator was. It had automatically descended back to the ground, so all she had to do was open the door and enter. Griff found the hatch Marth had opened and sent a small burst of lightning into the opening. Mira pushed the button and ascended to the top of the wall.

By now, Katrine and her teammate had jumped off the wall, using a wind spell to slow themselves, and were running to the safe.

"Oh no you don't, Katrine!" Griff called. He dashed forward and sent a wind spell after her. She smirked and dodged it with ease. Before Griff could respond, her teammate, a boy named Rindle, cast a lightning spell that hit Griff square in the chest. While his battle armor took the brunt of the spell, it still seized his muscles and sent him flying.

The landing knocked the air out of his lungs and his body ached from the blow. Pain flared in his wrist. He could still move it, though. Probably just a sprain. He laid on his back and stared up at the sky. He'd been here before. Taken out by the other team and using it as an excuse not to fight. He could do it again. He could stay here and blame it on being outnumbered.

No. Not this time. Griff fought to regain his composure. He'd battled against Korrun and the nightstalkers. He'd faced the magical forest protecting the shard this summer and walked away. He was a fighter at heart. He wouldn't stop now.

He grunted and stood, ignoring the pain in his wrist and the fire burning inside his lungs. *Fire*, Griff thought. Suddenly, he had an idea. He extended both hands, keeping his eyes on Katrine and Rindle. In one hand, he conjured a white orb of light. In the other, a large fireball. He sprinted forward, wanting to make sure he was in range. With a grunt of effort, he smashed his hands—and the two spells—together and pushed the new spell out with all his might. A swirling, fiery ball of light flew across the field and landed on target: a few feet away from Katrine and Rindle. They yelped in surprise as the explosion of light and fire blasted them away from the safe. They battled to regain their composure, only to walk blindly in opposite directions from each other.

Griff knew from experience that the effects of the spell would wear off soon, so he took advantage of them and flung a wind spell their way. Not too hard, just enough to knock them back off their feet. He wasn't trying to harm. Only buy his team time.

As they struggled back to their feet, Griff dashed to place himself between them and the safe. He eyed the wall and saw the elevator on the opposite side rise with a battered-looking Marth inside.

Yes! Griff thought. Eyes wide with panic, watching a scene unfold below him, Marth clutched the storm orb tight against his chest. *Just a little longer...*

Rindle was the first to recover from Griff's onslaught. He wiped his eyes and awkwardly aimed a fire spell at Griff. It was probably going to miss, but to show he was in control, Griff responded with a lazy wind spell, which sent the fireball whizzing off in the opposite direction.

Red lightning crackled in Katrine's hands. Her scowl matched the intensity of her spell. Her blonde hair, normally well-groomed and styled, was frazzled and dirty. Griff's sense of control faded at the sight.

Griff sighed as she widened her hands and the red lightning flashed and danced as it grew. "Oh, boy."

She raised her hands, ready to cast the spell, when suddenly—for the second time in mere minutes—she was lifted from the ground with another wind spell.

"Sorry! Sorry! Had to be done!" Marth cried, shoving Rindle to the ground and rushing toward the empty altar next to the table.

"Aha!' Marth screamed at last as he placed the orb in its rightful place.

Colorful sparks filled the air and the crowd erupted in screams. It was over. They won.

"NO!" Katrine screamed.

Griff knelt to the ground in exhaustion. "We did it," he laughed. "Oh, king's crown, we did it."

Griff met the rest of his battlegroup in the tent just outside the arena. Everyone, even Sadie, had grins the size of a warg's wingspan. Marth tackled Griff to the ground, and Vincent joined, squeezing the breath out of him. But he wouldn't have it any other way.

"Nice work, Griff! Way to figure out that riddle!" Marth said, rubbing Griff's already messy black hair and jumping off him.

"Yeah…" Griff said through pained breaths. "Good job to you guys, too."

"That's what I call some serious teamwork." Marth placed his hands on his hips proudly.

Just then, Kara threw open the tent flaps and jumped into Marth's arms.

She squealed with glee and said, "Good job out there, sweetie! You did *such* a great job taking charge and leading the team to victory!" She planted a firm kiss on his cheek.

Vincent offered Griff a hand up, and once he was standing again, he felt Mira come from behind, wrap her arms around him, and squeeze tightly. He turned to face her.

"Hey, listen. I'm really sorry for the way I've treated you lately," she said sorrowfully. "You're right. I need to trust you more. And I do. I do trust you."

She gently took Griff's face in her hands and pulled him toward her. There in the middle of the tent, in front of the whole team, they kissed. An enormous weight dropped off Griff's shoulders. He was back. His friendships were back. His relationship was back. For once since the last Altar Storm match several weeks ago, it seemed like everything was going to be okay.

"Aww, c'mon guys, that's *gross!*" Marth said.

CHAPTER 27

This time of year was supposed to be about joy, laughter, togetherness, and generosity. But that was all about to disappear.

Houses were supposed to be adorned with ornate and magical decorations. And on the tables … food. Lots of food. By the end of the night, however, Tyrell and the rest of the black cloaks would destroy everything this holiday stood for.

Tonight, instead of families coming together, they would be torn apart. Holiday trees with dancing magical lights would burn. Tears of laughter would turn into tears of mourning. And there was nothing he could do about it.

He flexed his fingers and bounced from one foot to the other, just to give his anxious body something to do. Most would have thought he was just trying to warm up against the colder winter air. His heart thudded so hard he was afraid someone in the crowd of black cloaks would hear it. A large, bull-like nightstalker with spikes that jutted out from its side snorted next to Tyrell, startling him. Its glowing white eyes lit up the immediate darkness around them. Tyrell gritted his teeth. Any time he was close to one of these creatures of Corruption, he had to force himself not to stab them with his dagger. Even after all this time, it wasn't easy. Ava grabbed Tyrell's hand to try and calm him. It didn't help, yet he held on anyway.

Korrun's voice stilled the swirling evil whispers in the night. "We've lost some good men and women recently. Some by the hands of the king's *battlemages*," he spat. "Others by their cowardice. They will pay. They. Will. Pay. But for now, we need more supplies and more people."

The flames from the torches flickered and danced, causing Korrun's wicked smile to disappear and reappear in the darkness. He turned and stared at the town on the hill in front of them. Another town that had rejected his invitation. Another town that would now have to unwillingly give up their people and possessions.

"Not everyone understands our cause just yet. So, when we *don't* have willing suppliers, we *take* what's rightfully ours."

A roar of agreement from black cloaks and nightstalkers pierced the midnight silence. They were ready for blood. Itching for a fight. Korrun turned to face his followers. Sly smiles appeared on the faces of many in the crowd. They cracked their knuckles, stretched their arms, and gripped their weapons tighter. It was time.

"Go get them."

Tyrell was immediately shoved to the side as eager black cloaks sprinted ahead, wanting to be the first to shed blood. Tyrell sighed heavily, then sprinted along with everyone else, locking eyes with Korrun as he passed. He gave Korrun a knowing nod, hoping it was convincing enough. He couldn't show enthusiasm for such heartlessness. But he hoped he could feign a readiness to follow orders.

Nightstalkers and black cloaks slammed against the thick wooden gate still decorated with garland that housed twinkling magical sparkles of silver and gold. Dangling just below that were magical icicles that never melted. Until tonight. Tyrell smelled the burning wood before he saw it. Mages at the front of the line laughed with every spell they cast, hurling balls of flame in almost every direction. As if celebrating their own twisted holiday, the mages ignited their handles, crafting weapons of blue, red, yellow and green—so much green—that it lit up the surrounding darkness with festive light.

One mage, a bald man with a long, black, braided beard, crafted a large green mallet. The burning gate was weak now, as the flames had taken hold and climbed higher. He swung his weapon with all his might, connecting the head of the mallet at the center of the gate where the two doors connected and locked. The door exploded inward with a dazzling display of magic and fire, sending splinters flying dangerously through the air.

Tyrell wasn't exactly sure what to expect on the other side, but he knew better than to expect a sleepy, unsuspecting town.

And he was right. As soon as the barrier had been breached there was a single shout from the other side, followed by a roar of battle cries. The men of the city were ready. Standing side by side, the looks of holiday cheer were replaced by fierce resolve. Every man wielded whatever weapon he could find. Some had crafted their own out of makeshift handles. While the black cloaks had a vast array of colorful weapons and spells at hand, the weapons the mages on the other side of the gate had crafted were all uniform: red. Red swords, spears, hammers, and daggers glowed like burning coals and illuminated the men's hatred for the black cloaks. Tyrell couldn't blame them.

The black cloaks at the front line didn't wait. They moved quickly. Decisively. They wanted blood and they weren't afraid to step into the fight to claim it. An array of spells were flung at the men of the city but bounced off the bright red shields. They returned the black cloaks' onslaught with their own, launching fire, red lightning, and intense wind spells back at them. The two groups collided. Screams and shouts echoed over the roar of the flames. The clashing of metal against metal rang across the battlefield. Warriors from both sides were flung through the air. Nightstalkers leaped over the black cloaks and joined in the brawl, their snarls sending chills down Tyrell's back.

Though they resolved to protect their own, the men of the city were outnumbered and unable to best Korrun's army of nightstalkers. They began to retreat, leaving their fallen behind. The black cloaks pursued with menace.

Tyrell and Ava found Kwame and Amina standing by the gate, refusing to go in. Amina clutched her spear tightly in both hands, but Tyrell knew it was not because she was going to join in the fight. It was in case the fight came to her. The Adebayo family and Tyrell watched the battle unfold, refusing to take part. Tyrell knew they would have to act soon, though, lest they be counted among the cowards, or worse, disloyal.

Suddenly, Ivar, one of the Forty-Two, dashed toward them, stopping just before hurtling into Tyrell. His breathing was heavy and his eyes were wide with panic.

"What are we going to do, Tyrell?" Ivar looked back to the some of the other members of the Forty-Two. "We won't kill innocents, but we don't want Korrun to catch wind either."

"I ... I don't know." Tyrell stammered. He looked to Ava. She shook her head. Suddenly, she flinched when she heard a man's scream cut short by a nightstalker's attack.

Kwame stepped forward. "Those who are *not* mages need to skirt the outsides of the town. Find the women and children in hiding and help them escape. *But do it discreetly.* If you see Veyla, tell her only to heal the men in grave danger, but also discreetly."

Ivar nodded. "And those who *are* mages?"

Kwame turned to Tyrell, his eyebrows raised, passing the weight of leadership with just a glance. Every eye followed. He needed to think of something. Fast. The battle was heating up and the black cloaks were winning. He thought back to his last raid. The one where he'd killed Liam to save the family. It had been risky. But it had been the right call. Suddenly, an idea sparked.

"Okay, listen. We need to show that we're active. That we're fighting, but we *don't* have to show competence. Sling spells, but make sure they hit *the wrong targets*. Do what you can to make everything look like an accident instead of sabotage. Make people trip. Cast a wind spell that hits everyone, including our own, to make it seem like it was collateral damage. Got it? We'll frustrate a lot of people, but we might be able to save others."

The corners of Ivar's mouth turned up in a mischievous smile. "Excellent, sir. I'll pass on the word."

Tyrell snatched Ivar's hand as he turned to leave. "Tell the mages *it has to look real*. If anyone catches us foiling Korrun's plans, we'll be fed to the nightstalkers. A lot of lives are on the line here. Meet back here at the gate if things go south."

Ivar nodded, then dashed off to pass the message along.

"Good job." Ava squeezed his hand. "That's very clever."

Tyrell heaved a heavy sigh. "It's only clever if it works. Let's go."

They rushed past the smoldering remains of the gate and entered into the chaos. Tyrell regrettably jumped over moaning victims, silently hoping Veyla would get to them soon. They approached a group of black cloaks looting one of the houses. He could hear them laughing and talking as though on a normal job. Tyrell gritted his teeth, swirled his hands, and sent a blazing red fireball at the bushes on the side of the house. Suddenly, the black cloaks whirled his direction. Tyrell's heart dropped at their glares, but then he raised his fist victoriously and forced a smile.

"I can't let you guys have all the fun, can I?" he called.

They cheered in response and flung their own fire spells onto the remaining shrubbery.

Tyrell turned to see Ava's look of horror.

"We gotta play the part, Ava. It was a bush, not a person."

She exhaled and nodded. "Okay. Okay, let's do this." She pulled the bow that had been strung around her torso off and nocked in an arrow. Tyrell placed a hand on her shoulder.

"No. Remember what your dad said? You need to help people escape. You can convince the women and children you're to be trusted way more than Ivar can. He looks like he belongs here. You don't."

The back end of a building with a blacksmithing sign hanging from the front suddenly exploded, and cheers from the black cloaks responsible for it could be heard.

Tears filled the corners of Ava's eyes and spilled onto her cheeks. "I ... I don't want to leave you."

He turned her toward her, locking eyes to show the sincerity in his next words. "I don't want to leave *you*."

Ava took some deep breaths, wiped the tears streaming down her face, then nodded, gritting her teeth in resolve.

"You and your mom go and see how many lives you can save. I'll take your dad and we'll play our part. And cause as much of the right type of chaos as we can."

A small laugh escaped at his words. Ava pulled the bow back over her torso and nodded again. She pulled him in close, ignoring her parents' looks, and hugged him tightly. "Please be safe, Tyrell." Then before he knew what was happening, she lightly kissed his cheek.

Dazed, Tyrell could only stand there with his hand over his cheek as he watched Ava and her mom disappear behind empty buildings.

"I take it you didn't see that coming. You should have." Kwame said flatly. He pushed his glasses farther up the bridge of his nose. "I'm going to pretend I saw nothing as we have a job to do."

"R-Right," Tyrell answered, forcing down the warm feelings fluttering about.

Together, Kwame and Tyrell sprinted forward to join with the rest of the black cloaks. Not paying attention to the debris on the ground, Tyrell almost slipped, his foot sliding forward in an awkward motion. His ankle griped at his negligence, but he did his best to ignore it.

He reached down to see what had tripped him, and his heart sank. Tattered and torn, Tyrell held a rocking horse head in his hands. Carefully sewn and stuffed, this must have been a present for an unsuspecting boy or girl. These kids should be sound asleep, or at least trying to, as they would have been eager to wake in the morning to see their holiday tree bursting with handcrafted toys like these. Instead, they were trying to survive the night.

Tyrell gritted his teeth and clenched his free hand. What he was doing mattered. Difficult as it was, it was the right thing to do. He released his grip on the stuffed horse head and watched it topple to the ground, settling in the dirt next to other toys and household objects that had been blown into the street by the black cloak's destruction. Then he saw it. A small, paper pouch with the words TWILIGHT ROSE SEEDS written in curling, artistic font. He stuffed the packet quickly into his pocket. One day he would give these seeds to his mother. One day when he was finally home.

Kwame, unaware Tyrell had fallen behind, stood just ahead watching the scene in the town square. Tyrell joined him and watched the horror unfold. Some black cloaks had forced their way inside homes and shops, taking what they could and destroying the rest. Others were locked in a fierce battle between the guardians of the town. Reflected spells screeched through the sky. Steel clanged against steel. Claws raked against flesh. Soldiers from both sides fell one by one.

Kwame reached into his pocket and pulled out an oval shaped, metallic object. He held it out and hesitated, staring at it as though it was an unusual food. He shook his head, muttering, "Here we go," then pulled out the circular pin from the top of the object and rolled it next to a man who was surrounded by nightstalkers.

Tyrell turned to him in panic. "What did you just thr—"

BOOM! The object exploded in fierce light. The force from the explosion sent all the people and objects in the surrounding area flying backward. Tyrell landed on his back. Hard. He ignored the pain and jumped to his feet in shock. Where the object had exploded now stood a two-story swirling vortex of horror. A tiny tornado that barely reached above the rooftops zigged and zagged forward into the battle. Those lucky enough to see it coming dodged out of the way just in time. Those who weren't were sucked in, then sent flying out.

Mouth opened wide, Tyrell, along with everyone else turned to look at Kwame, who stood watching and stroking his white goatee in fascination.

"Unbelievable," he whispered.

"What. Was. That?" Tyrell asked incredulously.

Kwame shrugged his shoulders. "Essence Grenade. I *am* an artifician. This is what Korrun recruited me for ..."

Kwame walked toward Tyrell and whispered, "And it follows our plan of sabotage without *looking* like sabotage, right?"

"Absolutely," Tyrell said. A laugh of disbelief escaped as he watched the tornado fling a group of badger nightstalkers into the side of a brick building.

"An ... essence ... grenade ... What else you got?" Tyrell asked eagerly. Kwame's chaotic inventions might just be the spark that could turn the tide. Or the match that would set Korrun's plans ablaze.

"Well, let's see." Kwame pulled out four more grenades. Each one with a differently colored string tied to the top. "I have a"—he checked the string attached—"another tornado one, but I think this one has fire in it."

"Too destructive," Tyrell said quickly.

"Then I have a water-lightning mix I've been itching to try..."

"Too lethal."

"Oh! I know!" Kwame stuffed the grenades back into his pocket and pulled out two with identical strings.

An eager glint flashed across his eyes as he pulled the pins on both grenades and launched one at a cluster of black cloaks and another at a group of townspeople.

"What were those?" Tyrell screamed at Kwame, hoping they weren't as lethal as the water-lightning grenade he had mentioned.

"Watch," Kwame pointed.

The essence grenades exploded in sync. Tyrell shielded his eyes from the blinding light, but as soon as he brought his hand back down, the ground at the explosion sites began to rumble. The debris from the battle bounced against the cobblestone street. Suddenly, a full circle of earth punched up through the cobblestones and rose to the height of the tornado from the previous grenade. It was a giant, circular, earthen wall, trapping its inhabitants inside.

"Brilliant!" Tyrell slapped Kwame on the shoulder.

Kwame said nothing, only looked at his new invention with pride, watching as the free black cloaks did what they could to rescue their comrades. Kwame waved a hand at them and shouted, "Sorry! Trying some new things out for Master Korrun!"

The comical moment didn't last long. A large fiery blast detonated Kwame's earthen wall that housed the black cloaks. Nobody inside survived. Tyrell looked around, trying to see what civilian could have sent such a devastating spell. The only problem was that it looked as though the spell had come from above.

Just then, a mage and their warg landed in the town square and flung spell after crushing spell, eliminating each black cloak it encountered. Tyrell didn't need to see the silver wolf's head on their cloaks to know: The king's battlemages were back.

More men and their wargs joined in the fray. Some of the men from the town saw the reinforcements and turned to fight alongside them. The black cloaks were no longer in control. Their laughter turned to shrieks of fear or pain that warmed Tyrell's heart. Korrun's followers dropped their loot and ran toward the city gates, but were met with more battlemages.

Kwame and Tyrell watched with glee to see Korrun's plans being foiled even further. A battlemage's lightning spell whizzed past them, pulling Tyrell out of his daze. The battle was coming to them. It was time to find Ava. Her heart might belong to the king, but her uniform marked her as Korrun's—and the battlemages targeted anyone in his colors.

"Time to go!" Tyrell shouted at Kwame. They turned and sprinted back toward the gate, hoping Ava and Amina would be nearby. Tyrell dodged an ice shard aimed at his chest. He rolled on the ground and cracked a lightning spell at the battlemage's feet, shooting dirt and debris into his face. The man rubbed viciously at his eyes, trying to recover his vision, when Tyrell hurled a powerful wind spell at him, knocking him off his feet.

Then he stepped in front of Kwame and cast a shield, protecting them both from a fire spell.

"Stay behind me!" Tyrell called back. Together they marched forward, Tyrell doing his best to deflect spells and disarm their mages. They slowly made their way to the gates, where the black cloaks fought to escape. The battlemages were fierce combatants, and the black cloaks were no match this time. They were spread too thinly around the town and the king's battlemages had their numbers and unmatched skills.

Suddenly Kwame snatched a black cloak from the crowd, pulling him behind Tyrell's shield. An older man with long gray hair pulled back into a ponytail. He wielded a spear that was now covered in blood. Ivar was back from his mission.

"Have you seen them?" Kwame asked Ivar, eyes wide with panic. "Ava and Amina? Have you seen them anywhere?"

Ivar shook his head. "We got separated when the battlemages showed."

"Daddy!" Relief flooded Tyrell at the sound of her voice. "Tyrell! Oh, king's crown, it's so good to see you!" Ava and her mother fought through the crowd and stood behind Tyrell's shield.

"Are you all right?" Kwame yelled above the noise. "How did it go?"

"We saved as many as we could!" Amina answered. "The battlemages came, and we left before they spotted us!"

The onslaught of spells were becoming too much and Tyrell couldn't make his shield any bigger. He didn't know if he could protect everyone or how much longer he could keep it up. He was getting tired, and the king's battlemages were just getting started.

"We need to move! Now!" Tyrell commanded. "We gotta push through this wall of battlemages if we're going to survive!"

Suddenly, a large ball of ice exploded onto Tyrell's shield, but embedded in the ice ball, was a brilliant white light. As the ice exploded, so did the light into the darkness. The powerful spell sent Tyrell flying back, knocking his entire group to the ground. Tyrell fought to regain his vision, but it was useless.

Blinded by the light, he scrambled to his feet, only to get gut punched and shoved back to the ground. Reeling from the attack, Tyrell could only clutch his stomach and writhe on the cobblestone street. His vision started to come back into focus, and he almost wished it hadn't. Standing above him with a look of fierce resolve was a battlemage, who had crafted a large, blue axe blade. He held it up high over his head, ready to swing it down and end Tyrell. The pain in his stomach was so overwhelming, Tyrell couldn't do anything but hope it would end soon.

A look of surprise suddenly dawned on the man's face. He dropped the weapon and sank to his knees. Randolph Falkenburg walked over, anger radiating from every feature on his face. He kicked the stunned soldier over and offered a helping hand up for Tyrell.

"Th-Thanks," Tyrell gasped, still barely able to breathe. He continued gripping his stomach as he helped the others around him. Randolph barely acknowledged his son before pulling his guns back out of their holsters and disappearing into the chaos, his shots joining in with the chorus of the other battle sounds.

Tyrell eyed the soldier nearby, writhing on the ground, blood spilling from his side. This was the same man who spared Tyrell's life back at the camp near the water. Thinking Tyrell was still fighting on Korrun's side, this man was going to make good on his promise to bring swift justice. Tyrell looked around and found an empty alleyway.

"Quick! Help me!" Tyrell called to Ivar. The older man cocked his head to the side when Tyrell snatched one of the soldier's legs, triggering a fresh wave of pained screams. "Ivar! Let's go!" Tyrell commanded, snapping the man out of his confusion. He nodded at the young mage's orders, gave his spear to Kwame, then copied Tyrell. Ignoring the cries and threats from the soldier, they dragged him to the alleyway.

Tyrell turned to Kwame and Ivar. "Find Veyla Vexley and bring her here." The two men nodded, then turned at once and disappeared back into the fray.

"Listen, I don't have much time. You know who I am. I am Randolph Falkenburg's son. I am *not* loyal to Korrun. I came here to get my dad. He's too far gone. Now, I am here undercover on behalf of the king. There are those here who do not willingly bend a knee to Korrun. We're going to fight back."

Just then, Kwame and Ivar stepped back into the alleyway with Veyla. She looked weary from battle. Her black cloak covered in blood, but Tyrell saw no open wounds. Likely she had been healing those on the battlefield. It was her gift. And now it was time for her to use it for an even bigger purpose.

"For now, though, I have a message I want you to take to the king. I know where Korrun's headed." Tyrell leaned low, ignoring the man's pained sputtering, and whispered in his ear. The soldier's eyes were wide with realization. "I'm hoping to see you and the other battlemages there."

The soldier locked eyes with Tyrell, fought through his pain, and muttered, "I ... will tell the ... king."

Locking eyes with Veyla, Tyrell only needed to give her a nod, and she understood. This man must survive this battle.

Leaving Ivar in charge of Veyla's safety, the rest of the group emerged from the alleyway and ran toward the gates.

"Oi!" a cocky voice called from behind. Tyrell gritted his teeth and turned. The blond boy, Kaden, and Theo marched with purpose toward Tyrell, ignoring his look of annoyance.

"What were you all doing in the alleyway? Huh? I demand answers!"

"Watch out, Kaden. Tyrell's been known to off black cloaks when they get in his way," Theo teased.

"I don't answer to you two, and we don't have time for this."

Tyrell turned his back and walked toward the ongoing battle ahead, looking for an opening. A rough hand clenched on Tyrell's shoulders and forced him around.

"You were talking to one of the king's battlemages, weren't you? What did you tell him?"

Tyrell knocked the blond boy's hand off his shoulder and slugged him in the jaw. Hard. Theo tensed and clenched his fist, but maintained his position.

"We don't have *time* for this!" Tyrell argued. His anger flared. Not just because he was being held up from protecting Ava's family, but because he was on the verge of being caught. Again. And with Theo and Kaden working together, it was only a matter of time before they stopped accusing and started taking action.

"If you *must* know, you two nosy little nobodies, the soldier in the alleyway is dying. We let him do so in peace. Now, for king's sake, leave us alone or you'll join him."

Tyrell turned to Ava and the others. "Let's go."

He didn't look back, but Tyrell pictured a look of shock on both the boy's faces. He wanted to watch Kaden nurse his jaw as he watched them leave, but kept his back turned instead. Though a battle around them raged on, that imagery gave Tyrell a deep sense of satisfaction.

By this time, the other black cloaks farther in town had retreated and joined in the battle at the gates. Stepping in to join Tyrell and the Adebayos was another mage from the Forty-Two. Doran was a fierce fighter whose personality mirrored the fire he brought to every fight.

"Trying to break through!" Tyrell called. Doran wiped the dirt off his brow and nodded. He marched beside Tyrell, crafting his own shield. Together, they protected those behind them as they moved closer to the battle. Ivar and Veyla joined them minutes later, Veyla exhibiting signs of exhaustion. She was too out of breath to talk, but the look she gave Tyrell was all he needed to know: Mission accomplished.

Soon, others from the Forty-Two joined. Those who were mages stepped to the front, shielding the others from spells. It was a slow, brutal fight. They stepped over the bodies of nightstalkers, black cloaks, and townspeople. The king's battlemages were in control of this area, and breaking through the crowd seemed impossible. What could he do? He had his people to protect. People who were all trying to thwart Korrun's evil schemes. They were on the same side as the battlemages, but he couldn't tell them that.

A screech from the air pulled Tyrell from his thoughts. A flock of large, eagle-looking nightstalkers swooped in from the night sky. Their razor-sharp wings raked against the battlemage's armor. The damage might have been minimal, but it sent them flying backward, nonetheless. Soon, a pack of feline nightstalkers joined the fray. Suddenly the attention was off Tyrell and his group and onto the new nightstalker forces. For all Tyrell cared, they were absolutely expendable. The more expended ... the better. The nightstalkers created a large gap in the wall of battlemages, giving Tyrell and his group the chance to escape. They sprinted past the gates, shields down, and out into the night. Away from the fight.

Tyrell glanced behind him. The town, once beautifully decorated in holiday spirits, was now scorched and splintered.

Suddenly, it hit Tyrell. Tomorrow would be his one-year anniversary of leaving his own town. His home. Also neatly decorated with magic and care. His heart sank even lower. He patted the pouch of seeds in his pocket, then clasped Ava's hand in his and together they retreated to their camp. A lingering thought stayed with Tyrell. One he knew he wouldn't be able to shake as he thought about his home: He just hoped all of this was worth it.

CHAPTER 28

The twinkling lights housed within the pine tree didn't come from Griff—a fact he'd almost resented had it not looked so beautiful. Lighting up the corner of the Driscoll's living room in a soft, warm glow, the tiny, magical balls of light slowly danced in a downward spiral until they fell like snow and disappeared before hitting the floor. It was a never-ending light show filled with complicated magic that captivated Griff, especially now as it battled back the early morning darkness.

Marth, the self-proclaimed champion of all things Christmas, had insisted the Driscolls incorporate the lights in their tree. Something they'd never had before. To Marth, it was tradition. To the Driscolls, it was one more reason to love magic. Before leaving to spend the holiday break at Marth's, the battlegroup had stayed the prior weekend with the Driscolls. When they weren't helping with decorations, Marth, Vincent, and Sadie learned about the non-magical art of blacksmithing, while Mira helped Leena in the garden. Griff was exhausted trying to find excuses to keep his girlfriend and mother from being alone together for too long. He'd never brought a girl home to his parents, but knew his mother well enough to know she wasn't afraid of making things awkward. There were plenty of embarrassing moments in his childhood he didn't want shared. And honestly, he was just as afraid of the "interview" his mother would inevitably put Mira through.

Then there was Runa. Ever since he'd discovered her egg, he had worked tirelessly to keep her a secret. Now, though, the secret was out.

After spending time with her for himself, Mr. Dingmann talked to Headmaster Aldamund about caring for the dragon. After the headmaster's approval, it was then that he suggested she no longer be a secret. After that, word about Griff's pet dragon spread like wildfire.

Mr. Dingmann and Griff agreed to train her—not to weaponize her, but to ensure she only ever acted in Griff's defense. She was still a dragon, after all. And while she might always see herself as Griff's protector, that didn't mean she had to stay hidden. Powerful and dangerous as she was, they didn't have to train the dragon out of her. They just needed to make sure she was good.

For months, Griff hid her like something to be ashamed of. Now, he played with her in his back yard. Kids and their parents from all over town stopped by and asked to see Runa. His dad had even hammered out a metal sign that read: "Beware of Dragon" that hung next to their front door.

Seeing the faces of the neighborhood kids light up when Runa nuzzled their tiny hands unshackled Griff from the burdens he'd carried with him this whole time. He felt so free having his secret come to light. There was no more hiding. No more sneaking around. He had the support of his family and friends. Sure, there was the occasional, "Why do you harbor a weaponized animal in your backyard?" But Griff's parents were readily available to back their son up if it was ever needed. Besides, Runa's surprisingly loving and whimsical personality usually won the naysayers over.

Now, she was curled next to the fireplace, enjoying the fire Gale had started the night before. He had brought Runa over to see if she could start it with her own flames, but to no avail. Only dark smoke puffed from her nostrils instead.

Griff wondered if developmentally she wasn't ready. But he also had his suspicions that she wasn't really interested in trying any new tricks. He could tell she was tired and perfectly content to be lazy. She had every right to be after the previous day had been filled with an endless supply of meat, chin scratches, and all her favorite people. Now, she slept deeply. Her chest rose and fell in a slow, steady rhythm. Tucked protectively under her chin was a large, stuffed dragon that Leena had crafted herself over the break. Runa fell in love the moment she saw it, gingerly carrying it around the house as though it was her own hatchling.

When Griff had walked into the living room earlier, she had peeked open a single eye, but when she saw who it was, she adjusted her chin on her stuffy and fell back to sleep. Griff was surprised she didn't leap from the floor with excitement when she realized he wasn't in his pajamas but was instead dressed in outdoor gear. Still, he couldn't blame her. It was early, the sun hadn't risen, his mother's newly acquired chickens hadn't started their morning commotion, and Griff was sure the food coma was still very much in effect.

It didn't take long, though, for the sleep to wear off. As soon as Griff heated up the stove and the sounds of sizzling stagmoose sausage wafted over toward Runa, she shook the sleep away and bounded toward Griff.

"Yeah, yeah, I thought that would get you up." Griff yawned and stretched. Runa, mirrored him with a wide, smoky yawn of her own. Her long, pink tongue unfolded out, then zipped back in after the yawn was complete. Then, almost like a cat, she stretched her back and unfolded her wings. They almost reached either end of the kitchen, scooting a chair across the wooden floor. It wouldn't be long before she would be too big for the house. And before she would breathe fire... Griff waved the smoke away and dismissed the thoughts just as quickly, hoping he wouldn't have to deal with either of those anytime soon.

"You get first bite, but only a bite, okay? You have to share with the rest of us. Including Sylva. He's going hunting too."

At the mention of Sylva's name, Runa's head perked and she looked toward the front door.

"Not yet, girl. Not yet. Soon, though, okay? You can even answer the door if you want. Just ... don't wake Mom right now. You wake her up too early, and trust me when I say, you won't be the scariest creature in this house anymore."

The snow crunched under their boots. The winter breeze tried to cut past the warm layers Gale, Griff, and Sylva wore. But they had come prepared. The dazzling white snow was almost blinding, reflecting the sun's rays back into Griff's eyes. They had borrowed some horses and rode straight out of town and deep into the woods. At first the horses reared up at the sight of Runa, but like every other time she encountered a skeptic, they came around quickly.

The two-to-three-hour ride had been mostly uneventful. Runa especially enjoyed the travel. She jogged most of the way, but sometimes would flutter just above them, taking the opportunity to practice her flying. Her excitable up-and-down antics provided the group with plenty of entertainment. Griff had never really pushed to see what her stamina was like, but clearly, she had a lot. When they arrived at the edge of the forest, Gale tucked his map away in his pack and hopped off his horse.

"Ahh, we made it!" He stretched out his back with a loud grunt. "Bram said we'd have no trouble finding game here. I'm excited to see what all's runnin' about out there."

He detached the cart from his horse and walked it into the shade of the forest, where he, Griff and Sylva fastened their lead ropes to the trees. They set out hay and some water before venturing farther into the woods.

The only sound that could be heard besides their own footsteps was the gentle swaying of the tall pines, the occasional tweet of an unseen bird, or the random muttering from Gale as he studied Bram's map—repeating stories about places to check out, and others he said were best left alone.

Even Runa seemed to understand that stealth was the goal, as she tiptoed through the snow, rather than bounding through it like she had on their way.

"We're gonna walk about another half mile, where we should stumble upon a small pond," Gale whispered. "Bet'cha we find a stagmoose or some deer or, I dunno, somethin' there."

Griff nodded, readjusted his bow hanging around his torso, then he and Sylva began whispering amongst themselves. They talked about Sylva's apprenticeship and all the tasks he had been assigned over the course of the semester. Surprisingly, it wasn't Runa that had caused them extra work. Instead, the baby wargs had created a lot of chaos for Sylva and Mr. Dingmann. Runa had been on her best behavior in the stables. So long as she stayed fed, it didn't seem like they would have to worry about any missing animals.

"Shh!" Gale commanded quietly, putting a finger to his lips. He pointed ahead to a clearing where a pond glistened in the late morning sun. A thin, delicate layer of ice clung to the edges. The kind that would crack under the faintest of pressure. In the center, the water remained unfrozen, the gentle breeze rippling the water, spilling it onto the ice.

Sylva pointed to the side of the pond, directing everyone's attention to the tracks in the snow.

"Stagmoose," he whispered.

While Griff had experienced a lot of new things in this past year, hunting a stagmoose was familiar territory. He lifted his nose to the breeze as it wafted a musky odor his direction. Definitely stagmoose.

"It's near," Griff added quietly.

In response, Gale pointed to the other side of the clearing. The bark was missing on a few of the trees, and more tracks led deeper into the forest.

"Let's circle around the clearing and see if we can find it resting nearby," Gale suggested.

Griff locked eyes with Runa. "If you want more stagmoose sausage, now's the time to be extra quiet. Deal?"

A wet tongue on his cheek was the only response she gave.

"Awesome…" Griff wiped the saliva off his face with his sleeve. "Let's go."

Slowly and quietly, they navigated through the snow, trees, and bushes, careful to make sure they didn't snap any twigs or rattle their arrows in their quivers. Runa stayed right next to Griff, only taking a step after he did first. She hunched low to the ground, her furry ears perked to listen for any trace of sound.

Gale signaled for everyone to stop. He cocked his head and listened intently. Quietly, he pulled his bow off his chest and nocked an arrow, though he didn't draw the string. Pointing the arrow toward the ground, he turned and whispered to Griff. "See that ledge up there?" He motioned with his head. About an Altar Storm's pitch away stood a small cliff overlooking the valley they were currently standing in. "I want you and Runa to head up to the cliff while—"

"—But Dad!" Griff hissed quietly. "She'll behave, I promise! She's well trained!"

"Just listen, son. Sylva and I will circle behind the stagmoose, and get it to run from *us* … toward *you*."

"Oh," Griff said awkwardly. "Okay, yeah. That makes a lot of sense."

Gale gave him an annoyed smile and shook his head. "It'll be too focused on escaping what's behind it, so that you can come in with a nice clean shot. If it's not a kill shot, you've got Runa and your magic to help. Got it?"

"Got it."

Griff and Runa quietly marched to the top of the hill, where not only was the view incredible, but it also gave him the vantage point to see the large stagmoose munching on some leaves. From here, he could also see his dad and Sylva stepping into their positions. Though Griff and his dad had hunted these beautiful animals for years, seeing one in real life never ceased to amaze him. Their large, thick, curved antlers intertwined with one another, making a breathtaking display of beauty and power.

Griff knelt on a single knee, pulled his own bow off his torso, and nocked an arrow in place. Then he reached down and felt his sword handle, to make sure it hadn't fallen along the hike up. Gale and Sylva were almost in place, so Griff calculated where he thought the stagmoose would run based off their positioning and angled himself in that direction, readying his bow for a shot.

Considering stagmoose were fast and easily spooked, Gale and Sylva rightly stayed just out of range and motioned for Griff that they were ready. Griff nodded and loosened his shoulders and neck.

Runa lifted her nose to the air and sniffed deeply. Her eyes widened and she hunched low to the ground. A low rumble vibrated deep in her chest. Oh no. She smelled the stagmoose! If she bolted right now, she would spook the unsuspecting creature and their entire hunt would be ruined.

"Runa!" Griff whispered sharply at her.

The stagmoose stopped mid-munch and perked its ears. It jerked its head to one side. Then the other. Griff, Sylva, Gale and Runa—king's crown— everything, even the whole world stood still, as if holding its breath. Waiting to see what would happen.

The stagmoose bolted.

Heavy as this creature must be, it was surprisingly agile in the face of danger. It crashed through the brush and dashed away from the cliff Griff stood on.

Griff growled with frustration. It was too far for his arrows now. But ... maybe not for a spell? He dropped his bow and arrow, eyes trained on the speeding stagmoose, and then quickly lifted his hand and flung a blue bolt of lightning at the beast. Snow exploded at its feet. It was a miss. But the stagmoose stumbled to the ground. Without waiting, Griff hurled another one, this one hitting its hind leg. It flailed wildly on the forest floor, flinging snow and dirt into the air. Its desperate bellowing echoed through the forest unanswered.

"Let's go!" Griff hollered at Runa. He quickly loaded his arrow back in his quiver, threw the bow back around his torso, and began his careful sprint down the hill. He didn't look to see if Runa followed. He knew she would. Instead, he kept his eyes on the beast, making sure it didn't escape. Finally, the stagmoose found its footing and started limping farther into the forest, desperate to flee the scene. It was slow now, but still frustratingly far away. Runa matched Griff's speed, staying right by his side. She was holding back. He knew if he'd allow it, she could close the distance in half the time or less.

His quiver and bow bounced on his back with every pounding step. He crashed between the bushes, shielding his face with his arms. The shouts of Gale and Sylva were nearby, though they remained out of sight. Griff hoped they would see him if all three converged near the stagmoose. He didn't want to get in the way of their arrows.

Griff passed the spot where his initial lightning spell had struck. A black scorch mark and some churned up snow scarred the otherwise still and pristine forest floor. A few feet later, Griff spotted the dark red blood against the shining white snow. His second lightning spell. He couldn't see the stagmoose now. The forest ahead became more and more dense. But he now had tracks and droplets of blood to follow.

Ignoring the low hanging twigs from the trees he passed, Griff sprinted farther into the dense woods. Gale and Sylva sounded like they were farther now. Perhaps they were trying to get the stagmoose to circle around. Griff would also have to be careful not to accidentally shoot them as well.

With every minute that passed, Griff began to wonder if they were going to lose their game. He couldn't see it, and his pace had slowed as he navigated the thick brush. Runa dropped back and lifted her nose to the air again.

"Smell it, don't ya?" Griff said breathlessly. "I've got a trail right here." He pointed to the snow. "C'mon, let's keep going."

Runa growled but obediently returned to Griff's side. He ignored the pangs in his side from sprinting through the snow in his winter gear and continued pushing forward. More blood darkened the ground, and a large section of disturbed snow told Griff that perhaps the stagmoose had fallen. It was slowing down.

Suddenly, a loud shout of pain came from ahead.

"Dad!" Griff cried. He unlatched his handle from its sheath and ignited his sword. Heart pumping at full force, he strained his way forward, the pain in his side disappearing in the adrenaline. He fought through the dense shrubbery, using his sword and fire spells as necessary.

He finally broke through the brush and into a clearing. His dad was propped against a nearby tree, nursing his arm. Sylva stood over a dying stagmoose, his arrow sticking out from behind the front shoulder. A direct kill shot. Sylva had already nocked another arrow in and had it trained on the stagmoose in case it had one final attack in it.

"You okay?" Griff sprinted toward his dad, whose breathing was shallow.

"Yeah ... I'm okay. Just ... it kicked me in the shoulder. I don't think it's all the way broken, but he got me good."

"It's dead now," Sylva said, walking over and putting his arrow back in its quiver. "How are you, Mr. Driscoll?"

"Aye, I'll live," Gale said in a pained laugh.

"Sorry, Dad. They haven't taught me healing magic yet. I ... I can't help you with that."

"S'all right," Gale muttered. He tried to stand, but screamed in pain. "Yeah ... I'mma need to rest some before moving."

Great. He couldn't walk.

"Can I see?" Griff tried to pull his dad's collar to the side, but another bellow of pain stopped him. Frustration and panic surged in him, but he tried to push those feelings to the side. He unsheathed his handle and crafted a small, yellow dagger blade.

"Mind if try to get a better look?"

His dad eyed the dagger cautiously, then finally, Gale locked eyes with his son, gritted his teeth, and nodded.

Carefully, Griff slid the magical blade down a few inches and slowly peeled the clothing back. A large, dark bruise had already formed by his collar bone and was spreading down toward his chest.

"Looks like a broken collarbone, Mr. Driscoll," Sylva finally said, peering over Griff's shoulder. "Mom sees 'em all the time."

Gale gritted his teeth and nodded in understanding.

An idea stirred in Griff. He looked at the carcass, then at their surroundings.

"Okay, Sylva, we gotta get Dad home, but we can't waste the kill either. Can you field dress it while I work on a wooden mat or something to put Dad on? I can try and levitate it back to the horses."

"Can you levitate the stagmoose *and* your dad?" Sylva asked. "It would be faster."

"... Not yet," Griff answered. He felt so helpless in the moment. It was a painful moment of realization: he still had so much to learn. Levitating one object was easy, but he hadn't quite gotten the hang of multiple items. Plus, he didn't want to risk his dad's safety trying something new either.

Sylva nodded. "Then in that case, I'm on it." He quickly pulled off his pack and sifted through its contents to find the gear needed.

"Hang tight, Dad. We'll get you outta here."

Knowing his dad was in intense pain, Griff crafted a bright yellow axe head from his handle. It didn't take long for him to hack down a few small trees and tie them together into a makeshift wooden mat.

Immediately after, he joined Sylva in dressing the kill. They worked together in silence as the sun passed overhead and disappeared in the afternoon clouds. They stripped the carcass nearly to the bones and piled the neat cuts of meat into a sack and gave Runa the remains, which she happily accepted. As they worked, Gale rested against the tree, clearly still in pain.

With the meat tucked away in Griff's pack, he levitated the mat over to his dad.

"Ready?"

Gale grunted. "No. But let's do it anyways."

Griff snickered, then reached for his dad's good arm. Another growl from Runa interrupted him.

"Runa! It's dead already!" Griff turned to issue a command to heel, but stopped. His heart leapt to his throat. This whole time she hadn't been sensing the stagmoose. She had been sensing another animal. A new threat she hadn't experienced before. Neither had Griff.

Standing on the edge of the clearing stood a pack of wild, hungry-looking wolf-like creatures. Though, only barely recognizably wolf-like.

Standing tall on each head were two slender, deadly-looking horns. Equally just as deadly were two long fangs that jutted out of their mouths and stretched past their chins. It was as though they flashed a permanent, devilish, mischievous grin. A grin that sent chills down Griff's spine.

Instead of four legs, they had six. The two extra jutted out from their midsections, too short to touch the ground, but tipped with deadly claws that showed a more deadly purpose than walking. Instead of fur, sharp, deadly bones protruded from their tails in awkward angles. They dragged deep lines into the snow as the tails swished slowly, confidently back and forth. These monsters, maybe ten to fifteen of them, eagerly eyed the carcass with a greedy, desperately hungry kind of look.

The largest of the pack, probably the alpha, stepped forward and sniffed the air. Then it made a clicking sound. Not a growl. Not a rumble. Just an eerie, high-pitched, clicking, which the rest of the pack echoed in response. The alpha sniffed and clicked some more, then turned his eyes toward Griff. Griff's stomach dropped. He had a pack full of meat.

"Y-You think if we let them be ... they'll just ... just take the carcass?" Sylva asked. Griff was glad to know he wasn't the only one terrified.

"I ... don't get the feeling that's all they're here for ... but ... well, keep an eye on them while I help Dad onto the mat."

"Aye."

Griff's heart pounded against his chest. His hands shook as he tended to his dad. Gale yelped and grunted in pain, but spoke no words of complaint. Gale's noises only sparked the pack's hungry curiosity even further. They stepped into the clearing. Runa confidently stepped forward in response. Smoke shot from her nostrils. Her vicious rumble echoed about the clearing.

"Yeah, they're not looking for a carcass," Sylva said nervously.

Immediately after securing his father to the mat, Griff stepped beside Runa. He swirled his hands and flung a large fireball at the ground near the alpha's feet. It didn't move. Didn't even flinch.

"Leave!" Griff shouted. He took a step forward. So did the alpha. Then it clicked some more. The pack responded in kind. Griff hurled a lightning spell. Then another fire spell. He screamed. He whistled and stomped his feet. But the others lined up beside the alpha.

"Sylva. Grab your bow. Now."

Griff turned to Runa. "Let me and Sylva handle this, okay?"

Runa didn't acknowledge his words, but stayed motionless, eyeing the monsters.

"Okay. I tried being nice." With a shout, Griff flung another fireball forward. This time, it wasn't a warning. The alpha yelped loudly when the spell connected. It flew backward, its body smacking a tree trunk with a satisfying thud. The others didn't flee. They took another step forward, filling in the vacancy and clicking louder in response. Another yelp as Sylva let his arrow fly. Griff didn't want a full-fledged attack. There were just too many of them. But they weren't taking the hint.

Suddenly, they lunged forward, sprinting toward them with a hungry, desperate look in their eyes. Griff let the spells fly. Some connected, some didn't. They kept coming. Griff unlatched his handle. It looked like he was going to have to fight close-range.

He ignited his sword and dashed forward. With a loud yell, he sent a gust of wind forward, flinging a few bodies back. He slashed one monster down, then another. Runa's snarls from behind Griff told him she was forced to join the fight as well.

A sharp shout from Sylva snapped Griff's attention away from the beast in front of him. Sylva had been knocked back and was being dragged by the arm. He looked more scared than hurt. The layers of winter clothes had cushioned the crushing bite. Griff hurled a shard of ice toward the creature and turned his attention back on the one in front of him. He didn't wait to see if his spell connected, but the sharp yelp that died quickly and Sylva's sigh of relief told him he'd made the kill.

The pack was circling them, each monster dashing in and out as they saw opportunity. With a flick of his wrist, Griff flung a large log their direction, but they easily dodged it. A groan from his dad forced Griff to whip around. One wolf-creature had broken from the fight and stood mere feet from easy prey. A single lightning spell was all it took to stop the threat.

Two wolves, bigger than the others, stepped forward. These were probably next in line for alpha, Griff guessed. They clicked and licked their lips with long, slender tongues. Griff lifted his hands, readying another spell. Runa, however, stepped in front of Griff and roared. She had just issued a challenge. One Griff didn't intend to let happen.

He opened his mouth to tell her to back down, but the air in his lungs was knocked out as he landed hard on the ground. He hadn't noticed the monster that had flanked him. A sharp, white-hot pain exploded from his ankle. The beast's teeth had found a lesser cushioned area and grabbed hold. Paralyzed by pain, all Griff could do was scream. His blood painted the snow red.

One of Sylva's arrows whistled by him, followed by a pained yelp. The creature immediately released Griff's ankle and collapsed on its side.

The pack circled tighter. Griff gritted his teeth and tried to stand. Sylva was an amazing shot, but he wouldn't be able to take them on by himself.

Runa's eyes narrowed, her mouth opened wide, and she bellowed her challenge to the pack once more. A white streak of light ignited from the tip of her nose all the way down her back and to her tail. Smoke poured from her mouth and nostrils. Without another warning, she stretched out her head, opened her mouth wide, and midnight black flames burst forth, engulfing the two wolves who had stepped into the circle. There was no yelp. No whimpers of pain. No clicking. They just died instantly.

Stunned by Runa's new ability, Griff stared in shock and watched as she sprinted to a cluster of monsters and released another surge of black fire, killing everything it touched. The beasts who watched their pack mates die, clicked loudly and nervously, taking several steps back. Griff shook off the paralysis and limped beside Runa. He remembered his time spent with Professor Coen in the training room. He set his jaw in place, spread his arms out wide. *I did it once. I can do it again.*

"Close your eyes!" Griff hollered, hoping everyone, even Runa, would listen.

In one, quick, fluid motion, Griff brought his two spells in each hand together and sent a dazzling bright fire spell that exploded in the center of the pack. Taking his own advice, Griff didn't see the explosion of his fire and light spell, but the startled yelps and clicks and the bright flash of light that lit up his darkened vision, told him he had been successful. As the light dimmed, he slowly opened his eyes to see the bony tails of the last monsters disappear into the shadowy forest.

The clicking sounds faded. All that was left were the charred bodies and an awful, smoky, fishy smell. Runa nuzzled Griff's hand with her head. He took her head in both hands and kissed the bridge of her nose.

"Runa. That was unbelievable. Thank you for saving us."

"Aye," Gale added through pained breaths. "You're ... gettin' ... a big hunk of meat when we get home."

Sylva walked up, dusting the snow off his jacket. "Yeah, I have *got* to send Mr. Dingmann a letter as soon as we get back."

"Speaking of ..." Griff eyed the late afternoon sky. "We *do* need to get back. It's getting late. And believe it or not, there are worse things here in these woods than *those* things." He winced as touched his ankle. "And I'd rather not meet them tonight."

CHAPTER 29

Griff never thought he'd be so happy to be back at the training room again. Seeing the large, old wooden door and the room's name engraved on the silver sign next to it brought him much needed relief.

He'd survived what was meant to be an uneventful, family-fun day of hunting—one that nearly turned tragic. With an arm around Sylva and the other keeping his dad's mat in the air, they had emerged from the forest without any further issues. Runa had pranced proudly next to Griff, standing a little taller after her new trick. Now she was back at the stables with Mr. Dingmann, where no doubt she was proudly showing off her new skills at his command.

Though Griff was happy to be back at school, ready to train with Professor Coen again, something felt off about tonight. The professor had met him in the second year boy's common room with a new set of magical armor.

"Here. Put this on. You'll need it for tonight," he had said ominously.

Questions rose in his mind, but Griff kept silent and obeyed, stepping back into his room to change. Their training sessions *had* been a little more intense compared to last year. Griff was learning more complicated magic, and it was probably an added safety precaution. In some ways, he was more excited, wondering what they could possibly practice tonight.

Professor Coen opened the door to the training room and allowed Griff inside. Griff didn't even have to step through the threshold before his heart sank. Sitting off to the side in one of the wooden chairs was Headmaster Aldamund, silently reading a book.

"Ah, Griff. Professor Coen. There you are." Headmaster Aldamund stood and tucked his reading glasses into his shirt pocket. "Welcome back, Griff. I hear you had *quite* the holiday vacation."

Griff smiled cautiously. "Mr. Dingmann?"

The headmaster smiled. "Indeed. Mr. Dingmann. Sounds like your dragon has gained a new ability!"

"Yes sir. And just in time, too."

"Very good. Well, I'm happy to hear she's taking to training and being accepted by the community." Headmaster Aldamund clapped his hands together. "Now, any other secrets you care to share with me before I explain why I'm here? No other ... secret pets or daring missions you've undergone?" He smiled genuinely, but knowing he had good reason to ask still stung. Griff had broken his trust more than once and Headmaster Aldamund had every right to wonder.

"No, sir. No more secrets. I've learned my lesson. The hard way."

The headmaster maintained his warm smile. "Funny how sometimes that's the only way we learn, isn't it?" He took a step forward, his smile disappearing as a more serious tone crept in. "How about your dreams? Have you seen anything more?"

"No, sir. I would come straight to you if there had been. I promise."

"I believe you, I believe you." The headmaster chuckled. "Speaking of learning the hard way, let me explain why I am here. Even kings and headmasters, people in authority, sometimes make mistakes and learn things the hard way. I myself have stumbled into that form of learning recently as well."

He placed a gentle hand on Griff's shoulder. "I should have accepted your offer to join my father's soldiers in search of the shard that night. Your help, I believe, would have made a difference. My uncle would probably not have another shard in his possession if you'd been there."

Griff's jaw dropped. He'd had every right to be frustrated after that night. And *he*, the headmaster, someone with so much authority, was acknowledging that he had been *wrong*, and it left Griff stunned.

"So I'm asking for your forgiveness, Griff."

"Sir ... you don't need to ask for forgiveness. I mean, I understand not wanting to risk a seventeen-year-old's life on the battlefield. I'm sure that was a difficult call to make."

"Mm. Yes, it was. And sadly, I believe, I made the wrong one. You know, you have so much to learn here at this school. From the professors and even the headmaster. But we can learn a lot from you as well."

"Thank you, sir," Griff said quietly.

"Now, to show that I have learned from my mistakes, I am here to help you train."

"Train, sir?" Griff asked, unsure where this was going.

"Indeed. I would feel much better sending you with the battlemages the next time a shard is on the line if you were properly trained. The way the king's mages were trained."

Griff's heart dropped. He was about to be put through the same kind of training as the king's elite. He didn't know what to expect, other than a world of pain and a lot of healing magic.

"Korrun has gone into hiding recently. My father's men have been actively patrolling his most recent whereabouts and stopped one of his attacks on a town. He's gone dark ever since. But my father did receive a message from someone on the inside. Someone who has infiltrated Korrun's ranks. We believe we know what direction he is headed. We think he has the location of another shard."

The headmaster locked eyes with Griff. "So, after speaking with my father—and yours—you will join the king's battlemages the next time we have the location of a shard. If that's what you still want."

Griff's face lit up. "Yes, sir! Absolutely. I want to help. I *can* help. I'll do whatever it takes to be ready."

The next words out of the headmaster's mouth made Griff wonder if he really knew what he was asking for.

Headmaster Aldamund rapped his knuckles on the chest of Griff's armor.

"Good. Professor Coen and I will make sure that you are."

CHAPTER 30

"Easy, son. Easy." Einar Falkenburg held his hand out toward Arthur. His son's face was red in anger. Tears streamed down his dirty cheeks, clearing dust and ash from them as they trailed to his chin. Sweat matted his straight brown hair, making it look greasy and unkempt. They were standing on the cobblestone street just outside the house he'd grown up in. Years spent here, building cherished memories of love, laughter, and joy. Memories that his son seemed to have forgotten.

The smoldering remains of their living room lay scattered across the street. Stuffing spilled from the handcrafted pillow Fedelma had knitted with Arthur's name on it. A table leg rolled back and forth in the morning wind. Shattered bits of brick and wood littered the ground, making it harder to walk on. Einar knew he'd have to be careful. Not only was his son now an enemy, but even the debris from their home threatened to betray his old ankles.

His neighbors had scrambled to leave at the first sign of trouble. From the moment Arthur blew out their living room into the street, they had all scattered. Though most had probably left town, Einar observed a few of them peeking from behind the bakery just down the street.

He frantically scanned through the wreckage that was once his living room, and finally found the journal. Einar breathed a sigh of relief. It was safe. It sat atop a bookshelf in the far corner of the room. If he survived this encounter with his son, he knew he would log this moment. For his daughter, and for all those who would come after her. So they wouldn't make the same mistakes that Arthur made now.

"Her? Really, dad?" Arhtur sobbed. "My sister instead of me? Why don't you *trust me*!" He floated his father's favorite sitting chair and flung it at the man. Einar flicked his wrist and sent the chair soaring over him with an upward wind spell. It crashed into nothing more than splinters and stuffing behind him, joining the rest of the debris on the street.

"You had to have seen this coming, son," Einar said sadly. "Your mother and I, we … we *wanted* to trust you. We gave you every opportunity to show responsibility. To earn our trust. You just…" Tears formed in the corners of Einar's eyes. His voice faltered. "You just never earned it."

Arthur huffed, staring at his father as the words sank in. "You … you're blaming *me* for Mom, aren't you? That … that was an accident! You said you forgave me! I … I didn't mean for her to die!"

"You went looking for trouble, Arthur!" Einar pleaded, hoping there was still some rational part of him that could hear reason. "You snuck out at night to get a nightstalker head for a *trophy,* of all things! Something you could proudly parade about for everyone to see. Do you not understand the lack of wisdom behind that?"

"Lack of wisdom? Lack of wisdom!" Arthur took another step forward. The vein in his neck bulged. "You want to talk about a lack of wisdom? Then why did Mom come after me like some hero and get herself killed? That wasn't *my* fault! She should have stayed home."

"YOU should have stayed home, Arthur!" Einar bellowed. The love Einar had for his son didn't dwindle from his arrogance and disrespect of Fedelma. But he would never let anyone, including his own son, speak ill of his late wife. Einar paused to let his words sink in, and give himself a chance to calm down. He wiped the tears from his eyes. Arthur had made his decisions. Lived in his own arrogance, pride, and folly. Now, he would have to live with the consequences of it all.

"I do blame you for the death of your mother. It *was* your fault." Einar stepped closer to his son. He would not show fear. "Many bad things that have happened in your life are *your fault.*" Another step. Another tear fell. "But ... son ... I love you. Still! And I *do* forgive you. But yes, it is your fault. And yes, I chose your sister over you to be the next Guardian. And ... and you'll never understand why, because you just don't have the ears to hear. You're clouded by your own arrogance and foolishness. And, son, if you're not careful, it will be the end of you."

The vein in Arthur's neck pumped viciously. No more tears fell. Instead, he furrowed his eyebrows and clenched his fists. They shook in fury, and blood dripped from the wounds he gave himself as his nails dug into his palms.

I am protector and defender, Einar recited sadly in his mind.

I wield my magic. It does not wield me.

Arthur's blood-curdling scream echoed down the street.

I brandish my power with wisdom and resolve.

Arthur raised both hands, red crackling bolts of lightning dancing over his blood-soaked palms.

I do not strike first, but I strike true.

With an enraged cry from its owner, the lightning bolts shot toward Einar. But he had been ready. With just a simple flick of his fingers, a silver serving platter zipped from the ground and guarded its owner. The red lightning smashed against it and bounced. Einar hated himself, but knew the angle of the platter was exactly where it needed to be, reflecting the spell back at the one who had cast it.

I do not seek battle, but I will end it.

Arthur's eyes widened in horror. His own furious spell was hurtling straight toward him. There was nothing he could do. No time. It pierced his side and continued through him until hit smashed into the old oak tree in their front yard. The side of the trunk exploded, sending splinters flying in every direction. Arthur yelped and tumbled to the ground. He landed with a scream. He grasped his side, trying to stop the bleeding.

Einar slowly walked toward him. The pain of seeing his son like this gnawed at his very soul. "Your actions have consequences, son. And they always come back to you, whether you like it or not."

Arthur scooted on the ground, whimpering as he dragged himself away from his father. He finally found his footing and stood. Einar watched as his son's eyes flicked toward the journal.

The same journal Einar had written in and studied each night, just before setting it aside to tuck Arthur into bed. The same journal Arthur was never allowed to read, though he often dreamed of the stories and legends hidden within its pages. The same journal he tried to steal today.

There was a look of longing in those eyes. Then a look of shame, when he met his father's gaze.

Einar knew this was the last time he'd ever see his son. All the shouting, destruction, the blood, the heartbreak—none of it hurt more than the look of betrayal Arthur gave him as he turned and limped away.

CHAPTER 31

Some said they were fishing. Others that they were hunting. Some just disappeared without telling anyone anything. But they weren't catching fish or stalking game. They were training. Across the river from their temporary camp, over the hill, and through some dangerous cliffs, Doran had found what used to be some sort of military base that had long since been deserted. Overrun with weeds, vines, and trash from before Day Zero, the place itself was hardly useful to the Forty-Two. One tree had grown straight through the rusted shell of a blown-out military vehicle. Tilted on its side and half-buried in soil, the vehicle was now a permanent cradle for the tree's roots. Now fully grown, the tree had burst through the side window, its trunk thick and solid, as if to say that nature had reclaimed this territory once again.

Having scoured every inch of the base, they couldn't find very much that was useful. Save for the metal door on the ground in one of the buildings. It took a while before they could get it open. The door was sealed tight, with a dusty number pad next to it. Kwame, ever the prudent artifician, realized the door needed electricity. Once Tyrell overloaded the number pad, a loud, metallic clunk signaled that the door, sealed for hundreds of years, had finally unlocked.

A stale, ancient aroma puffed through the door and overwhelmed Tyrell's senses. It smelled like an abandoned forge, ground to dust and festered in the sour, underground air. A set of stairs that led into darkness greeted them. They wound down them until another metal door blocked their path. This one didn't need a lock.

The rusty knob creaked as it turned and opened to a wide tunnel with some form of tracks on the ground. There were three sets of tracks running parallel to each other. Even the light from the mages' spells were unable to pierce very far into the dark to see where the tracks led. Realizing there was no reasonably close exit except for the one they came through, Tyrell and the rest of the Forty-Two decided this tunnel would be the perfect place to hide their training sessions.

They didn't know how long they would have in this location. The king's battlemages were hunting them. Ever since their first battle against them on the beach, the battlemages maintained a wide patrol of this part of the country. Messengers flew on their wargs to every town, warning every man, woman, and child to be on guard for the black cloaks.

Traveling by nightstalker was no longer an option. It was too risky, now, with their enemies patrolling the skies on their wargs. It slowed Korrun down. He moved his army farther inland in hopes of shaking their pursuers.

It had only been a few days, but Korrun was on edge. He tried to hide it, but Tyrell saw the cracks. Always watching, always observant, Tyrell could see the way his shoulders sagged a little more each day. His eyes grew darker. He wasn't sleeping as well. And he'd stopped giving his hollow words of inspiration laced with murder and deceit.

Because Korrun was occupied with staying hidden from the king's battlemages and trying to find a new path to their next location, this gave Tyrell and the Forty-Two an opportunity to get organized. Of course, it had been Ava and her father's idea. Once again, they wanted to force Tyrell to the front. To lead this rebellion. And once again, Tyrell reluctantly agreed.

He observed a group of mages wielding guns that they had borrowed from the weapons cache. Officially, they were signed out for patrols—at least, that's what they told the supply captain. Unofficially, they were being used to prepare for the war that no one suspected.

Even with essence crafted bullets, guns were loud. The supply captain warned that they were only to be used if they came across a squadron of the king's battlemages. Otherwise, the noise would give them away. But down in the underground tunnel, the stone walls and layers of earth above them dampened the sounds of their training, including the magical rounds being shot into the dark.

It was a beautiful sight to witness—seeing the multi-colored bullets light up the dark like a festive celebration. While the goal was for each mage to craft blue bullets—a sign of discipline and control—almost every color of magic was represented in their shots.

Understandably, some of the bullets were red or purple. Tyrell assumed those mages were angry or grieving, likely mourning loved ones lost to Korrun's foolish quest. Mages that were nervous, whether about getting caught training or nervous about wielding a gun, crafted yellow bullets. But it was the green bullets that worried Tyrell most. There was no room for mischief in this squad. He made a mental note of each one, determined to learn their true motivations.

"Here," Tyrell said, gently placing a hand on a woman's shoulder.

The woman, Elaine, gave a small, grateful smile. Once a housewife who tended to her garden and home, this petite lady was now intensely focused on mastering the skills of combat. She had a daughter safely away at Bergots, and her older son, Doran, stood across the room with the group without guns, waiting his turn. Elaine's husband had been killed trying to protect them from Korrun's attack. Fortunately, Elaine's parents were out of town at the time, and she silently thanked them, knowing at least part of her family was safe.

"You've got to steady your breathing," Tyrell said. "Close one eye and aim with the sight on top here."

Elaine nodded nervously. She took a deep breath, then let it out slowly, squeezing the trigger and blasting a yellow bullet down the dark tunnel.

"Not bad!" Tyrell said. "Now you just got to work on staying in control. Breathe. Let your magic flow naturally. Don't try to force it, okay?"

Elaine smiled. "Thanks, Tyrell."

He nodded, then turned to scan the rest of the group. Ava beamed proudly at Tyrell from her mother's side. A small number of those without magic brought swords and shields—just enough to sneak out of camp without suspicion. The rest stood to the side, awaiting Tyrell's instructions.

Some in the group were barely teenagers; others were old enough to be his grandfather. The rest fell somewhere in-between. There was a mix of age, magical abilities—or lack thereof—and combat prowess. Tyrell stood silent, the sounds of the gunshots echoing throughout the tunnel as he weighed the group and what little he had to work with.

Finally, he asked those with weapons from camp to pass them to the older, non-magical members and asked them to stand to one side. They would receive their training shortly. He hollered for the shooters to halt so he could address those in front of him. Once the echoes of the last shots faded, he asked, "Who here knows how to fight?"

Awkward silence. They all looked at each other. Finally, Elaine's son, Doran, stepped forward.

"Uh, yeah. I do."

No one seemed surprised at this revelation. Doran was a young man, physically fit, and his gruff personality all but gave it away.

"Any sort of military training?" Tyrell asked.

"No. More like street brawling for money."

Tyrell raised an eyebrow and glanced at Elaine, the sweet, petite, garden-tending housewife, who was now focused on her shots. Did she know this about her own son?

"Okay, then," Tyrell said. "I'm sure you can still help me demonstrate some things. Maybe you can even show us a thing or two as well. Stand here."

Doran stopped a few feet in front of Tyrell, who casually placed his hands in his pockets.

"Come at me."

"What?" Doran responded.

"Come at me, Doran. However you want."

"Um. Okay."

Doran took two strides and raised his fist in the air.

"Stop," Tyrell commanded. Doran obeyed, looking confused. He hadn't done anything but take a few steps.

"First lesson. I see someone coming at me in a threatening way. How should I stand? Feet together? Hands in my pockets or arms by my side?"

No response. Doran lowered his fist. "Hands up," he said confidently.

Tyrell nodded. "Good. If you find yourself in a hand-to-hand combat situation, you have to protect yourself. By having your hands up, you're protecting your face, your neck, your head. And you are more prepared for what's coming."

Tyrell shifted his legs, one in front of the other, raised his fists, and angled his body.

"See the difference? By spreading my legs more, having one behind the other, I'm not going to the ground easily. Angling my body makes me a smaller target and protects my organs from my assailant."

He looked around, seeing a few nods of understanding from the group.

"Let's see you get in the same position." They obeyed. "Good. Okay, Doran. Come at me again. Don't hold back."

Doran resumed his attack, taking the last few steps toward Tyrell, fist raised. As soon as Doran swung, Tyrell was like lightning. He stepped forward. Blocked with his forearm. Grasped Doran's arm, spun, and flung him over his shoulder. Doran's yelp of surprise when he landed on the hard stone floor stirred a few stifled laughs from the onlookers.

Tyrell didn't laugh. It didn't feel right. Sure, throwing Doran like a ragdoll had been fun, but teaching these lessons, his father's lessons, left a sour taste in his mouth. He felt guilty. Dirty. Wrong. How could he use the same teaching tactics as Korrun's second in command?

He's been corrupted. The man who taught me is gone.

The person who taught Tyrell everything he knew *wasn't* Korrun's second in command. He was Randolph Falkenburg. One of the top battlemages for the king. And *that* was where these lessons came from.

Tyrell walked over and helped Doran to his feet.

"Sorry," Tyrell said. "I guess I'm kind of a 'show' instead of 'tell' guy."

Doran caught his breath and dusted his backside off. "All good. All good. That was ... fun."

Tyrell smiled, then turned to the rest. "You saw the movements, yeah? Block, grab, turn, and pull them over. Practice the first three motions first—slowly!—then when you and your partner are ready, then you can practice the throwing. But ... just don't kill each other, okay? We need the numbers on our side."

He turned back to Doran. "Think you can help them from here? I've got to work with the others and their weapons."

Doran glanced at the older group awkwardly holding swords and shields.

"You're not planning on throwing *them*, are you?"

Tyrell grinned. "Only if necessary."

He clapped Doran on the shoulder as he passed, walking toward his next group.

Doran called after him. "Wait! Was *I* necessary?"

Tyrell decided to remain silent. His favorite response.

"You were *amazing* back there, Tyrell!" Ava squealed. She held his hand as they walked toward camp. The Forty-Two left in small groups to avoid detection. It would look strange if everyone arrived back at camp at the same time. He made sure he was the last to leave. Not only because he had been taught that's what good leaders do, but also because after all the questions, all the attention, and all the talking, he craved a few moments of silence. He didn't get the silence. But he did get something better.

"Thanks," he answered quietly.

"No, seriously, Tyrell. You make a great teacher. Watch out, after this is all said and done, they'll probably hire you to teach at Bergots!"

Tyrell laughed. "Never."

"No? Never?"

"Never. I've never done anything like this before. People looking up to me, wanting my opinions—my attention. Other than my brother, I've just never experienced anything like it. It makes me ... it makes me feel nervous. I don't like nervous."

"Well," Ava answered cheerily, gazing at the clear sky above and ignoring his moody tone. "You *are* a great leader, and I won't have you thinking otherwise."

Nature could be so misleading sometimes. The sky was bright and the sun basked the ground with a summer's glow. But the fog from Tyrell's breath that curled in the cold winter air told a different tale.

Suddenly he pulled her off the path and together, they sat under a tree. Sure, the shade was colder, but they could at least pretend it was a summer day.

They bundled close together as the breeze shifted and directed the cold toward them. Tyrell locked eyes with Ava.

"Are you sure about all of this?"

Ava cocked her head. "What do you mean?"

"This." Tyrell gestured broadly with his hands as if that explained everything. "The Forty-Two. The rebellion. Fighting back. Look. We could leave right now. Grab your parents and go. We could go back to my town. I could introduce you to the rest of my family. The ... good side of my family. I know my mom and brother would love to meet you."

Ava placed her hands on his. "And I *will* meet them." She paused, choosing her next words carefully. "But what about everyone else? Why should we get a happily ever after when Korrun is still rampaging about? He attacked on Christmas Eve, Tyrell. Destroying not just a holiday, but people's homes and way of life."

She shook her head avidly, then tucked her hands into her jacket pockets to keep them warm. "I can't sit back and enjoy life when I know there's work for me to do."

"What makes you think it's *your* work to do? Why not somebody else?"

"Maybe there is somebody else. All I know is that I'm here and I can't ignore what I see happening."

She turned to meet his gaze. She stared not just at him, but *into* him. It was like she could see directly into his very being. His soul. "Tyrell, it's my work because I believe in you. I believe you have what it takes to train me and teach me what I need to know so that I can step in and *be* that somebody when the time comes. You bring something out of me that makes me believe I can do anything. Be anything. And what I want more than anything is to right the wrongs that Korrun has brought down upon our world. And you make me believe it's possible."

Tyrell gently wiped a single tear from her cheek. All that passion, all that love she had for the world. For what was right. She could have been selfish. Like him. She could turn and run and choose safety. Instead, she was willing to risk it all to give everyone else a chance at what she was giving up.

She shivered as a breeze swept through, and Tyrell pulled her closer. Her head leaned against his chest and the familiar faint scent of roses drifted toward him. He didn't need to fight. He didn't need to flee. He just needed to be here. With her.

If only the rest of the world could fade to black and he could stay in this moment with her forever. He would give anything to have that. To have this moment with Ava over and over again. He would climb the tallest mountain, swim the deepest ocean. He'd kill a thousand nightstalkers if it meant never losing another moment like this.

Then it hit him. *This* is what she was fighting for. She was fighting for a world where not only they, but everyone, could sit under a tree under a clear sky and not have to worry about Korrun or the black cloaks ever again. They wanted the same thing. His heart pounded. He knew what he was about to do.

He lifted her chin and met her eyes. "Thank you for believing in me."

She didn't respond. She didn't need to. He closed the distance, his lips meeting hers. There was so much to do. So much to think about. So much to plan.

But not now. Now, in this moment, the world stood still, granting Tyrell and Ava this pure moment. All the cold from his body left, love and warmth filling its absence.

The sun shined brighter. The birds sang. Tyrell knew that this moment would eventually come to an end. But together, they would fight. Not just to survive, but to experience this again. To make a world where moments like this could last.

CHAPTER 32

Crumbled ruins lay broken and scattered around Griff. The few tall buildings still standing sagged and leaned against one another like weary, old giants. Once upon a time, these structures would have been a magnificent sight to behold. Even now, the fact that they were still standing spoke to their ingenious engineering. The holes blown out of their sides, blackened scorch marks or the massive cracks in the large concrete blocks told him that this was more than just from the passage of time and lack of use. Something violent happened here. And Griff only had one guess as to what it was.

The stars overhead twinkled brightly, almost happily. As if they had forgotten the horrors they must have witnessed in this city years ago. Chilly winds scraped grains of sand across Griff's face. And the particles weren't just in the air or gathering on top of his messy hair. The sand was everywhere. Like it was growing. Hungry. Devouring the city that had tried to remove it years ago. Removing it and replacing it with concrete, stone blocks, and imported grass.

Now, though, rusted metal skeletons of vehicles were half-submerged in piles of it. It danced along the streets in its supposed victory, spilling through the broken windows of a nearby boutique and covering the once immaculate tile floor. It scraped away at large, old signs, erasing the messages once displayed for the whole city to see.

But just past the city, bathed in eerie moonlight and like kings on their thrones silently judging the city they faced, stood ancient structures far older than anything Griff had ever seen. Though they were weathered and worn like everything else in this city, he believed their shape was intentional. Almost mistaking them for distant mountains, he finally recognized them as pyramids. It was hard to make out any details from the ground. He had to get a better view.

Having only the moonlight as his guide, Griff carefully wandered the littered streets, searching for the tallest building. One that was still safe to walk through. Unsure if he was truly alone or not, he resisted the urge to use his light spell and fumbled his way down the littered streets.

Ever since Griff had stepped foot in Solastran, he'd always thought the town felt a little cramped. Not necessarily in a bad way. But there was no denying Solastran housed a lot of people. And it was even worse just before school started in the fall. But walking the tightly-packed corridors in between buildings now showed Griff that he didn't know what cramped truly was.

He spotted it. Across the street stood a massive white stone structure that towered above the others. The enormous concrete blocks that made this building were still holding strong. Jutting out from the side facing him, and the pyramids, were large balconies. He needed to get to the top and stand on one of those for a better view.

He dashed across the street, nearly tripping over an empty glass bottle. Its hollow clinking sound echoed through the night like a haunting whisper down an empty hall.

Tall glass doors greeted him. One stood halfway open, as if closing a door to a building that would never be used again felt pointless. Griff stepped over the sand that piled between the doors and into the lobby. White tile covered in small piles of sand lined the floor. On one side of the room was a black tiled wall with what looked like a fireplace built into it. Carefully placed in front of it was a circular coffee table with worn, padded chairs around it, all waiting for guests that would never come.

On the other side of the room was a long desk, also decorated with black tile. A large wooden sign bore silver lettering in a language Griff didn't recognize. Was it the building's name? Directions? Maybe it just said, "Welcome." Either way, like the rest of the lobby, it was expertly designed to show elegance and affluence.

Just past the desk was a long, wide hallway with a restaurant and a shop. Amazed as he was at this strange place—echoes of another world, another age—he was on a mission. He squashed his desire to explore for the sake of exploration. Eventually, he found a door leading to a dark stairwell. *Finally.*

Strange. Even though he knew this was a dream, and even though he was only halfway up the flight of stairs, he still grew tired. And the muscles in his legs quivered from exertion. Still, he fought his way to the top floor and found an open door at the end of the hallway.

It was like a miniature house inside. There was a small kitchenette in the corner, a couch and some chairs in the middle of the room, and a large bed whose covers were ruffled as though someone dashed out of them and decided making it wasn't worth the effort. On one of the couches was a suitcase still full of clothes. Some neatly folded, others crumpled in a pile on top. The window to the balcony was open, the cold wind penetrating the room and blowing the curtains wide, perfectly revealing the ancient stone structures outside the city. The pyramids.

Griff stepped out onto the ledge and looked over the railing and down at the ground, fifteen stories below. He silently hoped it wouldn't give out on him. Knowing it was still a dream and that he would probably just wake in his bed thousands of miles away didn't help.

Instead, he shifted his gaze toward the pyramids, and as he did, something inside him leaped. It was that still, small voice inside him. That mysterious presence that always pulled him toward another shard. It signaled that somewhere, deep within those pyramids, a brother was waiting. Pleading. *Come find me.*

Griff couldn't tell which of the pyramids housed the next shard. But one thing was certain: one of them did.

He stepped back inside the room and scavenged for clues. The last occupant would have gotten along well with Mira, for they both clearly had a love for books. A few were tangled together on top of the sheets. Others were stacked haphazardly on the bedside table. None hinted at why the city had been abandoned. But at least they were written in his language. Griff leaned closer, blew the sand and dust from the cover, and read aloud, "'Business Leadership: Gritty Integrity' by Ron Ramin Bahrand."

The room's final occupant had been a businessman as the other books were either on business leadership, negotiation or closing sales deals. It all sounded boring to Griff. But jutting out from between the pages of one of the books was a restaurant menu, again in his own language. Scanning it made Griff hungry for food he'd never heard of, but more importantly, there was an address.

Suddenly, Griff jerked awake. His eyes popped open and he shot up from his bunk, banging his head on the wood above him, the message from The Deceiver still engraved in it.

He spoke aloud. Not to anyone in particular, though he didn't care if anyone heard it. He was too excited. It was clear this time. No guessing games. No star maps. He didn't care if he woke Marth or Vincent. He just had to speak it aloud to the darkness.

"I know where the next shard is."

CHAPTER 33

"Skies've been twitchy the last few days. Seen less birds. No wind. Strange," Captain Orin Ashdown said, spitting in the dirt.

"Probably nothin', Captain. King's crown, we ain't seen a calm day since Korrun's goons started marchin' around anyways. I say we take it while we can get it."

Rurik Oakfell, second in command, stood beside his captain, overlooking Solastran. There wasn't a single cloud in the sky, and only a light, ever so gentle breeze. The lake was calm, save for the random splash signaling a fish catching a fly that landed on its mirror surface.

A couple of months ago, Griff had been standing in this very spot, throwing sticks to Runa and moping about the last Altar Storm match he'd lost. So much had changed in so little time. His dad knew about Runa. So did everyone else. He'd won another match on the Altar Storm pitch. And now, he was standing with the first and second in command of the king's battlemages. Geared up with his newly-acquired battle armor from Headmaster Aldamund, he was ready for a grand, yet very dangerous quest for another shard. Once they reconnected with the rest of the squad awaiting them in Solastran, that was.

Having the entire squadron come to escort Griff away would have brought too much attention. And with The Deceiver still in hiding, it was quieter this way. Still, even Headmaster Aldamund and Professor Coen had to come and say their farewells in between the early morning classes.

Magnus snorted beside Griff, demanding another head scratch.

"Yeah, all right, all right," Griff said, giving in to his demands.

"We'll take it while we can," Orin repeated Rurik's line. He gave the skies one last suspicious glance, then turned to face Griff and the others. "Ready, son?"

"Yes, sir!" Griff saluted too eagerly, triggering an eyebrow raise from the captain.

"No need for any of that, Griff. But ... well, I appreciate the sentiment." He turned toward the professor. "Sure you won't ride with us, Coen?"

Professor Coen looked to the headmaster, who raised an eyebrow, then chuckled. "Absolutely not. I've done my time, and I think I'll be just fine hanging back here at the castle."

And with Professor Strickland, I'm sure. Griff knew better than to say anything though, which only made the thought that much sweeter.

"Aye, you sure have, Captain," Orin said, offering his arm in response.

"Aw, please. I'm not your captain anymore," Professor Coen answered, grasping Orin's forearm firmly. "Just a normal, everyday kind of guy, now."

Rurik laughed and looked at Griff. "If you'd seen what this man can really do, you'd know there's nothing normal about him."

"Oh, trust me. I know he's not normal," Griff responded.

All four men laughed to Griff's pleasure. Professor Coen offered Griff the same forearm grasping gesture as he did to the current captain of the battlemages. Then he pulled Griff into a bear hug so tight it threatened to crush his lungs.

"You be safe out there, all right? You're with the best of the best, but still. You watch out for yourself and don't make their job any harder than it already is."

Griff laughed with what little air he had left. "I'll do my best. Thank you."

The professor finally released, allowing Griff to breathe. He was both honored and embarrassed that Professor Coen had hugged him like that in front of the toughest men in all of Oriel.

"Remember, Griff," Headmaster Aldamund said as he shook Griff's hand. "You're the locator. That's your job. Don't try to be a hero or take risky chances. Find the shard, and give it to Orin. Then come back and do your homework. Deal?"

"Deal," Griff smiled. The headmaster trusted him. And he wasn't going to let him down.

The cold breeze rushed through Griff's long, messy hair. Winter was on its way out, but Spring was slow to take up the mantle. He was missing classes and flying on Magnus for an important mission. A mission he had been desperate to be a part of. It felt freeing and frightening all at the same time. The king, the headmaster, and over a hundred battlemages —all of them were counting on him. The weight of that trust was almost crushing. Except, well, he had asked for it. So, either he stepped up and showed he was worthy of their trust, or gathered up his books and his trunk and left Bergots for good.

For the second time in two years, Griff saw Bergots Academy shrink in the distance behind him as he flew away on a warg. Sure, just like last time, he knew that certain danger lay ahead, but this time, at least, his family was safe.

The soldiers flew in silence, resting their minds and bodies for what was to come. They'd been separated and had been patrolling Korrun's last known whereabouts for the past year, and Griff could tell that the travel and the random skirmishes were wearing on them.

Captain Ashdown flew at the head of the pack, his long, red beard trailing behind him like a battle flag rallying the troops. Then Rurik and his wife, Cerys—one of the few women within the king's battlemage's ranks—flew behind him. Encircling Griff on ferocious wargs had to be Oriel's toughest men and women. Griff was sure that if he were to ever face any of them one on one, it would be his undoing.

After about two hours or so of flight, Griff started to see the scars from the Corruption appear on the land. Dark, disfigured blemishes that tarnished the otherwise beautiful landscape. And it reached. Like black tentacles stretching forward, withering everything at its touch. The waters of the ponds, rivers, and streams it touched turned black. Trees laid dead and decaying. The grass was withered and scorched.

So far, these tendrils of Corruption hadn't reached Bergots. Griff didn't know if that was just happenstance, or if the king had some sort of powerful magic that kept it at bay.

The longer they traveled, the more signs of the Corruption he saw. The scars seemed to be closer together, like a growing, untreated infection upon the land. Any towns they passed were completely deserted—ravaged by blight, overrun by wild, disfigured growth, leaving nothing more than the skeleton of once thriving communities.

Suddenly, the sky darkened. White, puffy clouds converged out of nowhere and covered the endless sea of blue above them. If the sky was an endless sea of blue, it was now as if someone had spilled an endless supply of cotton balls across its surface—soft, harmless, even cheerful at first glance.

But it was strange how suddenly the clouds had appeared. Normally, that would have been a sign to take cover and prepare for a storm. But these weren't storm clouds. Not really. They drifted lazily above them, like the kind of clouds Griff would lie under on a warm summer day. They didn't *look* dangerous. But ... they had appeared so suddenly. The other soldiers noticed the activity above as well and sat straighter on their mounts.

"Are we in danger right now?" Griff hollered over the wind to the soldier on his right.

"Naw!" Yoren responded. "Might be somethin', but might not! Either way, I'm sure we'll be fine. Just keep your wits about ya. That's all."

"Yoren, you crazy old bat!" Isla, one of the other females in the squadron, said to him. "You know this has Corruption storm written all over it!"

Yoren cackled at her response. "Oh, I know. But it's always somethin' we can handle! King's Crown, remember that fire rain couple weeks back?"

Isla rolled her eyes. "I know where this is going," she said to Griff.

"That was a mighty fine rain!" Yoren continued. "Did good for me dry skin!" He held out his arm, showing the tiny burn marks sprinkled across it. "We'll be just fine!"

Griff didn't like it. Something about the clouds just felt off. It was like being smiled at by someone who wasn't really smiling. They *seemed* harmless enough. If that smiling person were to have offered their hand in greeting, Griff would have grasped it. But he would have wondered if their intentions were less than welcoming.

They flew another five to ten minutes in silence, almost as if they were pretending nothing strange had just happened. Almost. Every soldier, including Griff, watched their surroundings—especially above them—with vigilance. Were they being followed? By clouds?

Then the song came. Rising through the sounds of the rushing wind and the flapping of the wargs' wings, was a single note that came from an invisible harp without a strummer. Not too high of a pitch. Not too low. Somewhere in between the extremes, the note held long and beautiful, yet felt otherworldly. Ethereal. And it came from the clouds.

From out of the depths of pure white, a dark circle formed above one of the soldiers in the back. The single note grew in intensity while the dark circle followed the man. The song stopped.

Silence for half a breath. Then a thunderous rush ruptured the silence and out of the shadowy disc in the clouds came a column of wind. As fast as lightning and as strong as a hurricane, it slammed into the soldier and his warg and forced them all the way to the ground. The man's horrific screams were silenced when the column of air met the unforgiving ground.

Suddenly, there was shouting. Orin hollered instructions. Soldiers bellowed their understanding and passed the message down the line. The wargs flew faster.

Then the harp began its song.

Another shadowy circle appeared over a new target. This time toward the front. He barked orders at his warg and together they broke rank and rocketed to the side. It was no use. The warg was fast. But the disc tracked them easily. Almost lazily and carefree. The musicianless harp played its note as the circle followed. Now, however, it sounded like the tune was off. Hollow. Warped. Then silence. A scream. More silence. Two down. The wargs flew faster. The soldiers screamed louder.

Then the harp began its song.

Everyone desperately scanned the sky. Who would be next? This time, the smoky circle appeared over Griff.

Terror flooded Griff's veins. Cold sweat beaded on his forehead. He tried to order Magnus to fly, but his mouth was suddenly dry. Then he looked again. No. It wasn't over him. It was above Yoren. The twisted song echoed louder as the two of them locked eyes. Yoren's were wide with fear. The song stopped. Yoren took a deep breath. Then a strange calm appeared on his face. He gave Griff a nod. Then the wind struck and he was gone.

Then the harp began its song.

And then another note joined in. Just slightly higher in pitch, but this one didn't create a harmony. It twisted and warped the song further. And the two notes joined together, a second dark circle formed. Now there were two of them.

Orin barked an order and the soldiers passed it back.

"To the ground!" he had cried. Without hesitation, the whole squad dove. There was silence, then two more bursts of wind slammed their targets to the ground.

Then the harps began their song. This time, another one joined their haunting chorus. Now, there were three.

The silence hit just as the paws of the wargs touched the ground. The soldiers who had been targeted dodged the bursts of wind just in time. King's crown, those columns were wicked *fast*!

Orin pointed forward to a cluster of small, abandoned, metal buildings. A military outpost? Didn't matter. They needed to get under cover *now*.

The eerie song started again, another note joining. The storm was growing. It was greedy, and it wanted more. Griff searched the clouds but didn't see any circles above him. He hollered for Magnus to keep going.

Silence hit again, and this time, not all were fast enough to dodge. The burst of wind came hammering down and slammed into a soldier on the outside of the pack. He screamed in pain, but something even more horrifying happened next. He was taken into the clouds, still screaming.

Griff dared to look behind him and realized that there was no evidence of the previous attacks. No bodies. The wargs and their riders didn't just crash into the ground. They were lifted back up and disappeared into the clouds. There would be no body to go back to. No bodies to mourn over. They just … disappeared. A deep shudder ran through Griff's entire body, twisting his stomach in knots.

The squadron squeezed through the gates to the outpost, and they were ordered to split up among the buildings. Isla motioned for Griff to follow her as she joined Orin's crew. They were lucky enough to have found one of the few buildings with a door not overgrown with vines and shrubbery. Griff noticed some of the other groups had to blast their way through. He and the rest of their group jumped off their wargs and squeezed into the building together.

Old, dusty computer monitors and keyboards lined the tables against the walls. Just above the tables, stretching across almost the entirety of the wall were large windows that almost reached the ceiling. Scattered papers and trash fluttered in the breeze that drifted in through a few of the broken windows. This must have been some sort of command center.

"What now?" Griff whispered to Orin, almost afraid if he spoke too loud, the Corruption storm would hear.

"We'll wait it out," he replied in a low but steady tone.

The distorted song filled the air once again. Griff couldn't see the clouds, but knew that dark circles were forming. He just didn't know where. All the soldiers jerked their heads back and forth, scanning for signs of where the storm might strike. As the song played, it was like all the air had been sucked out of the room. Like everyone was holding their breath. Waiting. Helpless.

Then there was silence. A thundering rush announced the next attack and all the pillars of wind smashed into the building across the path from Griff. The screams from the soldiers and the cries from the wargs faded as they were pulled from the ground and disappeared into the clouds. Hardly any of the debris from the crushed building remained.

"It can crush *buildings*?" one soldier cried. Sharp whispers of panic filled the room. Even the battle-trained wargs began to whimper in fear.

"Wait! There's something here!" another soldier said, silencing everyone in the room. "A door! And it's unlocked!"

"Lemme see!" Orin ordered, marching through the tightly packed room. As soon as he reached the metal door, he briefly scanned the charred number pad before grasping the handle and flinging it open. A set of stairs led underground into darkness.

He took a few steps down to investigate, came back up, and said, "Everyone in!"

The soldiers and their wargs immediately followed as the song from the clouds played again.

Orin rushed to the broken window, whistled loudly, and barked orders for the others to follow.

"Let's go!" he cried from the back of the group. "The others are coming."

The storm's warped song faded as Griff joined the others down the twisting stairwell. Some of the mages generated a ball of light in their hands, which cast long shadows along the concrete wall. Some of the wargs had to squeeze their wings tight against their bodies to make the descent, but thankfully the walls on either side were just wide enough.

It didn't take long for Griff to reach the bottom, and when he did, he was amazed at what he saw. A large, underground tunnel with tracks. Scattered across the concrete floor were tables and training targets that had seen all sorts of trouble.

A message was burned on the wall high above them, like a battle cry or a war banner.

THE 42 WILL STAND WHEN KORRUN FALLS

"The forty-two?" Griff asked Rurik. "Who's the forty-two?"

"No idea," he answered. His wife, Cerys, rushed over and embraced him, pulling him into a tight hug. "Looks like this place was some sort of training facility for them, though. Nice to know we have others joining the fight."

"Hmm," Orin said, stroking his long, red beard. "I bet this is this group that infiltrated Korrun's army."

"Yeah?" Griff asked, his mind immediately trailing back to Cordelia, where Tyrell had saved his life.

"Why are you following him, Tyrell?"

"I owe you nothing. Especially not answers. But you owe me something. Keep this to yourself, deal?"

Maybe this whole time he *wasn't* actually following Korrun. Maybe there was more good in Tyrell than Griff had given him credit for. Griff had assumed that he had gone to be with his dad, but maybe there was something more at play.

In the distance, a muffled *crash!* shook Griff from his thoughts. The storm was still attacking. Looking for more victims. Thankfully, there would be no more bodies for this storm today. Everyone else had made it to the tunnel. There were hushed sniffles from those who had lost close comrades. There were quiet, angry conversations about the storm. The image of Yoren's silent acceptance on his face just before he was attacked haunted Griff's mind. But amidst the sadness and anger, there was a collective sigh of relief. The storm had taken its toll, but most of the squad had made it safely through the other side.

"Nightstalker's fury, we've never seen anythin' like that," Rurik said to Griff. "Glad you're okay, though."

"We lost some good men and women today," Cerys added.

Griff nodded respectfully in response. Any words of encouragement he could muster in his mind felt hollow. He really had no idea what to say in the midst of tragedy like this. Though it seemed like with each year, he was becoming more accustomed to it.

"You know," Rurik said, "Korrun's not the bad guy here."

He received a sharp look of surprise from his wife.

"Hold on, now. Here me out. Yeah, he's a bad guy, all right? But he's not THE bad guy. He's just the guy that's in the way of the real enemy."

Griff furrowed his brows in hard concentration, trying to follow, but he didn't understand. "If not Korrun … then who?" he asked.

Rurik didn't need to respond with words. He just pointed to the furious sounds echoing above. Then understanding hit.

The Corruption.

Not just the storm, but what *made* the storm. The magical plague that was corrupting all of life. *That* was the ultimate enemy. Korrun was just another obstacle in the king's quest for the shards. A barrier between the king and the total annihilation of the Corruption.

"What do we do now?" Griff asked, turning to the captain.

He heaved a weary sigh and wiped his face with his hands. "We wait."

CHAPTER 34

The storm was angry.

Though its tantrum was muffled by the layers of dirt above them, Griff could still feel it. It had tasted the king's battlemages, and it wanted more.

It was hungry.

They'd considered going deeper into the tunnel, searching for another exit. But there was no telling how far it went—or where it might lead. And, as Rurik put it, "These things usually sputter out eventually."

This one didn't. Not until the next morning. Griff didn't know if it had sputtered out from pure starvation, like Rurik suggested, never to be seen again, or if it had simply wandered off to look for new victims. Either way, everyone was much happier when they emerged from the tunnel and stepped into the light of a new day.

Frustrating as it had been to be stuck there, it gave the squad time to rest and mourn their losses. None of these soldiers were just a number. They'd had names. Families. Friends. And that night, while the Corruption storm laid bare its fury above, the soldiers had sat around small campfires and recounted memories of each person taken that day.

Rurik may not have been right about the storm sputtering out sooner rather than later. But he'd been right about one thing. Korrun wasn't the true enemy. Sure, he had his body count. Crimes that Griff hoped would be brought to justice. But he was sure it was nothing in comparison to the toll the Corruption had taken on the world.

After a scout had returned and confirmed that the storm had indeed disappeared, the soldiers and their wargs marched from the tunnel and continued their journey.

The first few hours back in the air were tense. Everyone scanned all around them, looking for signs of another attack. Nobody spoke. They barely blinked. Finally, when it looked like that storm was gone, for now, the tension in the air faded.

Several hours later, as the sun was setting and casting a golden glow across the land, a familiar city appeared on the horizon. One Griff had never visited in person, but recognized it immediately. He had visited this place in his dreams. Walked among its concrete giants. And there, standing a head taller than the rest of the buildings, was the white stone structure he had explored.

They were in the land of Khemria. A wasteland of shifting sands and forgotten cities on the edges of Oriel's borders. A harsh desert and even harsher death was assured for anyone who dared to venture too far. Haunting stories of this place were whispered among children at bedtime. It was a place where death awaited, yet myths and legends came alive.

There were no names for the abandoned cities in Khemria. Not anymore. There was no need. No one visited and nothing remained but destruction and debris. There was plenty of that to be had in the abandoned cities elsewhere in Oriel, with a far smaller chance of death there, too.

As soon as the ruins of the ancient city came into view, the presence in Griff's mind came alive. There was an eagerness in him that wasn't his own.

As they flew closer, the soldiers glided lower, staying just a few feet above the sands that covered the ground. When Griff had visited this place in his dreams, he'd felt the cold, grainy wind on his skin. It had felt dirty. Gross. But he had awoken in his bed clean and free from the grit. Now the wind was real, grazing against him and leaving bits of sand behind. It clung to him like before, but he knew this time it wasn't going to come off so easily.

The sun disappeared behind the pyramids, bringing with it the golden glow that illuminated the land. Darkness replaced the light and a deeper chill set in. Griff wrapped his cloak around him tighter as the temperature dropped. They were close now, and the stars had appeared to watch the rest of their journey. Finally, the squadron of soldiers landed their wargs on the edge of town. Silence that was so strong it was almost tangible greeted them. It was a harsh reminder that the stories the children told each other were just that. Stories. Speculation. Nothing lived here and never could. Not after Day Zero, anyway.

"What now?" Griff asked quietly to Isla, keeping his voice low over the whipping wind. He still had soldiers protecting his every side, a fact he was very thankful for now that they glided over the edge of this creepy city.

"You'll see," she answered, scanning the tops of the buildings.

A tiny flash of light materialized, then vanished in the blink of an eye.

"There!" Griff hissed. He pointed to the top of a building near the one he'd climbed in his dreams.

The light appeared again, this time in a pattern. Long flashes and short flashes broke through the darkness. Griff had no idea what it was, but Orin studied the light closely, nodding his head in understanding.

"Right," he said, then extended out his own hand and flashed his own pattern in response.

"It's a code we use," Isla explained. "The long and short flashes of our light communicate a message without having to shout at each other."

"Ah, I see."

Orin's hands were a blur as he sent out instructions with his sharp gestures.

"C'mon," Isla said. "Follow Orin to the top of that building." She pointed to their destination, a building just beside the one that had flashed with light. "Oh, and do it *quietly*."

Griff nodded and together, he and Magnus followed her instructions. Orin led a small team that glided through the compact streets, staying low and hidden. When they reached their building, Orin's warg quickly turned up, flying completely vertical, staying close to the building's walls. His warg was almost inches from walking up its side. Griff gripped his handles and clutched onto Magnus' sides with his thighs. Magnus followed the other wargs and Griff had to grit his teeth with all his might, lest he start screaming. Any moment, he thought he might fall off his mount and that would be the end to his quest. But just as soon as the thought infiltrated his mind, Magnus had landed on the rooftop. There, standing across the building top was King Aldamund and his own warg.

"Well, well," the king said, smiling warmly at Griff. "It's good to see you again, Mr. Driscoll. Glad you made it safely through Khemria."

"Y-yes, sir. You too," Griff stammered. Was he cold? Or just nervous? Probably both. This quest of Griff's—no, this *obsession* of his about finding the shards had mostly been in his mind. Now, though, with the king in front of him, suddenly it all felt real. Too real. The stakes were high. So high that it demanded a presence from the very king of Oriel to oversee it.

"Thank you for your service to the kingdom, Griff. Your information has been most helpful."

"I'm glad to hear it, sir."

"The information you gave us solidified some intel we received from an old classmate of yours."

"Tyrell?" Griff asked. "He's still with Korrun? How is he?"

"Well, he seems to be doing all right, for now. He's the one who told us they were coming to Khemria. Your intel pinpointed *exactly* which city they were coming to."

King Aldamund motioned for Griff to follow. Soldiers and wargs parted, allowing them passage to the front of the building. By now the moon had risen high in the sky, its faint, eerie glow washing over the entire city. It was both beautiful and disturbing. Griff tried to imagine this city prior to Day Zero. He imagined the city didn't sleep. It just changed. He pictured the crooked lamp posts straightened and lighting up the walkways. He imagined the smells of late-night meals wafting up to greet him. And lights from within the rooms that dotted across the skyline. He was sure he would have been mesmerized by the experience. Now though, the streetlamps were dark. The only smells in the wind were from the sand and dust that covered literally everything. And the windows which would have lit up the night sky were broken, shattered, or dusty.

The king didn't have to say anything as Griff took it all in. Instead, he waited patiently for the young mage. Then Griff saw it. At the far edge of the city were small campfires that glimmered in the middle of a town park. It was too far away and too dark to see the details, but Griff knew immediately who it was.

"Korrun," he whispered angrily. Even the presence inside him seethed. He had beaten the king's battlemages here and was probably already searching for the shard.

King Aldamund sighed sadly. "Indeed. Though I don't think they have been here long. We saw them setting up camp this morning."

Griff grit his teeth in frustration. The Corruption storm had put them behind. They could have gotten here before them and already started the search. Then, as if to confirm Griff's thoughts, he noticed tiny flames and balls of light sprinkled among the pyramids. They *were* searching already!

"So, what do we do, then?" Griff asked.

"Hmm. That is the question my men and I have been pondering as we waited for you. But fear not, I think we have a plan."

He smiled genuinely, probably to ease Griff's troubled mind. It did the opposite. How could he be calm, knowing what was at stake? And to know they were behind! Korrun was here and already searching for the shard. There was bound to be conflict. Nonetheless, Griff knew not to say anything. He was the king of Oriel, after all. And a good king at that. He had earned Griff's trust, and it was time to show that through his silence.

After speaking with the captains of the different squads, the king laid out his plan. Half the soldiers would attack Korrun's camp to be a distraction and hopefully draw Korrun's forces out of the pyramids to defend.

Meanwhile, the other group needed to get Griff closer to the pyramids, so he could do what he'd been recruited for: locating the next shard. So, Griff, the king, and their protectors would circle the pyramids on their wargs, protected by the cover of night. Conflict was inevitable. Griff had only hoped he wouldn't find himself caught in it. He was just a locator, after all, and he needed the presence inside him to be awake and ready to give directions.

"Men!" the king announced to all the soldiers on the surrounding rooftops. He didn't whisper. He didn't shout. He was calm, yet assertive. It didn't matter now if the black cloaks heard or not. The attack was imminent. "A shard from the Orb of Essence lies near. My brother, Korrun, wants to take it for himself. Tonight: He. Will. Fail."

Shouts of resolve and anticipation filled the air as the king's battlemages rallied around his words. King Aldamund's message wasn't a battle cry. It wasn't a reminder of the task. It was a statement of trust. Every mage there felt it. And every mage knew that the king of Oriel was placing his trust in their skill, camaraderie, and loyalty. They would make sure that by the end of the night, King Aldamund would have the shard in his possession.

Griff's chest swelled with pride because he knew the king trusted in *him* as well. *He* was the locator. The only one with a shard inside him, pointing him to its brother. Lives were at stake, and he wasn't going to be the weak link tonight. He thought back to his friends' disappointed looks in the Altar Storm arena after he'd failed to show up. He wouldn't be the weak link ever again.

With a roar that shook Griff's bones, the first squadron lifted from the surrounding buildings and dashed toward Korrun's camp. There was movement on the ground. Tents lit up as black cloaks were alerted by the king's speech. It didn't matter, though. There were just as many black cloaks as there were battlemages.

Fire spells blasted the ground from above as the king's mages launched the first of their spells. Surprised shouts and corresponding commands echoed across the hollow city. Some of the battlemages launched ice spells with balls of light embedded inside. They landed at the entrances to the tents. When they exploded, the light was so bright, it blinded even Griff from where he stood. Part one of their plan was working so far: disorient the enemy. There was chaos in the camp. Confused men and women tumbled over themselves, trying to fight an enemy they couldn't see. Either because they were blinded or because their enemy was shielded by darkness.

Griff bounced on his saddle, waiting for the king's command. They needed to hurry to the pyramids before it was too late.

"Steady," the king commanded his men. "Let the first squad do their work. Wait for the others to leave the pyramids."

The mages in Korrun's army began to launch a counter attack. Yellow, red, and green lightning spells discharged from the ground. Most missed as their targets were cloaked in the night. A few of them hit, sending soldiers and their wargs to the ground. Most of the battlemages stayed in the air, while a few landed to protect their comrades who were recovering from the fall.

Suddenly, nightstalkers of every breed swarmed the area. The king's battlemages who were on the ground drew their handles and crafted weapons. Then, dazzling blue shots lit up the darkness from those wielding guns. Blue arrows whizzed in between tents, felling a few out of the swarm. Controlled bursts of spells from the battlemages collided with the nightstalkers. Korrun's army retaliated with their own multicolored spells.

Orbs of light bobbed in zig-zag lines from the pyramids as the black cloaks tried to fall back from their search and form a defense. Griff smiled. Help was on the way. Perfect. The king watched his men a few minutes longer before he spoke.

"It's time! Fly to the south and circle back around!"

He had barely finished speaking when Griff and Magnus sprang into the air. Finally, Griff didn't have to sit still any longer. It was his turn.

"Let's go, Magnus!" Griff called, patting his side. "You got this!"

Griff eyed the pyramids off in the distance. The number of bobbing lights grew fewer and fewer.

"Okay, little buddy," Griff whispered to the presence inside him. "Just tell me where to go."

Together, Griff and Magnus followed the king south, then circled back around to avoid detection. The whole time, Griff locked his eyes on the pyramid. Which one was it? Which one housed the next shard? He didn't feel a stir. That still, small voice in the back of his mind only seemed eager, but it wasn't guiding him. Leading him to the next shard. He needed to get closer.

The king looked back at Griff expectantly. As if he were checking to see if he'd found the location. Griff shook his head and hollered, "Let's move closer!"

King Aldamund nodded and snapped the reins of his warg. It flew faster, and Magnus matched its speed. They were just above the southernmost pyramid now. And Griff gazed upon its beauty. The presence gave him no instructions. His stomach didn't flutter with a foreign joy not his own. An intrusive excitement didn't override his thoughts. This pyramid wasn't the one.

They circled on the backside of the next structure. It was the least impressive of them all. Unlike the others which still maintained their height and pyramid shape, this one was more like a large, stone mound than a pyramid. It didn't have nice, sharp edges or a point at the top. It was worn and weathered, barely noticeable compared to the giants next to it. This couldn't be the on—

"SKREEEEEK!"

Griff and Magnus jolted as something slammed into Magnus' side. Griff's feet were yanked from the stirrups. He flailed his arms, desperately searching for a handhold, clamping onto the only thing he could find: a clump of Magnus' fur. Magnus barked in pain, but continued to fly as Griff barely held onto his side. Griff found a ledge on the saddle and repositioned his hands off the warg's fur. Then the nightstalker fluttered into position for another attack.

It was a large, bat-like creature with the signature deep-black scales of a nightstalker. Its four wings beat out of sync with each other in forced, jerky movements. Yet, it flew steady alongside Magnus. Horrific and unusually long, skinny arms that were the length of its entire body reached for Griff, trying to yank him off. Pure dread gripped Griff's chest. The nightstalker unhinged its jaw and opened wide, revealing a gaping, black void lined with rows of jagged, dagger-like teeth. It could easily swallow Griff whole. And it was trying to do just that.

It screeched and yanked at Magnus' fur, dragging itself closer. A wet *click* sound emanated from its jaw as it became unhinged again and the mouth opened wide. Griff froze in fear. The wings jerked vigorously. Violent excitement radiated from the beast. One long finger extended out and caressed the side of Griff's face, then its mouth opened wider.

WHAM! The beast screeched in pain as a fire spell crashed into its back.

"Wake up, Griff!" Isla screamed. "We need you!"

Griff nodded. She was right. Time to step up.

He flexed his fingers and spread them wide, blue lightning crackling across his palm. He raised his hand high, ready to exterminate the horrifying beast. But as it fell, it grabbed Griff's leg, sending them both spiraling to the ground.

His screams joined with the nightstalker's screeches. The monster let go of his leg and its arms flailed about. Its wings quivered and jerked, but they were scorched from Isla's fire spell. They couldn't save the creature now, and its shriek carried a woeful realization of that fact.

Panic dulled Griff's mind. Ideas and plans on how to walk away from this fall unscathed melted into the background. The mound-like pyramid, once a background piece in the grand landscape of Khemria, was getting closer with every second. Griff would crash into the hard stones and his mission would be over before it began.

An idea finally sparked. Would a wind spell work? They'd used it before to soften landings when jumping from high places. Could he soften his landing enough to live? It was worth a try.

Griff roared from effort and terror, then swirled his hands and forced every bit of energy out of them. Powerful gusts of wind rushed from them, and suddenly, he slowed. The nightstalker continued to fall at the same speed, but now there was a growing distance between them. But Griff's wind wasn't strong enough. It slowed his fall, but he was still going too fast.

He flinched when he heard the sickening *crack!* of the nightstalker's impact against the pyramid. That was going to be him. It was like he was witnessing his very own demise right before it happened.

Then—Magnus. His wings were tucked, his ears were folded back. He had dived to rescue Griff. Griff clutched onto Magnus' fur for the second time. And this time, Magnus shifted his weight and rolled onto his back, forcing Griff to ride on his belly. Was he going to sacrifice himself for Griff?

Magnus flung his wings out wide and together they slowed even more. But it still wasn't enough. The pyramid was so close now.

"Magnus!" Griff screamed wildly. "Roll! NOW!"

Griff jumped, trusting Magnus would obey. He did. The warg tucked its wings and twisted right side up. Griff landed awkwardly, but clutched the warg's neck for dear life. Without missing a beat, Magnus' wings flew out and beat with purpose.

They slowed even more. But they were out of time. Magnus and Griff crashed into the side of the pyramid, halfway to the bottom, forcing Griff off his mount. Together they slid and rolled along the smooth stones until they smashed into the gritty sand at the base.

Pain flared all over his body. He was scraped and bruises were already forming on his arm.

But he was alive.

Griff groaned as he sat upright. His muscles ached. His mind hazy. He heard a whimper several feet away.

"Magnus!" he screamed, ignoring the pain and scrambling to his feet. He dashed over to the warg who was on his side, breathing heavily.

"Are you okay? What's wrong, buddy. Can you show me?"

Magnus whimpered quietly in response. Then Griff noticed his front legs twitch. He didn't dare touch them, but from the looks of it, they were both broken.

Several wargs and their riders touched down behind Griff.

"You okay, son?" King Aldamund asked as he surveyed the scene.

"Yes, sir. But ... Magnus isn't. It's his legs, sir. I think they're broken."

The king hustled over and knelt beside Magnus. "Poor boy. It'll be all right, though."

He gently placed a hand on each of the warg's legs and closed his eyes. A soft blue glow emanated from his hands, and Magnus' breathing slowed to a normal pace.

"You'll be all right, Magnus," the king said, smiling and patting his head. "Just stay here for now and let the magic do its work. Now." He faced Griff. "Any signs of the shard?"

Griff clenched his jaw and shook his head. He hated to disappoint the king, especially at a time when the stakes were so high. From the ground, Griff couldn't see all the pyramids. Having a warg's eye view was more suitable for scanning all possibilities.

Suddenly, his heart skipped a beat. A foreign excitement flooded his mind and thoughts. He was staring at the pyramid right in front of them. The unimpressive mound of rock.

Here? Griff thought. He felt a non-physical, excited nod within him.

"Actually, sir. I think the shard is in there." Griff pointed ahead and everyone's eyes followed.

The king raised his eyebrows in disbelief. "This one, here, you say?"

Griff nodded, doubt still trying to invade his thoughts.

"I saw an entrance on the opposite side, sir," Isla said.

"Hmm. Then let's go. Griff, come with me." The king jumped on his warg and held out a hand for Griff to join him. Once they were both on and secured, the king's warg darted several feet to the sky and flew them around to the front side of the pyramid. From their wargs, those guarding Griff and the king dispatched the few black cloaks that were on the outside, guarding the entrance.

The foreign excitement within Griff's mind grew when they landed at the entrance among the bodies of Korrun's followers. It was as if the presence was trying to pull Griff forward into the pyramid.

"This is it, sir. I'm sure of it," Griff told the king.

"Very good, Griff." He turned toward his guards. "It's here. Let's go."

Everyone hopped off their wargs and walked toward the entrance. Two torches, one on each side, illuminated a long hallway that led deeper into the structure. The shadows it cast danced along the stone walls. It was entrancing. Provocative. Inviting them in to see what treasures lay just beyond the light.

Suddenly, a swarm of black cloaks and nightstalkers emerged from the darkness within the pyramid, marching toward Griff and the others. They must have heard their comrades fall. It had been an easy, almost unfair matchup between the flying battlemages and the few black cloaks guarding the entrance. Now, though, the odds were stacked against them.

The squad of black cloaks stopped in the hallway just short of exiting the pyramid. They turned to their side and stepped back against either wall. Nightstalkers poured out of the pyramid and stood along the front side of the stone structure.

Then, another figure emerged. He had long, straight, brown hair that fell effortlessly down to his shoulders, and a stubbled beard streaked with more gray than before. But most notable was the narrow scar on his left cheek. Prancing at his heels was an alligator-like nightstalker, a permanent, malevolent smile twisted all over its fiendish face.

Korrun Aldamund had stepped out of the pyramid and into the moonlight to personally greet his brother.

CHAPTER 35

"Hello, brother. I was told I might find you out here." Korrun's twisted smile knotted Griff's stomach.

King Aldamund smiled somberly at Korrun. "I'd like to say it's good to see you, brother, but sadly, I cannot say the same."

Anger flashed across Korrun's face for a moment, but realizing all eyes were on him, he dismissed the emotion and returned to his smiling, arrogant façade.

"Well, that's sad." He turned to his supporters and raised his hands out wide. "What *good king* would not be happy to see his own brother?" he spat. The black cloaks laughed. Korrun faced the king again and said, "Hmph! Seems like the king of Oriel isn't quite the *family man* everyone thinks him to be."

"Korrun, it is in the best interest of our people that you please step aside and allow us through." The king stepped forward and the nightstalkers and black cloaks sank back into the stone walls. "You have a chance here to *do the right thing*! I implore you, brother. Do what is right and good!"

The leader of the black cloaks narrowed his eyes at his brother. "You and I have a *very* different definition of the word *good*," he spat. "And no. I will not step aside. I'm done stepping aside so that you can fail. *I* will not fail! *I* am willing to do what *you won't do* so this 'good' that you speak of can exist all throughout our land. But you refuse to see things my way."

Korrun crossed his arms in defiance. "So, no. If you want access to this pyramid, you will have to climb over bodies to do it. Mine included!"

With his final shout, Korrun thrust his hands forward, unleashing a spiraling vortex of wind and brilliant red lightning at the king and Griff. Immediately, the king conjured a large blue shield that covered them both. The spell rebounded and fizzled out into the darkness above them. The force of the spell's impact caused the king to slide a few inches backward in the sand. The king let down his shield to speak, but Korrun's eyes grew wide with realization, and he stepped forward.

"YOU!" He pointed at Griff. "You're the boy! You have something I need! And I will take it from you by any means necessary."

Midnight black flames erupted between Korrun's swirling hands.

Griff conjured his own spell. A ball of wind danced over his palms. He wasn't sure if he could counter Korrun's powerful magic, but he wasn't going down without a fight.

Korrun hurled the dark fire Griff's direction. Griff swirled his hands, enlarging his ball of wind into a large wall, hoping its upward bursts would push the spell away from him.

Suddenly, two nightstalkers blocked the path. They exploded in black fire and their bodies disappeared, their echoing screeches lingering long after their death.

King Aldamund lowered his hands, his eyes burning with focus. He had levitated the monsters into the spell's path, blocking Griff from its power. Two down, dozens more to go.

Breathing heavily, not from exertion, but from pure rage, Korrun flung the hair off his glistening forehead.

"Get them," he ordered, never taking his eyes off the king.

Korrun's words created chaos. A battlefield of once clearly divided sides immediately became a tangled mess of monsters, mages, and magic. Wild spells of red, yellow, and green zipped back and forth as though there had been no defined target. Horrid screeches and guttural growls merged with the screams and shout of black cloaks and battlemages.

Griff rolled under a red lightning spell, then blasted the black cloak in front of him with a large ball of ice. He shielded himself against a weak fireball, then flung the mage backward with a wind spell. The mage slammed against the wall of the pyramid and fell over, unconscious.

The king and his brother's battle raged on. Each mage displayed spectacular power and skill. Korrun bombarded the king with red and black spells, only for them to be deflected or dodged and responded to with equal power and force. They pulled away from the rest of the skirmish, as their battle was personal. There seemed to be an understanding between the two sides: let the brothers fight.

A nightstalker's claw barely missed Griff's leg, and he responded with lightning to its face. He quickly unsheathed his handle, its steel Night-flame wings reflecting the brilliant blue from his magical blade. He slashed at the monsters surrounding him, taking off multiple limbs in a single swipe. A non-magical black cloak got close enough to try stabbing Griff with their dagger. Before Griff could respond, the man answered to Isla's ice shard.

Griff dodged when he could. Sliced when he could. Conjured spells when he could. And shielded against the rest. Even then, there were times he wasn't quick enough. Thankfully, the armor he wore took the brunt of the damage. But the pain was still real.

No matter how fast he was, how many spells he flung, how many nightstalkers he cut down, it didn't make a difference. The king's battlemages were completely outnumbered. With all the skill they had, the numbers still didn't add up.

Eventually, Griff found himself surrounded. Monsters. Black cloaks. They stared at him with an evil, conspiring kind of grin. The other battlemages were too busy locked in skirmishes of their own, blind to Griff's predicament. The nightstalkers growled. The black cloaks laughed. Then they closed in.

"Ahoy!"

Griff knew that voice. A wind spell knocked several of the black cloaks onto their backs. Blue arrows streaked through the others. And from above, an excruciatingly hot, black fire incinerated the nightstalkers.

"*Runa*?" Griff called incredulously. "*Marth*?"

Kindra and another warg from Bergots slammed to the ground, spraying sand across the battlefield. Runa touched down next to them. Marth, Vincent, Sadie, and Mira jumped off the two wargs, then Marth rubbed Runa's head and said, "Good girl!"

"Wha—what are you guys doing here?" Griff asked.

"Talk later!" Sadie shouted, sending a fire spell whizzing toward a black cloak.

"Right!" Marth said. Even he knew now wasn't the time for conversation.

Mira pulled back her bow and sent a blue arrow into the chest of a monkey nightstalker that was scrambling toward them.

Vincent ignited a blue hammer out of his handle and swung it wide, flinging several black cloaks into the darkness.

Runa stepped beside Griff and swung her tail, knocking over a large badger-like nightstalker. It crumpled to the ground, then the dragon snatched it in her jaws and flung it across the battlefield.

Someone seized Griff's hand. He turned, swinging his sword, but stopped short when he saw Isla's wide eyes.

"I don't know who they are or where they came from. But *you* need to get inside the pyramid and get the shard. We'll hold them off as long as we can."

Griff nodded in understanding and hollered for his friends to follow. They dashed through the chaos, ducking and shielding as needed before they passed the torches at the entrance and finally disappeared into the dark hallway.

The echoes of battle faded behind them as they ran. The path curved downward, and Griff realized it was leading them underground. He conjured light and the others followed. The path curved, and once they realized they weren't being trailed, they paused to catch their breath.

"What ... how ..." Griff sputtered.

"We couldn't let you have all the fun, now, could we?" Marth said.

Mira rolled her eyes, then took Griff's hand in hers. "It may look like all I care about is school. But believe it or not, you're not the only one in this group that cares about this mission, Griff. We *all* have something to fight for." She paused and scanned behind them, listening intently. "When Headmaster Aldamund put us together as a battlegroup, he probably didn't expect us to go on quests for the king. But we *are* a team. And we fight for the things that matter. Altar Storm matches, or anything else. We fight *with* and *for* each other. So, yes, we're here to help."

"Well, how did you know wh—"

"How do you think?" Sadie said.

Griff paused and thought about it. "Professor Coen?" They all nodded. "He put you up to it, huh?"

"No," Marth grinned. "He just couldn't handle our constant nagging."

"*Your* constant nagging," Sadie corrected him.

"Well, we don't need to go pointing fingers. But either way, he eventually told us where to find you. Once we got here, Runa did the rest, didn't you *girrrl*?" Marth gave the dragon a scratch under her chin.

Griff looked at his friends. There was a fiery zeal about them. The way they stood. The way they looked at him. They believed not only in the mission, but they also believed in *him*.

He took a deep breath, then nodded. "Okay. Well, you're here now. So, let's do this. I believe the shard is somewhere in this pyramid. I don't know what to expect, but these shards like to … protect themselves. So be on your guard. Watch your backs. Keep your magic ready."

"Easy," Marth said casually. "Now, let's go already. The sooner we find this thing, the sooner we get home."

Together, they continued deeper underground. Deeper into the pyramid. Several minutes later, the air around them grew colder. The darkness penetrated deeper. Then they came upon a large stone arch with ancient lettering carved into the top.

"Think it says, 'Welcome to Happy Land, Where All Your Dreams Come True?'" Marth asked.

"Probably not," Griff muttered. He stepped forward toward the opening and paused, listening intently and peering into the thick darkness. He ignited a light spell and raised it high. It didn't do any good. There was a large stone wall that kept him from seeing any farther. It stopped about fifteen feet high, but it didn't connect to any ceiling.

"Mira. Arrow, please. Right there." Griff pointed through the arch and past the top of the wall.

She didn't ask questions. She didn't hesitate. Instead, Mira stepped beside him, pulled off her bow and launched a bright blue arrow that sailed upward. It took what felt like an eternity before it finally bounced off the ceiling.

"That's what I thought. This is a massive room. And I'm guessing there's not an easy way across."

"Think Runa could fly us across, one by one?" Marth asked.

"Think she's strong enough to lift me?" Vincent asked with a sly smile.

Marth chuckled. "Right. You'll just have to stay behind or meet us on the other side."

"She's not strong to fly *anyone* across yet, okay? I was just impressed that she flew this far already. Let's not push our—or her—luck," Sadie said.

Griff nodded. "Yeah. One day she'll be strong enough to carry us *all* on her back." He thought back to her mother on the island. "But not today." He eyed his comrades. "You guys ready? You don't have to do this," he said, looking to his teammates.

"C'mon, already. You're wasting time," Sadie said, pushing past him. Vincent smiled, then followed. They walked through the arch and were immediately met with their first decision.

"Right or left?" Marth asked.

"Or do we split up?" Mira said.

"No way," Marth said. "Have you never read those ghost stories where the group splits up and then they all end up dead? We stick together."

"I prefer non-fiction," Mira said defensively, hugging herself tightly.

"C'mon." Griff nudged her gently to the left. "Let's stick together."

The first several twists and turns proved to be uneventful. Then Griff held up his hand and the others halted. Something felt off about this stretch of hallway. It was too clean. Too straight.

"Lemme see your pack," Griff asked Vincent. He took the large bag from his friend and tossed it in front of him. It landed on the stone floor with an echoey *thud*. White lightning flashed from one wall to the other, crackling wildly and loudly.

The group jolted backward, almost toppling over each other. Had they stepped into the hallway unawares, they would have all been dead.

"King's crown, that was *frightening*," Marth said, out of breath.

"Yeah, and I have a feeling that's not the end of the terrors," Griff said. "But I have an idea. Remember last year's Altar Storm match between Milo's and Erian's group?"

They thought for a moment, and understanding dawned on the group. Together, they stood back-to-back, each person facing a wall. Griff had tucked himself in between Marth and Vincent and faced forward. They all conjured shields tall enough and wide enough to cover themselves and the person next to them, while Griff's was wide enough to protect the entire group from any frontal attacks. The hallway was wide enough for them to spread out just far enough for Runa to squeeze in the middle.

As one armored unit, they shuffled down the stretch of hallway. Sadie screamed when the first bolt of lightning hit, but thankfully, she maintained her shield. Runa whimpered, but waddled along with the rest of the group. It was working. The lightning fizzled out upon impact, then another bolt would take its place.

The air crackled with electric tension. The flashes of bright white illuminated the fear painted on their faces. It was like walking through the heart of a summer thunderstorm. But they were close to the other side now. Inching slowly forward, their shields weathered every strike. Then with Griff's final step, crossing the threshold onto the other side of the hallway, his foot sank as the stone tile compressed underneath his weight.

Suddenly, the whole maze, not just the hallway, flashed in an overpowering, awe-inspiring brilliant display of bright white light as lightning in every room, every corner, struck. Sharp *cracks* and angry sizzles exploded against the penetrating silence. Then all went dark. Silent.

Nobody moved. Nobody spoke. Then, off in the distance, a loud chorus of harsh, guttural howls broke the silence.

"What. Was. That," Marth whispered, his voice trembling.

"Um. I ... I'm not sure," Griff said. "But I'll bet we'll find out."

"Hmm ..." Vincent said, a slight tone of fear slipping through.

"I'm ... I'm just glad we didn't split up," Mira noted.

"Yeah. Whoever set this up must've expected groups to be searching for the shard," Griff said.

Mira shuddered. "This would have narrowed the numbers substantially."

"Well, no backing out now," Griff said.

"Let's keep going," Sadie said, stealing Griff's next words.

They crept forward together, their shields lighting up the dark pathway. As they moved, they listened intently. Waiting for the next strike of lightning or another trap to spring. Nothing happened. There were no sounds. No sparks or hums. Not even a strange, wrong feeling in the air.

"You guys good with shields down, now?" Griff asked. They all looked around, carefully examining their surroundings. Finally, everyone agreed. They extinguished their shields and continued slowly with Griff and Runa leading the way. Sure, they moved at the speed of Professor Erebus' history lectures on a rainy day, but it kept them alive.

Silence hung heavy all around them. With each movement, Griff expected another burst of sound or light to announce their doom. Yet, they moved down more passageways without a single event. Until they rounded a corner and reached a dead end.

For the first time since they entered the maze, there was something else besides ominous, never-ending blackness above them. Strung across the top were thick, winding vines with purple flowers that glowed faintly against the dark. Some of the strands had fallen and dangled listlessly over their heads.

"They're beautiful," Mira whispered, reaching out her hands to touch one.

Griff snatched her hand before she made contact.

She wheeled around to him. "What in the king's cr—"

"—Don't touch it, Mira! Remember the last shard I went after? The whole forest came alive. These vines didn't grow here on their own."

Understanding dawned on Mira's face. "Right. Sorry. *C'mon Mira, get it together,*" she hissed at herself.

"All good. Just … be careful please." He squeezed her hand, and she kissed his cheek.

"Thanks for looking out for me."

Griff nodded then looked at their surroundings. "All right, clearly, we chose the wrong path. Let's go back the other way. I saw a hallway that looked promising."

"Well, hold on now, Griff," Mira said, her eyes furrowed in concentration as she examined the stones along the side wall. "I wouldn't take everything at face value in this maze. You said it yourself, these vines didn't grow here by themselves. Maybe this is a test or a trick. Might be a hidden door nearby or something."

They tested Mira's theory, careful to avoid the low hanging vines, but they found nothing.

"Well, we gave it a good try," Marth said.

"Hmm," Vincent agreed. He pulled off his pack and dug through it. "Anybody got some food? Mine's gone."

"'Course it is, buddy. You can have some of Sadie's though!"

Sadie smacked Marth's shoulder and simply said, "Mine."

Vincent chuckled and leaned against the back wall. His weight pushed it forward an inch or two, and Griff heard a metallic *click*. A few paces back, one of the walls suddenly swung sideways, blocking their way back. They were trapped.

"Uh ... guys!" Marth shouted.

The floor started to quake. The front and back walls began moving closer to each other. Closer to the group.

"It's going to crush us!" Mira screamed.

Runa whimpered loudly and spun around in tight circles.

Vincent backed away from the sliding wall, and a vine from above came alive and whipped around his torso, pulling him a few feet off the ground. He bellowed in pain as sharp thorns suddenly erupted from the vines, piercing his skin. More vines awakened and snaked around him, their retractable spikes surfacing as well. Their goal was simple: either shred Vincent to pieces or make sure he stayed to watch the walls come together.

Sadie blasted the vines above with a fire spell. They dropped Vincent, but the sparks from her explosion rained on the group.

"Careful, Sadie!" Marth said. "I'm not dying by fire today either!"

She scowled, but Griff knew Marth was right. The walls were getting closer. The room was getting smaller. Vincent struggled to his feet, small patches of blood soaking into his shirt. More vines came alive and wriggled toward them, their glowing purple flowers pulsing with hunger.

Griff snatched the handle from its sheath and ignited his blade. He sliced through the vines like hot steel through old cobwebs. Runa jumped in the fray, shredding the thick strands with her claws and teeth.

The grinding of the walls grew louder as they moved closer to the group. Panic surged through Griff's body. Of all the ways to die, this was low on his list.

"What—what if we..." Marth's eyes were wide with horror as he scanned their tiny room, looking for any clues to help them escape. "What if we climbed *through* the vines? The walls are getting close enough we might can get a hand or foot on each side!"

"There wouldn't be enough time!" Sadie called, sending a controlled burst of lightning upward.

"And there's no need!" Mira said. "Look!"

She had pulled up one of the stone tiles, revealing a slick, polished, obsidian slide that led underneath the maze. The wall behind Griff pushed him forward. Only a minute or so until the two walls crushed them.

"Nice work!" Griff said. "Let's go!"

Runa had to squeeze her wings hard against her side, but even she was able to fit in the hole after everyone else. Griff was sure to be the last one, slicing any vines that tried to latch on last minute.

The walls were so close now. Griff could have braced a hand against each one. Instead, he extinguished his blade and jumped through the hole, allowing the darkness to swallow him. He slid several feet down before his bottom hit the cold, stone floor. A loud, echoing, crunch was heard as the two walls crumpled the stone tile Mira had lifted.

Griff leaned his head back against the obsidian slide and took a deep breath. His heart slowed.

"That … that was *too* close."

Nobody responded as they all processed their narrow escape. Sadie tended to Vincent, bandaging the worst of his wounds from the supplies in her pack. Runa sauntered over and laid next to Griff, placing her head in his lap.

"You did good, girl. Really good."

"Well," Marth said, "it looks like we don't have to worry about wandering through the maze anymore." He motioned around them. They had slid down into a vast hallway, as wide as an Altar Storm pitch. It was hard to tell how long it was, as the corridor stretched indefinitely, the shadows on either end swallowing the path whole. Mira's light spell could only penetrate the darkness so far. It was like they were on an island of light, surrounded by a vast ocean of darkness.

Then Griff noticed the smell. Wet. Musty. It was like walking into a flooded grandmother's house. Drops of unseen water echoed into eternity. The air felt thick. Moist. Almost tangible.

"We're not going *through* the maze," Marth said at last. "We're going under. I think we just cheated this deadly little game."

"Hmm," Vincent scratched his chin. "I don't think it'll be tha—"

Chittering sounds echoed from behind them. Griff leapt to his feet and ignited his sword again. His heart thumped harder. The chittering got louder. Closer. Whatever it was, there was more than one. Could have been a dozen. Could have been hundreds. Either way, Griff wasn't about to find out.

"Let's go!" he commanded. The battlegroup turned and sprinted forward into the vast ocean of darkness, unsure of what they would find. Regardless, it had to be better than what was behind.

Mira led the way, her light spell pushing back the darkness and illuminating their path. The group moved quickly, but it didn't matter. The chittering grew louder and other sounds joined the horrific chorus. Scraping. Grinding. Snapping. Sounds that came out of nowhere and everywhere at the same time.

"We gotta go faster!" Griff called from the back.

A high-pitched, raspy shriek rang out behind him. He turned to look. His heart sank into his stomach. His blood froze. But he kept running.

It was a nightstalker. But not like one he'd ever seen before. Twisted. Warped. Its body gleamed with deep black scales, thick as armor—something a normal blade wouldn't penetrate. Enormous claws lined with jagged, bony spikes snapped as it surged forward. Two tails, each with a stinger dripping with poison, were raised high and ready to strike the moment it was close enough. Its eyes, two on top, the rest along its skull, glowed with an eerie, hollow hunger. Then there were its fangs. Sharp and twisted. Made to kill.

Worst of all were its legs on top of its back. There were eight of them and they lined either side. The monster leapt, its grotesque upper limbs catching on the ceiling. It flipped its tails under its belly and continued to sprint right-side up, the second set of legs just as fast as the first.

It was right above him now. With a loud hiss, it tucked its top legs back in, falling toward Griff. He dove, but was too late. One of the jagged pinchers scraped across his shoulder as he rolled. A scream of pain escaped his lips, but he forced himself to stand, ignoring the searing, white-hot wound and the blood that spilled from it.

Instead, he swirled around, bringing his blade full circle, slicing the deadly pincer off the beast. It pulled back and shrieked in pain. Griff used the opportunity to blast it with a wind spell. It flung backward into the swarm of other scorpion nightstalkers that took its place.

"Guys!" Griff called. That was all he had time to say. Two more nightstalkers chittered toward him, tails poised to strike. They hissed in anticipation, but Griff's bright yellow lightning arced between them, flinging them to the side. He turned to see another poisonous stinger speeding toward him. He couldn't cast in time. Couldn't swing his sword fast enough.

Suddenly, Vincent's large hammer smashed into it and sent the monster flying into the dark. Sadie rushed in with a blazing red fire spell, scorching the row of creatures in front of her. Runa stepped beside her and gushed black fire. Mira's blue arrows streaked through the darkness, shrieks of pain confirming her kills. And Marth sent wave after wave of wind spells to keep the masses at bay.

What had been like a single, writhing mass of bodies now broke apart. They spread out with terrifying purpose. Some continued to charge forward against the onslaught from the battlegroup. Others used their top row of legs to scuttle along the sides and ceiling of the corridor. They were trying to surround them.

One launched itself at Sadie, crashing into her and sending her to the ground. It rolled away, but another pinned her to the floor. One tail struck, but Sadie whipped her head to the side just in time, and it crashed against the stone floor. The other tail stabbed, narrowly missing her neck. Then the monster met Vincent's hammer.

Suddenly, Marth roared in pain and sank to his knees. Blood immediately drenched the back of his pant leg, the stain spreading quickly. Before anyone could get to him, he screamed again. Another swipe with the nightstalker's claw opened a fresh wound on his arm.

A stinger dripping with poison pointed right at Marth, but Mira felled it with an arrow. Monstrous heads turned as they smelled the fresh blood from Marth's wound. Sadie launched an ice spell, creating a tall, frozen wall between Marth and the nightstalkers. But they were starting to climb, digging their sharp legs into the ice.

Terror gripped Griff. Their magic wasn't enough. Their weapons weren't enough. For every one nightstalker killed, two more stepped in their place. Adrenaline coursed through Griff's body. Anger, fright, and desperation fought for control. Then, a sense of purpose and power engulfed those lesser emotions. It didn't come from Griff, but from the foreign presence inside him. He felt the power rise.

"Shields!" Griff bellowed. His group obeyed without hesitation. They surrounded a wounded Marth, Runa stepping into the middle as they ignited their shields. White winds churned powerfully around Griff. Any nightstalkers that rushed him were violently flung backward. Pure white lightning crackled and danced within the gusts. Fire of the same color ignited and extinguished, bursting out of the sphere of wind and lightning. It was a beautiful and deadly dome of controlled chaos. The power inside him grew. His fear melted away, and zealous confidence surged in its place. The dome expanded. The winds strengthened. The lightning flashed brighter. The bursts of fire exploded more forcefully.

With an angry shout, Griff flung his hands wide and the sphere of chaotic magic blasted outward, incinerating all the surrounding night-stalkers. Shrieks and hisses melted along with their bodies. Ash rained from the ceiling where the monsters once hovered. A few of the night-stalkers toward the back remained, but they quickly chittered away, their claws scraping against the ground as they fled.

The horrific echoing sounds of the beasts faded, and then there was silence. Griff heaved a sigh of relief and wiped the sweat off his brow.

Marth stood and limped toward Griff. He wrapped his arms around him and squeezed tightly. Vincent and Mira rushed over and joined.

"Well done!" Vincent said, nearly crushing Griff.

"C'mon, Sadie!" Marth said, gritting through the pain of his fresh wounds. "Get in on the action! You know you want to!" Even with blood spilling from him, Marth couldn't help but crack a joke.

Sadie crossed her arms and glared at him. "Don't be stupid. Marth, you need help. And ... good job, Griff."

"Okay ... thanks, guys ... but ... I need to breathe."

Finally, they released their hold on him, and he sucked in a lungful of musty air.

"That was close," he said. He turned to Marth. A sting of guilt washed over him when he saw the blood. "You okay?"

Marth winced as he lightly touched his wounds. "Think so." He plopped on the ground, then laid his head on the floor.

Sadie walked over. "Here, I've got more bandages."

Griff was amazed to watch Sadie patch up Marth. The person who annoyed her the most with his incessant chatter. Their team was really coming together.

I'm sorry, friend, Griff thought as he watched Sadie work quickly to stop the bleeding, his moans of pain bouncing off the walls. *You shouldn't have to pay the price for following me. I promise, I'll get us out of this.*

"We better keep moving in case there are other ... things ... like that lurking around," Griff finally said once Sadie had finished her work.

The presence inside him fluttered again. Trying to pull him forward. There was an excitement. They must be getting close. Griff ignited a light spell and rushed forward.

"Hey! Wait up!" Marth grunted in pain as he stood. "Never mind! You keep going, I'll catch up!"

A minute later, Griff appeared in front of an ancient, ornate wooden door. More unfamiliar letters were scrawled across the top, but Griff didn't bother to try and understand what it said. The presence inside was nearly screaming into Griff's mind. They were so close.

As the rest of the battlegroup caught up, Griff grasped the rusted metal handle and pulled. The archaic hinges groaned with the weight of the door. A dark stairwell that wound upward greeted them. This led to another door that mimicked the first. When Griff opened it, torchlight poured into the dark stairwell.

With Griff's first steps into the room, the presence inside him surged with triumph. They were here. This was the place. This was where the shard had been hidden this whole time. But Griff's heart sank when his eyes adjusted to the light.

A girl Griff had never seen before gasped when they entered, stepping back as two other figures moved forward. One was a black cloak Griff didn't recognize, but the other—blond hair, stocky, and that smug, know-it-all grin—Griff was all too familiar with. Kaden Horter. Hot anger flooded Griff as he eyed the dark cloak his old tormentor wore.

As disappointed as Griff was to see one of his peers donning Korrun's colors, the gut-punch came from the other person standing beside the girl: Tyrell Falkenburg—and the shard he held in his hands.

CHAPTER 36

Ava smiled at Tyrell. Then he did something he hadn't done in a long time. So long, as a matter of fact, that when he did it, it felt foreign. He smiled, too.

He gazed into those brilliant hazel eyes that gleamed with fresh joy. She was always a happy, excitable person. But this happy was different. Because things with *him* were different. Better. She giggled as she dragged him toward the edge of camp. Not toward the pyramids. Only select groups were permitted to go there. And only when Korrun allowed it. No, they were going to the city to scavenge and look for supplies. At least, that was the story they told anyone who needed to know. Ava had brought her spear to make the story more believable.

Tyrell was holding out information on Ava, too. But it didn't take long for her to piece things together. He had planned a date. Something neither one had ever experienced.

And it felt strange to do something ... romantic—the words almost making Tyrell gag—while they were stuck wandering around the whole land of Oriel, masquerading as Korrun's black cloaks. But wasn't that the whole point? They were risking everything so moments like this could exist. So life could be beautiful again. Tyrell wanted to show Ava a glimpse into the reality they were fighting for.

A cold yet gentle evening breeze caressed the two and they huddled closer together as they wandered the streets of the long-forgotten city.

"Where are you taking me, sir?" Ava giggled a little too loudly.

Tyrell smiled again. This time, it felt good. Natural, even. "You know me. I am a man of few words. You'll not get any more out of me than you already have."

They passed a narrow alley cluttered with large, rusted, metal cannisters that were used for trash before Day Zero. Now, they were perfect hiding spots for things far worse. He checked their surroundings. An old habit. Even after a year of being in Korrun's employ, he was still used to the night being the enemy. Being afraid of the things that lurked in the dark was as standard as breakfast. It wasn't something someone shook off easily, even if the things in the night were on your side.

A few more twists and turns, and then they stopped in front of a set of tall, wooden double doors. The small panes of glass embedded in it were cracked or missing. The ancient lettering painted above the glass was chipped and faded.

"After you," Tyrell said, the door creaking as he pulled it open.

Ava smiled, then brushed past him and stepped into the room. She gasped and covered her mouth in pleasant surprise.

The walls were lined with dusty leather benches and marble tables. Some of the tables had cracked or broken completely over the course of time, but others had held strong. A curved glass display case sat next to the counter with three empty shelves, probably used to exhibit baked goods or other treats. One side was shattered, having left dusty shards scattered across the floor. Thankfully, a well-aimed wind spell from Tyrell during his earlier visit had pushed them to the forgotten corners of the shop.

Behind the countertop hung a menu written in the same foreign language. One of the lines holding it up had snapped with age, leaving the whole thing drooping at an awkward angle. On top of an expensive piece of rusted machinery sat a neat row of ceramic mugs, still upside down as though they had just been washed and ready for the next patrons. Dangling above it all, in a spectacular, spiraling display, was an old chandelier with missing crystals that swayed faintly from the cold drafts.

It was beautiful and depressing and disgusting all at the same time. The furniture and decorations were gorgeous, but dusty, broken, and forgotten. Once upon a time, the place would have exuded smells of freshly baked goods and rich coffee. Now, even with Tyrell's earlier wind spells to clear the air, the place smelled of dust and mold. Of age and abandonment.

Tyrell brought Ava over to a table that had been dusted with a wind spell and the bottom fold of his cloak. Several candles sat on top in the shape of a spiral. He didn't know what he was doing when he placed them earlier. He just thought it looked better than a square or a triangle. He lit the candles with a quick, carefully controlled swirl of flame. The room glowed and came alive.

"Wow, Mr. Romantic," Ava said, her smile widening. She leaned her spear against the booth beside theirs and Tyrell offered his arm, which she used to ease herself onto the leather seat. "You really shouldn't have."

"Maybe not," he said, removing his pack from his back and scooting in next to her. "But ... well ... you're worth the effort."

The candlelight danced in those hazel eyes that Tyrell couldn't get enough of. The cold draft disappeared as the heat from the tiny flames grew.

"What are you thinking right now?" she asked.

"That ... you make me a better man."

She slapped his shoulder.

"Ow! What was that for? What did I say?"

"No, seriously, what are you thinking?"

"Are you gonna hit me again if I tell you the same thing?" Tyrell said, rubbing his shoulder. He wouldn't admit it, but nightstalker's *fury*, she had a solid strike.

"So, you think I make you a better man, huh?" she teased, though her eyes sparkled with curiosity.

Tyrell opened his mouth to speak, to pour out his heart and lay bare his soul to her. To share all the thoughts and emotions she forced him to feel. What better moment to be more vulnerable, to lay it all out there, than now, in this place that he had meticulously prepared for her?

But he never got the chance. *BOOM!* A not-too-distant explosion rattled the few remaining windows of the café. Then another. It came from Korrun's camp. Tyrell and Ava locked eyes, their fears the same: The king's battlemages? Another attack? Tyrell blew out the candles.

"Mom! Dad!" Ava shouted, shoving the recently polished table forward so she could stand. She snatched her spear from the booth.

"C'mon! Let's go!" Tyrell said, already at the door and flinging it open.

Faint screams echoed down the winding streets, fueling their sprint even more. The faces of the Forty-Two flickered across Tyrell's thoughts. His friends. His new comrades: Ivar. Elaine. Doran. Veyla. Ava's parents. They were all in danger. But from who? The battlemages? Probably. Tyrell had told them which direction they were headed, after all.

If so, what would he do? Was now the time for the Forty-Two to step up and fight back? Was this the night they turned against Korrun and brought the weighty hammer of justice down on him? He had more questions than answers, and the adrenaline coursing through his veins did nothing to provide clarity. It only muddled things further.

When they reached the outskirts of camp, they were greeted with chaos. Tents were ablaze. Spells from invisible riders in the sky rained down around them. The black cloaks were fighting back. The mages retaliated with spells of their own. The non-magical black cloaks launched arrows randomly into the night.

A soldier had been hit by a spell. He struggled to regain his ground, but others and their wargs surrounded them. It *was* the king's battlemages. A part of Tyrell cheered internally. They were here to stop Korrun.

Hopefully once and for all. However, they would attack each black cloak without discrimination. That included him and his friends.

Tyrell ignited a shield that covered him and Ava just as a fire ball streaked toward them. The explosion forced Tyrell to slide back, but otherwise, they remained unharmed. He extinguished his shield and sent a flurry of spells forward. Wind. Lightning. Ice. Anything to stun. He wasn't going to take down an ally, even if they thought *he* was an enemy.

The soldier dodged and readied another attack. Then a crab-like nightstalker smashed into him and readied its razor-sharp claws to finish the job.

"Ha!" A disgusting, arrogant shout of victory pulled Tyrell's focus away from the nightstalker. He looked over to see Kaden kicking an unconscious soldier.

Tyrell grit his teeth. "He's *out*, okay? Keep … keep fighting!" He almost felt bad for encouraging him to do such a thing. But he couldn't stomach the disrespect. Plus, he must have gotten lucky. Any one of the king's battlemages should be able to dispatch him quickly.

A battle cry alerted Tyrell to another soldier behind them, a bright blue magical blade already in motion to kill. Tyrell flinched, readying himself for the pain, then a bright flash of light illuminated the darkness around them, and the soldier was flung to the side, a tendril of ice wrapping itself around him.

"I call it my 'ice rope grenade,'" Kwame announced proudly as he hurried over to embrace his daughter.

"Whatever you call it, I'm glad it works!" Tyrell said, shaking his hand. Then Tyrell pushed him to the side and blasted a battlemage and his warg that had swooped toward them.

Two members of the Forty-Two suddenly appeared: Ivar and Doran. Ivar's long, gray hair clunk to his sweat-soaked face. But otherwise, the old warrior seemed to be unscathed. Doran, Elaine's son who was only slightly older than Tyrell, wasn't even breathless, but a swollen left eye told Tyrell that he'd seen better days.

"These guys are everywhere!" Doran said. "I wish we could just tell them we're on *their* side!" He clenched his fists.

Suddenly, Kwame tossed another essence grenade. It didn't explode when it landed on the sandy ground next to an unsuspecting black cloak. It separated. Smaller fragments of the grenade now surrounded Korrun's follower as he readied another spell to fling at the soldiers in the air. Loud *pops* and small flashing bursts of fire and lightning blasted from within the fragments. The mage yelped and covered his eyes, but he was already blinded. He ran at full speed in zig-zagged lines, ignoring the small patches of flame eating away at his cloak.

"Disorienting essence grenade," Kwame said slyly. "Still working on my sabotage techniques."

Doran was not impressed. "Tyrell. *Now* is the time. We've been training and readying ourselves for this very moment. The Forty-Two must stand with the king."

All eyes looked to Tyrell. Was Doran right? *Was* this the moment? He knew everyone was thinking it. Tyrell gazed out over the battlefield and locked eyes with others from the group. They were watching him closely. Waiting for the moment when he would fling off his cloak and announce his true loyalty.

But were there enough of the king's battlemages here? *Could* they actually defeat not only Korrun, but the black cloak forces as well? The battlemages had skill. The black cloaks had nightstalkers. His heart pounded against his chest as the seconds slowly ticked. Still with no answer. Finally, Tyrell lowered his head.

"I ... don't ... know," he said eventually.

Doran growled in frustration. He swirled around and marched into the middle of the madness, dodging spells almost with ease. With a single hand, he unclasped his cloak signifying his loyalties and threw it high into the sky. With the other hand, he launched a larger-than-needed fire ball that consumed the cloth immediately.

"I am not a black cloak!" he roared. "I FIGHT FOR THE KING!" He turned and incinerated a group of beetle-like nightstalkers. Their hisses ended abruptly with their deaths.

"Who will join me?" Doran's eyes were wild with fury. He looked to Tyrell. Tyrell could only look back, once again silent. The other Forty-Two looked on with curiosity, but mimicked Tyrell's response.

The chaos continued. A few battlemages rallied around Doran, and together, they fought a group of black cloaks and nightstalkers. It didn't take long before they were pulled in opposite directions, leaving Doran to fend for himself.

The swarm of black cloaks and nightstalkers suddenly parted and Randolph Falkenburg walked out. He easily deflected Doran's spell and continued walking calmly toward him. He stopped just feet from the young mage.

"Traitor." There was no anger in his voice. He didn't shout. There was hardly any emotion at all. It was a simple statement of truth.

Quick as lightning, Randolph unholstered his guns and bright blue light flashed in the night, followed by loud, echoing *booms* that rang through the air.

Doran had crafted a shield. But he wasn't fast enough. His wild, angry eyes transformed into panic. His shield flickered and died. He placed a hand on his stomach and pulled it back. Red. Red all over. He stumbled backward and landed on his side, gasping for air.

Randolph holstered his guns, then walked toward Tyrell, his face a blank canvas.

Tyrell watched with panic as the skirmishes around Doran persisted. The battles between man and monster, black cloak and battlemage intensified, blocking Doran's twitching body from Tyrell's view.

"Come with me, Tyrell," his father said.

"Where?" Tyrell strained his neck trying to see Doran, but it was no use.

"No time. Follow me if you want to prove your loyalty." Randolph turned and walked to the edge of camp. Toward the pyramids. Tyrell didn't know what his father was up to, or why he wanted to bring him along, but it must have to do with the shards they were looking for.

He remembered his ancestor, Einar Falkenburg and his daughter. They had been the last two guardians of the shards in their family. Until now.

Tyrell looked into Ava's eyes. They were still wide with shock at Doran's fall. He caressed the side of her head with his hand.

"Ava, look at me."

Tears formed in the corners of her eyes, but she broke her gaze and listened. Her hands were quivering. Tyrell hated what he was about to say. He wanted to stay and protect her. To make sure she got through this fight. But he knew she'd be safe with the others, and he had a mission to accomplish.

"I'm going with him. I think it's about the next shard. I've got to do something. Steal it if I can. Stop them if I must."

She stopped shaking. Ignoring the sounds of the battle around them, she grasped the hand that caressed her and stared into Tyrell's eyes.

"I'm going with you."

"Absolutely not. This is *dangerous*, Ava."

"Yeah. Yeah it is," she said sadly. "But just because it's dangerous doesn't mean it's not worth doing."

She was right. King's crown, *she* had been the one to convince him to stay and help her find a way to stop Korrun. This had been her mission before it was ever Tyrell's. She could have left with him. They could have escaped, but she chose to stay.

Tyrell looked to Kwame and Amina. Kwame held his hands up as if to say, "Don't look at me, this is *her* decision."

Tyrell huffed, then said, "Okay. Let's go."

Ava stabbed her spear into the ground, then rushed over and embraced her parents. Kwame kissed the top of her head and squeezed her shoulder.

"I'm so very proud of you, my girl," he said. "Whatever happens, know that we love you."

Amina squeezed her tight and said, "Go get 'em, honey."

Tyrell gave each of them a nod, then turned to Ivar, who had been keeping an eye on the battle, allowing them the moments they needed.

"You guys be safe," Tyrell said. "Hopefully, when I'm done with what I need to do, it'll be time. Time for us to finally step up."

Ivar nodded his understanding and tightened his grip on his spear.

Tyrell retrieved Ava's spear from the ground and handed it to her and the two dashed past the chaos, doing their best to keep a low profile and avoid any conflicts. Two teenagers who appeared to be retreating were far less threatening to the battlemages than a pack of murderous nightstalker rabbits or a black cloak dual-wielding essence crafted whips.

Their conversation amidst the battle had taken too long. Randolph had walked with purpose to the pyramids, not once pausing to wait for his son. Tyrell and Ava sprinted to catch up. Tyrell's mind reeled with questions and possibilities of what he was about to find. He didn't get a chance to ask what this was all about. He had no clue what he was walking into. Other than a pyramid.

A nightstalker's screech pierced the darkness somewhere above the pyramids, followed by panicked shouts and a warg's yelp. Tyrell just hoped the battlemage somehow survived.

By the time he and Ava reached Randolph, he was at the entrance of the smallest structure. They could barely even call it a pyramid in comparison to the other magnificent constructs surrounding it.

"I see you brought your girlfriend," Randolph said. He wasn't teasing. He wasn't denying her entry either. It was another simple statement of truth. Perhaps this was a feeble attempt to connect to his son? Tyrell ignored him, and together they entered the pyramid.

They walked down the long, dark hallway in silence until Tyrell couldn't stand it anymore.

"So what is it, huh? Why are we here? Is it the shard?"

Randolph nodded. "It is. But it's protected. We'll let our troops fight for us while *we* work on retrieving it."

They rounded the corner and stopped at the back of a group of black cloaks and nightstalkers. Tyrell and Ava stayed where they were, while Randolph marched to the front next to Korrun and his pet. Standing in front of an ornate stone arch, Korrun had just finished giving instructions when someone else rounded the corner behind Tyrell, shouting.

"Sir! Sir!" Kaden said, out of breath. Theo stood beside him.

"What are you two doing here? You're supposed to be watching our backs!" Korrun spat.

"Master Korrun ... the king. The king is here."

Korrun rolled his eyes. "Yes, I am aware. He and his men are out there fighting somewhere." He turned toward the arch, ready to cross the threshold and retrieve the shard.

"No, sir! He's *here*! Right outside this pyramid," Theo explained.

Korrun paused, and placed a hand on the arch. He took a deep breath, then turned and smiled. "Then why don't we go say hello?"

He addressed the rest of the group. "NO ONE! And I. Mean. No. One. Touches that shard until we take care of my brother. It's MINE! Understand?" He glared at the group.

Tyrell's stomach twisted under his cold stare. He could feel Ava squirm beside him as well. The group called back their understanding, then Korrun said, "Well, then. Let's go!"

The black cloaks shuffled around the corner and down the hallway. Tyrell and Ava held a slow pace, allowing others to push past them, until they found themselves at the back. Closer to Korrun. Closer to the shard.

The group halted just before the entrance, then parted to allow Korrun and his pet to pass, being the first to greet the king and his men.

Tyrell and Ava eyed each other, then Tyrell nodded. They slipped back into the shadows, down the hallway and around the corner. They didn't speak a word until they stood before the ornate archway. Even then, their voices barely rose above a whisper.

"It's in there somewhere. Maybe we can steal it before Korrun's finished with his business out there," Tyrell said.

"Or maybe the king will end it completely."

Tyrell nodded.

Ava continued. "Tyrell, this ... this could all be over tonight. No more hiding. No more pretending. No more war."

He squeezed her hand. "I hope you're right. Maybe then ... you and your family could visit Whisperspell? Meet my family?"

She smiled warmly. "I'd love nothing more."

Tyrell sucked in a lungful of air, afraid of what stood on the other side of the arch.

"Here we go."

"Watch it!" Ava cried from across the room. Another stone tile sank to the ground and disappeared beneath the boiling hot lava. Ava hugged her spear as she watched from the entrance. Sweat drenched Tyrell from head to toe. His legs quivered from exhaustion, but he was almost across, paving the path of safety for Ava.

After all they had already been through to get to this point, Tyrell thought surely this had to be the room with the shard. Only to find one more deadly puzzle: cross the room of stone tiles. It seemed easy enough, until Ava took her first step and the tile sank, and lava took its place. Water and ice spells didn't work. They sizzled out immediately and the lava remained. He couldn't use a wind spell to fling himself across. Ava would be left behind. They had to cross the room the way the Guardians had intended.

But a strong wind spell put enough pressure on the tiles to see which were safe. And which were not. A few moments later, Tyrell finally landed on solid ground on the opposite side of the room. He was safe. Ava crossed over as well, following the path Tyrell had laid out for her. She heaved a heavy sigh of relief when at last she jumped into his arms.

Then, she kissed him. Not the gentle, romantic kind. It was the "we're alive" kind that was messy and forceful. It didn't matter to Tyrell, he was just as happy as she was that they had made it.

Eventually, he turned and pulled on the rusted metal handle and the wooden door creaked open. They stepped into the room, hand in hand, and marveled at the sight in front of them.

The room was large and circular. Doors were placed every few feet around the room with unlit torches in between them. *Were there multiple ways here from the maze? Some probably safer than others?* Tyrell wondered.

In glorious display in the center of the room, surrounded by thick, ornate columns that almost looked like ancient sentries, was a pedestal that glowed with a white light so intense that Tyrell had to shield his eyes until they could adjust.

It was the shard.

"We did it!" Ava shrieked, her nails digging into Tyrell's arm.

He hissed in pain, then smiled. They did it. They found the shard before Korrun. Ava clutched Tyrell from the side and squeezed him tight. He leaned his head on top of hers. Together they stared at the brilliant piece that hovered above the pedestal.

"Let's get more light in here," Tyrell said, flinging small orbs of fire toward each torch. The room burst to life with a warm glow. Tyrell and Ava smiled at each other, sharing in the joy of sweet victory.

The worn-out hinges on the door behind them creaked. Tyrell's heart jumped to his throat. He spun, readying a spell as the door slammed shut. But then he paused.

"Kaden? Theo? What are you two doing here?" He lowered his hands, but not his guard.

The blond boy pulled his hood down. He and Theo were both drenched in sweat from the maze as well. But Kaden smiled. It wasn't a warm, friendly one, either. There was a darkness that filled the expression.

Suddenly, a sharp, crackling sound filled the air. Like lightning without thunder. It sounded like it came from everywhere, all at once. Tyrell froze. Even the two black cloaks' menace faltered. A distant roar rumbled, a reminder that there were other monsters lurking in the maze besides the two that stood in front of him.

Ignoring the fear bubbling up, Tyrell grit his teeth and refused to show any more emotion.

"What are you doing here?" Tyrell repeated, taking a step forward.

Kaden laughed. "Exactly the question I was going to ask *you*, Falkenburg. Oh, and thanks for solving all those puzzles for us back there. Made things *so* much easier. So. You gonna tell me what it is you and your little girlie here are up to?"

They stared at each other. Theo clenched his fists. Kaden remained silent, waiting for an answer from Tyrell. Tyrell refused to give it to him.

Finally, Theo spoke. "Didn't Master Korrun tell us *not* to touch the shard? That it was his?" An evil, mischievous grin grew with each word.

Still, Tyrell said nothing.

"I've got another question for you, Falkenburg." Kaden took another step forward and wiped the sweat from his brow. "How in the king's crown did the king's battlemages know our location? Huh?"

"You're asking the wrong guy, Kaden. I don't know how they found us."

"I think I do." He sauntered closer, head held high, shoulders back, that smug look filling his features. Tyrell promised himself that by the end of the night, that look would be wiped off his face.

"I saw you," Kaden whispered.

"You've seen a lot of me."

"No. I saw you and your little group of misfits. You were talking to a battlemage in that alleyway at our last little scuffle. I called you out for it, and you slugged me."

Tyrell snickered, infuriating Kaden even further.

"You told him where we were headed, didn't you?"

Tyrell didn't answer.

"DIDN'T YOU?"

Tyrell stepped forward, inches now from Kaden.

"I don't know what you're talking about. But how dare you accuse me."

He wanted to slug him again. To fling spell after spell on the two boys until they begged for mercy. Instead, he turned, walked to the shard, and grabbed it off the pedestal in open defiance. Kaden clenched his fists, his face turning bright red. Theo closed the gap, standing next to Kaden, his brows furrowed in anger.

Then, another door opened.

CHAPTER 37

"Marth?" Tyrell said. "Wha—what are *you* doing here?"

Marth and his battlegroup stepped into the light. Well, Marth *limped* into the light. Fresh blood stains had soaked through his pant leg, and there was a gash across his leather sleeve. Even in this condition, and in this place, it was good to see his old childhood friend again.

Then, a dragon with deep black scales and brilliant ruby eyes followed. At first, Tyrell thought it was a nightstalker. But it didn't have those hollow, lifeless white eyes. This was a real dragon. And it ... sat obediently! With only a word from its master, who was still in the shadows, it obeyed. Then Marth spoke.

"Tyrell? Wow! Crazy seeing you here, mate! Long time ... long time..." Tyrell could tell Marth sounded guarded. They had been best friends growing up. He could read that boy like a children's book. Granted, anybody could, as he was never known to hold anything back.

Another mage stepped in front of the group. It was the boy from Cordelia. The one he'd saved from the stagmoose nightstalkers. The dragon stood when he moved, but sat back down with a word from the boy. What was *he* doing here? And how did he have a dragon for a pet?

Tyrell looked around the room. Things were already messy, and now with Marth and his gang, it only got messier.

Kaden stepped forward. "Well, well, well!" He seemed genuinely surprised. "Lookie who we've got here. It's the famous Griffina. The only mage from our old hometown."

The black-haired boy took a step closer, ignoring Kaden's awful jabs.

"Kaden." He didn't sound surprised. Only disappointed. "Why are you following that monster out there? I heard your family gave up pretty quickly to follow him. Why?"

"Oh, come off it, Griff! It was that or die! Plus ... Father's always been a businessman." Kaden stood taller. "We supply Master Korrun with leather. We get not only our lives, but *exclusive* rights to the *new king's* leather market."

Griff shook his head. "Trading integrity for ambition. Yeah. Sounds about right."

Kaden's face turned bright red. He clenched his fists and took a step. Griff crossed his arms and raised a brow as if to say, "You really wanna do this?"

Then Kaden eyed Griff's dragon. "You ... you wouldn't ... wouldn't know success if it slapped you right in the face!" he said at last.

Griff sighed. "I don't have time for this right now, Kaden. I wish I could say it was good to see you. But it really wasn't."

Distant shrieks alerted the room. Were there more monsters in the maze? They had already killed the ones along the path here. How many more were there?

Ignoring the far-off monstrous sounds, Griff faced Tyrell, his eyes drifting toward the shard. Tyrell knew what he was going to say before he said it. And already his mind was reeling with how to answer.

"Tyrell. We came for the shard. We're here to bring it to the king."

All eyes turned to him. Marth and his battlegroup looked on with hope. He could tell they hoped there was still good in him. Kaden and Theo eyed him suspiciously. They'd been on to him this whole time. Watching his every move. Theo wanted revenge for Liam. Kaden wanted to use Tyrell's downfall to climb within Korrun's ranks.

And then there was Ava. She'd been by his side this whole time. Speaking truth and love into him. She didn't stare at him with suspicion. She didn't even look to him with hope. She didn't have to hope. She *knew* there was good in him. King's crown, she was the one who brought it out in him. He didn't care what the others in the room thought. Only her.

The room stilled as Tyrell walked to Griff. Some of the battlegroup tensed, not sure if a battle was about to ensue. No one spoke. The torchlight seemed to glow brighter, more intense with every step. Finally, Tyrell extended his hand and dropped the shard into Griff's.

"NO!" Kaden and Theo screamed together.

"I knew it!" Theo roared angrily. "You were never with us, were you? You treacherous little—"

The brunt of Ava's spear smashed into his mouth.

"I wouldn't finish that sentence if I were you, Theo," she warned.

He pulled his hand from his mouth, blood spilling onto the stone floor.

He growled, green lightning crackling in his palms. Faster than Theo could hurl his lightning bolt, Tyrell flung fire at the boy's feet, burning right through his boots. With a wail of pain, Theo's spell skewed wide, bouncing off a wall and up into the ceiling, where it fizzled out.

While everyone watched in horror, Kaden took the opportunity to slam into Griff.

"Give it to me!" he screamed. The shard tumbled out of Griff's hand and bounced toward the black-haired girl who had been standing next to Griff.

The dragon sprang to its feet, but from the ground, Griff held out his hand. "No! Stay!" It obeyed.

Kaden scrambled to beat the girl to the shard, but she was faster. The fact that she was a girl did nothing to stop him. He punched her in the gut. Hard. Her howl of pain echoed in the chamber before she doubled over. Kaden's fist smashed into her jaw, and she collapsed to the ground, gasping for breath. The shard fell from her grasp and landed with a *clink* at her feet.

"Mira!" Griff shouted.

Tyrell watched as a fire flashed before Griff's eyes, and he slammed Kaden into a wall with a wind spell. The other girl with fiery red hair and a giant of a boy rushed over and picked Mira up and carried her toward the door they had entered.

Suddenly, more screeches and shrieks came from the maze. They were coming from another door yet to be opened. The room froze. The sounds were getting closer.

"Vincent! Take Mira back!" Marth called to the giant. "We've got this!"

Tyrell eyed Vincent, then jerked his head to the door they had entered through. "Go that way! Once you pass the lava room, you'll be safe. We killed everything else along the way."

"Lava room?" Vincent asked.

"Stick to the floating tiles and you'll be fine. Just ... trust me."

Vincent nodded, and he and the red-haired girl disappeared through the door with Mira over the giant's shoulder.

Theo capitalized on their moment of distraction and rushed over, snatching the shard before Griff could recover. Then he unsheathed a handle and ignited a brilliant, red-bladed axe. He stared at Tyrell with a wicked look. The crimson glow from his weapon accentuated the blood-smeared grin.

"Please, Tyrell. I *dare* you. Come and get it."

The shard in his hands had been invitation enough. But Tyrell stepped forward, eager to accept.

"Tyrell!" Griff called. The boy now stood over Kaden, who was whimpering for mercy. Griff unsheathed his own handle and tossed it to Tyrell. He snatched it out of the air and gave it a quick glance. Beautiful craftsmanship. The steel crossbar had been molded into dragon wings.

Tyrell didn't need a weapon to stop Theo. His magic had always been weapon enough. But he stared at the boy who had challenged him. Who held the shard. This was now more than just about the mission. It was about justice. About proving to Theo what he should have known all along: that Tyrell was better. That he'd *always* been better. That he should have never stuck his nose into Tyrell's affairs. And if he wanted to challenge Tyrell with a blade, then by a blade Tyrell would take him down.

A blue glow washed over Tyrell as he crafted a curved, sickle-like blade. Theo's grin grew wider, and he tucked the shard in his pocket.

Tyrell heard Marth mutter to Ava behind him. "I'm assuming you're Ty's girlfriend, but hopefully you know better than to step in the middle between those two. Ty is a proud dude." Ava snickered but said no more.

With Griff handling Kaden, it was just Tyrell and Theo. And that was exactly how it needed to be.

Tyrell dashed forward, blade raised high. As expected, Theo readied his own blade, bracing for a side swing. It was exactly what Tyrell had hoped for. At the last second, he pivoted, spinning around until he was behind him. His sickle blade followed through with a clean, shallow cut across Theo's back.

Theo stumbled forward, crying out in pain and surprise. He'd been faked out. Humiliated in a battle that had only just begun. And Tyrell could see that only made him angrier.

Theo gripped his handle tighter, his knuckles turning white. He screamed and dashed forward with quick, slicing motions. Tyrell dodged and blocked them all. Instead of gaining confidence with every missed attack from Theo, fear began to grow. And his blade exposed that to the room—shifting colors from the confident blue to yellow.

Theo was fast. Strong. And exceptionally good with his weapon. He may not have had the training that Tyrell did, but *someone* had taught him well.

Rolling just in time to avoid a fatal strike in the chest, Tyrell turned and sliced the side of Theo's leg. He screamed, then kicked him in the face, blood shooting from Tyrell's nose. His blade extinguished. Bright stars covered his vision. A blurry shadow with a red glow towered over him. He rolled just in time as the ax blade slammed into the stone where Tyrell had just laid.

He tried to shake away the pain—and the stars—so he could regain his sight. It helped. Slightly. He brought his sickle up to block, parrying the ax to the side, then kicked upward into Theo's chest. The mage slammed into one of the columns surrounding the pedestal. A sharp *crack* echoed across the room as Theo's arm collided awkwardly into the stone. He screamed, dropping his handle to the floor, the blade extinguishing as it fell.

Tyrell regained his stance and walked forward, reigniting his sickle blade, its color turning deep red. The mage nursed his arm as Tyrell walked toward him. His eyes were wide with fear.

"No ..." Theo whispered. "No!"

He scrambled to his feet. Whimpering, he turned and ran to the nearest door. Tyrell raised his blade, intending to throw it. Intending for death. Theo flung open the door and came face to face with the leader of the black cloaks. Surrounded by nightstalkers.

"M-Master K-Korrun," Theo whimpered. He bowed low before his master. Although Korrun had a calm menace about him, Tyrell could see he hadn't made it through the night completely unscathed.

His battle armor had random tears and scorch marks. Dust, sweat, and debris covered his body. Even then, he steadily took in the scene. He saw Tyrell with his blade raised, ready to throw it at Theo. He saw Griff binding Kaden with rope. Then he looked back to Theo. The boy sputtered and sniveled before his master, the blood from Ava's attack pooling at Korrun's feet.

"You're *weak.*"

With a casual flick of his wrist, a powerful gust of wind lifted the mage and slammed him into the stone wall on the far side of the room. Tyrell's stomach twisted when Theo fell from the wall and landed on the floor. Lifeless.

Tyrell was about to give into that same temptation. To end Theo's life. But to see someone else do it was a stark reminder of the weight his actions had. Guilt squeezed his insides and wouldn't let go.

Behind Korrun was an army of black cloaks and nightstalkers. And everyone looked hungry for a fight. Korrun stepped over the pool of blood from Theo's wound when he had bowed before him in loyalty earlier. A devotion that been repaid with indifference. Then his pet alligator nightstalker splashed through the pool and stood proudly next to its master.

The last Tyrell had seen of Korrun, he was walking out of the pyramid to meet his brother. The king. If Korrun was here … where was the king? Could it be that the leader of the black cloaks actually bested his brother?

Tyrell looked to Griff, whose eyes were wide with fear. Rightfully so. This was the leader of the black cloaks. The king's brother. And a powerful mage with an army at his back. It was just Griff, his pet dragon, Marth, and Ava. There was no way they lived through this moment.

Korrun had the attention of all. He breathed calmly. Deeply. As if drinking it all in. Finally, he spoke. His eyes boring into Tyrell's.

"Where is the shard?"

Tyrell didn't answer. Not out of defiance. Fear had muddled his mind. The previous events twisting together in an unsolvable puzzle as he thought about his answer. Where *was* the shard? Who'd had it last?

Ava stepped forward. She eyed the alligator nightstalker, clenched the spear in her hand, and said, "It's gone. And you'll never see it again."

"Ava! What are you doing?" Tyrell hissed.

She turned to face him, uncompromising resolve etched on all her features.

"It's time, Tyrell. Time for us to step up. Time for us to fight back."

Korrun raised his eyebrows in playful amusement. It was like a kitten biting at a lion's paw. Korrun knew it. So did Tyrell. As masterful as she was with that spear, Ava was playing a dangerous game she was bound to lose.

"Is that so, Tyrell?" Korrun teased. "You ready to fight back?"

From across the room, Korrun's presence loomed over Tyrell. Fear surged through Tyrell's veins, fear driving it forward. He couldn't let Ava do this to herself.

"N-no sir, Master Korrun." The words tasted bitter coming out. He wiped his face with his sleeve, the bleeding wound on his lip refusing to close. "I'm not here to ... fight you. I know where the shard is. And it's ... it's yours."

Tyrell walked over to Theo's limp body and rummaged through his pocket.

"Tyrell, no!" Ava begged. "Don't do this."

He grabbed the shard and held it out in his open palm. "It's the right thing to do, Ava."

Her mouth fell open in disbelief. Tyrell looked around the room. Marth showed a look of betrayal. Griff's brows were furrowed in confusion. And Kaden, though he was bound, had a curled smile of victory.

Heart thumping loudly in his throat, Tyrell crossed the room, every eye on him. A cold sweat formed on his forehead and he wiped it with his free hand.

"No ... no, Tyrell," Ava whimpered. He hated betraying her trust like this. *This will all be over soon. I promise,* he thought at her.

He stood before the leader of the black cloaks and the pet monster at his side, its hungry yellow eyes fixed on the shard.

"I present to you, another shard of the Orb of Essence," Tyrell said.

Korrun reached for it, and as he did, Tyrell snatched his hand back. The look of confusion on Korrun's face gave him just enough time.

"Griff!" Tyrell shouted. He tossed the shard to the boy, who caught it and immediately stuffed it into his pocket. "Go! Now!" Tyrell said. He brought his fist upward, connecting with Korrun's chin. Tyrell faced Griff's handle toward the ground and generated a yellow staff that he used for support as he brought both feet up and kicked Korrun square in the chest. The leader of the black cloaks landed on the stone floor, dazed. His pet scuffled over to check on him. Tyrell extinguished the weapon and pitched the handle back to Griff.

"Hurry! Go!" Griff nodded as Korrun regained his composure. But instead of turning and running, Griff stepped beside Tyrell and shouted.

"Runa! Fire!"

The dragon flared its wings wide and roared. A brilliant white line formed from the tip of its head and traveled all the way down to its tail. Then deep black flames poured from its open mouth, spewing across the room. Toward Korrun. Toward the nightstalkers and black cloaks that were storming into the room.

Korrun had ignited a shield just in time. He gritted his teeth, tense with effort to keep his magic alive.

A loud wail rose above the dying screams in the room. It was Korrun's pet. Unable to get behind the shield in time, the beast's hardened scales were no match for Runa's black fire.

"NO!" Korrun screamed, though he kept his shield intact.

The torrent of flames died and the dragon closed its mouth. Any beast or black cloak that had been in the room died, save for Korrun, who had extinguished his shield and crawled over to the ashes of his recently deceased pet. He breathed heavily through his nose. His fists clenched and loosened. His mouth twitched with fury.

He looked to Griff. To his dragon. He snarled, stood, and raised his hands.

But Ava was quick. Fierce. Strong. She rammed the butt of her spear into Korrun's stomach, knocking the air out of him. Breathless, he barely dodged as her spear grazed against his left cheek, just under his scar. His eyes widened as she stepped forward, launching a new onslaught of strikes. Korrun didn't even have time to wipe the blood from his fresh wound.

Tyrell was just as shocked at Ava's boldness as Korrun was. He shook himself from his stupor and locked eyes with Griff.

His hand slipped into his pocket. He pulled out the small paper packet, feeling the tiny seeds rattle inside. After giving them one final glance, he tossed it to Griff, who caught it with a puzzled look.

"Go," Tyrell said.

Griff hesitated briefly, then gave him a nod of respect and understanding before he and his dragon disappeared through the door. Marth hesitated, taking a final look back at his childhood friend. There was an ache in his eyes, as though he wanted to stay and fight. Finally, he too gave Tyrell a nod and followed the others into the dark.

He turned and faced Korrun, who was staggering, trying to catch his breath while dodging Ava's relentless strikes.

This could all end tonight.

She was right. Now was their chance.

Crafting the largest fireball he could manage, Tyrell shouted, "Ava! Move!" She dove just in time as he flung it toward Korrun. The man rolled to the side and slid beside his pet's ashes. He gave them a quick glance, hate flickering across his features.

Black cloaks and nightstalkers poured into the room, but Korrun held up a hand as he stood.

"MINE!" he screamed wildly. He leapt to his feet. "Get the shard!"

Several black cloaks dashed across the room and disappeared into the maze.

A strand of hair dangled over his face and he blew it away.

"You killed my pet. You stole my shard. You betrayed my trust. Now. I'm assuming you wouldn't have done that if you'd known—"

He took a step forward. Eyes narrowed. And the evil grin that spread across his face sent chills down Tyrell's spine.

"—that I am an *expert* in vengeance."

Black and red lightning flickered between his hands and he turned to Ava. Tyrell sprinted, pumping his legs hard. He crafted a shield and dove in front of her. Korrun's lightning flashed across Tyrell's vision before slamming into his shield. It knocked Tyrell into Ava and the two flew across the room, slamming hard into the unforgiving stone wall. Ava's spear clattered to the ground, rolling until it stopped at Korrun's feet.

He flicked the spear into his hands with his foot and swung it around. Testing it. Then he slowly walked toward the two crumpled traitors.

Dazed and weak, Tyrell tried slinging fire balls his way, but they were easily deflected. Korrun moved closer, using the spear like a cane.

"I love the taste of vengeance," Korrun whispered. He ran the blade of Ava's spear across his thumb and smiled at the blood that spilled.

Pain flooded Tyrell's body. Fear penetrated his every thought. Ava whimpered and tried to reposition herself against the wall. Her breathing was heavy. Forced.

The leader of the black cloaks stood over them and watched their pain in silence. They couldn't move. Couldn't fight. Couldn't breathe. He lifted the spear casually and pointed it at Tyrell.

"You will feel this. I promise."

Tyrell gritted his teeth and closed his eyes. He swore upon each of the nine shards that he would not show weakness. That he wouldn't cry out in pain. He would take his death with honor and hope that Ava would be spared.

Korrun's angry shout pierced the silence. Tyrell braced for the white-hot pain of the spear's blade.

It never came.

Only a gentle whimper.

Realization struck him before his eyelids flung open.

Ava.

His heart sank. His blood froze over.

In both hands, she held the shaft of the spear. That was all there was to grab. The blade was buried so deep in her body it couldn't be seen.

"No ..." Tyrell moaned softly in disbelief. She looked to him, pain and fear painted across her features.

"NO!" Tyrell screamed. "Ava ... AVA! S-stay w-w-with me! Please! No. Not like this. Not like this!"

He scrambled to his knees. His hands shook. Tears streamed down his face. He didn't know healing magic. But he had to try.

Gently placing a hand just above the spot where the blade punctured her abdomen, he felt the wet warmth of the blood through her shirt. He closed his eyes and focused all of his magical energy into his hands. He didn't know what he was doing, but he had to try something. Anything.

A dim, yellow light glowed from his hands, but then it disappeared. He could feel his magic slip through his control like trying to catch water with a fishing net. He stared into her wide, pained eyes and tried again, his magic radiating purple. Still, he failed. Time and time again, he forced his magic to his palms, but without knowledge, without control, it was useless. He pulled his hands back and his heart shattered.

He couldn't help her.

He stared helplessly at the only girl he'd ever loved. The one who believed in him. Who gave him a purpose when he had none. The one who showed him love time and time again.

And he couldn't do anything for her.

Ava's lips trembled, bright-red blood dripping from them. Her tears glistened in the torchlight. Her breaths were short. Sharp. Tyrell caressed her head in his hands, bringing his forehead to hers.

"I ... I don't know what to do," he whispered helplessly.

"N ... nothing," she breathed. "'s okay, Tyrell."

"You can't go." His tears spilled onto the ground, but he didn't care. "P-please. Don't leave me. I ... I need you."

Her breathing grew shallow. Blood continued to spill from her wound and her mouth. A forced, shallow grin appeared on her face, and she locked eyes with him. "This isn't the ... end. Only ... only a new ... beginning."

"No. No. There is no beginning without you now." He grasped her hands in his and squeezed tight. "I love you, Ava. You hear me? I love you! Please ... stay with me. We'll ... we'll figure this out."

"I ... love you too, Tyrell. More than life itself. I'm sorry ... our time was cut short." She tried to reposition herself and cried out in pain.

"Don't move," Tyrell whispered to her. More tears fell with his next words. "It'll ... it'll all be over soon."

"We ..." She coughed. "We did what we could. Hopefully it was enough."

"You were so brave, Ava. You did what I couldn't do."

She squeezed his hand gently. Only because that was all the strength she had left in her. "I did what I believe *you* can do. Only, next time, you'll finish the job."

She motioned for him to come closer, and when he did, she kissed his cheek.

"I love you, Tyrell Falkenburg," she whispered.

Then she was gone.

Everything inside Tyrell broke. An agony he'd never experienced before ripped through his heart, shredding his very soul. He screamed, not caring who heard it. He placed his head against her chest, his tears soaking into her shirt. There was no heartbeat, and its silence was deafening.

"I told you, you would feel this," Korrun whispered silently. He had taken a few steps back to watch their final moments. There was no emotion on his face. No sly grin of satisfaction. No sense of victory.

He had delivered his vengeance a hundred-fold, and now he was on to whatever came next.

Vengeance. Tyrell stood and wiped the tears from his eyes. Vengeance was his heartbeat now. This room would probably be his grave, but not before *this* stain on the world received his due. And Tyrell was going to make sure he fulfilled Ava's final wishes. He would finish the job.

He roared in hatred and fire swirled about his hands. Korrun smiled and took his stance. That smiled fueled Tyrell's rage even further. He hurled his hate in the form of a fire ball from each hand. They merged mid-air, growing into a singular sphere that headed right for Korrun.

Tyrell wasn't finished. As soon as the spell had left his hands, he swirled them again, flinging lightning into the gigantic ball of flame. Korrun's eyes widened at the power of the newly merged magic, but instead of fear, amusement flickered across his features. He dodged the ball of storm and fire, a move Tyrell had expected. Before Korrun could even regain his bearings, ice shards hurtled toward him, slicing his arms and legs.

He growled in pain. Tyrell stepped forward, tears of sadness and hate streaming down his face. He would have his vengeance. And he would make sure to do it slowly. Methodically. Ever so painfully.

Fire ignited once again in Tyrell's fists, this time though, there would be no spells launched. He allowed the flames to dance around his clenched hands. As Korrun wiped the blood from his arm, Tyrell sprinted.

"Oh? Hand to hand? My favorite." Korrun's smile grew wider.

Tyrell mustered all the force he could into a single flame-fueled punch, swinging his fist in a wide circle. It connected with the dark shield Korrun had created. Pain shot up his arm, but Tyrell ignored it. He whirled around until he was behind Korrun and slammed his elbow in between Korrun's shoulder blades. The man stumbled forward.

Tyrell dashed forward at the opening and hammered his fiery fist at the base of the man's neck. Korrun hit the ground. Tyrell kicked him in the ribs as hard as he could, knocking the air out of him. The leader of the black cloaks rolled, using a wind spell to push him to his feet.

Korrun took a slow, steady breath and blew another strand of hair from his face.

"Not … bad," he breathed. "Not bad at all. It's a shame that you'll have to die, too."

Black energy crackled and popped between his palms. But the energy didn't just zig and zag like lightning. It also didn't blaze and burn like fire. It didn't dance and sway like water. It was like a mixture of all three. A ball of midnight black energy swayed and darted, zigged and flashed. This was something new. Something evil. And it continued to grow. Fear overwhelmed the hate that fueled Tyrell, and he took a step back, the fire in his fists extinguishing.

"You've had your shots. It was only fair. But now, it's time you recon-nected with your girlfriend."

Tyrell's tear-stained eyes grew wide as Korrun stepped over the ashes of his recently deceased pet and closer to Tyrell. Would his shield be strong enough to withstand this power? He was backed into a corner.

Korrun raised his hands over his head, the dark spell sizzling and danc-ing treacherously. Tyrell conjured his shield, forcing what little energy he had left into it and hoped against hope that it would hold.

"Wait!"

Korrun lowered his hand and glared at the man who would interrupt him.

It was Randolph Falkenburg.

"Master Korrun, I have another solution for you to consider."

"There is no other solution than the death of this boy."

"You're right to want that." Randolph stared emotionlessly at his son. "I want that too."

He took another step between Korrun and Tyrell. "He's taken advan-tage of your trust. Stolen *your* shard. Kept you from your mission. *But*

... we need more men. Men with magical abilities as strong as this boy's." Randolph stepped closer to his master and whispered, "Let's *turn* him."

Rolling his eyes, Korrun said, "We've been *trying* to turn him! Everyone who stays around the Corruption gets turned. That's how it works, Randolph."

"No, Master Korrun. I mean, turn him like you did *me*."

Understanding dawned on Korrun and his smile grew wider.

"Death would be a mercy for the boy, Master Korrun. Let him feel the pain in a cell. Relive his worst moment over and over again. And all the while, we'll *force* him to be exposed to the Corruption. And just like me, he'll come to see reason."

Adrenaline, hate, and grief muddled Tyrell's thoughts. Had he heard that correctly? His dad didn't run from his post. He'd been captured, broken, and turned by the Corruption. That's why he vanished. That's why his family was the shame of Whisperspell. It had been Korrun wielding the Corruption against his father this whole time. His father wasn't to blame. Korrun was.

"Interesting suggestions, Randolph." The leader of the black cloaks extinguished his spell. "How do I know you're still loyal to me and not just trying to save your son?"

Before the words made sense in Tyrell's mind, Randolph turned and launched a blue bolt of lightning that struck Tyrell's shoulder and sent him flying backward. He hit the wall with a loud *THUD* and stars immediately filled his vision.

He'd landed next to Ava. Squashing the pain that arched across his body, he reached over and held her hand. One last time.

I love you, Ava Adebayo. And I always will.

His lips trembled and warm, wet tears slid down his cheeks. He wished it was a nightmare. One he would wake up from to find her sitting next to him, waiting for him to wake. But the surging pain in his shoulder told him the nightmare was real. And there was no going back.

Grief and pain stole his will to fight. To live. He allowed the black cloaks to bind his hands and levitate him through the maze and out of the pyramid. The king and his men were gone now, so those who survived the night waited by the opening for their leader.

Cold air stung at Tyrell's tear-stained cheeks when they finally flung him onto the sand. The sun was starting to rise on their destroyed camp. The black cloaks kicked Tyrell in the ribs and commanded him to march in front. He received angry or quizzical looks from most of the black cloaks. But then he spotted Kwame and Amina pushing their way through the crowd.

Tyrell's heart hung heavy when their eyes locked. A look of urgency filled Ava's parents' features, and they strained to see each person as they emerged from the pyramid.

Kwame looked to Tyrell. Tyrell barely had the strength look back.

"Ava?" he screamed, panic in his voice. He scanned the line exiting the pyramid. "W-where's my daughter, Tyrell? WHERE'S AVA!" he shouted.

Tears welled in Tyrell's eyes. His voice trembled when he had finally mustered the courage to speak to Ava's father. "I ... I'm so ... so sorry..."

Kwame fell to his knees and wept bitterly. Amina dropped beside him, embracing her husband and joining him in his grief. Their only child was taken from them. They had every right to their pain. Tyrell didn't think he could have been more broken than he already was. But to deliver the news to Ava's family only broke him further. Weak from his sorrow, Tyrell collapsed in the sand and cried. The sand stuck to his face. The rising sun's rays brought warmth to his skin, but offered no comfort. It taunted Tyrell. A promise of a new day filled with hope in a world that had nothing left to give.

Tyrell welcomed each blow from the black cloaks' boots. They shouted at him to stand. To march. Let them. They could beat his body all they wanted. They could try to break him. He would endure it all. Not because he was strong, but because there was nothing left to break.

CHAPTER 38

"They're coming!" Marth called from behind. The dark hallway lit up behind Griff with a flash of yellow light. Sharp yelps echoed down the corridor.

"Never mind! That'll slow 'em down!"

Griff was glad to see Marth's earlier injuries hadn't held him back. Even so, his thoughts drifted to the twilight rose seeds in his pocket. Back to Tyrell. Was this his way of saying goodbye?

It hadn't felt right leaving him and the girl to face Korrun. Guilt weighed heavy on him, as though by leaving, he'd endorsed their death.

He did his best to shake the uneasy thoughts about them from his mind. He was still on a mission for the king. Now, questions about what he would find when he left the pyramid surged through his mind. Where was the king? He was supposed to be fighting Korrun. He was supposed to *win*! If Korrun had been there in the cave with them, then there could only be one conclusion. The king was dead. Dread flooded Griff's thoughts as he thought about the ramifications of such an event. He did his best to block them out.

They had made it through the lava room with ease. Runa had enough space to fly across, and since the path had already been crossed by Tyrell and Ava, Griff and Marth only needed to jump across the floating tiles. Marth was tougher than Griff gave him credit for. The boy would grit his teeth and jump, only grunting quietly as he landed on his bad leg. Then together they sprinted down hallways, passing the dismembered bodies of more scorpion nightstalkers.

All the traps had been sprung by Tyrell. Even the ones that could have started back up didn't. They passed by a wall covered in familiar vines. Some had been scorched; others sliced. Even then, some were left unharmed. None of them came alive like the ones Griff and his battlegroup had experienced.

As he passed them by, it reminded him of the previous shard he had found. It felt like an eternity ago, and yet, he remembered it vividly. The forest had sprung to life to protect the shard. Or was it to test him? Either way, he was thankful that, like before, his path back had been clear.

Other than the black cloaks chasing them.

Just as Marth caught up to Griff and Runa, green lightning zipped past Griff's ear.

"Whoa! These guys are fast!" Marth shouted. "Don't they know we have a *dragon*?"

"You'd think that would be enough!" Griff huffed.

They retaliated with their own spells, not sure if they hit. But that wasn't the point. They just needed to get out alive. Preferably with a low body count, but the persistence of the black cloaks chasing them might quickly change that.

Griff skidded to a stop when he reached a stone archway that led to another corridor.

"Hey!" Marth called, almost slamming into Griff. "What's the hold up?"

"Careful," Griff pointed. Inside the room was a hole that stretched into eternity. If Griff had the time, he would have shined a light or dropped a stone to see how far down it went. But time was one thing he was very short on.

Crossing the stretch of hallway was a narrow walkway. There would be nothing to steady yourself on. You either had to have incredible balance, or you died.

The sound of the horde of footsteps pounding against the stone floor grew louder. The black cloaks were close.

"Well, nothing else to do but walk." He turned to his dragon. "Runa! Fly, girl!"

She obeyed immediately, stretching her wings out, and with two flaps and a glide, she landed on the stone platform on the other side.

Griff checked his pocket to make sure the shard was still there, then shook his head and took a deep breath. "Here we go."

One foot in front of the other, that was all he could do. He told himself not to look down, but how could he not? A thin stretch of stone as wide as his foot was the only thing that stood between him and death. Or a life of forever falling.

The footsteps grew louder. Marth eventually joined Griff on the narrow ledge and began walking with purpose.

"Uh, I don't mean to rush you, Griff, but they're almost here!"

"Doing my best here, buddy!"

His foot slipped. He cried out as his body lurched into the darkness. He reached blindly to grab hold of something and barely caught the ledge. His fingers wrapped tightly around it; his feet dangled into the unknown.

"Coming!" Marth screamed. He sat on the ledge and scooted to Griff's position. He reached down and snatched him by the arms and pulled him back onto the ledge.

"There!" one of the black cloaks screamed.

They had made it. Some started walking across the room, but a wind spell from Griff launched them off and into the never-ending darkness. Their screams faded, but no sounds of impact were heard. Chills erupted down Griff's arm. If he wasn't careful, that could be him.

Runa whined from the other side of the room, but sadly, there was nothing she could do. With Griff and Marth in the way, she couldn't risk her fire. And she would knock them off if she tried to fly around the tight corridor.

Marth turned to face Korrun's army, still sitting on the ledge, and crafted a shield, then held it in front of him. He scooted backward as he blocked the spells while Griff mimicked his motions and steadied him with a free hand. Some spells were so powerful they nearly knocked them off, but together, they held strong. Whenever one black cloak tried to jump on the ledge, Marth would lower his shield just enough for Griff to launch a spell.

Seconds ticked into eternity, until finally Runa was standing over them. They jumped to their feet and both ignited their shields. Marth turned to run, but Griff grabbed his arm.

"Wait! I have an idea."

Together, the two mages extinguished their shields and hurled their most powerful fire spells, not at the black cloaks, but at the ledge. The two giant orbs of flame met on either side of the stone and exploded outward, crumbling the middle of the walkway before the entire thing gave way and collapsed into the unknown.

Angry outbursts came from the squad that was now stuck on the other side of the room. They would have to find another way through the maze before they could get to them.

"Nice work," Griff huffed. "Let's go."

It only took a short sprint until the two mages and their dragon made it to the starting archway, where Vincent, Sadie, and Mira stood waiting.

"You okay?" Griff asked breathlessly.

Mira nodded. "Yeah. Fine, now." She looked him up and down. "How about you?"

"Yeah. Fine, now."

"You got the shard?" Vincent asked.

Griff patted his pocket and nodded grimly. He should have felt a surge of joy at the weight of the shard in his pocket. Even if it was just from the presence inside him.

They had just snatched it right out from underneath Korrun's nose! But there was a cost. Guilt flooded back into his mind as he thought back to Tyrell and the girl, silently hoping that they had somehow escaped. He would make sure that whatever happened to them, it would be worth it.

"We gotta go. Now."

They sprinted down the hallway and out into the night. The cold air slapping at his face was a welcome relief. All that running. All that fighting. It soothed his burning, aching body. Bodies of nightstalkers, black cloaks, and battlemages were scattered about, but the fight was over. There were no moving bodies left just outside the pyramid.

"Where to?" Sadie asked. She stood beside Vincent, her hands at the ready.

Griff surveyed their surroundings. The first rays of sunlight were starting to peek over the horizon, turning the pitch-black night sky into a gradient of deep purple and dark orange.

Smoke billowed from Korrun's camp, and the ash from the fires rained down on the city ahead. The air was thick with the smell of charred wood and burned fabric. Something for which Griff was grateful. Even if the king was dead, he hoped that Korrun's forces had been completely demolished in the process.

A loud roar forced Griff and his group to jump. They whirled around and each readied themselves for another battle. Runa snarled and flared her nostrils, smoke billowing from them.

"Griff!" King Aldamund shouted. He jumped from his warg as Magnus, the other wargs, and their riders landed and dashed over to him. He squeezed him in a tight embrace and then said, "I'm so glad to see you alive!"

"Sir, I'm ... I'm so glad to see *you* alive!" Griff replied. "I saw Korrun in the pyramid and ... and I was afraid of what happened to you."

The king chuckled. "Ah, yes. That would be frightening, I'm sure."

He eyed the smoldering camp behind him, then turned his attention back to Griff. "You see, my brother does not like to lose. Games, challenges of wit, and battles to the death above all. He lured me back to the camp and summoned his nightstalkers to surround me. Then he disappeared. He knew he was losing and did what he could to escape. We just finished the fight and came to help you. But it looks like you survived the pyramid ... mostly unscathed. Well done, boy."

"Thank you, sir. And we didn't just survive ..." Griff reached in his pocket and retrieved the shard, holding it out for all to see. Its fierce white light glowed brightly, illuminating the king's face.

"Well done, my boy! Well done!" The king gently plucked it from Griff's palm and tucked it back into a hidden pocket in the waistline of his trousers.

"Sir, Korrun is still in the pyramid and I'm sure he's headed this way. I'm ready to fight if you are, sir."

"Ah, yes." He placed a hand on Griff's shoulder. "We came to claim a shard. Not lives." He looked around at the scattered bodies. "Well, not *intentionally* claim lives. Korrun will live for now, but we must return with this shard to keep it safe. I'm sure my brother's pursuits will have slowed after last night. Let's get you back ho—"

"—But sir! Tyrell's in there, too. He and some girl were fighting Korrun when I left."

The king paused. His face scrunched in thought. Then he clenched his jaw and said, "Tyrell's father is Korrun's second-in-command. I still believe there's a small shred of honor in my brother. Killing Randolph's son is very unlikely. Even so, if we lose this shard, far more lives will be at risk than just one. I'm sorry, son. But we need to secure this shard and get you home."

Griff heaved a sigh of mixed emotions. Relief mingled with guilt. He would have fought to rescue Tyrell and the girl. He would have fought to the death for the king. Nightstalker's fury, he almost *did* die for the king. But home was where he wanted to be.

The king addressed the rest of Griff's battlegroup. "I'm not sure who you all are, and how you made it here. But I can see you all helped Griff—and me—with this mission. Thank you."

They all nodded and smiled. Marth bowed awkwardly low.

"Time to go!" the king said, eyeing the pyramid.

Mira joined Griff on top of Magnus, while the others saddled with the battlemages. The wargs from the Bergots stables were found one pyramid over, and soon Griff, Runa, the king, his battlemages, and Griff's battlegroup soared through the sky in formation. Griff sucked in lungfuls of the clean, crisp air as they flew above the smoldering battlefield, clearing the smoke and ash the higher they ascended.

Every inch of his body groaned in complaint. His muscles ached. His wounds throbbed. His joints were stiff. Drained of energy, Griff could hardly fight the drooping of his eyelids. As the ancient city and its pyramids faded into the horizon behind them, Griff's body demanded sleep, but he knew that such luxury was still a long way off.

The next afternoon, Magnus barely landed on the outskirts of Solastran before Gale and Leena Driscoll charged him.

"Whoa, whoa. Easy there, Mom!" a weary Griff said.

Runa and the rest of the wargs landed, all looking as weary as Griff felt. Leena fussed over the scrapes on her boy before he could even dismount. Then, Gale placed a hand on her back, and she stepped to the side, next to Runa, who solicited a head scratch from her. Gale didn't fuss over Griff as though he were a toddler. Instead, he grasped him in a giant bear hug and lifted him in the air.

"I am so proud of you, son."

"Thanks ... Dad ..." Griff breathed.

Gale set him back down and straightened his shirt. "Sorry. Couldn't help myself."

"You should be very proud of your boy, Gale," the king said, walking over and shaking his hand. "The mission was a success. All thanks to Griff and his friends."

Gale beamed proudly as he and the king entered through the gates of Solastran. A gentle hand slipped into Griff's and squeezed. It was his mother's. He smiled at her, and they walked behind the rest of the battlegroup.

There was no parade for them as they walked the streets of Solastran. No confetti or cheering of their names. Their mission had been secret. So had their victory. Instead, most of the citizens of Solastran went about life as normal. And normal was everything Griff desired right now.

Sadie and Vincent held hands as they walked. Though the king's healing magic had done wonders for Vincent's puncture wounds from the vines, he continued to keep Sadie's bandages around his torso. Though Marth had also received the same treatment as Vincent from the king, his limp was suddenly and conveniently back.

Mira paused to let Griff and his mother catch up, then she grabbed his free arm and said, "Your son is a real hero, Mrs. Driscoll."

"Thank you, Mira. I think so, too." Leena squeezed Griff's hand again.

The two women in Griff's life stood on either side of him, bragging about his bravery and the strength he displayed during the mission. The way Mira clung to Griff and the way Leena smiled made Griff feel invincible. Until the faint sting in his shoulder from the scorpion nightstalker reminded him he wasn't.

That night, the king joined the Driscoll family and Griff's battlegroup for a stagmoose steak feast. Runa laid across the living room floor, shredding her own steaks that she had earned on the mission. Stories of the journey, the battles, the traps in the maze—all of it—were shared among the group. Sadie had taken it upon herself to keep Marth's exaggerations to a minimum.

As Griff shared his final moments in the room with Tyrell, the king asked that they pause for a moment of silence. Their celebrations that evening had been at the expense of others' grief.

They chose not to speculate on Tyrell's fate, other than to recognize that his bravery came at a cost. Whatever that may be. Shortly after, the celebrations continued. Life would move on. Not to forget those sacrifices, but to honor them. Not by living in sorrow, but by living on.

While the king and Gale talked business about the sale of Gale's newly forged weapons, and Mira and Sadie helped Leena with the dishes, the rest of the battlegroup stepped out onto the back porch with Runa.

A few crickets chirped from the edges of the yard as if, through song, they were begging for spring to arrive. The newly acquired chickens and pigs shuffled in the barn as they settled in for the evening.

Solastran quieted as the streets emptied and the beds filled. The stars glistened in the cloudless sky. The air was crisp and cool, but not unpleasant. It had been almost a year since the attack on Cordelia. Almost. So much had happened in the last ten months. And Griff felt stronger because of it.

"Back to school tomorrow, eh?" Marth said, finally breaking the silence. As usual.

"Mm-hmm," Vincent replied from the rocking chair. His eyes were closed and his hands were crossed comfortably on his chest. He was the true picture of peace. Sleep would surely take him soon, considering he'd had four helpings of everything the Driscolls offered, with more available if he wanted it.

"Think they'll make us do the next Altar Storm match? Last year they didn't when Griff went off to play hero."

Griff snickered. "I dunno. I hope not. I think healing from this level of exhaustion is gonna take some time."

"Agreed," Vincent added, still refusing to open his eyes.

Runa slipped off beyond the lamplight, into the far corners of the yard where she couldn't be seen. Griff sighed. He'd have to get the special shovel after she was done taking care of business. Thankfully, she was house trained. Not that it would matter much longer anyway. He took a seat in the chair next to Vincent, his aching bones complaining with every movement.

"I'll probably take a few tardies in Professor Erebus' class and take some naps. I can afford a few skips in History," Griff said.

"Not me," Marth chimed in. "I've been out of those for a long time. Least. Favorite. Class."

"Yeah, but you can tell he at least *tries* to make it interesting," Griff said, coming to his defense.

"Trying and *succeeding* are two very different things, good sir."

"He's not wrong," Vincent chuckled.

The door to the back porch opened and Mira stepped out.

"Your mom said she's got it from here, so I'm free now."

Marth and Vincent exchanged looks, then, as awkwardly as they could make it, they strode past the couple and stepped back inside. Runa trotted proudly back into the middle of the yard and began curiously sniffing at a toad.

Mira walked over to Vincent's chair and rocked beside Griff.

"I'm really proud of you, Griff," she said, barely above a whisper. "You told me the stories of fighting for your town last year. But they just felt like stories. Ones you hear of brave heroes just before being tucked in for the night. But ... to actually experience that for myself ... well, I just. I guess I gained a new appreciation for my boyfriend." She turned to him and smiled.

The toad didn't appreciate Runa's presence and tried to hop away. Instead, that only strengthened her curiosity. She cocked her head and followed it across the yard.

"I'm sorry for the way I treated you earlier, after we lost that Altar Storm match. You were so focused on the bigger picture of what was happening outside of school. I guess, with the shards and Korrun and everything being this ... distant threat that almost didn't feel real, I was so focused on what I could see right in front of me. My Altar Storm performance. My chance to do something good for my family once I'm done here. I guess I was blind to the bigger picture."

Griff reached over and squeezed her hand. "That's what makes us a great team. You keep me grounded. There was nothing I could have done about the previous shard. You did what you could to pull me back into the here and now. The things I could control."

Just then, the door to the back porch opened again, and this time, the king of Oriel stepped out. Griff and Mira immediately stood, their rocking chairs still swaying from the sudden movement.

King Aldamund sucked in a lungful of air and let it out in a *whoosh*. He patted his tummy and turned to Griff and Mira.

"Griff, you need to be careful. I might invite your mother to come and cook at the castle full time! I've *never* had stagmoose steak cooked so exquisitely."

Griff laughed. "Well, sir. Lightstone is quite a long way away from here. I'm afraid I would miss my weekend meals too much!"

"Well, I could see why!" The king chuckled. He stepped closer. "Excuse me, Ms. Dunn, but could I have a private word with Griff?"

"Absolutely, your majesty." Mira curtsied awkwardly, then disappeared back into the house. As soon as she opened the door, the sounds of Marth and Gale's laughter burst into the night. The door closed, diminishing the raucous noises from inside, and Griff and the king were left to … mostly silence.

"Please, have a seat, Griff." The king motioned to the rocking chairs. Griff sat in one and the king in the other. Apparently, tonight was the night for important conversations in rocking chairs. It could have been worse.

"Well done, Griff. Truly. You showed bravery and strength that matched my battlemages. You retrieved the shard. Fought against monstrosities most only experience in their nightmares. Well done."

"Thank you, sir." What else could he say? Any words that bubbled up in his mind felt too small or weak for what they had all experienced. He wasn't so sure he deserved all the praise. Not when others hadn't made it home. And not when there was still more work to do.

"Your Majesty … we retrieved a shard from the pyramids. I found one being guarded by Runa's mother. I've witnessed Korrun recovering two: one from the lava cave, and another from the ocean. I …" He hated acknowledging this to the person who was actively seeking *all* the shards. "I have one … inside me. How many are left to find? Are we close?"

"Well, now. Don't forget about the one Korrun found after attacking your town. Remember telling Professor Coen about that one? He went down into some catacombs and broke open a casket?"

"Oh, right!" Griff started counting on his fingers. "So … Korrun has … three. And we have three as well, when you include the one inside me? Do you have any more that I don't know about yet?"

"I'm afraid not. I have the two you have given me, and the one inside you."

"So, then, there's three left to find."

King Aldamund nodded. "Indeed."

"And once we find the rest, what is your plan, sir? If … if I may ask."

The king sighed. Not at Griff, he could tell. It was more like an old man remembering a sad story.

"I've been looking for these shards for so long. Researching, studying, testing the one shard I had."

King Aldamund stood and stared up at the stars, his hands clasped behind his back. It didn't feel right to stay seated while the king of Oriel stood, so Griff rose and joined him. Runa had grown bored with the toad and sat at the bottom of the porch stairs, licking her claws with her long, skinny tongue. Her evening bath routine.

"My goal is the same as my brother's. It's a dream we've shared for as long as I can remember. I told you that we had stories, myths, legends about the Orb of Essence that had been passed down our family line. But I haven't told you everything.

"You see, my family is more than just a royal line. Sure, we have had kings ruling Oriel for quite some time. However, we were more than just royalty. We were Guardians."

"Guardians?"

"Aye. Guardians. Guardians of the Shards. Part of a secret organization that sought to keep the shards from the Orb of Essence away from the public. They were too dangerous in the wrong hands. An ancestor of mine was one of the first guardians, and he passed his shard—and the story—down the family line."

"So your brother knows about as much as you do?" Griff asked.

King Aldamund nodded. "Since we've ... gone our separate ways, I'm not sure what else he's learned. Clearly, he's gained more knowledge, as he's beaten me to some of the other shards. But yes, we heard the same stories growing up."

The king scratched his beard, his mind a million miles away.

"Once upon a time, Korrun and I both desired the complete annihilation of the Corruption. We saw the havoc it wreaked upon our world. And with the legends we grew up on, we believed that the Orb of Essence, when whole again, would contain unimaginable power. Power to create. Power to destroy. And we wanted to wield that power to destroy the magical plague that is undoing all of creation.

"Over time, it became clear: Korrun's end goal wasn't the eradication of the Corruption. That was merely a steppingstone to power and control. My parents realized it too."

Runa, now finished with her evening bath, folded her wings and flopped onto her side with a dramatic *huff*.

The king snickered at the tuckered-out dragon, then continued. "Korrun became obsessed. Mad, even. The shard we protected suddenly was in danger. Not from the threats outside, but from within.

"My father, the king, eventually sent Korrun away from the castle. And ... as I'm sure you can imagine, Korrun didn't take too kindly to that.

"Before he left home, he vowed the next time he stepped foot on Lightstone soil, it would be to claim the final shard. No matter the cost."

The king sighed, long and heavy, then remained silent. Together, Griff and the king stood quietly on his back porch, staring at the sleeping dragon. The crisp evening wind caressed Griff's face and teased his hair.

Finally, he looked to the king. "I'm ... sorry to hear that, sir. I don't have a sibling, but I imagine the pain that must have caused you."

The king smiled. "That's very kind of you, Griff. Yes, the pain of losing my brother that night was unbearable. But my desire to bring peace and healing to the world was stronger than my pain."

He turned to face Griff. "We *do* share the same desire to rid the world of the Corruption. But ... he's willing to do whatever it takes. Even if it means embracing the darkness. And there are some lines that I refuse to cross."

"I respect that, sir. A lot. It's one more reason why I choose to follow you. I believe you'll win. And you'll win the *right* way. But ... what about the other shards? Do you have any leads? There's still three more out there somewhere, and I don't want Korrun to get them."

The king smiled warmly. "Your loyalty means the world to me, Griff. Thank you. As for the other shards ... well, I have a hunch that I must investigate. But just know that you are now as much a part of this as I am. So, when the time is right, I will call upon you again."

"And ... and what about the shard ... inside of me?"

"What about it?"

"Once you have all the other shards, how ... how will you get this last one?" He touched his chest where the shard resided.

"Oh my boy!" The king laughed, then placed a firm hand on his shoulder. "As I said, my brother might be willing to embrace the darkness, but I am not. You need not worry about that. I promise you. You are safe."

Relief flooded Griff's mind. That anxious thought that lurked in the dark places of his mind this whole time was finally gone. He felt free. Light.

"Now." The king removed his hand, took a deep breath and released it slowly. "You are headed back to school tomorrow, yes?"

Griff nodded.

"Then I shouldn't keep you up. You need to go back in and celebrate our victory with your battlegroup. We will have more time to talk about the other shards, but for now, rest in your victory. We can talk again soon."

A clatter arose from the living room, and Vincent's roar of laughter echoed into the night. Griff turned to peer through the window, but the curtains had been drawn. He turned to address the king, but he was nowhere to be found.

Griff eyed Runa, who had raised her head and cocked it in curiosity, then he asked, "Where did he go?"

CHAPTER 39

Laughter and a swelling tide of indistinct chatter rose above the clinking of forks and knives against their plates. The smell of warm cinnamon cakes drifted through the Dining Hall, and the morning sun shone through the room's large windows, signaling the start of another day of classes.

Most of the students had no clue what had happened these past few days. They continued going to class, writing their papers, and gossiping about the different relationships around Bergots. They practiced their magic, slept soundly in their bunks, and complained about staying up too late the next morning.

Griff wasn't sure how to feel about it all. He should have been happy. He'd survived another battle and made it off the battlefield alive. Somehow the hardest part of it all was pretending it hadn't happened.

On the other hand, it did happen. There were still three more shards to be found. And going through the motions of classes and papers felt incredibly mundane and useless. But it was what the king requested, and so, as much as possible, Griff tried to force himself to be present. To put in the work. Learn what he could, knowing anything might help him in the weeks, months, maybe even years to come as they searched for the remaining shards.

And then, once they found them all, there was still Korrun. He had three in his possession. At some point, he would either have to give them up voluntarily, or he would die trying to keep them. There would be no other options.

"How many plates is that, big guy?" Marth's voice cut through Griff's dark thoughts.

Vincent smiled as he sat, and held up four fingers.

"Four!" Marth shouted. "If I ate as much as you, I'd be as big as the stables! Where do you put it all?"

Vincent dropped his fork and flexed his unusually large bicep.

Marth shook his head. "Fair enough."

"Hi sweetums!" Kara Thorson placed her plate between Marth and Griff. Griff gladly scooted his chair closer to Mira, giving Marth plenty of space to add a chair for his girlfriend. Sadie and Mira both rolled their eyes as Kara plopped in the chair and kissed Marth on the cheek.

"Did you see they had mangos today? They *never* have mangos! I wonder where they got the mangos!"

"Yeah, Kara. Mangos," Mira said, annoyed. "Good stuff."

Kara took a dainty bite, then placed a hand on Marth's arm. "Mmm, that is *delicious*."

"Right? Really good!" Marth said with a wide smile.

"Now, you know you're still in trouble for leaving me all by my lonesome self and not telling me where you went." She playfully slapped at his shoulder. "You're not off the hook yet!"

"Well, sweetie, it all happened so fast. We had to catch up to Griff and the king," Marth whined.

"That's fair." Kara leaned in. "You know, the whole school is talking. They're saying you guys are legends. That you were up against a horde of nightstalkers, twenty to one, and you *still* beat them!"

Griff stopped chewing his food. How did the whole school know they did anything? Did someone from Solastran see them walk into town with the king? He eyed Marth, wondering if his limp had "magically" returned and he'd spouted off a few clues when asked about it.

Griff swallowed. "We didn't have time to count them, Kara. We were just trying to stay alive,"

A look of awe dawned on her face. She took another bite of mango. "That's incredible. And to think Korrun's army was all the way out in Ashrock Wastes."

"We didn't fly to Ashrock Wastes, Kara." Mira rolled her eyes.

Kara held up her hands. "Sorry, that's just what Katrine told me. Is telling everybody, really. Watch out, Marth, I think she's making you out to be the hero of your little adventure ..." She narrowed her eyes playfully at him. "I'm keeping my eye on her ... and you!" Kara sat back in her chair and crossed her arms.

"You don't have to worry about her, Kara. You're my one and only sweetums, okay?" Marth patted her hand.

A bell tolled in the distance. Chairs screeched across the tile floor and students rushed to throw away their trash and pack up their things for class.

Griff sighed. Could he skip out on Professor Strickland's Ethics class? He felt like he was a pretty ethical mage. But, sadly, he was almost out of absences, mostly to take care of Runa. Or nap.

He snatched his bag and rushed to catch up to Mira, who was already to the door. Not paying attention to the bodies he passed by, he accidentally bumped into Connor Ofner.

"Sorry Connor!"

Thankfully, the boy didn't fall. He held his potted plant with the green and purple leaves in one arm, and his bag in the other.

Connor smiled at Griff. "Okay! It's okay!" Then Connor slowly reached over and squeezed Griff in a giant hug, and wouldn't let go.

"Good to see you too, Connor. All right, I gotta head to class!"

Connor smiled and waved as Griff disappeared through the door.

Mira, of course, didn't wait for him, but continued rushing through the crowds to get to class first. By the time he caught up to her, she was already grabbing a seat in the front row. Professor Strickland wasn't even in the room yet.

Griff yawned, then reached down and pulled out his copy of *Wizards and Wisdom* textbook, opening it to chapter fourteen, titled, "Magic and Medicine."

He stared at the page. Then blinked.

Giant, red, scrawling letters stared back at him from the page.

DID YOU MISS ME?

EPILOGUE

Tyrell stared at the bowl of black water in the corner of this cell. He was *so* thirsty. The air in their new location was incredibly hot and arid. His dry throat longed for a drop of that water. He'd lick the dew off the grass if he could. Sadly, he was trapped.

Sure, he could have melted the metal bars of his jail cell within minutes, burst through the wooden wall and out into the deserted town Korrun's army resided. But surrounded by weathered, wooden buildings with signs that read, SALOON, SHERIFF, BANK, and GENERAL STORE, he'd have to face a horde of nightstalkers and what remained of the black cloaks. He wouldn't survive against those odds. But did he even want to?

With Ava gone, it was suddenly as though he were missing his own heart. The thing that kept him alive. That pushed blood through his veins and gave his life purpose. She was gone. The remains of the heart that now beat inside his chest were shredded. Weak.

Out of spite, Tyrell refused to drink the black water. And in the moments he felt weak, when the dark liquid called to him, beckoning a single taste, it was the hope that his end was near that kept him strong.

When he was bored, he would read and reread the flyers posted on the warped wooden wall just outside his cell:

"WANTED: You and Your Friends! Posing like an outlaw in our fully immersive town will get you sent right to jail! Our Sheriff with the keys is always on the watch! Take a picture and post it to your socials for a chance to win an annual pass to Yeehaw Yonder Years! Because we all know, a one-time visit is never enough for true cowboys and cowgirls!"

As minutes and hours passed, desperation for any distraction would kick in and he would move to the next flyer.

"COWBOY CHILI COOKOFF! You ain't never had a bowl of chili until you've had Clyde's Canyon Chili! Come for the chili, stay for the showdown! Cowboys and Outlaws go head-to-head in our dinner theatre inside the SALOON. Kids' meals are half-priced when dressed like a cowboy, and DOUBLE if dressed like an outlaw! Yeehaw!"

A cheesy picture of a child wearing a cowboy hat and fake, bushy handlebar mustache was printed alongside the flyer. It always made Tyrell laugh. Not because of the silliness of it. But because they had no idea what a real showdown was. There were no fake weapons and cheap overacting in a genuine showdown. The danger was real. The screams, the blood, the loss. All of it ... real. If they had been through what Tyrell had experienced, would that even be an attraction? Probably not.

Suddenly, the door to the jail house flung open. Korrun and Randolph stepped inside holding a ragged, but very much alive, Doran. In shock, Tyrell fell to his knees, grasped the metal bars, and watched. They dragged him by his arms, swung the neighboring cell door open, and tossed him inside. He grunted as his body bounced on the concrete floor.

Korrun slammed the door shut, and Randolph locked it tight. The leader of the black cloaks stared menacingly at Doran, the second scar on his left cheek a reminder of the girl who put it there. Of her desire to fight.

"If I can't motivate loyalty in you, then I'll force it." Korrun sneered. "Once you turn, you'll make a great fighter. Until then, get comfortable in that cell."

Doran moaned as he rolled on the floor. He was alive, but just barely.

Korrun turned, whipping his cloak about him, and stepped out into the dusty street. Randolph remained. He stared at the man on the ground before him, then looked to Tyrell. He placed the key to the cell in his pocket, then walked over to his son.

"How are you doing?"

Tyrell mustered what little saliva he had and spit on his father's shoes.

"How do you think? And why would you care?"

Perhaps he could use his last bit of energy to launch a giant fireball at his father. They would die together, but it would be his final act of revenge before joining Ava.

"Believe it or not, I do." Randolph knelt, coming face to face with his imprisoned son. "More than you know."

He stood again, and turned, facing the door. "Being in here will do you some good, son. It'll give you time to consider your next actions. Who will you join? What side will you fight for?"

Randolph paused by another tacky flyer with a woman in a frumpy dress. "Maybe it'll give you time to read." He turned back to Tyrell. "The choice is yours."

Before Tyrell could snap back with a hateful line, Randolph disappeared through the door. It closed with a *bang*, forcing Tyrell to jump.

Another groan from Doran snapped Tyrell from his hateful thoughts. There were no walls between the cells, only metal bars. If he was going to be stuck here, at least he could speak with one of the Forty-Two. He stood and faced the man on the floor.

"You're alive," Tyrell said blankly.

"Doesn't feel that way," Doran said, refusing to sit up.

"How?"

"Veyla."

Of course! The healer in the group. "How did she get away with *that*?" Tyrell asked. "You showed your true colors that night. I would have thought they wanted you dead."

"Korrun lost a lot of soldiers that night. He actually asked *her* to heal me. Now he's going to turn me." Doran, still refusing to sit up, turned his head to examine Tyrell's cell. "I guess like they're trying to turn you."

"Yeah, well. They won't."

"Hmph," was all Doran could say. He continued to lie on the ground, his breathing slowing as he stared at the ceiling.

Tyrell sat against the bars that connected Doran's cell to his. He leaned his head back and took a deep breath. Then he cocked his head to the side. Something was on the floor in front of his cell that hadn't been there before. Tyrell crawled over, dust covering his pants as he did so.

It was a book. He reached down and picked it up, turning it sideways and slipping it between the bars. No. Not a book. A *journal*. He flipped open the first page:

THE JOURNAL OF EINAR FALKENBURG AND FAMILY.

I am protector and defender.

I wield my magic; it does not wield me.

I brandish my power with wisdom and resolve.

I do not strike first, but I strike true.

I do not seek battle, but I will end it.

—The Guardian's Creed

Tyrell's heart thudded in his chest. Einar's journal? Questions flooded his mind as he thumbed through the pages. All of Einar's notes, his stories ... they were all right here. And filling in the margins were other comments from the rest of his family, including his dad's. Something thumped on the ground as the pages turned. A key. The same key he had seen his father place in his pocket. Where the journal must have been stored.

A grunt from the neighboring cell snapped him from his thoughts. Doran sat upright and leaned against the back bars of his cell.

"So ... what do we do now?" he asked.

Tyrell gazed at the key in one hand and Einar's journal in the other. He clenched his jaw and grasped the key tight.

"We fight back."

THE ADVENTURE CONTINUES...

Six Shards of Essence have been discovered. Three more remain.

Griff has returned to the safety of Bergots, but Tyrell's world has fallen apart.

Don't miss the epic conclusion to the Corruption of Essence series in:

GRIFF DRISCOLL
AND THE ORB OF ESSENCE

SUBSCRIBE to my newsletter to stay up to date on the next installment in the Corruption of Essence series! More info at www.Brandon-Harriman.com

THANK YOU for joining Griff and Tyrell on their journeys through the land of Oriel! If you enjoyed the adventure, would you consider leaving a review so more people can experience the magic and mystery Oriel has to offer? I truly hope you had fun alongside Griff and Tyrell, and I hope you are as excited as I am about their story moving forward!

ABOUT THE AUTHOR

As a baby, Brandon Harriman could barely get the Miami sand out of his diaper before he was whisked away to the Southern charm of North Alabama. Growing up in Decatur alongside his twin brother, Brandon traded salt air for sweet tea, and developed an early love for reading.

That love of reading frequently had him tuning out his teachers (much to their displeasure) to dive headfirst into the magical worlds of books like *Harry Potter*. In hindsight, he probably should have paid more attention in class, but he recognized the pull a good story had on his focus.

Brandon earned a business degree from Harding University before completing a Master of the Arts with a dual focus in Youth Ministry and Pastoral Ministry at Grand Canyon University. After six fulfilling years as a youth pastor in Sarasota, FL, he and his wife, Annette, along with their son, Jayce, made the move to Tulsa, OK. As part of the discussion to leave Florida, Brandon decided to pursue his dream of writing young adult fantasy novels full-time while embracing the role of stay-at-home dad. Since then, the Harriman clan has grown with the addition of their daughter, Haley.

When Brandon isn't exploring the fantastical worlds he creates, he's busy being playful at heart. Whether it's board games, video games, sports, or assembling (and inevitably stepping on) Legos, he's always up for some fun. He's also an unapologetic beach lover, with a passion for tropical weather, deep-sea fishing, and snorkeling.

Thanks to the unwavering support of his family and friends, Brandon has completed his debut novel and, at the time of publishing, is hard at work finishing The Corruption of Essence series.